MARRIAGE ACCORDING TO RETT

The average age American women got married was twenty-five. I was twenty-seven. I had seen the men that women over thirty had the opportunity to date, and it wasn't pretty. If I didn't get married soon, I would probably never get married.

I hadn't been looking for a husband, but when Greg came along I knew we'd get married. I just had this quiet feeling; our relationship felt so right. Is that the feeling that people who marry their high school sweethearts have? It must be. But I don't think I could have appreciated how right things felt with Greg if I hadn't had the close-but-not-quite experiences with Alex and Ryan.

I don't believe that we each have only one soul mate, but I do think finding someone who is as attracted to you as you are to him, who you can laugh with and still have something to talk about years down the road, is as rare as a four-leaf clover, and if you manage to find him, you should count yourself very lucky. That doesn't mean there aren't moments when I'd like to push Greg down a long flight of stairs. Happily, these moments are infrequent, and most of the time I consider myself fortunate indeed.

Plus, after seeing Jen and my girlfriends date one self-absorbed loser after another, I really appreciated how good Greg was to me. He was so sweet. He wasn't into football or porn or getting wasted with his buddies. He didn't spend all his money on beer and electronic equipment. I wasn't about to let such a good guy get away.

But why hadn't we had the forethought to elope?

And why were wedding dresses made to make our asses look like the hindquarters of a wildebeest?

Books by Theresa Alan

WHO YOU KNOW

SPUR OF THE MOMENT

THE GIRLS' GLOBAL GUIDE TO GUYS

Published by Kensington Publishing Corporation

Who You Know

Theresa Alan

KENSINGTON PUBLISHING CORP.
http://www.kensingtonbooks.com

First Trade Paperback Printing: May 2003
First Mass Market Paperback Printing: March 2005
10 9 8 7 6 5 4 3 2 1

Printed in the United States of America

For my mother and father,
Evelyn and Don,
and for Sara.

Acknowledgments

I'm grateful to my agent, Alison Picard, and editor, John Scognamiglio, whose suggestions helped improve this book considerably. To my sister, Sara Jade, who was the first person to read the manuscript and has been my personal cheerleader for years. To Mom, Dad, Heather Frank, and James Ritter, for their support. To Jenny Atchley, for encouraging me to submit the manuscript, and to Susan Arndt, Rob Allen, Dixie Darr, John Gress, and Jen Daumler, for keeping me in good food, good wine, and good spirits.

RETTE

The Cruel, Self-Esteem Crushing Job Search

Going into the job market armed with nothing more than a degree in English is like trying to fight a five-alarm fire when you're soaked with lighter fluid—you're just not going to get very far.

It had taken four months and forty-two résumés, but at long last I'd gotten called for an interview. Four months is a long, long time when your fiancé is busy with graduate school and all you have to entertain yourself with is daytime television and a massage wand, AKA the Magic Wand. (I'd had to invest in the Magic Wand despite our tight budget—it's difficult to explain developing carpal tunnel while unemployed.) The sound of drills, blenders, and electric shavers now produced a distressingly carnal reaction in me.

The interview was an hour away, and every synapse in my body was twitching with nervous energy. I tried to read but couldn't concentrate. I got up from the table, paced, sat down again. I flipped through a Victoria's Secret catalog. Wonder-bras. This is not something I understood. Maybe when I lost the thirty-five pounds that snuck up on me in high school and college, I'd get it. But right now, the idea of purposely making a part of your body look *bigger?* Incomprehensible.

I reached up to grab the cordless phone off the wall and dialed Avery's number.

"Explain the concept of thong underwear to me," I said when Avery answered. I made a face at the annoying Victoria's Secret model who looked so pleased with herself.

"Rette, I'm afraid thong underwear is one of the great mysteries of the world."

"I spend a good portion of my life trying to keep my underwear from nesting between my buttcheeks, and here's a product whose sole purpose is to wedge its way between the fleshiest parts of my body." I was dying for some coffee, but my nervous stomach couldn't handle caffeine's caustic effect. The months of unemployment had proved corrosive to both my ego and my digestive system, and I did not want to go to my interview with the gases in my stomach doing a miasmic tango. "Guess what? McKenna Marketing called yesterday. I have an interview today." I padded across the wood floor to the sink to rinse out my cup. The floorboards creaked mournfully, straining beneath my weight. Greg's cereal bowl was in the sink, unsoaked of course. How hard was it for him to rinse it out and put it in the dishwasher? Why did he not realize that after a few hours corn flakes and milk could produce a bond stronger than love?

I turned on the faucet and the ancient water pipes groaned with exertion. Our apartment was old and ill-tempered, and I absolutely loved it.

"An interview? That's great. I had friends who looked for a job for six months before getting an interview."

This was why I loved Avery. Unlike, for example, my

family, Avery could always make me feel like slightly less of a loser. My younger sister, Jen, had majored in marketing, and even though she got execrable grades and her résumé was overflowing with grammatical errors, she managed to get a job two weeks after she got her diploma. She and my parents were astounded by my lack of progress in my job hunt.

"Are you nervous?"

"That's an understatement. I've sent out forty-two résumés and this is the only place that called. Why did I quit teaching?"

"Because you hated it."

"Oh yeah." I walked back over to the table, collapsed into the chair, and started looking through the Victoria's Secret again.

"You need to visualize yourself acing the interview and getting the job. I'm serious. You should look in the mirror and tell yourself you're smart, you're talented, and you're going to get this job. You need to say it like you mean it."

"Yeah, Ave, that's pretty much just not going to happen."

"I know it sounds corny, but it's the power of positive visualization. It works."

"Yokay." This was short for "yeah OK," which was short for "yeah right, not in this lifetime, nice try though."

"I'm going to be late for work, I'd better get going," Avery said. "You're going to do great. Stop by my office when it's over and give me all the details."

"Will do. Talk to you later."

Avery and I sometimes called each other six times a day to say absolutely nothing. I had begun to look forward to reporting my day's events to her or, more likely, the nonevents—random thoughts I'd had, new ideas for the wedding I wanted to get her opinion on, new ideas about what I wanted from a career and from my life. Meeting Avery was the only good thing that had happened since the move.

When Greg asked me what I thought about moving to Colorado so he could get his master's degree in engineering at the University of Colorado at Boulder, I was torn. On the one hand, I liked Colorado and had been looking for an excuse to get away from Minnesota and its entirely inhuman winters. On the other hand, Jen had moved to Colorado three years ago to follow her ski-bum boyfriend, and I preferred my little sister when she was thousands of miles away, not a mere few blocks across town. It had a little something to do with her astonishing beauty, staggering self-centeredness, and the fact that any time I was around her I felt like the fat, frumpy older sister that I was. But I'd said yes, and we moved, and I'd spent the last four months marinating in feelings of failure and rabid self-contempt.

Things with Jen hadn't been as bad as I had worried they might be. She was the one who introduced me to Avery, for one thing, and I was grateful to her for that. I can honestly say Avery is the only tall, skinny blonde I don't despise. Avery was the kind of person who did everything spectacularly well, but somehow you didn't hate her for it. Her meals, for example, looked like something that should be photographed for a gourmet cooking magazine. Can you imagine, taking the time to lovingly arrange a sprig of decorative parsley atop the entrée before gorging yourself silly?

Avery knew about stuff that was completely alien to me. She's a vegetarian and cooked food I couldn't even spell: Seitan, kreplach, kasha, avial, kabocha, aspic—these were not foods found at your neighborhood Denny's or Village Inns back in Minnesota, I can assure you.

Avery was the one who told us that the apartment above her was for rent, which is how we found this place.

Avery was also the one who let me know about the job opening at the company where she and Jen worked.

Which just goes to show you that the saying is true: Getting ahead in this world is all about who you know. But like an idiot, instead of spending my years in college networking and brown-nosing, I'd worked my butt off to get good grades, routinely pulling all-nighters to finish epic essays and making myself sick with stress every time exams rolled around. What had all my hard work gotten me? A career that paid about half the salary of the average construction worker.

Being a copy editor for a marketing company wasn't my dream job, but right now I was willing to launch a career as a llama wrangler, a ticket taker at a movie theater, or one of those people who stands in the bathroom handing out towels (which begs the question: Is this really a needed service? Is it harder to reach an extra three inches to grab a towel yourself? I think not), anything to get my butt off the couch and some money in my pocket.

It would be cool to see Avery every day, but Jen? Every time I looked at her, I could feel my few remaining shreds of self-esteem wither. We looked like a set of before and after pictures: We had the same long, thick red hair and brown eyes, but she was two inches taller and at least thirty pounds lighter. It wasn't Jen's fault she was stunning, but she had a way of igniting my insecurities as no one else could.

Jen and I would never be good friends; we were just too different. I consumed books with the same voraciousness I attacked fattening foods, while she never read anything more substantial than a greeting card and was on a perpetual diet. Plus, there was the fact that Mom adored Jen, while I never measured up. Mom didn't give a hoot about good grades (she'd never done well in school and found it odd that I could be content to sit still with a book for hours on end), and she was constantly giving me admonishing glances, explaining to me that I might fare better with the boys if I put on a little lipstick and maybe didn't read quite so many books. Pardon my blistering resentment.

I mean I don't want you to get the idea that Jen and I hated each other or anything. Jen's beauty and sparkling personality were as intoxicating to me as they were to everyone else. It was a love/hate thing with myself, a fiery internal battle of jealousy, curdled self-esteem, and a burning wish to be a lot more like the person I aspired to be, a person with my kindness and intelligence but Jen's looks and perfect figure (incidentally, my ideal self also had a dazzling fashion sense that would make my mother glow with pride rather than shake her head and roll her eyes and give me the kind of withering looks that made me want to promptly hurtle myself off the nearest cliff).

But if nothing else, Jen and I were good drinking buddies, and sometimes in a new town, all you need is someone who can help distract you from your loneliness.

AVERY

Dancinfool

I believe there is a certain order to the universe, an organized plan; I believe that from the chaos comes meaning. Just as the unruly spattering of notes of music on a page are transformed into a symphony when you interpret it and put it all together, there is a method behind the madness.

What the method to this current madness was, however, unclear. My horoscope this morning had provided no warning this was coming.

It was all the fault of my caffeine addiction. If it weren't for my dependence on coffee, I would have been safe in my office right now and not standing here waiting for the coffee to brew and listening to Jim from the sales department tell me he was bringing over a bride from the Philippines. What was the proper response to such a statement? What was I supposed to say?

What I did say was "Well, that's great, Jim." I nodded and smiled and willed the coffee to brew faster while he went on about how beautiful she was and how they had such similar philosophies about life.

I watched the coffee dripping slowly, a caffeine udder. I couldn't exactly leave now with an empty cup. Why did I ever get hooked on coffee in the first place?

I never would have poisoned my body with such a toxin like caffeine in my dancing days, but now that I worked in an office, coffee gave me that artificial jolt of energy I needed to make it through the day.

I looked at Jim, letting his figure blur. His aura was orangy red, a good sign. Maybe he really was happy. Maybe this would all work out after all.

When the coffee was ready at last, I poured myself a cup, told Jim I needed to get back to work, and bolted back to my office, feeling better than usual about being single.

If I let myself think about this poor woman who was going to marry Jim, I'd start crying. I couldn't let myself think about it; I couldn't let the toxic thoughts consume me. *Everything happens for a reason, everything happens for a reason,* I reminded myself.

Even though the whole thing was sad, I couldn't wait to tell Jen, my officemate, about Jim's overseas bridal shipment.

It was always rewarding to share gossip with Jen. She'd been cracking me up since our cubicle days when she'd hurl paper airplanes made out of pictures downloaded from bestiality Web sites across the walls of our cubicles. Several times a day she would wedge her way into my cube and whisper scandalous tidbits about coworkers: "Avery, I have such dirt to dish, you would not *believe.* "

Jen and I had recently been promoted from peons to low-level grunts at McKenna Marketing, and our promotions had been marked with a move from cubicles to a cramped, windowless, bathroom stall-size office we shared, making it easier than ever to share the latest rumors.

At 8:30, only half an hour late—unusually early for her—Jen came rushing into our office holding a liter of bottled water in one hand and her briefcase in the other. Jen always made a big show of taking work home with her. She didn't do any work while at work, so I found her pretense of being a slave to her job hilarious.

"My day is ruined before it's even begun," she announced, dumping her briefcase onto her desk. She collapsed into her chair and swiveled theatrically around to face me. "I got trapped into having a conversation with Lydia in the hallway. I saw her coming, but I had no place to hide, and I had to hold an entire *conversation* with her."

"How is our fertile co-worker?"

"*Glowing* as usual. You'll be happy to know that the little fetus is an absolute *Rockette*. Lydia's *latest* craving is for apple butter on melba toast. And the nursery is almost done, and it is *just perfect,* absolutely just *so adorable.*"

Lydia was a nice woman, but she was hopelessly superficial. Talking to her was like holding a conversation with a Pop Tart—there just wasn't a lot of substance.

Jen turned on her computer. She stared at the screen contemptuously as the computer booted up. "It's only eight-thirty in the morning, and I'm bored and ready to go home. Please tell me you have gossip. How is Art?"

"I haven't had a chance to check my e-mail yet 'cuz, Jen, I've got some serious heavy-duty dirt. I'm serious, you are never going to believe this: Jim is bringing over a mail-order bride from the Philippines."

She arched her eyebrows and looked at me. "No way! That is *hilarious!*" she roared. Her hysterical laughter was contagious, and I couldn't help but laugh right along with her.

Jen did nothing halfway. When she laughed, she really laughed—a knee-slapping, head-thrown-back kind of laugh. She made this *aah-aah-aah* noise that was really more of an absence of sound—all you could hear was a few choking breaths between convulsions.

"I can't believe he'd tell you about it," Jen said when her laughter had abated enough for her to speak. She dabbed at the tears in the corner of her eyes with the tips of her fingers. "You'd think he could at least lie and pretend he met her while traveling. We'd still know she was marrying him for his money, but at least it wouldn't be quite so obviously gross."

"You know something? I read this article that said the whole mail-order thing became popular in the seventies, which just happened to be when American women discovered a little thing called feminism."

"Here's to being single," Jen said, raising her bottle of water. I clinked my coffee cup against it. "Speaking of, check your e-mail already."

I logged on to my Yahoo! Personals account. For a moment, I felt guilty about laughing about Jim when I, too, had turned to such unromantic means of finding a date. The moment passed.

At least people using the personals knew what they wanted and weren't selling themselves to escape their grim socioeconomic plight. I didn't really think I'd find my soul mate online, but it had been nearly two years since the divorce, and I hadn't gone on a single date that entire time. I'd been wary about getting into another relationship. I knew from experience that marriage was highly overrated, but Jen had more or less forced me to try to get back into the drama of dating. She created an account on the Yahoo! Personals and would respond to guys' ads, describing what *I* looked like. When they wrote back detailing the salacious acts they wanted to perform on me in unlikely locations, she'd forward their responses to me, cackling with laughter.

She thought her ruse was hysterically funny, but I thought it was sort of mean, or at least in bad taste, and definitely creepy.

To get her off my back, I made up my own account and even browsed through the ads every now and then. I hadn't really planned on responding to one, but eventually I found the ritual of reading them somehow therapeutic—it was nice to have constant confirmation there were other single people out there. At work, absolutely everyone except Jen was married. Or, like Jim, getting married, no matter what it took. We single people were a freakish minority.

Of course, the ads could be depressing, too. Most were not particularly appealing, and not everyone posting an ad was single. Many of them were along the lines of "I want to have sex with someone who is not my wife. If you respond, you could be that person!" Others said things like, "ISO a woman who enjoys golden showers. Must enjoy being urinated on." A little repelling, no doubt, but, on the other hand, this was not the kind of information you want to find out about a guy late in the game, like right before you're going to get peed on, for example. This is the kind of stuff you want to know *right up front*.

This being Colorado, a lot of the ads were guys in search of women who liked mountain biking and skiing and skydiving. I liked working out, but I wanted to be firmly on the ground when I did it. Before marrying Gideon, I'd dated my share of sports fiends, and I'd learned my lesson. I didn't want to spend my vacations rock climbing and mountain biking and camping with only a stream to bathe in, if, that is, I could fight my way through a fog of mosquitoes and gnats. With the personals, I could make my desires known right away.

Over the weeks, a few ads had mildly interested me, but only one made me feel like maybe there was hope of meeting a decent guy after all.

He went by the moniker "ArtLover," and his profile said that he was a 6-foot, 170-pound nonsmoker with hazel eyes and brown hair. His ad read:

> I'm not a Versace model with an Austrian accent, but I'm not a swamp monster in need of delousing either. I enjoy theater, film, good books, and good conversations. By day I'm a mild-mannered accountant; by night I'm an amateur painter. (Alas, the Louvre is not reserving a space for me just yet . . .) I've spent one too many Saturday nights at home with my dogs. My dogs are sick of me!

He seemed modest yet not lacking in self-esteem, funny but not trying too hard. And there was something so endearing about a guy with dogs. He would be caring yet firm, playful yet responsible. (All those walks on freezing cold winter nights!)

We'd been e-mailing each other for a couple weeks, and I was falling for him a little more each day. I was surprised how much I'd gotten to know about him in our daily e-mails. He'd told me all about his travels and his parents and his brothers and his friends. He told me about his frustrations at work and what he enjoyed about his job. He was a good writer, and he always managed to put a smile on my face. He hadn't demanded my measurements and my picture as some other guys insisted on, which suggested a certain depth of character. Plus, we had a lot in common. Though I'd grown up in Colorado and he'd grown up on the East Coast, I'd gone to New York for high school and college, so we could talk (write) at length about the cultural differences between the turbocharged East Coast and laidback Colorado.

I loved that he was an artist, but not a starving one. I

imagined him immortalizing me in one of his paintings. It would happen like this: He would ask me to pose for him. I would feign resistance at first, then relent. In his dusty, ramshackle studio above his garage, I would lie naked on a velvet couch, my legs extending across the couch, my blond wavy hair fanning out in soft wisps around my head. He would position my body just so, his fingers lightly grazing my skin . . .

My e-mail let me know, with an excited exclamation point, that I had new mail.

> To: Dancinfool@yahoo.com
> From: ArtLover@yahoo.com
> Good morning! What a gorgeous morning it is. If there is anything better than drinking a good cup of coffee while looking out over the mountains, I haven't found it yet. I always feel so at peace looking at the mountains. It's why I moved here. That, and the people. Back East, people wouldn't stop to gaze at the mountains unless it could somehow help increase their stock portfolio. It's a lot more relaxed out here.
>
> To answer your questions, my favorite ice cream is Ben and Jerry's Phish Food; I was in 11th grade science class when the Challenger blew up—we watched the footage over and over and my teacher cried, which almost made me cry; and my favorite book is Catcher in the Rye. (Not very original, I know. To make things even more groan-worthy, my dogs are named Holden and Phoebe. You're never going to write me again, are you? Well, I have to fess up to every cheesy detail about myself since I'm sure you'll extract it from me someday.)
>
> OK, a question for you: Are you just a fool about dancing?

I loved that he thought I would discover all the details about him someday, that our relationship would last long enough to extract every last one of his secrets. I smiled and hit REPLY.

> To: ArtLover@yahoo.com
> From: Dancinfool@yahoo.com
> I've done foolish things in every area of my life. The one my mother still likes to silently torment me about was my decision to major in dance in college. Technically I proved her wrong about how worthless a degree in dance was because I managed to get a job as a dancer after college. For two years I danced on a cruise ship before realizing I really wasn't making a career out of dancing but out of looking passably sexy in a sequined leotard. When I quit that job and returned to Colorado (and lived with my mother for a few months, if you can imagine such a fate), she was quite satisfied that she'd been right all along. There weren't exactly a lot of openings for dancers in Colorado, and that was when I got a job doing market research. You know those annoying people who call you up while you're eating dinner to ask you questions about your favorite dishwasher detergent? I did that for one cruel, horrible year. Then I became a marketing support specialist, which means I ran around doing miscellaneous grunt work—ordering stress balls, mugs, and pens; reserving trade show slots and hotel space for meetings and retreats. Since I got my promotion, my job is to write the questions the researchers ask and take the data they gather and put it into graphically scintillating reports with colorful charts and pulled quotes. It's a living, but ever since I got into marketing my life has been like an issue of Cosmopolitan without the cleavage: My sentences are sprinkled with words italicized for enthusiastic emphasis and every other sentence I utter ends in an exclamation point.
> I have to say, I miss living in New York. Or maybe it's college in New York I miss, when I was always sur-

rounded by artists and writers and dancers and comedians who were all as broke as I was. We'd have seriously funny conversations, talking late into the night over cups of espresso about politics and books. The people I spend my time with now—my coworkers—talk about their stock portfolios, the lavish equity they're building in their homes, their $35,000 SUVs. Since I don't own stocks, a home, or a new car, all I can do is nod and smile and wish we could talk about something more substantive than money or the latest episode of ER.

Of course what I miss most of all is dancing. I still dance at home on the hardwood floors of my apartment and go out dancing at clubs whenever possible. When I'm dancing, that's the only time I don't think at all, about anything. I really let myself go. Maybe that's foolishness of a sort. Maybe that's the smartest thing I can do.

I read over what I'd written. Why was I telling someone I didn't know about my failed dreams and my annoyance at my mother's lack of faith in me? For all I knew, he could be lying about everything. He could be a twelve-year-old boy or an eighty-year-old woman. Somehow though, I trusted him. We hadn't talked about meeting in person yet, but I sensed we would meet one day. Part of me didn't want to meet him because I didn't want reality to interfere with my fantasy, but then again, it would be nice to have someone to go out to dinner with, to snuggle and laugh with. I already knew I liked Art's personality; after that, everything else would fall naturally into place.

Just before I could hit SEND, I heard Jen say, "Good morning, Sharon!" I quickly minimized my browser, feeling guilty, like I'd been caught surfing porn sites. I turned to face my manager, the other pregnant woman in the office. It was a fertility epidemic around here.

Her smile was fake as usual, so perhaps she hadn't seen the bold Yahoo! Personals banner at the top of my screen.

"How is the Expert project coming?" Sharon asked, rubbing her belly ostentatiously. She'd begun wearing maternity clothes in her second month. Jen and I made it a point to never bring up the baby because it amused us to see how she always managed to work it into every conversation. Also, knowing she was dying to talk about it made us even less interested. I realized pregnancy was a big deal, but let's be honest here, she was not the first woman to do it.

I feared, irrationally, that she would want to use my computer to show us something, and my secret would be discovered. I'd only told two people about being reduced to surfing the personals: Jen and my neighbor, Rette.

"Right on schedule," Jen said brightly. Jen was always extra bubbly around people she didn't like.

I'd read in studies that good-looking people succeeded faster than average-looking and ugly people, a fact that rather wounded my ego since Sharon and I had started at McKenna Marketing at the same time, and she was making her way up the ranks far faster than I was, yet she wasn't what you'd call good-looking. She had a round face, limp hair parted down the middle, a long nose, and a chin that had no discernible end but just sort of faded into her amorphous neck. She was bottom heavy, with thick legs like Doric columns. She was wearing a dress with large yellow sunflowers that ended midthigh.

Though she wasn't beautiful, Sharon knew how to play the game. How to kiss up and brown nose and schmooze. For some reason, I kept believing that if I worked hard, somebody would eventually notice and reward me. But my chance to prove myself once and for all was finally coming. When Sharon went on maternity leave, I was a shoo-in to fill in for her.

I had to look to the future, because if I kept thinking about the past, all I'd get was bitter. I'd start thinking that it wouldn't be so bad if Sharon had a degree in marketing or there was some understandable reason she'd gotten promoted above me, but her degree in elementary education was as irrelevant to this job as my degree in dance. All of our experience came on the job, with the occasional training seminar thrown in once or twice a year. She wasn't particularly good at her job; I knew I could do better. Back when she was a grunt like me, she often pawned her reports off on me to do and then she'd take the credit for my work. Yet she'd gotten three promotions by the time I'd finally gotten one.

I had trouble paying attention to what Sharon said in the best of circumstances, but right now I was too painfully aware of the browser minimized in the corner of my screen to hear a word she said.

"So you'll have those reports ready by the meeting tomorrow?" Sharon asked.

"Of course!" Jen said.

This was an audacious lie. There was no way we'd have those reports done.

Expert Appliance had hired us to revamp their product line. To determine how to market the products most effectively, our department was doing the research to see what features consumers wanted in appliances like refrigerators, dishwashers, and washing machines. Our marketing department was producing marketing and sales collateral, and IT was designing Expert's new Web site.

This was the biggest project McKenna Marketing had ever done. We were staffing up to meet the demand, but even with the new hires, we couldn't meet our deadlines, and we were falling hopelessly behind.

"Great," Sharon said.

As soon as Sharon was out of sight, Jen said, "God! I thought she would never leave. Let me just say now that women with cellulite-ridden elephant thighs have no right whatsoever wearing those kind of dresses, particularly ones covered in gigantic sunflowers."

I stifled a smile. Jen said out loud all the bitchy things I felt guilty for even thinking, which was precisely why I loved her. I opened my Internet browser and finally sent my message to Art.

"So how is Art?" she asked.

"Wonderful, as usual. His dogs are named Holden and Phoebe."

Jen looked confused.

"From *Catcher in the Rye*, one of my all-time favorite books. I just like him more every day."

"Ooh, he's literary, too. And you're such a big reader," Jen said.

That was true, though these days my tastes hardly ran toward the literary. I'd become more of a romance novel kind of girl.

"I need to find a man, too. I can't let Dave think I'm a spinster. But I don't think I'm ready to try the personals."

Dave was Jen's on again/off again boyfriend. They broke up about every other month. He'd move out and stay with a friend for a month or two; Jen would go out with several new guys, find them wanting, and welcome Dave back into her life, suddenly managing to forget all his faults.

It would be a stretch for anyone to think of Jen as a spinster, to put it mildly. She had an amazing body and every item of her wardrobe was intended to emphasize this fact. Jen drove a twelve-year-old car, her five credit cards were practically transparent from overuse, and her apartment was microscopic, but her clothes were always stunning. She was the kind of woman whose T-shirts never wrinkled or frayed, the kind of woman who looked head-turningly good in a sweatshirt and jeans. She had brown eyes, and today she wore her striking red hair in a messy sort of ponytail bun that said clearly, "Look how I can just throw my hair up and still look gorgeous."

"I wish Tom would ask me out already," Jen said.

"Jen, for the record, you're asking for trouble if you date a coworker, but if you insist on dating Tom, why are you waiting for him to ask you out? Why don't you just ask him yourself?"

"In some ideal feminist world, women could ask men out and things would work out, but that's just not the way the world works."

"Maybe he's not asking you out because he's smart enough to know that it's not a good idea to date a coworker."

Jen rolled her eyes.

Tom worked in tech support, and Jen was constantly discovering software updates she absolutely *could not* live without. Jen's latest strategy was to purposely make her machine crash, so he'd have to come up and take a look at it. Despite her efforts, Tom had yet to ask her out.

"Do you know how long it's been since Kitty's gotten any? It's been . . . oh my God, it's been a month. Shoot me now. Take me to a nunnery! This is tragic!" Kitty was Jen's nickname for the area of her body her bikini bottoms barely covered. I found it more than a little disturbing that she referred to that region in the third person.

"I've read that after about three months of celibacy, you don't crave sex anymore. But the desire comes back right away when you start dating again," I said.

"Celibacy? Don't use such cruel terms. I don't want my sex drive to go into neutral. I'm too young."

"Think of all the work you could get done if you weren't trying to get laid all the time."

"What work is it exactly that you think I need time to devote myself to?"

"Don't you have any hobbies you wish you had more time for?"

"Yes, sex. So you see just how dire the situation is."

It was about 9:30 when Jen and I stopped talking and started pretending to work. I went back for three more cups of coffee in an attempt to caffeinate myself to the brink of functioning. Not that my new job wasn't infinitely better than harassing strangers over the phone into answering quantitative questions about their favorite shampoo brands, but it got pretty dull all the same.

JEN

Office Romance: How to Royally Screw Over Your Career

All was chaos and misery. How was I supposed to get any work done in such an environment? Jim from sales was buying a bride from overseas and my officemate Avery was trying to get herself some nookie by begging for it over the Internet. My own love life was in absolute shambles despite my heroic efforts. Where was gorgeous Tom from IT? Why hadn't he come to heed my call for help? Did he care at all how much effort it took to think of new ways to get my computer to crash or new programs I absolutely had to have installed just to lure him up to my office? The efforts I went to for love!

Of course I'd always thought Tom was magically delicious, but until four weeks ago I'd had to restrain my lust in the name of monogamy. No more!

Since Dave and I broke up for the fifth, and absolutely last, time, I'd lost six pounds. There was nothing like brutal rejection to get a girl to lose her appetite. But it was the best thing; it really was. I was so over his gambling, titty-bar-going, drunken bullshit. Yeah he was hot and

had a great body and was so much fun. You don't realize how boring most guys are until you break up with
your boyfriend. During the times Dave and I were separated, I went out with men who were so excruciatingly
dull, Dave's DUI's and unpaid credit card bills and absolute avoidance of housework seemed like no big deal.
Endless dinners talking about the real estate market
and foot surgery would send me running back to Dave
with open arms. But did Dave's exceptional talents in
oral sex make up for the fact he ravaged my credit rat-
ing? (I know, it was so stupid for me to cosign his car
loan, but I was in love and what was a girl with a properly cared for clitoris to do when Dave pointed out that
we were, after all, going to get married someday and our
finances would essentially be combined anyway, and in
any case, his gorgeous brown eyes and sexy smile were
asking so sweetly?) No. Did toe-curling neck-kissing abilities make up for the fact he almost never took me out
to dinner and absolutely never made me dinner at any
time during the three or so years we lived together despite all the gourmet meals I spent hours planning and
preparing? No. Did the way he could always make me
laugh, no matter how much he was acting like an asshole, make up for all the nights he blew me off to hang
out with his friends? No. But god I missed the way he
made me laugh.

Okay, of course I still loved Dave. We had our share
of trouble, what couple doesn't? We were together for
five years, with stretches of separations and time-outs
here and there. After I graduated from the University
of Minnesota, I moved out here with him and we moved
in together. Even with all the fighting and the occasional broken window, I always knew we'd work it out.
We were young, we both had some oats to sow. I wasn't
worried.

But I had to face the truth, and the truth was Dave

and I were toxic together. Now I was twenty-five and the pressure was on. I didn't want to be some old biddy when I had my kids. I needed to find a good man who would be a good father to our kids, and I needed to do it fast. Even if I met a guy soon, we'd need a year to date and a year to plan the wedding and then a year to be a young married couple without kids. Then I'd promptly get pregnant and nine months later I'd have our first kid with hardly any time to spare before I turned thirty.

I needed a guy who could support me while I raised our kids. I used to think I wanted to be some big career woman. Then I got a job, and let me tell you, work *sucks*. Maybe there were some people out there who had careers that challenged their creativity and helped them learn and grow in some fulfilling sort of way. Maybe there were people who'd managed to get jobs with managers who weren't complete idiots. I wasn't one of them. Screw my career. I just wanted to be a good wife and mom.

It really was the best thing that Dave and I had broken up. Dave was not the kind of guy who would be a good father to our children even though, god, they'd be soooo cute. A bartender and ski instructor who'd never finished college couldn't afford to let me stay home with the kids.

Speaking of men in upwardly mobile careers, where exactly was Tom? Didn't he care about the loss of productivity? How was I supposed to get any work done if my computer crashed every time I opened Photoshop? Did he need to know I didn't actually need to use Photoshop because Avery did all the graphics?

How was I supposed to concentrate on work when I was in the midst of a fertility and romantic crisis? And who could work in such a managerially dysfunctional environment anyway?

McKenna Marketing reminded me of the double-blind studies I learned about in psychology class in college. That's when doctors prescribe patients pills, and neither the doctor nor the patient knows who is getting the placebo. That's the way things worked around here. Absolutely no one knew what was going on. Orders were issued without the order-giver having any clue how things work in the real world. We order-takers nodded dumbly and tried to look busy, never really understanding what it was we were allegedly getting paid to do. The amount of work my manager Sharon assigned and the time we were given to get it done in was so wildly unrealistic, there seemed no point in even trying. Sharon was only another hapless cog in the McKenna Marketing machine. I understood that she took her orders from above and was not nearly as important as she thought she was, but it seemed to me that she should be the one to let the higher-ups know what could and couldn't be accomplished in an eight-hour workday instead of always saying, "Yessah, yessah, we'll get it all done, sah."

"Tom!"

"Hi, I heard your computer crashed again." He stood in the doorway, his thick arm muscles rippling Adonislike from the sleeves of his T-shirt. "It may be time to get you a newer machine. You've been having a lot of troubles lately. What's the latest issue?"

"Every time I open Photoshop I crash."

"What on earth do you need Photoshop for?" my evil officemate Avery asked.

I gave her a look, trying to telepathically communicate to her that just because her vagina was cobwebbed and decayed like a long-forgotten ancient artifact, she didn't need to foil my plans. Honestly. She could really be pretty if she tried, and then she wouldn't have to go to such extremes to find a guy. She never wore makeup for one thing, and she never did anything with her hair. She was totally skinny but hid her figure in these loose cotton pantsuits or flower-child long skirts and flowing blouses. She did have nice features—a gorgeous long neck and cheekbones to die for, to start with. And her eyes were a stunning shade of blue. If she would only wear some makeup to play them up! And right now I could count not one but *two* scraggily eyebrow hairs. I wanted to leap across the desk and pluck them out myself.

"I'm adding some visuals to the Expert reports."

"Maybe you just need some more memory. Do you know how much memory your machine has?" Tom said.

I shook my head.

"I'll just take a look." He leaned over me and typed in some things on my keyboard. I sat, immobilized, my heart racing with him so close. "Wow, that's a lot lower than I would have thought. I wonder if your memory may have been dislodged. Has anyone moved the case recently? I'll just check out the motherboard. Excuse me." Tom crawled under my desk.

I rolled my chair out a little, but only a little, to give him room, but not too much. Like all the guys in the IT department, Tom always wore jeans. But nobody made jeans look as good as Tom. The denim was drawn tight over his muscular thighs, and I had the ideal vantage point from which to enjoy them fully.

He'd started working at McKenna Marketing five months ago. Of course I'd thought he was hot the moment I'd laid eyes on him, but I hadn't truly lusted after him until I had a chance to talk to him at a company picnic in August. That's when I found out that, before he'd gotten this boring office job, he'd worked as a firefighter, a white-water rafting guide, a blackjack dealer at a casino in Blackhawk, and a carpenter. And he was only twenty-eight! When he got sick of making crappy wages, he started going to night classes to get his associate's degree in computer science.

Plus, he and his girlfriend had broken up two months ago. Just enough time for him to be *so* over her.

We were perfect for each other.

"Avery," I asked, "are you going to Rios tomorrow night after work?"

"I haven't decided yet."

"You have to come so you can buy me a drink to celebrate my breakup from Dave."

Avery shook her head and smiled. She kept right on working as she said, "We'll see."

"How about you, Tom, are you going to come out with us tomorrow night? You can bring your girlfriend," I said.

Tom came out from under the desk. "I don't have a girlfriend, thank god. I broke up with her a while ago. She was a sweet girl, but man, what a psycho."

"Oh really, that's a shame. You two made such a cute couple."

He shrugged.

"So what about tomorrow night?"

"I have some plans with some buddies of mine."

"Oh," I said. "Where are you going? You guys should stop by Rios if you can, it'll be fun."

"We'll see. I'm going to see about getting you some more memory. I'll be back."

"Thanks so much," I said.

"No problem."

I sighed. It was far more interesting to watch Tom's blue-jean-clad ass than it was to type up a report on features people wanted in an oven. Alas.

RETTE

The Interview

Bound in my nylons, navy blue suit, and high-heeled shoes, I tried to coax my car into transporting me to my job interview.

My sorry-looking '87 Subaru always had to pull this shit when I had some place important to be. The engine finally turned over, but it wasn't happy about it.

I couldn't complain. It was amazing that the car made it all the way from Minneapolis to Boulder. Still, I prayed it would cling to life for a few more months, at least until I could get a decent job. It was a long shot, as the Subaru had repeatedly made it clear that death was imminent.

On the drive from Minnesota, Greg had driven behind me so he could rescue me lest my car conk out for good. The Subaru made it, but various features in the car went quietly kaput, the most troubling of which was the demise of the driver's seat. At one moment I was driving along the interstate in a seated, upright position, and in the next instant I heard a little snap and I was suddenly supine and staring at the sky through the sunroof. It took me a long moment to understand what had happened, then I screamed and bolted upright, relieved to discover that I hadn't drifted into oncoming traffic. It was twenty miles until the next gas station. Twenty miles of driving without any back support whatsoever is harder than it sounds. At the gas station, Greg wedged a block of wood in to get the back of the driver's seat to be almost but not quite upright. Now when I drove I had to sit at an unnatural angle that made me feel as if I were manning a lunar space module.

Then there was the matter of the sunroof. It wouldn't latch. I had tied it down with a shoelace, but it still didn't close completely. Greg used electrical tape to seal the gap, but rain always managed to drip through anyway. Because of Colorado's frequent afternoon thunderstorms, I'd gotten used to driving smashed up against the driver's side door to avoid getting completely drenched. At stoplights, with my face mashed up against the window, I tried desperately to avoid the gazes of the drivers who pulled up beside me and observed my contorted position with confusion or amusement.

Today, happily, was sunny, and the fact that I wouldn't arrive at my interview sopping wet seemed a good omen. I popped in an Indigo Girls tape and sang along with Amy and Emily.

I had just turned onto the highway when a rock hit my windshield. For a moment I thought the popping sound was a gunshot and the glass shrapnel that whizzed by my eye was a bullet. The crack in the glass burned its way across the windshield, making it hard to get a clear view. The splintered glass changed its trajectory, fashioning a complicated web. Like I wasn't jittery enough.

My heart pounded furiously against my full-coverage support bra as terrifying thoughts seared through my head: What if the glass hadn't missed my eye and I'd been blinded and then spun wildly into traffic, leaving a trail of blood and carnage, my dead body hurled from the car into a Mack truck that, upon impact, exploded into a firestorm of destruction?

Okay, the good news: I wasn't dead. The bad news was that, now, in addition to being forced to drive at an entirely unnatural incline because of my busted-up driver's seat, I could only see through the bottom part of the windshield like you do in the winter when the defrost has only cleared the first couple inches.

Oh well. The car was worth about fifty cents with or without a cracked windshield.

I found McKenna Marketing without further hazard and the human resources director started me off with two hours' worth of spelling and editing tests. By the time I'd handed in the battery of exams, I was more frazzled than ever. My lipstick had worn off from chewing my pencil nervously, my hair was disheveled from slapping my head in an effort to kick-start my brain into thinking, and my eyebrows were furrowed tightly with stress. As the HR director alerted the managing editor that I was ready to see her, I took deep breaths and struggled to gain a modicum of composure.

"We're so glad you could make it," Eleanore, the manager of the editorial department, boomed as she stormed into the waiting area. She had wild, dyed-to-cover-the-gray blond hair and a huge, artsy medallion hanging from her neck. She wore a tremendous amount of makeup, which somehow seemed to accentuate her wrinkling, crepey skin. She was tall and perilously skinny.

Eleanore was flanked by her assistant, Paige, for whom the effort of uttering her almost inaudible greeting seemed to make her so nervous it heightened my own already epic anxiety, and Sharon, a marketing manager who I noticed, despite my nervousness, had made some truly unfortunate fashion and hairstyle decisions. Why on earth would a pregnant woman with ponderous thighs and sallow skin think a short yellow dress with large sunflowers was a good idea?

They led me into a conference room where the three of them sat on one side of the oblong table and I sat across from them. I cleared my throat more often than necessary.

"As I explained over the phone, our company is growing rapidly, and we need another editor," Eleanore began. "Paige has been putting in all kinds of overtime to get the job done. That's what's expected at a growing company, but even with all our hard work, there just aren't enough hours in the day to get through all the brochures and reports generated by the McKenna Marketing staff. So, tell us about your interest in editing marketing materials."

Ouch. "Well, I'm not an expert, but I love learning about new things." True. "I really enjoyed editing for the business journal in Minnesota." False. "That's why I worked there every summer when I was in college." False. I worked there because they paid me seven dollars an hour, which, since it had the distinction of being more than minimum wage, seemed like a lot of money at the time, plus Mom was friends with the publisher. I hoped she didn't notice that I didn't actually answer her question.

"What was it that you enjoyed about the business journal?"

"Well . . . I, uh, learned a lot. I enjoy making things clearer for the reader, cleaning up poor grammar, and checking facts." Not entirely false.

"You *enjoyed* fact checking?" Eleanore and her entourage laughed a mirthless, corporate laugh.

"I know that sounds weird. I guess I just like taking pride in my work and making sure things are accurate. Some of the stories I worked on were pretty complicated, and I liked . . . it was kind of like putting a complex puzzle together, and I don't know, call me weird, I think that stuff is fun. Editors are kind of, I don't know, not like regular folks. We can debate for hours over whether a hyphen should be put between two words. That is not most people's idea of a good time."

"Why did you quit teaching?" Eleanore asked.

"Well, my fiancé . . ."

"You're getting married?" Eleanore said. "Paige just got married eight months ago."

"Great, great," I gushed.

"When are you getting married?" Sharon asked.

"August fifteenth."

"Congratulations," Eleanore said.

"Yeah, it's exciting." Smile, smile, enthusiasm, enthusiasm. "So, teaching was difficult, but I enjoyed it." True, false. Oh god, did I say difficult? Shit. I meant challenging. *Challenging.* "But when my fiancé wanted to leave Minnesota to go to graduate school, it seemed like a good way to get out . . . to see some other parts of the country."

"Margarette," Eleanore said, "where do you see yourself in ten years?"

The question threw me. What exactly was it that I wanted to do for a living ten years from now? Did I want to move up and become a manager? Would I be editing business shit I wasn't interested in? I cleared my throat. It was taking me too long to answer. "That's an interesting question. I'm not sure exactly. I know I want to be working in the editorial field. I want a job where I'm always learning and growing and being challenged. It's hard to say where I'll be in ten years because things can change so much. I used to think I would teach English until I died, but . . . I don't know. I think it's important to be open to change." I sounded like a job-hopper, an aimless Gen X slacker. "And yet, stability also is good, too. Stability and change. It's a juggling act, sort of." What mentally deficient imbecile was this argument going to sway? And tell me I didn't just end a sentence with a preposition while interviewing for an editorial job. Why did they mock me by continuing to ask me questions when I was clearly an unemployable loser?

They grilled me for forty-five more minutes and told me I'd either get a rejection letter or a phone call in the coming weeks. I thanked them profusely for the opportunity to meet with them. I couldn't face Jen and Avery after failing so miserably, so I left without stopping by their office. The fake smile I'd had plastered on all morning melted from my face the moment I left the building.

On the drive home I reviewed every stupid thing I'd said. The emptiness I felt in my stomach and chest swelled into an uneasy nausea.

Small Victories

In the dark weeks of unemployment, I often thought that my life was like decaffeinated coffee: utterly pointless. Then I'd think of that thirteen-year-old girl who weighed 680 pounds and died of a heart attack in front of the television she never left. Her body was covered in bedsores and there was feces caught between the folds of her flesh because sometimes it was too difficult for her to haul herself to the bathroom. Her story was a sad one, no question. But sometimes I'd think to myself that, you know, even on my worst days, *damn*, at least I wasn't trapped in front of the television shitting on myself; at least I didn't go around with shit caught in my flabs of fat.

It's important to celebrate the small victories in life.

Feigning Nymphomania

As soon as I got home I peeled off my constricting interview suit and got into my beloved, battered sweats. I had just started making dinner when Greg came home.

"Hey, beautiful," he said, wrapping his arms around me and kissing my neck. "This is what I like to see. The wife in the kitchen making my dinner." He smiled his goofy, lopsided grin that had forced me to fall in love with him.

"Soon-to-be wife and don't get used to it." I said it lightly, but I wasn't kidding about that last part. Since we'd moved in together, Greg had been busy with classes (he'd had to finish a pre-rec this summer, so three days after we got here in June, he'd become nothing more than a blur of textbooks and notebooks and calculators), and I'd been bored and unemployed, so I'd taken to doing most of the cooking and cleaning. It was important that Greg realized that once I finally got a job, he'd have to start doing a much bigger share of domestic duties.

"How'd the interview go?"

I groaned. "Let's just say I no longer feel above doing temp work."

"You're going to find something soon, don't worry. What are you making?"

"Chili and cornbread and salad. Wanna cut salad ingredients?"

"Salad?" Greg whined. He was not a fan of vegetables.

"Some of us need to lose weight so we don't look repugnant in our wedding dresses."

"I don't want there to be an ounce less of you in the world."

"You won't love me if I'm skinny?"

"I'll always love you."

"Good. Cut the carrots." I chopped the garlic and onions for the chili. I wasn't much of a cook, but I had a few simple recipes that I was capable of making. I would have liked to have made vegetarian chili to cut down on calories, but Greg firmly believed in red meat at every meal. So I compromised with low-fat ground beef, which was wickedly expensive.

Watching Greg cut carrots made me smile. He looked so cute, concentrating so intently. Greg had kind hazel eyes and, compared to me, was a giant at six-foot-two. He was thin, too, all elbows and angles.

"Greg, what are you doing?" I asked. He was chopping the carrots into huge pieces. "Do the words *bite size* mean anything to you?"

"Are you dissing my carrot-cutting abilities? Were you aware that *Gourmet* magazine has offered to pay me thousands of dollars to photograph my exquisitely shorn carrots for their cover?"

"Really? That's fabulous. When do we see the dough?"

"Oh, well, I turned them down of course. I didn't want to sell out. My carrots are only for the eyes of my beloved."

"Oh no, please, sell out. I'm ready to sell my plasma and root through strangers' garbage for aluminum cans to recycle. At five cents a can, we could be out of debt, who knows, maybe before our eighty-sixth birthdays. So what do you want to do tonight?" I asked.

"I have to go back to campus. We have a group project to work on."

"Oh," I groaned. "We never spend time together anymore. We never have time for sex these days." Since Greg started grad school, we were down to having sex only once or twice a week. It wasn't like I was starving for it: In the long, dull hours of unemployment, I was up to masturbating approximately fourteen times a day. While I still appreciated Greg's gentle caresses, the efficiency of the Magic Wand was astonishing and reliable, and I was growing increasingly dependant on its ferociously intense, insistent throb. I needed to get a job soon, if only to keep my relationship with Greg intact. Greg's friends had warned him not to move in with me. They said women never wanted to have sex post-cohabitation. I loathed Greg's friends and would feign nymphomania to prove them wrong.

I pretended to pout.

"Guess we'd better do something about that." He set the knife down, put his hand behind my neck, and pulled my lips to his. The kiss was delicious, but I was really hungry and not at all horny. Although the pertinent region of my anatomy was nearly callused from overuse, I didn't feel I could say no when Greg took my hand and led me to the bedroom.

We quickly got out of our clothes, as mechanically as if we were getting ready for a doctor's examination. I lay on the bed on my back and Greg practically leapt on me, kissing and groping me with puppy-like eagerness. I clenched my jaw and willed myself not to shout, "Oh, just get on with it already, I'm starving!"

Greg's attempts to arouse me were thorough, if ineffective. "Come inside me," I whispered in the most vixenish voice I could muster.

"You're not ready."

When we'd first started dating, I'd loved how we could engage in foreplay for hours, and he never seemed the slightest bit bored or put out by it. But right now, my stomach was growling, time was of the essence, and I'd already given myself three orgasms that day (far fewer than usual as I'd been busy with the job interview). I could do without for one evening.

I wondered if McKenna Marketing would call. Maybe I was being too hard on myself. Maybe I had done better than I thought.

God, I was so hungry I was even salivating over the thought of the dinner salad awaiting me just a few short feet away. Oh Christ, we hadn't eaten the vegetables I bought for that ratatouille recipe I'd meant to cook last week. Nuts. We did not have the money to squander on wasted food, and yet week after week I replaced clear plastic bags of gelatinous murk with clear plastic bags of fresh produce. It was a vicious cycle of good intentions. I knew I should eat more fresh . . .

Just then, something strange happened. Greg's urgent fingers had managed to find just the right spot, and my worries about the day suddenly vanished. All I could think about was how good his fingers felt. I let out a little moan. Greg smiled. To him, a moan was the equivalent of a standing ovation. He continued on, thus encouraged, and I applauded his efforts.

Bravo, bravo! I thought, as Greg kindly inspired the day's fourth orgasm.

AVERY

Possibility

Driving home from work, I studied the people in the cars beside me. The woman with her outreached arm, a cigarette dangling from her fingertips; the teenage boy who looked so young, his entire future ahead of him, a gamut of possibilities; a good-looking guy in his early thirties. I imagined what would happen if he rear-ended me—gently of course. We'd get out of our cars. He'd be all concerned. I'd say, "Don't worry, what's one more scratch. There is no need to get the insurance agencies involved." He'd be so moved by my kindness that he'd say, "Let me at least take you to dinner." I'd agree, and we'd go to a fabulous restaurant where we'd laugh, I'd say witty things, he'd say intelligent and sweet things, and we'd live happily ever after. He wouldn't be rich, merely comfortably wealthy. He'd have a nice home and car and like to travel. He'd tell me I was beautiful.

Or maybe a tire on my car would blow and I'd be stranded along the side of the road. He'd pull over to help me. He'd be a professional of some sort, but despite his white collar, he'd know how to fix my car because mechanics was his hobby as a teenager (maybe he paid his way through college working at a garage during the summer). While he worked on my car, we'd talk. It would turn out we had a lot in common. We'd laugh. I would be struck by his amazing smile. He'd ask me out. He'd take me on a picnic by a creek in a forest. We'd drink wine and eat grapes, Brie and bread, and gourmet chocolate. We'd live happily ever after.

Gideon was not the man for me; it just took me a few years to figure that out. There were lots of single men out there. There was a world of possibility.

Now I just needed a date.

The story of Gideon and me might sound very romantic if you didn't know the ending.

We met five years ago when I was helping facilitate a focus group. Participants earned forty dollars for an hour of their time. They watched a twenty-minute pilot of a sitcom, discussed what they liked or didn't like for thirty minutes, and then filled out a profile of themselves.

It was unusual for a lowly teleresearcher to assist with a focus group, but my manager at the time thought I had potential. (Unfortunately, she was fired under mysterious circumstances, and with her went all my chances for advancement.)

When gorgeous Gideon walked in, I stared at him with the fawning gaze of a groupie meeting her rock star idol for the first time. Then I dropped the entire stack of handouts I'd been holding. Fifteen years of dance training and in the presence of a good-looking guy, every shred of grace I'd developed vanished. The papers billowed out around me and I scrambled to collect them. Gideon helped me pick them up.

"Here you go," he said. He had long, dark hair and a disarmingly sexy smile.

"Thank you," I mumbled.

While the pilot was shown, there was blessedly little I could do to further embarrass myself. I sat in my corner behind the focus group members, trying to hide my smile. It had been such a long time since a man had gotten my heart racing, and I rather liked it.

During the discussion portion, when it was his turn to comment on the program, he talked about how the women in the sitcom were simpering idiots and Hollywood needed to come up with some stronger roles for women characters. He was sick of women in TV shows always being young and pretty and stupid.

Not only was he gorgeous and considerate, he also noticed how women in television were objectified. He was a perfect, perfect man.

From the profile he'd filled out at the end of the discussion, I learned that Gideon was Single/Never Married and twenty-four years old, which was a year younger than I was at the time. It surprised me to see that he hadn't gotten past high school. He spoke so eloquently I thought he must have had at least a master's degree in something esoteric and highly intellectual.

The profile said he worked at an art boutique and as a part-time model, and under hobbies and activities, he listed jogging and watching movies.

The form also contained his address. He lived in my neighborhood, not far from me.

I couldn't stop thinking about him. Over the next few weeks, I started visiting all the art boutiques I knew of in Boulder. At first, I wasn't conscious of what I was doing, but then I began going to boutiques as deliberately as a spy on a reconnaissance mission. In three weeks I'd covered all of them but hadn't found him. It occurred to me that I might have gone to the boutique where he

worked but on a day or at a time he wasn't on the schedule. So I went to them all again, on different days at different times. I felt vaguely like a stalker, but I couldn't
help myself. For all I knew he could have had a girlfriend or been gay, but I hadn't been so attracted to
someone in a long time and visiting art galleries wasn't
a bad way to spend my time, so who was it hurting?
Except I never did run into him.

So then I got extreme.

I devised a plan that involved me jogging in our
neighborhood at different times of day, hoping to run
into him. This plan had many flaws. For one thing, what
were the chances I was going to run into him? For another thing, I hated jogging. I found it a monotonous
way to work out.

I began by jogging two miles a day, very slowly. I made
sure I looked casually adorable whenever I jogged. For
the first few weeks I kept looking for him and expecting
to see him. Soon though, I stopped worrying so much
about meeting Gideon, and I began to actually get into
the running. I enjoyed feeling my endurance improve,
and I began to push myself more and more. I hadn't
pushed myself physically like that since I'd danced in
college. I had grown complacent with my yoga work-
outs, doing the same routine day after day, and I loved
that I had found a workout that excited me again after
such a long exercise rut.

Three months after I first met Gideon, I almost never
thought about him anymore. Then one Saturday I saw a
man with long, shampoo-commercial beautiful hair jog
past me. I sped up to get a better look—it was him!

If I'd bumped into him right away after I'd begun jogging, I probably would have been too nervous to talk to
him, but now I wasn't particularly invested in getting to
know him, and I didn't feel any shyness. "You're Gideon?
Right?"

He nodded.

"Maybe you don't remember me. I work at McKenna Marketing."

"Yeah, sure, I remember you."

"So you live around here?"

He nodded again.

"I'm Avery."

He gave me the slightest smile.

We jogged in silence for a while. I was in decent shape, but keeping up with him wasn't easy. Finally he stopped at a drinking fountain in the park. I waited, worrying that if I had kept on going that would have been rude, and worrying that waiting for him was presumptuous.

"You're a dancer," he said.

"I *was* a dancer. Wait, how did you know that?"

He pointed to my feet, which had gone to third position out of habit. "You carry yourself well. You're very graceful."

"Thank you." I was suddenly very conscious of how I was standing. I shifted my feet awkwardly.

"Ballet?"

"Years of it, but I was never that great at it. I was more into modern and jazz."

"Cool."

I nodded. I nodded some more. "Well, I guess I should get going. Maybe I'll see you around."

"Yeah." We looked at each other, then the ground, then each other. We nodded and smiled. I was just about to turn to leave when he said, "Hey, do you have plans for tonight?"

"Not really."

"I was going to make spaghetti for dinner. Would you like to join me? I live just a few blocks from here."

I couldn't believe it. After all my scheming and plotting to meet him, not only had we finally met, but he'd asked me out for a date. It was fate. We were meant to be. "That sounds great." I turned to go, then turned back. "I'm . . . I'm a vegetarian so if you could leave the meatballs out of mine, that would be great." I braced myself for him to say, "Oh, why are you a vegetarian?" or make some kind of smart-alecky comment. I'd been veggie since I was thirteen and I'd spent most of my lifetime defending what was apparently a very threatening alternative dietary lifestyle to some people. But all he said was "Cool."

I was in love.

For us to meet like that—what were the chances if destiny didn't mean for us to be together?

My heart soared all afternoon with the knowledge that I had found my soul mate.

The gods of destiny weren't around to help me make the right decisions about what to wear, however. As soon as I got to his place, I wanted to run home and change. He opened the door in a blue silk shirt, meticulously pressed black pants, and expensive black leather shoes; I was wearing a long loose cotton skirt and blouse. He looked like he belonged on a runway in Milan, and I looked like I belonged in the parking lot of a Dead concert selling beads.

Gideon didn't say much over dinner. I asked him a lot of questions, and he told me that, just like me, he'd grown up in Colorado and had lived in New York for a while. He was there for nine months before going broke. He'd gone there to make it as a model, but it wasn't until he came back to Colorado that he started getting any work. He did mostly ads for local department stores. Even so, the pay, he explained, was unsteady, and he'd taken a job at the boutique. He didn't know anything about art, and he didn't have any experience in sales, but the owner of the boutique thought he had the right look.

"Do you like it, working at the boutique?" I asked.

"Yeah it's okay. Rich people, you know, they're a trip. They think nothing about dropping seventy grand on a canvas with some scribbles on it. The opening nights are fun. Afterward, I get to help Glenda, that's the owner, finish up all the wine and finger foods. That's my favorite part."

I spent the entire evening staring at him dreamily, awed by his beautiful, delicate grace.

"Why are you smiling? You've been grinning like, all night."

I couldn't tell him that it was because I was just so happy. "It must be the wine," I said.

"Well, have some more." He grabbed the bottle and filled my glass. "Your smile is beautiful."

One year later we went to a justice of the peace and vowed we'd be together till death do us part. Two years after that, we got quietly divorced. There was no fighting, no arguing over who got what. In fact, we never argued during our marriage. But then we never really talked, either. My marriage with Gideon was a marriage of silence. I would've welcomed fighting; I would've welcomed any kind of communication at all. I'd never felt so lonely as when I moved in with him. I was so lonely in my marriage that making the transition from being married to being single was easy. I don't know exactly when it happened, if there was one exact moment or a gradual decline, but at some point, when I tried to talk to him about my work, my dreams, my day, he would look so bored and uninterested that I would cut my story short. After a while, I rarely talked at all. How had I managed to marry such a stranger?

In the first few dates you have all your stories to share, all your jokes to tell. You see movies you don't want to see and laugh at jokes that aren't funny. Then, a few dates down the road, you have sex, and it's good, and you wonder if this could be love. The next dates have a lot of sex and not so much talking, so you don't notice that it's because you don't particularly have much to say to each other. You're grateful someone finds you attractive and wants to spend time with you. You mistake your gratitude for love.

Maybe Gideon was right. Did we ever truly love each other? Did we ever really like each other? Or were we so eager to be a part of a "we," to have a companion for Saturday nights and occasions like holidays and office parties that we ignored the fact that we didn't really get each other? Gideon was good-looking, he was intelligent, he was sweet and caring and the kind of guy I couldn't wait to introduce to my friends and family. I really thought I loved him. It had been easy for me not to notice that we didn't get each other's jokes and that we didn't really have anything to talk about. I was so enthralled with the idea of him, of the person I made him out to be in my imagination.

I even made myself believe it was a good thing that we were so different. I'd never read a fashion magazine in my life, and he wanted nothing more than to make it as a model. He read every men's magazine and knew the names of every designer. He always dressed better than I did. He even wore designer pajamas to bed. I liked wearing sweats and a T-shirt at night, but he liked me in silk negligees. Some nights I'd placate him, but the silk was too expensive to clean and I never slept well in it. I felt like an actress, someone pretending to be

stylish. Why, I would ask, does it matter what I'm wearing when I'm *asleep?* He would argue something about
the clothes making the man. He exhausted me with his
dedication to style, to every little detail. One time when
we were going to the clubs, I was wearing a black outfit,
and I didn't feel like putting my stuff from the brown
purse I brought to work every day into my black purse.
When we were getting ready to go, Gideon looked at
me. "You're not going to bring your black purse? Your
brown purse doesn't match."

I dutifully changed purses, all the while thinking,
weren't guys supposed to be oblivious to things like
whether your purse matched your outfit?

It wasn't that we didn't have fun together. We got that
part right. We went dancing all the time. After a couple
of drinks, in the darkly lit clubs, I would watch him
dance and be enthralled with him, with the way he carried himself, the way he smiled and moved. His easy
confidence was enticing. We would go home and make
love hungrily; then in the morning we'd make love again,
slowly this time. It took a long time for me to realize
what was missing from our relationship. In Gideon, I
had a lover and a companion, but I didn't really have a
friend. Gideon never really got who I was.

I hadn't realized how unhappy I was until Gideon told
me. We had gone to see some mind-numbing movie and
went to Wendy's for dinner afterward. We sat across
from each other with our plastic forks in hand. I looked
at my salad and strained to think of something to talk
about.

"Avery, you're a good person . . ." he began.

I let out a little laugh. I knew what he was going to
say. I'd known the end was coming without knowing I
knew. I couldn't look at him, so I turned to watch the
people waiting in line to order their food. The caustic

colors, the vinyl seats, the plastic silverware, and Styrofoam plates seemed to mock me. After a long moment, I managed to ask if there was someone else.

"No. No."

"Why this sudden change then?" I said, my voice shaky. "Is it someone from work?"

"There is no one else. I swear. It's . . .You and I never laugh together. I don't know . . . I don't know if I ever really loved you."

For the next several weeks, those words seared through my mind a thousand times a day.

I don't know if I ever really loved you.

I don't know if I ever really loved you.

I don't know if I ever really loved you.

It didn't seem as though divorce should be so easy. But since we didn't have any kids and didn't own much, it was just a matter of signing some papers. I agreed to let him keep the apartment because I couldn't afford the rent on my own. I found a new apartment a few weeks after we decided to separate, and I moved out a couple of weeks after that. I hadn't wanted to live so close to Gideon, but I fell in love with this apartment, and I could actually afford the rent, no easy feat in Boulder.

There were downsides to living alone. Never having enough whites to justify a load of laundry, for example. Every creak and noise took on new significance when there was no one to blame them on. Every night I came home from work and flung open the shower curtain, half expecting to find an armed maniac hiding in the bathtub.

After a couple of weeks, I brought an eight-week-old kitten home from the animal shelter.

I named her Martha. All she did was eat, sleep, and play. Watching her luxuriate in endless naps reminded me not to take life quite so seriously.

Martha liked chewing on everything from books to cords, and she liked to sharpen her nails on everything except the scratching post I'd shelled out fifteen bucks for. It was, however, impossible not to love her.

She seemed to grow every day, jumping up to higher and higher places in the apartment. I could throw anything across the room—a hair scrunchy, a pencil, a stuffed mouse—and Martha would bound across the room with a charging warrior meow and leap on the object with a Jackie Chan tumble, only to utterly lose interest in the item a moment later, abandoning it entirely.

I reviewed with her the basic concept of the game catch, but she inevitably fell asleep before I finished my tutorial. We played with her toy mouse, and though I tried to encourage her to bring the mouse back to me to throw again, she was only interested in the mouse while it was in transit, and after a while she was too tired to even muster enthusiasm for that. After a few minutes of play, she'd lie down and bat at it halfheartedly and half-asleep.

Martha spent most of her day dazed in a light sleep. Her stupor was occasionally interrupted by short bursts of energy in which she bounded around the house in crazed loops. She paused long enough to eat a few kibbles of food before collapsing again in fatigue.

Her goal was to let no surface go unadorned by cat hair. In the first few weeks I had her, she couldn't leap up to the counter, but soon she was surveying the apartment from the top of the fridge and the highest bookshelves (knocking several books over each time).

She often got these bursts of energy at three or four o'clock in the morning. She liked to turn over the garbage and wrestle noisily with paper or plastic that spilled onto the floor, ripping and growling at it as if it were a menacing burglar. She would race over my sleeping body, and, though she was light, anything that leaps on you from the dresser while you're deep in sleep is as jarring to wake to as a bucket of ice-cold water or the sound of a lawnmower being revved up right outside your window.

I would fall back asleep, only to be awoken an hour later by Martha sucking savagely on my neck. I tried to explain that her nursing days were over and no matter how hard she sucked on my neck she would never be nourished with milk, but despite her lack of results she was determined to find comfort by nursing on my jugular vein. I would toss her off me and she would return within seconds. I grabbed her and held her at arm's length while she struggled to regain access to my neck, then I let her go and dove for cover beneath my quilt and pillow. The determined Martha gnawed at me through the quilt. Kittens look harmless, but their teeth can be painful and are entirely unconducive to slumber.

I would go off to work the next morning wearing a turtleneck to hide the hickeys given to me by my kitten, which symbolized the state of my life more than I cared to think about.

JEN

Wallowing 101

I was far too depressed to eat; that much was obvious. I poured myself another glass of red wine and surveyed the damage. Half a dozen bags from the mall littered the living room floor. Shopping therapy.

Every time we broke up, I went on a shopping spree. I know material things don't solve problems, but I felt better for a while anyway.

I got a slinky black dress and black lace bra and underwear. I already had about six black bras, but I couldn't help myself. I look *good* in black.

This absolutely had to be the last time we broke up. I could not afford to max out my credit cards again. I was still in dire financial straits from helping Dave out with his car and credit problems. It was so unfair—I drove an old car, never traveled, lived in a shithole of an apartment, but still didn't make enough money to buy a few new outfits every now and then without maxing out my credit cards. I needed a better job, a job that paid a livable wage. My chance was coming. When Sharon went on maternity leave, I'd get the chance to take over her spot for a couple of months. I just needed to make sure she picked me.

I drained my glass of wine.

Must not call Dave. Must not call Dave. God, I missed him already. He was so bad for me. Why couldn't I fall for a sweet nerd like Rette did?

Why was it that you can know you're making a mistake, but you make it anyway? It was like when I used Sun-In in eighth grade. Even girls with light brown hair ended up with orange-streaked locks. I, with my dark red hair, ended up with hair that looked like a fire engine streaked with rust and decorated with bright yellow yarn. *Very* attractive. I had suspected it wasn't actually a good idea, but the lure of inexpensive highlights had just proven too much. It was like getting wicked drunk to feel a little peace and clarity when all it ever brought was a heinous hangover.

Dave was totally irresponsible. He was even worse with money than I was, which, let me tell you, is saying something. Although, maybe in a way, I liked being the responsible one in the relationship. Everyone always thought of me as Miss Irresponsibility. That's what I got for having a brainiac overachiever for a sister. I wasn't like a total failure in school; it only seemed like that because Rette was such a flaming teacher's pet. Also, my little stay in the hospital my freshman year in college certainly didn't help my grades any. The deal was, I was scared of gaining the freshman fifteen, and I went a little overboard and got a tiny little case of bulimia. Only my mother knows about it; not even Rette knows. But you can't miss that many classes in college; it destroys your GPA. Believe me, I know.

Anyway, as I was saying, in a way I liked being the responsible one. When Dave went to buy his car, I had to cosign because he couldn't have credit after having some little credit problems, and it was kind of cool that he had to depend on me. But let me tell you, being responsible got *old*. Dave absolutely never took me out. I paid for everything. Once, I lent him my last thirty dollars, money I was going to use for groceries, and I found out the next morning he'd spent every dollar of it, one dollar bill at a time, stuffing it into a stripper's G-string. Boy, was I pissed. But it all worked out in the end 'cuz without any food in the house, I lost three pounds!

These days though, I was so over wanting to be the strong one in a relationship. I wanted a man to take care of me. This nurturing crap was overrated.

The only way I was going to get over him was if I found someone else. What the hell was Tom's problem? He wasn't dating anyone, and I was easily the cutest single girl at work.

I got a piece of paper and titled it "Strategies to get Tom to fall in lust with me." I considered a moment, then scratched out "lust" and wrote above it "love." It wasn't easy to strategize after half a bottle of wine, but I came up with (1) be beautiful (easy), (2) be funny and sincere (no sweat), (3) be patient and demure. Let him come to you. (Fie! Who's got time for patience? I don't want to be one of those old biddies that has to have a kid with the help of medical science at the age of sixty-two!)

What if I was over my prime and no man would ever look at me again?

This was stupid, making myself cry. It was the wine. You know what they say, "Poor me, poor me, pour me another drink."

What if I didn't meet anyone good enough to marry? The kind of guy who, if I came down with some hideous disease, would love me enough to stick with me till the end, no matter how gnarled and useless my body became.

Dave wasn't that guy. So why did I miss him so much?

RETTE

The Itinerary

8:59 A.M. Consider getting out of bed. Opt to stay in bed and stare at ceiling. Think about eating potato chips and French onion dip.

9:41 Get out of bed. Pour bowl of Raisin Bran. Feel righteous for not eating chips and dip. Notice that the phone does not ring with job offer. Flip through classifieds. Get depressed.

10:02 Change into sports bra, shorts, and gym shoes. Do fifty sit-ups and twenty sets of leg lifts. Get hungry. Determine that Raisin Bran did not provide enough energy to enable rigorous workout.

10:31 Snack on carrot sticks. Feel deprived. Notice how carrot sticks do not taste like pizza or a burrito or ice cream or brownies or a Snicker's, yet despite all this suffering the body persists on being frumpy and lumpy. Notice that phone has still not rung with job offer.

10:40 Turn on TV. Do not drink coffee, though want to desperately. Remind self that cantankerous stomach is a sign to take better care of self.

10:45 Become bored out of mind with soap opera. Hate all the commercials for brownie mix, fried chicken, Taco Bell, and candy bars. Continue to crave chips and dip.

10:49 Put step aerobic tape into VCR.

10:51 Cramp up. Pause video. Decide to finish when carrots are more fully digested.

11:02 Flip through want ads.

11:04 Become discouraged. Call Avery. Get answering machine.

11:05 Attempt to push chips and dip out of mind. Be unsuccessful.

11:06 Decide to eat lunch now and finish workout in an hour. Eat a salad and an apple. Use ranch dressing with all the fat because of new scientific evidence that says low-fat products are actually worse for you. Feel righteous for not eating a Whopper with cheese and fries with a chocolate milkshake.

11:26 Decide day has proven exhausting. Take nap. Feel certain things will be different after a good rest. Secretly hope a phone call for a job offer will disturb slumber.

The phone did finally wake me up, but not, sadly, with a job offer. It was just Avery, inviting me downstairs. She wanted to see how my interview had gone the day before.

I went downstairs and knocked on her door. I couldn't wait to come back home and check messages.

"You're just in time. I'm baking scones," Avery said. I followed her as she led the way to the kitchen. "Work was making me crazy so I came home for lunch to do a little baking. Baking always makes me feel better."

Avery must not get upset often or else she didn't eat the fruits of her baking therapy because she weighed about eleven ounces. No, the reality was that she probably ate all she wanted. We fat girls like to think skinny girls must starve and suffer to avoid our fate of crowbarring our way into size twelve jeans, but the truth was probably that they never bothered to count a calorie as they mowed their way through grocery carts full of lard-laden delights.

Her counter was covered in flour and measuring cups. I watched as she added the oats and the blueberries to the bowl.

Avery had enviable domestic skills. Her home was impeccably decorated. Every silk flower, every throw pillow, every picture frame, every detail was coordinated and classy. All of her furniture looked like it belonged in a modern art museum.

"I'm on a diet," I said.

"What on earth would compel you to do that?"

"I have a wedding dress to squeeze into."

"You do realize Marilyn Monroe, sex goddess extraordinaire, wore a size sixteen."

"A sixteen? Really? Well, she had her fat arranged better."

"You are hopeless. You look just like the woman in Rembrandt's *The Bather*, did you know that?"

"I didn't know that," I said. "I've never even heard of that painting."

"Well, she's gorgeous. She has your color hair and your voluptuous figure . . ."

"Voluptuous. Voluptuous is a transparent euphemism for *fat cow*. Do you get sick of me bitching endlessly to you? I promise I'll get some other friends soon; then I can spread my bitching out a little." I sat down at her table. She set a cup of coffee in front of me and set down small matching china saucers with cream and sugar. She used an entire dish to put the cream in instead of just pouring the cream from the carton into the coffee. Can you imagine unnecessarily messing up another dish that would have to be washed? She cracked me up.

"So, how'd the interview go?" she asked.

"I don't think it went very well."

"I'm sure you did great. It would be so wonderful if you worked with me. I could use a close friend at work."

"What about Jen?"

"Jen is a blast, but I don't know if we're close friends. I mean I wouldn't call her in times of crisis."

I nodded. Jen was the type you could always count on to have a good time, but she had a short attention span. She only liked to hang around for the fun stuff.

"Jen has always been like that. It bugged me until we were both in college together," I said. "It's supposed to be the older sister who teaches you about orgasms and blow jobs and draws diagrams of the clitoris and that sort of thing, but she was always the accelerated one when it came to fun stuff. She did a great job of corrupting me." It was funny: We'd never hung out in high school, but when we ended up at the same college, suddenly we went out together a lot. Until Jen got to the University of Minnesota two years after I did, the most scandalous thing I'd ever done was get tipsy with the girls in our dorm room. Then Jen got there and I tried pot, saw my first porno, and spent a good number of weekends in a state of drunken debauchery. Jen had been the ringleader of every crazy thing I did in college.

"I believe it," Avery said. She went over to the oven and pulled the scones out. They smelled divine. "Sure you don't want one?" she asked, transferring the scones to a plate.

"Well, they have fruit and oats. That's very similar to being healthy."

"Exactly."

As Avery finished up in the kitchen, I glanced across the room and noticed a black and white photo of her on a bookshelf. She was standing in a dance studio next to several other dancers. The other dancers looked stuck up and pissed off. They were smiling rigid, toothless smiles, and their hair was pulled back into such severely tight buns it looked painful. Avery, on the other hand, had a friendly, genuine smile. Her curly hair had been much longer then, and it was pulled back into a loose ponytail, framing her face with tendrils of blond curls.

Avery set a scone in front of me and sat down.

"Avery, yum, you've outdone yourself." I savored another bite before changing the subject. "So how is Art?"

Avery looked down at the scone on her plate and smiled. "Good."

"Are you two ever going to meet?"

"I think so, but I'm not in any rush."

"Why not?"

"I guess I'm scared. I kind of don't trust myself to get into another relationship." She paused, stared out at nothing in particular, as if she were carefully weighing each word. "When I was in New York I dated a guy I later found out was a drug runner; my first love cheated on me left and right; and Gideon was a total disaster." She spoke slowly, cautiously, nothing like the verbal diarrhea I, Mom, and Jen used, always saying the first thing that came into our heads and regretting it later. "I'll probably end up dating a convict or rapist next. E-mailing Art is really fun; I just don't want to ruin anything."

"The whole thing is so romantic. I'm sort of jealous."

"Why?"

"Anything could happen. It's so exciting."

"Or nothing could happen."

Avery and I finished our scones and talked for another twenty minutes or so before Avery said she needed to get back to work. I didn't want her to go. I didn't want to face my quiet apartment all alone.

"Is everything okay?" Avery asked.

"I'm fine. It's just . . . Greg is going to be gone tonight, and I'm just so sick of being all alone in my stupid apartment."

"Come over for dinner tonight."

"Avery, that's sweet, but you don't have to."

"I love to cook. It'll be fun. I'll see if Jen can come."

"Yeah? Are you sure? I love your cooking. It's a date."

The first thing I did when I got home was check my voicemail for messages. Nothing. Nada. I was clearly unemployable. I would have to go to trucking school or one of the technical colleges they advertised endlessly in commercials on daytime TV.

AVERY

The Hug Club

I had Jen and Rette over for dinner. I made grilled vegetables, polenta, and Gorgonzola cheese, building a vegetable pyramid of Portobello mushrooms and zucchini on top of the polenta and topping it with the cheese, and arranging the asparagus, grilled tomatoes, and peppers around it in a circle. I drizzled a rich cream sauce over it all.

"Avery, you are such a domestic goddess. It looks gorgeous," Rette said.

I opened a bottle of red wine and poured each of us a glass. "Thanks."

"So not like I'm going to get the job, but just in case, tell me everything about this great company of yours. Ave, you've been there the longest. What's the scoop?"

"The scoop. Well, the company is six years old now; I've been there for five years. It was founded by Morgan McKenna. He's a small, wiry man with a sort of . . . I think some people think of him as being kind of abrasive. He's super smart, and you know how sometimes really intelligent people don't always have the best people skills? He has a Ph.D. in psychology, which is kind of strange because he seems much more interested in statistics than people. Morgan is kind of . . . he's very particular. Everything has to be cleared through him."

"Avery, sometimes you're so nice it's too annoying for words," Jen said. "He's a micromanaging control freak. He still acts like it's a company of ten instead of a company of more than a hundred. Everything still has to go through him; it's ridiculous. It's a total bottleneck. You can't get anything done; it's impossible to get anything done by our deadlines, and Morgan never seems to notice that he's the one holding the project up for three weeks."

"Even so, never, never send something out without his approval. A long time ago, more than four years ago, Sharon sent something to the printer without his approval. He'd seen the next-to-last draft—Sharon incorporated his changes and assumed it was good to go. But after it went to print, it turned out there was something Morgan didn't like, and he just went nuts, screaming and yelling. He was so furious; I thought Sharon might get fired. He kept ranting about how he'd already said that nothing could go out without his approval, didn't we respect him at all?"

"Any other characters I should watch out for?"

"There are eight VPs at McKenna, and they are all men, but you probably won't ever see any of them because we're not important enough," Jen said. "On the McKenna Marketing food chain, we're like, swamp algae."

"There are fourteen managers, three of whom are women: Eleanore, Sharon, and Pam," I added. "They all report to Glenn, the VP of marketing. Pam is the one manager I really like. She's incredibly hard working and always puts in insane hours and she's just really nice and very competent."

"The corporate mafia there," Jen said, "are three close friends known as the M&M gang because their names are Marc with a *c*, Mark with a *k*, and Mary. Marc and Mark both worked in the IT department and are something managerial. Mary works in marketing and is about as genuine as a silicone implant. Mark with a *k* is also known as Killer Mark because he'll start screaming at you for like, no reason at all. The M&M gang are all really good-looking, but they basically have the IQs of rotted logs. God forbid you ever need to get the IT department to run stats for a report. Marc and Mark are all arrogant, like their department is the most important, and therefore they can't be bothered to help anyone else get their jobs done. And when they finally do do what you ask them to, they always get it wrong, and when you point out that what they gave you wasn't what you needed, Marc goes blank and Mark goes ballistic."

"Sounds *great*," Rette said.

"I know sometimes I think . . ." I started. "You want some more wine?"

"Please," Jen said.

I poured her another glass. "Sometimes I think about my life and I just wonder, how did I get here? This was never how I expected my life would turn out. I went to a performing arts high school in New York, right? And then majored in dance in college, and I was never taught how to write a résumé or fix a toilet or balance a budget. I never worried about that stuff. I just thought about dancing and writing and pottery. I never even considered a future after dance. After I quit my job on the cruise ship, I came home, got the job at McKenna, and spent a year sort of picking up the pieces of my life after breaking up with Marcos, this guy I'd dated on the ship. McKenna was just this job I was going to have until I figured out what I was really going to do with my life. Then I met Gideon and put all my energy into that relationship, and I've been licking my wounds since the divorce. And now here I am, five years later, doing an eight-to-five job working in marketing, and I have no idea how I got here."

"So if you could be anything, what would it be?" Rette asked.

"Really, I don't know, that's part of the problem. Something creative. I was thinking I could see if I could work for Pam doing some writing."

"Have you ever thought about getting a job somewhere else?"

"I've thought about it fleetingly sometimes, but never very seriously," I said. "I'm just too loyal. My mom's like that too. That's why we stay with guys who cheat on us. We just keep thinking things will get better if we work hard enough. Anyway, I'm not really sure what other kind of job I'd want. It's a little bit pathetic when you think about it—I'm thirty years old and I have no idea what I want to be when I grow up."

"I majored in marketing, and *this* is *not* what I signed up for," Jen said.

"Well, you guys have cheered me right up. Ave, could you pass me the wine and maybe some arsenic while you're at it?"

It was only about nine in the morning when I heard Jen's machine shutting down. "Not again, Jen," I said. She stuck her tongue out at me and called down to IT.

A few minutes later, another guy from IT, Les, knocked on our office door. Jen was obviously disappointed. Les was a little overweight and had oversized eyeglasses and a shaggy, recklessly unfashionable haircut, but Les was, after all, a man, and Jen never let an opportunity to flirt pass her by, so she recovered quickly, smiling brightly.

"Hi, Les. Are you coming to Rios with us tonight?"

Les beamed and looked at Jen adoringly. "I'd love to come."

"All you guys in IT are invited. I think Tom said he was going. You might just want to remind him he's invited. We'll be there right after work, around 5:30."

She explained what had happened and he told her some possible problems. "So what do you think is wrong with my computer?" He told her a few possibilities. She oohed and aahed at his techy language. He practically glowed from the attention.

I shook my head, envying Jen's talent to make every man think he was irresistible, and I returned to the chore of going through my e-mail.

I'd spent half my morning hitting CONTROL D to delete e-mails from Lydia. They were supposed to contain funny e-mails to brighten our day. One out of every twenty of Lydia's e-mails might elicit a *huh*—not a full-blown *ha* and certainly not a full-fledged laugh—but an occasional *huh* was not worth struggling through the e-mail jokes that dragged on for an eternity and had a punchline that wasn't worth the time it took to focus my eyes on the screen, let alone wade through a Russian novel-length epistle.

Lydia never stopped smiling. She clearly spent years and years as a cheerleader. But beneath her dumb exterior lurked a killer closer, someone who could get companies to buy ten times the service they wanted or needed from us and got them to pay ten times more than what they wanted to pay. And after they signed on the dotted line, they would thank her for her help.

She was the one who had sold the Expert account and promised this outrageous deadline, so even though we'd maintained a superficial friendship for these past few years, when I saw her in the halls, I wanted to lash out in violent, entirely unprofessional ways to express just how much she'd ruined my life.

At last I finished going through my office e-mail and went to my personal e-mail account to check on Art.

> To: Dancinfool@yahoo.com
> From: ArtLover@yahoo.com
> *I'm afraid today's note will have to be a short one. It's 1:30 in the morning as I'm writing and I'm ready to collapse. My brother had a really bad night tonight. He went to pick up the kids, and I'm not sure what happened, but he was just a wreck afterward. I've never been through a divorce, so I can only imagine what it's like to have your wife leave you, especially when you have two little kids together. They've been divorced for six months and separated for much longer, and it's just not getting any easier for him. It's especially hard for him because she lives so close and he sees her so often when he goes to pick up the kids. So I spent most of the night just listening to him. I think the hardest thing for him is getting used to living alone. He got married right after college, so he's never had to live by himself. My brother is the reason I moved out here nine years ago. He went to school and I was his roommate for a short time before they got married. I wish I could think of things to say to him that would make him feel better. I feel so powerless to help.*

> To: ArtLover@yahoo.com
> From: Dancinfool@yahoo.com
> *Just listening, being there for him, that means everything.*
> *In case it helps any, you can tell your brother the good things about living alone. In fact, sometimes I worry I*

*like living alone too much. It's nice never having anyone
eat the leftovers I was planning on eating, never cleaning
up after anyone but myself, never having to watch stupid
action/adventure movies I hate in the spirit of compromise, even though I almost never did get to watch the art
films I liked. I know I sound like a bitter divorcée, but
I'm not angry with my ex, I'm angry with myself for not
being true to myself.*

I felt it was rather brave of me to admit these things,
particularly that I wasn't a fan of action/adventure movies.
But I wasn't going to lie to myself or anyone ever again.
If he didn't love me for who I was, forget it. Being alone
just wasn't that bad.

*Sometimes it's hard for me to imagine why I stayed
with my ex as long as I did. The other day, though, something happened that made me ache to be in a relationship again.*

*What happened was this: I burst out of my office, late
for a meeting and not paying attention to where I was
going, and I nearly ran into one of the guys who works
in our IT department. His hand briefly, gently touched
my arm to keep me from barreling into him—he sort of
steered himself around me. Now, this guy is not good-
looking, but the feeling of his hand briefly grazing my arm
electrified me. I don't mean sexually. I'm not sure if I can
explain it, but I guess his touch made me realize that I
couldn't remember the last time I'd gotten a hug or a back
rub. I couldn't remember the last time I'd held somebody's
hand. I suddenly ached for human contact. I'd forgotten
how amazing it is, the warmth of another person's touch.*

Have a wonderful weekend. I'll type to you Monday.

I hope I didn't sound desperate, but running into Les
had been such a jarring experience, and I wanted to

share my feelings about it with someone. It was nice to have a someone I could tell these random thoughts to.

We usually restrained ourselves to writing each other once a day, but he must have been online because he wrote back within minutes.

> To: Dancinfool@yahoo.com
> From: ArtLover@yahoo.com
> *Human touch is truly powerful. You made me think of something from my childhood. When I was growing up, my mother jumped on every fad. She did the macro-biotic diet, Jazzercized, did yoga, tried every diet made, and nowadays, Prozac is her trend of choice. Anyway, the point of my story was to tell you about this one fad of my mother's when I was about eleven. She had this hug group, and they would actually have these meetings where they got together and discussed the importance of hugging. The leader of the group handed out this flyer that Mom stuck to the fridge that said you needed to be hugged at least 12 times a day just for survival, 15 times for peace, and 20 for true happiness—something like that. I remember thinking that a lot of things in the world managed to survive without 12 hugs a day, but you'd need at least a hug or two to be happy. That did make sense to me, even then.*
>
> *I hated when we had those meetings at our house. Those people would hug anything, and the women would wear the most god-awful perfume. After the first time my Dad and I got mauled with a barrage of hugs, we made sure we were well hidden during the meetings. Happily, this phase of my mother's didn't last long. How much can you discuss hugging anyway?*
>
> *You know, I know we've never met, but writing you is very therapeutic. You have a good head on your shoulders. I have no idea what you look like physically, but it's*

hard for me to imagine not being attracted to you. I'm
already hot for your brain.

Smiling, I printed off his e-mail and put the print out
in my purse to take home and save with the others. He'd
echoed my thoughts exactly. Maybe meeting online first
was actually better than meeting in person. We were free
from the prejudice of outward appearance and could
focus on each other's personality. I definitely liked his
personality. I loved how he was there for his brother,
helping him through this difficult time. He was so sweet,
so sensitive, so articulate, so funny.

Sharon appeared at the door of our office, rubbing
her swelling belly. "Thank God it's Friday! So are you
going to join us for drinks after work? Well, of course
I'll be drinking ginger ale," she said with her I'm-a-preg-
nant-woman-and-don't-you-forget-it smirk.

Sharon had asked us earlier in the week to join her
and her husband for some drinks after work tonight.
Jen and I had held off letting her know if we'd go, always hoping something better would come up, which it
hadn't. I didn't feel like going out, but I knew I should.
Now that I was no longer safely coupled off, I got invited
out less and less, and when I did go out, I felt freakishly,
alarmingly single. But how was I going to meet anyone
if I spent every weekend with takeout and a romance
novel?

"Yeah, I'll probably go," I said.

"Yeah, yeah, me too," Jen cooed.

Back when I was with Gideon and still had a semblance of a social life, there were five of us couples who
would regularly go out after work for drinks, barbecues,
and dinner parties. Sharon and her husband, Mitch;
Lydia from sales and her husband, Dan; Pam from marketing and her husband, Joe; me and Gideon; and Jen

and whoever her beau du jour was. If she and Dave were separated, she would date one of the vast stores of guys she kept in reserve, all of whom were madly in love with her. Her seamless transition from one boyfriend to the next assured her continued invitability at all outside-the-office functions, whereas I had been mired in an abyss of solitude for nearly two years. No one liked adding a single person to the mix—I was like a neutron threatening to rage out of control without a balancing proton to keep me in check. Now, with both Lydia and Sharon pregnant, I could see that I was drifting farther and farther from normalcy. I wouldn't have anything intelligent to add about diaper rash remedies or the breast milk/formula debate, and soon, no doubt, Lydia and Sharon would tire of me and my only friends would be Oprah Winfrey and Danielle Steel.

"See you two tonight then," Sharon said and turned to leave.

I rang Pam's extension.

"Pam, what are you doing tonight?"

"Working. That's what I'll be doing all weekend. This Expert account is going to be the death of me," she said with a laugh. She didn't sound bitter or angry, but I could hear the fatigue in her voice.

"Well, we're going to Rios. Maybe you can stop by for a drink if you don't get off too late."

"I appreciate the offer, but if I don't get off too late, I'd really like to spend a quiet night with my husband."

"Of course, I understand. Hey, how are the kids?"

"Good, really good. Rebecca's in her second month at Cornell. She was a little homesick at first, but she's really enjoying it. Jackson has two more years at Columbia. Audrey's into your usual sophomore dramas. She's in drivers' ed now."

"You're kidding? She's driving?" I'd met Audrey only

once, about a year ago, but she'd seemed impossibly young. Maybe Audrey was small for her age. I knew she had asthma because Pam had been called out of the office on emergencies a couple times. Maybe the asthma made her smaller than other kids her age. In any case, I could barely envision her riding a ten-speed.

"Joe is teaching her. She says I make her nervous. She claims I clutch my heart in a panic-stricken sort of way that makes her too anxious to concentrate. All lies of course."

I laughed at the image. "It's too bad you can't make it tonight. Let's do lunch sometime."

"That would be great."

"Have a nice weekend. Don't work too hard." I knew that last part was futile. Pam always worked like a horse. She was a truly talented writer, and she generated an amazing amount of material. I would have loved to work for her as a copywriter or something. But since what she did—deliver products promised by sales to clients—wasn't a revenue-generating department, it, like editorial, rarely got the budget for additional staff.

Pam was attractive for her age, but she'd aged a lot in the past year. No matter how talented she was, I doubted she would be hired if she were applying for a job at McKenna Marketing today. These days Morgan wanted a young, energetic company filled with people who looked like they belonged on an episode of *Friends*.

After work, the seven of us met over at the Rios for appetizers and drinks. After a few glasses of ginger ale for Lydia and Sharon and a lavish number of margaritas for the rest of us, Jen, Lydia, Les, and Sharon's husband, Mitch, went to play pool. When Sharon got up to use the bathroom, I was abruptly alone at the table with

Lydia's husband, Dan, in a suddenly awkward silence. It occurred to me that in the three years since I'd first met Dan, we'd never had a conversation, just the two of us.

"So," I began, groping for a conversation topic, "a baby on the way. Pretty exciting." Lydia and Dan made a cute couple. I'd always been a little jealous of their relationship. I'd gone to a dinner party at their place one time—this was toward the end of things with Gideon, when I was feeling acutely lonely in my marriage—and I'd been struck by the happy pictures of Lydia and Dan around their house. On the coffee table was a framed photograph of them smiling beside a sign that said "Welcome to Rocky Mountain National Park." Lydia's hair was blown back by the wind; Dan's friendly smile seemed so content. On the bookshelf was a picture of them sweaty and smiling after their run in the Bolder Boulder and another picture of them playing with their dogs. On the refrigerator were several photos of them held up with smiley face magnets: one in which they were on a mountain with their arms wrapped around each other; another of them at Disney World; another of them fishing off a pier. Soon the house would be filled with pictures of them with their kid, who would no doubt be a cheerful, adorable child with an infectious giggle.

"I couldn't be more excited. I've been trying to knock her up since we got married seven years ago, but she kept putting it off," Dan said, smiling. His smile caught me off guard. Until then I had never really noticed just how good-looking he was. "She'll be such a great mom. She's so giving, so considerate, you know?"

I nodded. Lydia wasn't the most exciting person in the world, but she was nice. She'd be the kind of mom who would smile sweetly down on her dimply faced kid as they baked Christmas cookies together. She'd say something like, okay, you can have just one, but you have to save room for dinner! The kid would eagerly agree to this arrangement and devour the cookie happily, miraculously not spilling a single crumb.

"Like this week she knew I was really busy at work and didn't have time to go out to lunch, so she made my lunches. Isn't that sweet? Today it was tuna fish on wheat and an apple. She's just really supportive, you know? We just can't wait until the kid gets here. It's going to be so much fun. I mean it will be work, we know that, but we both just love kids."

I nodded. All at once I ached to be a part of a "we," to be the other half of a good-looking man's "we." I wanted a man to pack a lunch for, the kind of man who hours later would still appreciate the gesture.

"Is it hard that she travels so much for work?" I asked.

"Oh, it's awful, but, on the other hand, whenever she gets back from a trip, we fall in love all over again. It keeps our relationship fresh. She hasn't been required to travel as much lately, and we both hope she won't have to start traveling a lot again when the baby arrives. She talked to the VP about sticking to the Colorado and Wyoming areas for a while. He wasn't too happy about it since she's one of the top salespeople, but he doesn't want to get an anti-family rap, so it looks like he'll let her stick to local gigs, at least for a while."

Over Dan's shoulder I saw Sharon coming back from the bathroom. She stopped at the pool table to tell Mitch something. I watched Mitch put down his pool stick and start walking back to the table with Sharon. Just then, Jen came behind me and announced there was a good-looking guy up at the bar who would be perfect for me.

"Who?"

"Just come on, trust me."

When we were far enough from the table she said, "I can't believe you almost foiled my getaway plan for you.

I saw Sharon was about to make her return, and, being the kind of friend I am, I swooped in for the rescue."

"There's no guy?"

"Don't be such an ingrate. There is a guy, but I have dibs on him."

"Like you need another guy. Both Les and Tom are totally hot for you."

"Yeah right. Do you see Tom here?"

"He had plans with his friends, he told you that. But he's into you, I can tell."

"He would have changed his plans if he was into me. Blue shirt," she whispered as she sat next to a nice-looking blond guy in a blue shirt.

The guy was not my type, so it was no loss that Jen flirted outrageously with him while Les cast unsubtle glances at her from the table.

Since Mitch and Jen had abandoned the pool game, the others had returned to the table. I sat beside Jen on the barstool, quietly sipping my margarita, watching from across the bar as Dan lovingly rubbed Lydia's shoulder.

JEN

Catastrophes

I woke up with a searing headache. As I pried my eyes open, I had the strangest feeling there was someone else in bed with me.

Must focus.

How much did I drink last night? I'd never hallucinated before. That couldn't be . . .

Les opened his eyes and smiled. "Good morning beautiful," he said.

My tired eyes shot open. I realized with horror that I was naked, and, worse still, it appeared that Les was naked, too.

"Les?"

"Isn't it a beautiful day?" he asked, and leaned toward me, as if to kiss me. I reared back.

"Les? What happened last night?"

He laughed. "You're joking, right?" He tried to tickle me, but I slapped his hand away.

I rolled over on my back, setting off a maelstrom in my head. I gripped my palm to my forehead in an effort to keep it from exploding. What on earth had happened? Les had given me a ride home from the bar because I'd had too much to drink. Okay, I remember that . . . I invited him in for a drink . . . I got us each a beer . . . He sat down on the couch, and I lay down on the couch with my head in his lap . . . We talked . . . He began stroking my arm . . .

I looked over at Les, who was still smiling happily.

"Les, you know I was wasted last night. You're not going to tell anyone about this, are you?"

His smile faded. He looked confused.

"Les, promise me you won't tell anyone about this."

"I promise."

"I'm not feeling very well. Would you please go? Please?"

"Yeah, of course. I . . ."

I turned over and covered my eyes with my hand. As I listened to him get dressed, all I could think was, I've slept with a fat man named Lester. Or did I sleep with him? Maybe we just slept slept. Naked, granted, but otherwise innocently slumbering. Yes, that was most certainly what had happened. Even if that was all that had happened, if anyone found out I was fraternizing with a naked fat boy, it would *ruin* my chances with Tom and it certainly wouldn't help my chances for a promotion. Weren't managers supposed to be responsible and do things like only sleep with their accountant husbands?

"Can I get you anything before I go? Some water? Some aspirin?" he asked.

"Oh god, yes. The Advil's in the medicine cabinet in the bathroom. Bring five, no six."

Tell me I didn't sleep with a fat man named Lester. Tell me I didn't sleep with a fat man named Lester . . .

He brought the handful of pills and a large glass of water.

"Can I call you?" he asked.

"Call? No! I mean Les, you and I are just friends. Acquaintances really. We work together. I was drunk. This was a mistake."

My head felt like it had lost a fight with a chainsaw and Les's presence was doing nothing to curb my nausea.

"I'm sorry I . . ."

"Please, just go."

I listened to him leave. He shut the door quietly behind him.

RETTE

Hindquarters of a Wildebeest

I always hoped I'd be the kind of person who would have an affair with a dark-eyed stranger whose name I never bothered to get to know. Maybe we'd be on the Eurail going through Italy or France and we'd have sex in the bathroom without ever saying a word.

The thing was, I was getting married before I'd done crazy stuff like that. I'd only seriously dated two other guys besides Greg. I was too shy and too self-conscious to flirt. While Jen, flirt extraordinaire, never missed a school dance, I spent every dance at home with a book in one hand and a candy bar in the other, under the admonishing eye of my mother.

As soon as I started my job and I had a normal schedule, I'd start working out regularly. I'd finally get serious about getting in shape.

True, I had said this once or twice or three million times before.

I was nine when I went on my first diet. It didn't go well. For about three days I worked out and starved my-

self, then I ate Fritos and chocolate chip cookies for a
week straight.

When I was eleven, I stood in front of the mirror
with *Seventeen* magazine opened to the special Beauty
Plus section. The article, complete with illustrations of
thin, healthy girls measuring themselves, detailed the
proportions of the ideal body. My waist, according to
this, should have been ten inches smaller than my bust,
and so on. I was mostly proportional, though on a large
scale, but I was a little thick-waisted. I made charts and
goals. Over the years, I started many, many diets, not
based on any fad, but merely a regimen of serious deprivation to the point of near starvation (or at least so it
felt) and then binging, a cycle I repeated so many times
over the years that my metabolism became schizophrenic,
terrified of a mythical starvation conspiracy, and eventually, my body refused to let go of my bloated fat cells,
clinging to them like a drowning person to a life pre-
server.

Now, I had thighs that were dimpled like the hood of
a car thrashed by a hailstorm, slashed by angry lines
and riddled with bumps that reminded me of the mottled
flesh of a burn victim. My breasts were stretch-marked
and had begun to sag; they were the breasts of a middle-
aged mother of three. I had never experienced living with
the taut body of a young, nubile woman who starred in
romance novels and Aerosmith videos. I went from awkward preteen to fat old hag. And it would only get worse.
One day I'd be a brittle old woman with breasts like week-
old balloons. Every elastin will have waved a little white
flag and quietly retreated.

I had always been plump. Not obese, but not skinny
either. Sort of round. I was never athletic. As kids, while
Jen took ballet and gymnastics lessons, I took piano lessons or sat around reading books from the library.

In high school I still wasn't overweight, just curvy, or,

as my mother put it, solid. I used to binge all the time. Sometimes after a binge I'd kneel at the toilet and put my fingers down my throat and I'd try to puke, but I couldn't. I would gag, but that was about it. I was such a loser I couldn't even be a successful bulimic like Jen. She was even hospitalized for it, but I have to pretend I don't know. Jen didn't want Mom to tell me. Jen was able to confide in Mom because secretly she knew Mom wouldn't really disapprove. The only thing our size-six mother disapproved of were woman who were over-weight.

I didn't binge too often anymore, but every year I'd put on a few more pounds. It was a simple mathematical calculation that I knew well. If I wanted to maintain my weight, I needed to consume as many calories as my body needed to fuel itself every day, which was about 2,200 calories. If I wanted to lose weight, I had to consume 500 fewer calories each day, or between 1,500 and 1,700 calories a day, to lose one pound a week. Instead, I ate just a few more calories each day than I should have, and these extra calories hung out until they caught up with other lingering calories until they hit that hideous number, 3,500, and were able to gleefully ring up another pound on the scale.

Being with Greg didn't help. He could put away ridiculous amounts of food without gaining weight. He was eight inches taller than me and had a metabolism that worked at a frenzied pace, while my metabolism plodded along lugubriously. Plus, Greg loved me exactly the way I was. While I became frantic with desires of thinness around Mom, Jen, and any of the latest women's magazines, my lust to be svelte virtually disappeared around him. No matter how many times I tried to pick fights or get him to admit he'd prefer it if I were buff and fat-free, he insisted I was gorgeous the way I was. The bastard.

I really wanted to believe him. One of my favorite lines from Margaret Cho's show, *I'm the one that I want,* is about how for her, being ten pounds lighter is a full-time job, and she, for one, is turning in her pink slip. She's right; it takes so much damn energy for some of us to be a few pounds lighter than we are. There are times when I just genuinely want to be able to love myself the way I am. But as for me, a little feel-good feminist doctrine can compete only so much with an entire society that tells you fat is bad and thin is good. An entire culture or one mother.

No matter how many self-help books you read or how much you work on bolstering your self-esteem from within, you just can't help wanting to show off to your parents. I'd heard of people—and not just ones on daytime TV—who said that their parents called them dumb, useless, and the like. I would have taken a razor blade and ended it all right there if my mother had said anything like that to me. No, she was much more subtle, just a glance, just a slight frown or questioning look brought me to my knees.

While Jen went to just about every dance in high school—sometimes going to two or more homecomings at various high schools in the area a year—none of her relationships lasted more than a few dates. Until Dave, Jen had never been serious about anybody.

I, on the other hand, dated a senior named Alex for most of my junior year. He asked me out right after homecoming and we broke up just before prom (he didn't go with anyone else; my guess was that he couldn't afford to take me and breaking up with me was the honorable way to get out of it). We'd already decided not to do the long-distance thing when he left for school in Florida. He was just ending it a little before I'd expected. The problem with his timing is that in the photographic catalog of Jen and my high school history, Jen is featured in a gazillion prom photos, homecoming pictures, and Saddie Hawkins shots, whereas it looks like I was a complete loser, when in fact I was only mostly a loser.

Alex happened as a fluke, really. I was at a party with my two honors-geeky friends Julia and Ann. The guy hosting the party—I don't know his real name, everybody called him Schroeder— invited me in the hopes of getting Jen, who was a freshman at the time, to come. As soon as Schroeder said, "Hey, I'm having a party this weekend, wanna come?" I became giddy, wondering if perhaps I was turning over a new, nongeeky era in my life, if perhaps I'd underestimated the ability of my fellow classmates to judge me not by looks alone, but my wit, my intelligence, my *je ne sais quois,* and then he said, "See if your sister wants to come. Her name's Jen, right?" As if he didn't know.

Anyway, I didn't care that my presence was requested only to get Jen there. I'd been invited to a party, and I wasn't going to turn down the opportunity. I brought two friends and Jen brought two friends. I walked into Schroeder's parents' modest brownstone like Cinderella attending her first ball. When someone handed me a plastic cup of flat, warm beer, I felt like I'd been given Miss America's tiara.

As Jen flirted with what can only be described as a herd of boys, who stood around her in a horseshoe shape and never left her side, my geek buddies and I hid out in the basement. I thought we had the place to ourselves, and I was entertaining Ann and Julia by making fun of the drill team's dance numbers, overexaggerating wildly, including grinding my pelvis even more lasciviously than they did, which, believe me, wasn't easy. Ann and Julia were dying laughing, which was part of the reason I loved them—they found me hilarious—when I heard the clapping behind me and saw Alex. I'd seen him around. I knew he was a senior, not in the popular crowd but well above the sewer-dwelling stratum of the high school social structure. I was high on the unusual self-confidence inspired by Ann and Julia's laughter, so I did something I almost never did, I talked to a boy without stammering, stuttering, or acting like the shy, book-reading dork I was.

"I was just practicing my moves. I was thinking of trying out. I think there is no better way that one can serve her school than to put on low-cut sequined uniforms and do high kicks."

"Really, when you think about it, you're not just doing a service to the school, but the whole community really."

And off we went. Before the end of the night, he asked me if I wanted to go to the school's battle of the bands contest with him the next weekend, and I said yes and gave him my number. He called the next day and from that moment on we were inseparable—either attached through sound waves via telephone cords or together—for most of the next year. I said to my mom and Jen on every possible occasion, "my boyfriend" or some version of "I have to get ready for a date. Oh, did you hear, I have a *date*. Me."

When we got to the part of the relationship when we were ready to have sex (he was ready eleven seconds after meeting me; it took me about a month), I spent the first several months wearing as many clothes during sex as humanly possible and insisting that the room was bump-into-walls dark. No matter how much he insisted I was beautiful, I just couldn't buy it. What's funny is that I wasn't even that heavy then. Maybe ten pounds over my ideal weight. Eventually, however, hating myself so acutely simply became too exhausting, and I eased up on myself until it was more of a low-grade self-disgust that I had toward my appearance.

By the time I got to college, I'd at least gotten over

the fear that a guy would run screaming from the sight of my naked body, thanks in part (inadvertently) to Alex (not because he made me feel good about my looks, but because he helped remind me that I was a smart, funny woman who had a lot more going for her than just having a body made for *Baywatch*). Plus, I finally figured out that it would take a lot more than a few extra pounds and a little jiggle to stop a guy from getting laid.

Enter Ryan. It was the middle of my junior year in college, and I was at a bar with Jen and some of my friends and some of her friends. We'd all gotten in thanks to the fake IDs created by a friend of a friend of Jen's.

When the waitress came to our table and told me that the guy at the end of the bar wanted to buy me a drink, I promptly said, "Wait, are you sure he wants to buy *me* a drink?"

"Yep, he said the pretty red-haired girl in the green shirt." (Jen, the only other redhead at the table, had been wearing black.)

I accepted another beer and turned to look at him, fully expecting someone who looked like he'd be cast in the part of *Über Nerd* in the teen movie of the week, and instead saw Ryan, who was actually really cute. He had a little bit of a potbelly, but he didn't carry himself like someone who was sorry for being imperfect. He looked like someone who ate, drank, and had sex with gusto, and couldn't always be bothered with something as confining as self-control, something I found strangely sexy.

We waved to each other, and later, he pulled up a chair to our table to talk to me, *me*—amidst a table of gorgeous women.

Like the night I'd met Alex, I was unusually outgoing and feeling atypically good about myself on the night Ryan came into my life—thanks to the thrill of being bought my first drink by a man I didn't know plus the drinks themselves, which had bolstered me with a liquid confidence. We laughed a lot that night and had a great time.

Ryan had never finished college and was in a rock band, although he made most of his money by teaching guitar. Though our interests were about as different as could be—mine were academic and future-thinking, his were street-smart and about living life in the moment—we ended up dating for two years, and sleeping together on and off for another year after that. Our relationship had many faults, but we always laughed and the sex was always good. It helped that he was a little overweight himself. I realized that I loved him despite his imperfections, and it helped me grasp that maybe it wasn't such a stretch to believe someone could love me even if I wasn't perfect.

People, that is, other than my mother.

Mom had never been more proud of me than when I'd gotten engaged. She'd beamed for weeks after we announced the engagement. She'd taken an interest in the wedding that she'd never shown in anything else I'd ever done.

Before the engagement, Mom and I talked to each other on the phone every other week. Now that I had a wedding to plan, Mom sometimes called a few times a day. She would mail ads for dresses she thought would look good on me, all of which I found virulently repugnant, and she constantly offered advice, little of which I wanted. Mom and Dad had eloped because they'd been young and too poor to afford a wedding, so this was Mom's first wedding. She'd been storing up visions of an elaborate reception since she'd eloped twenty-eight years earlier, and she was spewing all of her ideas my way.

Since Greg had proposed, Mom's crusade to get me

to lose weight had spiraled out of control, though she feigned subtlety. If she saw me eating something, anything, with too much enjoyment, sometimes she'd say, "Think of the wedding pictures" or "Think of the bridal gown." More often, she would watch me eat and give me a look like I was a drug-addled prostitute who murdered small animals for sport. She did not hide her disappointment in my appearance well.

I was determined to find a wedding dress before she came out for Christmas—I did not want to go shopping for a dress with my mother. It was bad enough going shopping with Jen. Jen thought shopping for a wedding dress was a blast. If there were an award for the capitalist of the year, Jen would have been a serious contender. She'd at least get an honorable mention. She loved shopping as much as I hated it. It was simply not a good way for a fat, poor person to spend her day. You'd think as the bride I could get excited, but frankly I found planning all the petty details that went into hosting the most expensive party of my life rather dull.

I was late for my appointment because of little Ms. Capitalist who was hungover from partying the night before. I might've been jealous—it had been forever since I'd gone out and had fun—except she didn't look as though she'd had a particularly good time. Her hangover made me feel both righteous and dull.

Three other women had appointments at the boutique at the same time I did. Five "bridal consultants" flitted around giving advice and agreeing with everything we brides-to-be said. The women trying on dresses were positively emaciated. One of the brides-to-be was a size two. She looked damn good in everything she tried on. Wedding dresses are made for the clinically anorexic. Even the other women, who were size eightish, looked bloated in the white silk sample gowns, which, though they were allegedly all size ten, nobody could zip up. I didn't even try. White's a horribly unflattering color. Why hadn't someone had the forethought to make the traditional bridal gown a slimming shade of black or some color that wouldn't make women's skin look so sallow?

I stood in front of a mirror on a platform the size of a car tire because the dress was way too long for a shrimpo like me. I sensed that all the skinny bitches were saying, What loser would marry that lard-ass blubber butt? Perhaps they weren't using those exact words, but that was the gist of it.

"Ooh, this one looks great on you," Jen said, the lying bitch. "I'm so jealous. I wish I was getting married. I want to have at least one kid before I'm thirty."

"Yeah," I said, grimacing at my reflection.

Why wasn't I more excited about this? Maybe because marriage and bridal registries were supposed to come after I had broken the hearts of a string of exotic lovers around the world. The plan had been that I would spend my twenties in a high-paying, fulfilling career. After spending years accumulating adventures, I would settle down maybe in my late thirties, to having just one live-in lover.

The reality was that I was too terrified of getting herpes to sleep around, and as for travel and excitement, I hadn't even made it out of the States. One spring break spent in Florida and a couple of weekend trips to Chicago were as far as I'd gotten.

My plans for an exciting life dwindled quickly after college, when suddenly my friends began getting married one after the other. Some of my friends had bought houses; some were already having babies. Things were getting out of control, and despite myself I'd been knocked over by the nuptial domino.

The average age American women got married was twenty-five. I was twenty-seven. I had seen the men women over thirty had the opportunity to date, and it wasn't pretty. If I didn't get married soon, I would probably never get married. It's better to be a divorcée than a spinster. Divorcées might be failures, but at least people knew somebody had loved them at one time. Eventually I'd meet somebody who would give me herpes and cheat on me and beat me up and then stalk me when I broke up with him.

I hadn't been looking for a husband, but when Greg came along, I knew we'd get married. I just had this quiet feeling; our relationship felt so right. Is that the feeling that people who marry their high school sweethearts have? It must be. But I don't think I could have appreciated how right things felt with Greg if I hadn't had the close-but-not-quite experiences with Alex and Ryan. Alex was fun and sexy. As I realized later, well after we'd broken up and I'd gained some perspective, he wasn't a particularly nice person. And Ryan had never really been my intellectual equal, not like Greg.

I don't believe that we each have only one soul mate, but I do think finding someone who is as attracted to you as you are to him, who you can laugh with and still have something to talk about years down the road, is as rare as a four-leaf clover, and if you manage to find him, you should count yourself very lucky. That doesn't mean there aren't moments when I'd like to push Greg down a long flight of cement stairs. Happily, these moments are infrequent, and most of the time I consider myself fortunate indeed.

Plus, after seeing Jen and my girlfriends date one self-absorbed loser after another, I really appreciated how good Greg was to me. He was so sweet. He wasn't into football or porn or getting wasted with his buddies. He didn't spend all his money on beer and electronic equipment. I wasn't about to let such a good guy get away.

Why hadn't we had the forethought to elope?

Why were wedding dresses made to make our asses look like the hindquarters of a wildebeest?

AVERY

Romance and Other Marketing Ploys

I did not want to get out of bed Saturday morning. Something about going to the bar made my mood sour. Maybe it was something to do with the fact that nursing two margaritas throughout the evening had left me sober enough to notice the desperation that filled the air like humidity, heavy and thick. I'd been sober enough to watch Les watch Jen, sober enough to calculate the chasm of difference between thirty (my age) and twenty-five (Jen's age).

Eventually, however, my rumbling stomach managed to motivate me to get out of bed.

I sat at the kitchen table with a bowl of yogurt and fruit and flipped through the newspaper. As usual, I started with the horoscopes, then the comics, then the celebrity gossip. Eventually I'd glimpse at the serious news, doing my best to avoid reading anything depressing. If a headline talked about rape, murder, war, or robbery, I didn't read it. I used to read everything, and

I'd end up crying in my cereal bowl and be sad all day. I flipped the page and froze when I saw Gideon smiling up at me from an ad for men's cologne. He looked gorgeous as always. His long dark hair, his dark eyes courtesy of a Cherokee grandmother. He was thin, but his muscles were well defined. It was easy to see why I'd been so proud to be seen with him, why I'd wanted to brag to everyone, "Look! This gorgeous guy actually wants me to be his wife!"

I quickly shut the paper and pulled a stack of e-mails from Art I'd printed off at work from my bag.

As soon as I began reading them, my mood lightened. I'd been a lot happier since I'd begun writing Art. It gave me hope that someone decent was out there. All weekend, I actually looked forward to going into work Monday so I could hear from him again.

It was hard for me not to look around my apartment and envision smiling pictures of me and my future boyfriend, Art or whoever he was, taken from a variety of interesting vacation spots. If things worked out between Art and me, we'd go camping in the mountains, vacation in Hawaii, go to museums in Italy and France. He'd tell me little-known facts about the artists and their work. As an artist, he'd be able to point out things that I might not see on my own. We'd make a cute couple. I had no proof, but I felt fairly certain he was quietly good-looking, with a friendly smile and beautiful eyes.

By noon I officially began feeling guilty for squandering my day and I put on a T-shirt and shorts, threw my exercise mat on the floor, and started with some stretches. I used to do yoga every day, but now I was down to two or three times a week.

After warming up I went into the downward dog position, feeling my muscles lengthen. I breathed slowly, letting my tension drain away. I stretched further, as far as I could go. I loved that moment when my mind stopped fretting over quotidian details and all I could think about was how good my body felt.

When I used to perform, there was always that moment before the music started and the spotlights went on that I was sure I wouldn't remember what the first step was and I'd be standing there, motionless, like an idiot. I would stand/sit/lie there in whatever strange pose, straining to remember the first step, and until the music started, I couldn't have told you if you held a gun to my head what the first move was. My mind was that blank. But then the music would start, and the lights would come on, and my body always knew the right step, and I would get to this place where my body and mind were working together in a way they never did in any other area of my life. Throughout the performance, it seemed as if my body were acting on its own accord, as if the steps were programmed into my limbs. It wasn't until the music stopped that I would realize just how intensely I'd been concentrating. Even though I worked hard and long at the office, nothing I did there challenged me like performing once had.

After an hour or so of yoga, I went for a jog. I came home and showered and changed, then I called Rette. "What'cha up to?" I asked.

"I just spent several hours inducing clinical depression by trying on wedding dresses. Now I'm not cleaning, not working out, not going to the library to search for jobs on the Internet, and I'm certainly not doing a damn thing about the wedding. I was thinking about how I should be doing these things, however. Does that count as being productive?"

"You are strategizing, really."

"Oooh, yeah, that's exactly what I'm doing, strategizing. How about you?"

"I went jogging and decided that was accomplish-

ment enough for the day. I was just about to read a romance novel. I have to read about someone else's love
life since mine is a desolate wasteland."

"Oh, please. You have the mysterious Art. Sometimes I
wish I could go back to the excitement of first falling in
love."

"Excitement? Torture is more like it. I want to skip
right to the part where you are comfortable walking
around naked in front of him because you know he'll
love you even though gravity is doing horrible things to
your body."

"When do I get to that part of the relationship? I
don't walk around naked even when I'm all alone. My
thighs would chafe and the skin on the back of my arm
would flap like a bird preparing for liftoff."

"Very funny. You're beautiful, Rette. I know it and
Greg knows it. You're the only holdout."

"It's true I was lucky to score a guy who doesn't mind
fat women."

"You're not fat."

"Whatever. This stupid wedding is going to kill me.
Why didn't we elope? All the saleswomen at the bridal
shop were fawning over us, telling us all these lies about
how we looked like fairy princesses. I look more like
Cinderella's fairy godmother."

We talked for several more minutes. Rette kept cracking me up with tales of her bridal woes.

I ordered Chinese takeout for dinner and ran a bub-
ble bath. I read my novel for a while, laid it on the edge
of the tub, and called my mother on my cordless phone
to ask about her blind date. She'd signed up with a dating agency a month or so earlier, and this week she was
supposed to have gone on her third arranged date.

I hadn't told her about Art. Even though I thought it
was great that she'd gone to a dating agency, I was embarrassed I couldn't find a guy the traditional way. She

was older; it made sense for her to go through a dating service. But I was young enough that I should have been able to find a guy in a more romantic milieu. The women on *Sex and the City* were in their mid-thirties to early forties, and they scored dozens of dates every week.

"So how was the date?"

"Oh honey, it was . . . not good. He didn't seem like a healthy man. His aura was a very murky green."

"I'm sorry."

"It's okay. If this doesn't work out, I have three more dates left. And I've been thinking about teaching a gardening class at the free university. It might help the business, and who knows, maybe I'll meet someone."

"How are things going at the shop?"

"It's a little slow; it always is this time of year. We're just getting our poinsettias stocked up." Mom owned a flower shop. She'd started the business using some of the insurance money she got after Dad died. Gardening had always been her biggest passion. Her yard could rival any small botanic garden.

"How are you doing?"

"I'm good. Nothing very exciting. My boss is going on maternity leave soon, so I'm working really hard in hopes that I'll be asked to fill in for her."

"That'll be great."

"Yeah." I couldn't think of anything else to say. When had my life become so boring? "Well, I guess I should let you go. I'll talk to you later. I love you, Mom."

"I love you too, honey. Sleep well."

I hung up the phone and stared at the few lingering bubbles clinging to the top of the bathwater. My father had died when I was three, so for as long as I could remember, it had been just Mom and me.

She dated a few men when I was a kid, but nothing ever got serious. I liked it that way. I liked having her all

to myself. We would spend our weeknights and weekends baking and painting and gardening. We'd make
huge bowls of popcorn and watch *Fantasy Island* and
Love Boat together.

Mom met Carl when I was twelve. I didn't like Carl or
his put-on smile. I didn't like his pock-marked skin or
the way he made his unfunny jokes at other peoples' expense, trying in his sad way to feel better about himself.
Mostly what I didn't like was who my mother became
around him, fawning and skittish, straining to create a
semblance of familial happiness that wasn't there.
During weekday nights and weekend days I escaped in
dance practice. On Saturday nights, Mom and Carl would
go out to dinner and a movie, leaving me home alone
with a TV dinner and my resentment.

I wanted my mom to be happy, but I knew, even
then, that Carl was not the right man for her.

When they were first dating, every time he saw me
his smile was so forced I thought he might bruise a dim-
ple. I went away to a performing arts high school in
New York shortly after they were married, so after that,
I only saw him a couple of times a year for holidays. We
tolerated each other from a polite distance until he left
Mom for another woman when I was twenty-four.

Mom was so devastated; she hadn't been able to date
at all in the nearly six years since the divorce. Now, just
like me, she was finally ready to test the water, dip her
toe into the icy-cold dating sea, trying to muster the
courage to take the plunge.

I got out of the tub, slipped on my robe, and took my
book out onto the couch in the living room. The book
was about a beautiful stage actress, Cassandra Davis, who
was in hiding from a violent man who'd become obsessed
with her. She'd fallen in love with Michael just before Ajax,
the mentally unbalanced criminal, had begun stalking her.
Before meeting Cassandra, Michael, a world-renowned

wildlife photographer, had never wanted to settle down. Now, his only goal was to make Cassandra his bride.

Cassandra fled the country to escape from Ajax's violent threats. She loved Michael too much to endanger him, but he loved her too much to let her go. So when her attempts at going into seclusion brought her to Italy, France, Greece, Brazil, and the Bahamas, Michael always found her and followed her, over oceans and mountains and jungles. I always wanted a love like that. An overcome-all-odds, journey-over-mountains-and-oceans love.

I thought my first love, Marcos, was that kind of love. Marcos was a musician on the ship where I worked after college. He was half-Hispanic, half-Irish, and he had striking good looks. Just thinking about his smile could still make me melt.

On the day we met, he approached me while I was warming up for practice. I was doing the splits, arching back to grab my leg to get a better stretch and loosen my back muscles.

"Ouch," he said.

I came out of the splits and sat in a *Z* position, my right leg against my left knee and my left foot behind me.

"I've seen you dance. You're amazing," he continued.

"Thank you."

"My name is Marcos. I play the piano on the ship. You're new."

I nodded. "This is my third day. My name is Avery."

"Ah, to be new again. To not know who's sleeping with whom, who hates whom, who to watch out for."

"Sounds kind of interesting."

"Let me take you out to dinner tonight and I'll pull the veil of innocence away."

"I have to perform tonight, but another night would be fun."

"We dock at an island Saturday night, so neither of us will have to perform. Should we plan on Saturday? Say eight o'clock?"

"It's a date."

He picked me up just before eight as he promised. He was holding a single red rose.

"You look stunning," he said. I was just wearing a simple sundress and sandals, but I smiled, feeling beautiful.

"Thanks for the rose. Let me get it some water." I got a Styrofoam cup from the bathroom and filled it with water. It wasn't the most elegant vase, but it was all I had.

"Ready?" I asked.

He nodded, smiling.

We had a simple dinner—he had jerk chicken, I had a salad with fried plantains and poblano goat cheese—and far too many piña coladas. We spent the rest of the night dancing outside, under the stars, in the cool night air. His breath on my neck, and his hands on my arms, my back, my waist—it made me feel so alive, so awake, so aware of every sensation—the smell of the night air and the sea breeze and the lingering remains of coconut suntan oil from the beach goers earlier in the day; the sound of calypso music and the waves hitting the shore; the sight of women in bright flowing sarongs and the strings of lights decorating the restaurant behind Marcos. As we danced, I could clearly see our future together: We'd have gorgeous, musically gifted children and a glamorous, adventurous life. As artists, we wouldn't be wealthy, but we'd live rich, full lives, and grow old together but never stop dancing or listening to music and creating music of our own. We might even come back to this tiny island to retire, to spend our last remaining days in a land of endless sunshine.

That, of course, has always been my problem: I never remember to take into account the possibility of rainy days in my plans.

Marcos was charming and fun and very romantic. On our evenings off when we docked at an island, we spent the nights dancing under the stars. We'd spend our mornings making love and our days playing on the beach or shopping in the small towns. Some nights he would say he needed to work on his music, that he was almost finished writing a new piece. I'd fallen in love with him in part because of his passion for his music, so when I wouldn't see him for days in a row, I never questioned it was because of his dedication to his art. Except he never let me see the end result of all these evenings he spent alone "working." One night when we were docked and he said he was working I went off the ship and was wandering down the beach when I saw him dancing with another woman on the deck of an outdoor bar. That's when I finally figured out he wasn't spending all those nights slaving over his piano. He cheated on me several more times before I realized his cheating wasn't a challenge our relationship needed to overcome, it was bullshit. Even then, he was such an addiction, the only way I could give him up was to quit my job and move back to Colorado.

I dated a few guys over the next year, but it never got serious with any of them. Not until Gideon. Both Marcos and Gideon had a kind of music pulsing through them, making them seem more alive, more vital than most people I knew.

Maybe there's no such thing as romance. Maybe it's just a concept created by marketing executives to sell perfume and candles and novels and expensive dinners and weekend getaways.

Somehow though, despite all the pain, I still believed in love and happily ever after. But I also knew that there was something worse than being alone, and that was settling for less than you deserved. It's funny though, how the two men I'd loved had been so full of themselves they had no room left for me.

Every relationship called for some sort of compromise. The challenge was knowing when you were giving so much you were compromising yourself. It was a challenge I had yet to overcome.

Kodak Moment

I fell asleep on the couch early; it must have been before ten o'clock. Another exciting Saturday night.

I woke up Sunday morning at 6 A.M., feeling well rested and full of energy. I began cleaning the house, starting with cleaning out Martha's litter box.

I was wearing my flannel pajama bottoms and a stained sweatshirt. I pulled my hair back into a greasy ponytail. I wasn't wearing any makeup, and two large pimples on my chin foretold that my period was right around the corner. Ordinarily, I would never leave the house looking so bad—Gideon lived just a few buildings down from me. But Gideon would never get up before noon on a Sunday morning, so I knew I was safe.

I brought the litter box out to the Dumpster and heaved the litter into it just as a gust of wind rushed by, causing the litter to whirl back into my face in a vile dust storm. I was half blinded by the litter and coughing up the ammonia-filled dust I'd inhaled when I turned to see Gideon in the leather coat and tight black jeans he only wore when he went dancing at the clubs. Beside him was a tall, thin woman wearing a black patent leather cat suit and platform shoes. She had blond hair—blond-blond, not dishwater blond like mine but an unlikely cascading platinum sheen—to her waist. It was obvious they were just getting back from the clubs while I, with such an exciting social life I'd gone to bed at ten the night before, was cleaning out the cat litter box at 6 A.M. on a Sunday.

Gideon nodded his head almost imperceptibly by way of greeting. I waved feebly in return.

JEN

As You Climb the Ladder of Success, Only Let the Right Boys Look Up Your Dress

I peeked out from my office door and looked down the hallway first right, then left. There was no sign of Les. I took a deep breath and hastened down the hall to Sharon's office door. Ordinarily I would rather poke my eye out than go to lunch with Sharon, but if I wanted a chance to take over for Sharon while she was on maternity leave, I needed to market myself.

"Ready for lunch?" I asked.

"Are we ever. Boy, get pregnant and you just can't stop yourself. You're hungry all the time."

Whatever, Sharon, you were a lard ass well before you were pregnant, don't blame the kid. I smiled understandingly.

"I invited Lydia along, is that okay?" Sharon asked.

"Great!" Oh, dear god. Could my day get worse?

I left Sharon's office and immediately my question was answered. Yes, my day could get worse. There stood Les in the hallway, with a smile as moony and enthusiastic as a puppy wagging its tail.

"Hi, Jen," he said.

"Hey, Les," I said, avoiding his gaze. It looked like he wanted to talk, but out of the corner of my eye, I saw Lydia coming down the hall. For once, I was happy to see her because she gave me a good excuse to ignore Les.

"Happy Monday!" Lydia said.

"Ready?" Sharon was standing at the doorway of her office, slipping her enormous, duffle bag-size purse on her shoulder.

"I told my husband we'd meet him at the Sink for lunch," Lydia said. "Is that okay? Me and the kid are craving pizza like crazy!"

How was I supposed to kiss up to Sharon with Lydia and her husband in my way?

Two pregnant ladies and an accountant as lunch companions and a lovelorn fat boy named Lester lusting after me. What had I done to deserve this?

"Great!" I said.

The only good thing about going to lunch with two pregnant women was that it made me feel very skinny. Watching them hoover up their pizza made me totally lose my appetite.

Sharon spent the entire meal complaining about the shiftless teleresearchers in her employ and about how she had eight million and one ways to single-handedly turn McKenna Marketing into a Fortune 100 company but the villainous Morgan McKenna thwarted her every innovation due to his ignorance and lack of forward thinking.

"And my back is absolutely *killing* me. My doctor gave me this special pillow to sleep with between my legs—"

I suppressed a shudder.

"—but it's just not helping. I know I'm not the first pregnant woman to suffer from back pain. You'd think they could do *something*. I mean, they can sew limbs on people and grow hearts from pigs for human use, don't you think they could do something to help my back? I mean the pain is *unbearable*. Sometimes I don't know how I get through the day."

"But just knowing you're carrying a child makes the discomfort bearable, don't you think?" Lydia gushed. "And I've been getting so many back rubs and foot massages, I'm thinking about being pregnant all the time!" Lydia rubbed Dan's shoulder. He wasn't bad-looking; he had a good job. Why could Lydia land a good man but I couldn't even score a date? I was way prettier than her. It just didn't make sense.

"I just feel guilty; I was the one who knocked you up." The three of them laughed. It took me a moment to remember to laugh too.

I strangled a lemon over my glass of water. It was infuriating. It was almost time to go back to the office, and we'd spent the whole hour talking about pregnancy when what we were supposed to be doing was discussing my ample credentials for advancement.

"I can't wait to have kids," I said. "Sharon, I just don't know how you do it all, managing so many projects and such a large staff while you're pregnant. If you ever need any help, I'd be glad to assist. I've been looking for some more challenges." There, I'd finally said it.

"I'd love some help. Thanks for offering."

"You're in for it now," Lydia joked. This time, I didn't forget to laugh with everyone else.

When I got back to my desk, I felt a little better about my job, but I was feeling worse about my boyfriend status. There was nothing like a happily married pregnant couple to make you reflect on just what a sad and pathetic life you led.

After a couple of hours of work, I was dying for some water, but I was afraid to leave my desk lest I run into Les. On the other hand, Tom was a huge caffeine addict, so the chances of running into him in the kitchen were good.

Eventually, my bladder insisted I depart from the safety of my desk. Warily, I snuck down the hall to the bathroom. Victory! I made it without Les seeing me.

I returned from the bathroom using similarly diversionary tactics. This time, they were unsuccessful.

"Hey, Jen."

My heart seized as I turned to face him. "Les!"

"I was wondering, can I take you to lunch tomorrow?"

"Shhh!" I said in a loud whisper. "I can't. I've got plans."

"How about Wednesday?"

"No, I can't go to lunch with you Wednesday, not Thursday, not Friday, not ever. Do you want people to think we're a couple? Do you want me to be the butt of office gossip and destroy my career?"

"Of course not. I hadn't thought of it that way. Of course, you're right."

"You haven't said anything to anyone, have you?"

"No, of course not."

Thus assured, I relaxed a little. "Look, Les, you're a great guy, but we can't be seen talking to each other or going to lunch. We can say hi in the hallways, but that's it."

"Can we get together after work? I'd love to take you to dinner. I . . ."

How many drugs was this man on? What was it with the egos of men that a guy like Les actually thought he deserved a woman like me? "Look Les, I'm getting over a serious relationship." I was whispering so softly, Les pulled in closer to hear me. I pulled back and indicated with a pointed sweep of my eyes that we were not alone and he had to be more discreet. "It's been hard, and I've been drinking a little too much. I haven't been making the best decisions lately. What happened the other night happened because I'd had too much to drink; I was lonely. It's too soon for me to think about getting into another relationship, but even if it weren't, there is no way I'd date a co-worker." *If, that is, he looks like you.*

"I can quit my job."

"No!" I yelled, then quickly remembered myself and returned to a whisper. I was trying to be nice and let him off easy, but he was just not getting a clue. "Les, you're a great guy, but there is no possibility of us being a couple. Ever. Under any circumstances whatsoever."

"Oh," he said.

"I'll see you around." I didn't want to hurt him, but there was obviously just no other way.

I nearly jumped when I stepped into my office. Tom was standing there, talking to Avery.

"I was just telling Tom about the Halloween party I'm having next Saturday night. He said he didn't have anything to wear, but I said you were thinking of going as Scully from *The X-Files* and he could easily pass as Mulder. All he'd need to do was wear a suit and you'd give him a badge that said FBI."

I stared at Avery. This was the first I'd heard of a Halloween party. "Yeah, I mean that was just one idea I had. So Tom, what do you think?"

"Sure. That sounds cool. I'll pick you up, say around eight?"

"Perfect," I said.

"Saturday," he said, pointing to me just as he left our office.

It took me a moment to remember to breathe after he left. I turned to Avery. "What Halloween party?"

"I've been thinking about having one, and when

Tom came in here to check out what was wrong with my e-mail, I figured what better way to get you together?"

"Scully? That is so unsexy."

"I had to think quick of something you two could go as together. I said you were thinking of going as Scully but needed a Mulder. I believe some thank-yous are in order."

"You're right. Of course. Thanks, Avery. You're the best." I smiled, feeling practically human for the first time all day.

The prospect of seeing Tom at the party cheered me, but only a little. Why had I slept with his overweight coworker? What if he found out? What if anyone found out? Why was I behaving so stupidly? I was glad Dave was out of my life. I just needed to be in a good relationship to ground me, a relationship with a guy like Tom.

RETTE

The Cruel, Self-Esteem Crushing Job Search, Revisited

I spent far too much time waiting like an expectant lover after a promising first date for the phone to ring. Why wasn't McKenna Marketing calling? The rejection was excruciating. And none of the other résumés I'd sent out were getting me interviews. The worst was having to explain, over and over to Jen, Avery, Mom, Dad, and Greg, that no, no one was interested in me, there had been no new developments in the job front, I was just a big old unemployable loser.

I felt like my life was on hold. I wanted my future to begin. I fantasized about paid sick days and having health insurance. I envisioned getting a stressful, high-paying job and wearing nice suits like Jen did, or getting a job editing for a small magazine and eventually getting a better job at a bigger magazine where I'd earn scads of awards and endless critical acclaim.

Looking for work was about as relaxing as a shopping mall parking lot at Christmas time. When I wasn't fantasizing about becoming a senior editor at the *New*

Yorker or Random House, I fixated on our albatross of debt.

I made millions of budgets and long-term financial plans. Even in the best case scenario, it would be years before Greg and I could put a down payment on a home. Mom had told me over and over that the only way to get ahead was to invest in a house. Getting ahead seemed preposterously abstract when we were struggling so hard not to fall further behind.

Every time I sent out a résumé, I felt as hopeful as if I'd bought a lottery ticket. The chances of getting a decent job were equivalent to my chances of winning a zillion dollars. Who knew how many people applied for each job I applied for? Maybe they hired from within or hired the boss's nephew's friend.

I was so desperate, I entertained the idea of becoming a technical writer. I had no interest in it, but the pay was decent and it was at least tangentially related to my major. Of course the ads specified that I needed years of experience and knowledge of computer programs I'd never heard of. It was quite depressing to realize I wasn't even qualified for jobs I didn't want.

Practice

I flipped through the pages of *Bride's* magazine. I loved all the intricately designed dresses, the lace, the fabric, the satin shoes, the veils, the gloves, the flowers, the sophisticated, emaciated models who always looked so content.

The wedding itself terrified me. In my fantasies I was an elegant, demure bride who would host an event that would be talked about for years to come. The reality was that I hated the idea of everyone watching me walk down the aisle and say my vows. I hated public speaking. How could I say my vows in front of everyone I cared about and, more important, the people I didn't particularly care about but wanted to impress?

The wedding was ten months away and I was already having trouble sleeping. How could I relax with images of stumbling over my vows or my dress falling off plaguing me? Or tripping on my way down the aisle. God, what if I broke my leg and the wedding, all the months of planning and all that money, went to waste because I needed to be rushed to the hospital? What if one of us got sick or I broke out in hives the day before the wedding? What if I got a really terrible hair cut? For sure at least three of my nails would break the week of the wedding.

Why was I worrying about my wedding when it was still months away? I didn't handle stress well, never had. Even as a kid I came home from kindergarten with side-splitting stomachaches if I ever missed a question on a spelling test or if little Freddy Hanson called me Carrot Top. I suffered from allergies, tension headaches, gastrointestinal problems, and an increasingly serious weight problem. I was an evolutionary reject. In any other era I would have been mercifully exposed on a mountainside long ago.

I was already in training for the big day, practicing looking graceful and skinny in high heels. I paced up and down the living room floor trying to feel elegant and bridal despite the oversized, faded sweats I wore to train in. I tried not to wince in pain from the constricting shoes as I imagined myself as a glamorous model striding down a catwalk. Just as I was losing myself to the fantasy, I lost my balance, and my shin went careening into the coffee table. I fell to the floor, gripping my damaged shin. "Shit! Shit! Shit!"

Someone knocked at the door. I fought through my pain to teeter over to the door, my feet screaming for me to free them from the vise-like shoes.

"Should I ask?" Avery said, eyeing my sweats-and-heels ensemble and following me inside.

"I'm scared I'll trip when I walk down the aisle, so I'm practicing."

"I thought you hated heels."

"I do, but weddings aren't about comfort, they're about beauty."

"I thought they were about love and commitment."

"Whatever, yeah, that, too."

"Isn't the wedding like ten months away?"

"I really need the practice," I said, collapsing on the couch beside Avery, rubbing my bruised shin. "Oh my god, these shoes are torture. In college I used to waitress, you know? And being on my feet for hours gave me this bunion that makes these shoes even more unbearable. I only waited tables for six months, but the job left my right foot permanently deformed. Only surgery can correct it. Mine isn't bad enough to go through all that. So I just have to buy shoes that are like a size too big for me. What I want to know is, why don't shoemakers notice that women's feet don't come to a point at their toes? And why do they make shoes so damn skinny?"

"I don't mean to gloat or anything, but you do realize that you're talking to someone who had the good sense to get married at the Justice of the Peace?"

"Yeah yeah, okay. But didn't you ever want a big wedding?"

"Sometimes I wish we had. But we didn't have any money, and the important thing was that we were in love and I was marrying a gorgeous, sophisticated, wonderful—at least so I thought—man. So have you decided what you and Greg are going as for Halloween?" she said, changing the subject.

"I have some ideas." Historically I'd tried to ignore Halloween, but I wasn't going to let Avery down.

Halloween was a holiday for people with creativity

and enough self-esteem to look ridiculous. I could never think of anything creative, and I didn't like spending money or time hunting through thrift stores to come up with props. I wasn't the kind of person who saved old stuff and had yarn and glue and paint stored in some closet and could miraculously transform it into some clever costume.

"I'm so bad at Halloween. What are you going as?" I said.

"It's going to be a surprise. So what are these ideas of yours?"

"I was thinking we could go as literary characters. I could go as Hester Prynne and wear a scarlet *A*. But I'd need a bonnet and an apron. I thought Greg could go as a savage school boy from the *Lord of the Flies*, but we'd need to get him a conch."

"I have a conch and an apron."

"You own an apron? And a conch? That's amazing. I wish I kept handy things like that around."

"It's not handy. I'm just a pack rat."

"Are you inviting Art to your party?"

"I think it would be awkward to meet at a party."

"You're just chicken. Don't lie."

"That could very well be. I guess I don't want to find out he's human. I like the Prince Charming I've made him out to be in my head."

"Men usually are better in theory," I agreed.

Masks

It would not be inaccurate to call me a social misfit. I preferred to spend my weekends at home reading or watching a video with Greg than going out and partying. So of course I wasn't going to attempt to go to Avery's Halloween party sober. Beer was another thing I wasn't supposed to drink, yet another substance that had a nefarious influence on my stomach, but I had vats of Maalox and Pepcid to appease my ornery internal organs.

Getting myself to the party wasn't the only obstacle. I had to plead and cajole Greg into going. Like me, Greg was opposed to looking like an idiot, but I finally convinced him that he would have a blast and his costume would be brilliant, and besides, what else were we going to do for Halloween?

I had to explain my costume and Greg's costume about four hundred times. Greg joked that graduate school had turned him into a savage. It was cute the first time, but it lost its appeal by the eleventh time I'd heard it.

One of the main reasons I liked to be in a relationship was to avoid confronting social situations solo. However, I ditched Greg as soon as he started telling the story about his boss at his last job. The punch line was not even funny. The first time I heard it, we were on our second date. I'd laughed, which only encouraged him. It was the beginning of a new love. I was giddy and happy then. So sue me.

The house full of smiling strangers made me tense. I tried to chug my beer, but all the beer-guzzling talents I'd developed as an undergraduate had faded, and I had to settle for sipping my beer demurely.

I surveyed the room, looking for Avery. There were the usual random goblin/scary types, someone in neon green with a sign that said "Toxic Waste," a woman with a lampshade on her head and a nightstand around her waist that was a one-night stand, and an assortment of other costumes, all of which were better executed and more creative than my frumpy Hester Prynne. Avery caught my eye from across the room, but it wasn't until she smiled and came toward me that I recognized her.

Her makeup was amazing: her body, face and clothes were splattered in paint, splashes of green, blue, and black that somehow wove together beautifully. I could barely distinguish her face.

"Quit hiding in the corner," she said. "I want to introduce you to some of my coworkers. They don't work in editing, but maybe they can somehow put a good word in for you anyway."

"You look awesome. What are you?" I asked.

"I'm supposed to be a Jackson Pollock painting."

"Of course. You look so good."

"Thank you, Rette."

"I can't believe I didn't think of that. You look exactly like that. You look great."

Avery introduced me to Lydia, who was good-looking in a bland, wholesome way. Her nurse's costume strained over her pregnant belly.

"Where's Dan?" Avery asked.

"He wasn't feeling well, so I brought my cousin Ben as my date. What are you supposed to be?" Lydia asked me with a toothy smile.

Didn't anyone fucking read anymore? Why did I live in such an illiterate country?

"Hester Prynne. From *The Scarlet Letter*. The book. By Nathaniel Hawthorne. It's a great work of literature?"

Finally, a look of recognition passed across her face. "That was made into a movie with Winona Ryder, right? She's so great, don't you think?"

"Mmm."

"I dressed as a nurse because *ER* is my favorite show. I never miss Thursday night 'Must see TV.' "

I smiled and thought, *How embarrassing for you to admit that.*

Thankfully, just then Jen and her latest boyfriend had finally shown up dressed as Dana Scully and Fox Mulder from *The X-Files*.

"Jen is here," I said. "I should probably go say hi. It was nice meeting you."

Jen looked gorgeous in a green pantsuit with a badge pinned to her lapel that read FBI.

"Sorry we're late," Jen said.

"No problem. You look great." Next to Jen, I felt even frumpier and more old-fashioned. Hester Prynne was about as sexy as roadkill. Everybody knew who Jen was supposed to be. *The X-Files* were just slightly more hip than an eighteenth-century literary character.

"I'd like you to meet Tom," Jen said. "He works in our IT department, but before that he was a white-water raft guide, a blackjack dealer, a carpenter, and a paramedic. Doesn't that sound exciting? Tom, tell her that story you were telling me the other day about when you were a paramedic."

"Oh yeah, that was kind of interesting. I was telling Jen about how, this one time, we had these two whacked-out cases right in a row. First we were called to the home of an eighty-eight-year-old woman with pneumoxia—that means that she had too much liquid in her lungs and not enough in her blood." Tom was cute in a rough way. He said "wit" instead of "with" and his hard gestures emphasized his muscular arms. "She was blue, just blue from lack of oxygen. We needed to get an oxygenating valve to force air into her lungs, but all of her veins were collapsed. I mean she was so sickly, we had no way to get the valve in her. There was nothing we could do, except there's this procedure an EJ stick, an external jugular stick—you *jam* it right into the patient's jugular. It can be really dangerous if it's not done right. You only do it if the patient is absolutely going to die without it because if you don't hit the caroted artery, it cuts the flow of blood to the head. I mean you're jamming a huge needle into a patient's neck. None of my partners had ever done it; *I'd* never done it. Ken and Jim were like,

I'm not going to do it, what if we mess up and the family sues us? But I was like, she's most likely going to die anyway, why not give it a shot? So I took a needle and stuck ten cc's of epinephrine right into her neck and instantly, instantly the woman turned pink and started moving, started talking, asked what had happened. This had all happened in moments; we were still at her house. It's kind of unusual to see a patient reanimate right in front of me. Usually they're unconscious when we pick them up until after we've dropped them off at the hospital. Our job is to just keep them alive while transporting them. So it was kind of cool. I was feeling really high, like I'd really saved a life instead of just helping somebody cling to life till I got her to the hospital. So I'm feeling good, we're on our way home, we stop at a stop light, and this man knocks on the door to our ambulance. For a second I think he's going to try to steal the ambulance or I don't know what, but he gestures to indicate that he can't breathe, and sure enough he's turning blue. My partners and I get out of the cab and walk around to the back of the ambulance to give him some oxygen. We give him some oxygen, and the guy says he's feeling much better, and then he dies, just collapses right there."

Why did Jen get all the exciting guys with interesting pasts?

"So me and my two partners immediately go to work, and the guy revives within seconds. He never knew that he had died, he only knew that suddenly three big guys are holding him down, shoving tubes down his throat and needles into his arms. He starts fighting us off, he pulls the IV out of his arm as he reaches up to get the tube out of his mouth. Obviously if you've just died, you don't want to engage in heavy exercise, like wrestling three people, for example. I need to inject him with some Valium, but I also need to get the IV back in and the tube back down his throat. I'm practically sitting on the man's face. My partners Ken and Jim are holding his arms down, and I get the IV in in record time, then we inject him with some Valium. But get this: while all this whole big struggle was happening, the guy's daughter had driven by and recognized her dad's car and she gets out of the car screaming, oh my god, oh my god, that's my dad—she's just wigging out. We tell her he's going to be okay, we're taking him to the hospital. I guess she had a cell phone to call the rest of the family and they must have lived like right there, because by the time we'd stabilized him and gotten to the hospital, this guy's whole family is there. That's really rare for us, too. Usually the family doesn't show up until long after we've come and gone. We never get any credit for keeping people alive. But here we could see what we'd done. All these teary-eyed family members, the wife, the daughter, the teenage son, it was pretty cool."

"That's amazing," I said.

Jen beamed proudly.

"Yeah, that was pretty cool. We got a few interesting cases a year, but mostly it was just really grueling work. A lot of crazed drug addicts, a few grotesque car accident victims, and zillions of heart attacks."

Greg came up to us and gave Jen a hug and Tom an enthusiastic, "Hey! How's it going? I'm Greg, Rette's fiancé. Nice to meet you." They shook hands and Tom agreed it was nice to meet him, too. For a moment there was a lot of awkward nodding, then Tom asked if Greg had caught the Broncos game, and off they were, rambling on about such and such a play and who was going to win some upcoming game. Greg never watched football on TV, but somehow he managed to be conversant on the subject. He never talked sports with me so it was strange to see him be able to suddenly discuss it with such enthusiasm.

I was instantly bored out of my mind, but Jen looked enthralled by their conversation. Jen moved as though she expected to be caught on film at any moment, as if she felt watched and admired. She ate neatly, taking small, ladylike bites, and her eyes were always animated. She was captivating. Did she ever shut it off? Did she ever tire of performing? She could pretend to be fascinated by the most boring person. It was a skill that served her well.

Greg and I went up to our own apartment at two in the morning. The party had been fun, but I was exhausted. Even though I'd taken a Pepcid before drinking, my stomach rumbled irritably. It was bloated and distended and I felt like a woman nine months pregnant with twins. I did not feel at all sexy, so when Greg put his hand on my breast and tried to kiss my neck, I found his touch repulsive.

"My friends warned me this would happen. They warned me not to move in with you," he said.

"Don't be a jerk. I'm tired and my stomach hurts. We never have sex anymore because you're always busy with school. We'll make a sex date for tomorrow night. Wait, what time is it? Tonight I mean."

I wanted to talk more, but he just grumbled and turned away, slamming his head down into his pillow.

AVERY

The Party

I'd forgotten how much work it was to throw a party, but the turnout was good, and my costume turned out well. Even so, I wondered what it would have been like if Art had done my makeup. I imagined his gentle hands lovingly painting whimsical spatters on my face, neck, and arms.

I was pouring myself a beer when I saw them. Marc, Mark, and Mary had actually come. I'd invited them thinking I could get on their good side by pretending I wanted the honor of their presence when I knew they'd have a hipper party to go to. But they didn't. They were at my party with their stunning significant others in tow.

Mary was dressed as a genie, wearing a bikini that displayed her ample bust and small waist, and sheer baggy pants that exposed every leg muscle she'd earned from jogging. On her head she wore a square hat in the same shimmery pink as her bikini. Sheer material flowed out from the hat over her thick honey-colored hair. Her husband stood beside her wearing a pirate's uniform. Mark was with his live-in girlfriend (it wasn't enough that she was astonishingly good-looking, she was also a surgeon) and Marc and his wife, who smiled a practiced smile of a former high school prom queen. All four wore '70s disco attire, the kind of tight clothes in unforgiving fabrics that only a brave few could pull off. I thanked them for coming. Mark patted me on the shoulder and said it was good to see me as he walked past me to talk to someone more important. Marc, his wife, and Mark's girlfriend followed, leaving me alone with Mary and her husband, Todd.

"Wow, a ton of people came," Mary said beaming. "Quite a shindig you've got going. I'm sorry we're late. I could *not* decide what to wear. The only thing I could think of was my cheerleading uniform, the one I wore in college—I still fit into it, thank god!—but I wore that last year. Mark was just about to pick us up when Todd came home with this costume. He knows my taste so well. It's perfect." She put her hand on his chest and gazed at him admiringly.

"It's a beautiful costume," I said. I was now completely out of ideas for conversation. "So, how did you two meet?" I asked.

"We both went to school at Hartwick College," Mary said.

"I've never heard of that."

"It's a small college in New York."

"Interesting. Why did you decide to go there?"

"I literally just threw a college guidebook in the air and it landed on the page describing Hartwick, so I sent off an application just for the heck of it. I know now that I went there to meet Todd."

They were young, successful, gorgeous, and dazzlingly

in love. Surely I'd spent enough time with them by now, hadn't I?

"Well, help yourself to a beer. They're in the cooler. I should refill the snack trays."

I watched them go, hand in hand. I picked up a mostly empty tray of crackers and cheese and went to the kitchen. I was arranging the crackers when Lydia cornered me.

"Did you get a chance to meet my cousin?" she asked.

"Cousin?"

"He's straight. He's single. He just got transferred here from Iowa. He works in a hospital."

"Lydia, you are not trying to set me up."

She peeked out the kitchen door and we both covertly looked at Ben, who was sitting on the couch next to some guy.

"Admit it, he's cute," Lydia said.

He was kind of cute, though he had a beard. I wasn't a big fan of beards. He had nice brown eyes. His hair was thinning, but it didn't look bad on him. He wore a Renaissance-era costume.

"He's okay. You didn't say anything to him about me, did you?"

"I may have mentioned that I had a gorgeous, blonde, single friend, I'm not sure, I can't remember."

"You realize I'm never going to speak to you again."

"I'm going to remind you that you said that when you ask me to be a bridesmaid in your wedding. Come on, I'll introduce you."

"That's not necessary—" It was too late. She dragged me into the living room and introduced us. Ben and I smiled dumbly at each other and Lydia made an entirely unsubtle getaway.

"Are you supposed to be a character from Shakespeare?" I asked.

"I'm just an average Renaissance man," he said with

a smile. "I'm a member in a Renaissance revival group. We meet on alternate weekends and reenact life in the Renaissance. We do things like build our own bows and arrows. We do archery and have feasts and generally celebrate Renaissance times."

"Oh how interesting," I said. "How did you get interested in that?"

"I minored in history in college and focused on the Renaissance. I think it was such an important and intriguing era in terms of art and literature and culture. I have to admit, I'm not a fan of modern artists like Pollock."

"He's made some important contributions to modern art and, anyway, he's the only artist whose work I could reasonably reproduce."

"You actually make it look really cool. Are you an artist?"

"No, I got my degree in fine arts in New York. I majored in dance, but I took a lot of art and writing classes, some photography. Anything that I couldn't possibly make a living at in real life."

He laughed and I felt myself warming to him. So he was a little eccentric. Originality was interesting. We talked for a few more minutes until I saw newly arriving guests to greet, and I told him I needed to circulate.

I was so exhausted by the end of the night, I'd forgotten about Lydia's plot to get me together with Ben until he was leaving. I walked him to the door.

"It was a wonderful party," he said.

"I'm glad you could make it."

"Would you maybe like to go out sometime?" he asked.

"Sure."

"I'll get your number from Lydia."

"Great. It was nice to meet you."

"It was nice to meet you."

I waved to him as he walked to his car. A date! My first date in five years. I wasn't sure how attracted I was to Ben, but it would be good practice for meeting Art. When we finally met, I wanted it to be flawless.

JEN

Kitty's Discontent

I wanted Tom desperately, and God knows Kitty needed some attention after months of deprivation (surely that little incident with Les didn't count. In fact, I'd nearly managed to forget about it entirely), but before Avery's Halloween party I'd masturbated rigorously and explained to Kitty that that would be all she was getting tonight. We had to be on our best behavior lest Tom think us absolute sluts.

Even so, after a few drinks, I was ready to tear off his clothes. Instead, I opted to get to know him a little better, and I took him aside to ask him why he'd broken up with his ex.

"She cheated on me. With my coworker."

"Really? That's so awful."

"It's going to be a while before I can trust women again."

"Sure, I understand," I said. I waited for him to ask me about my ex. I wanted him to know that I had only recently broken up with my boyfriend. I didn't want him to think I'd been dumped, which I had, or that I'd been single for god-forsaken amounts of time, which, compared to Avery, I hadn't, but he didn't ask, and anyway, if I told him the truth about Dave driving me nuts with his alcoholic, partying, titty-bar-going ways, I would sound un-understanding, and if I told Tom I was ready to commit but Dave wasn't, that would scare him off for sure. So maybe it was a good thing the topic never came up after all.

Even so, it seemed I messed up at some point, though certainly I have no idea how. I laughed at his jokes and asked him question after question about himself, but at the end of the night, not only did Kitty not get any action (a little teensy bit of action would hardly be slutty, it would be merely advertising what I had to offer), I myself didn't get so much as a kiss. He gave me a polite hug good-bye and said he'd see me at work Monday. He didn't even promise to call!

Monday morning I went to work with a horrible hangover. I'd had a little too much wine during my festival of loneliness and feeling sorry for myself the night before. To add to my misery, in my stupid attempt to further my career, Sharon was treating me as her personal slave. I was already swamped with work on the stupid Expert account, but I pushed that aside and tried to keep my head from exploding as I typed in Sharon's ROI numbers for her report for her meeting later in the day.

Even though I felt like someone who'd taken a particularly harsh beating from Xena the Warrior Princess, I tried to look adorable and sexy for when Tom stopped by to tell me what a great time he'd had Saturday night and how he couldn't wait to see me again.

Except all the lip gloss I'd dutifully reapplied each hour went to waste—I didn't see Tom all day. Well, maybe the network had gone down and he was really busy. Or maybe he didn't want to seem overeager. That must be it.

I went to Tae Bo after work, and as I punched and kicked and sweated my ass off, I began to finally begin feeling like something close to human.

After class, I raced home to check my messages. Not a single person had called. Was it possible that Tom didn't like me?

I poured myself a tall glass of ice-cold Absolut Citron and wallowed in self-pity until I couldn't take myself anymore and called Avery.

"What's up?" I asked.

"Nothing. You?"

"I'm bored out of my mind. Tom hasn't called."

"I'm sorry."

"Me too. I wish I'd find a decent guy already. I want to have kids when I'm thirty, which means I'm going to have to find a guy really soon."

"Thirty is five years away."

"I know, but it takes so long to date and plan the wedding, I'm running out of time." It occurred to me just then that Avery was thirty and single. Oops. "Do you want kids?"

"I'm not sure. I used to think I did, but now I just can't imagine doing it. I think too many women have kids because they think they're supposed to, like it's the accessory they need to finish off the picture of their perfect life: husband, career, kids, house, dog. Do you know Elaine in sales?"

"Yeah."

"Her kid's daycare ends at six, but Elaine is constantly working until seven or eight. So she'll pick up her three-year-old from daycare, plunk him in front of the TV in her office, give him a granola bar for dinner, and ignore him completely until she's done with her work. She does this all the time. I'm not saying the mom has to take all the burden of raising a kid, but if neither the mom nor the dad pays any attention to the kid from seven in the morning to eight at night Monday through Friday, I don't know, I just don't think that's right. Why did they even have the kid if they had no intention of ever spending any time with him or giving him a balanced meal? My mom worked full time, but she made sure her evenings were for me. We'd cook a nice meal, talk over the dinner table, watch videos and eat popcorn together, just hang out. I don't know, I just think if you're going to be a parent, you should do it right, and I'm not sure I can do it right."

"Our mom worked. She spent time with us, but I'm not sure how balanced our meals were. At least she cooked. If it were up to Dad, we'd have eaten frozen pizza every night of our lives. Everything Mom cooked involved hamburger meat: tacos, chili, sloppy joes, or plain old hamburgers, and every now and then for like a big-deal Sunday dinner she'd make meatloaf. The only vegetable we ever had was corn."

"Corn's not a vegetable; it's a grain."

"Really? Huh. Oh, and for fruit we'd have Jell-O."

"Please tell me you're kidding."

"You know, with like slices of real fruit in it."

"Yeah congealed in it like samples of human brains at the science museum. Gross. Hold on a second, I've got another call."

Moments later she clicked back. "Jen, it's Rette. I'm going to put us on three-way."

"Sounds kinky."

"Hello?" Avery said.

"Hey, Rette," I said.

"What are you up to?" Rette asked.

"Drowning my sorrows in Absolut Citron. Stupid Tom hasn't called since our date Saturday."

"Did you guys have fun?" Avery asked.

"I thought so."

"Well, if it's meant to happen it will happen," Avery said. "Speaking of things happening, or in my case not happening, do you think it's weird that Art hasn't asked me to meet him in person yet? He's hinted that we'll meet each other someday."

"Why don't you suggest it?" Rette asked.

"I don't know. I guess maybe because I feel like if he did want to get together he would have said something already."

"Maybe he's overweight and scrambling to get in shape before you actually meet him," Rette said.

"Maybe he looks like the elephant man," I offered. "Hey, do you guys have e-sex?"

"What's e-sex?"

"Electronic sex. Like phone sex only through e-mail."

"How would you type and . . . do that?" Rette asked.

"No! Gosh no," Avery said, at practically the same time. "We just talk about our days, the small little moments. We talk about our families and work and places we've traveled and movies we've seen."

Hello, hadn't we started this conversation talking about Tom? How had we gotten so very off track?

"Everything will be fine, Ave. I should get to bed, it's getting late. Bye Rette, bye John-Boy."

"See you tomorrow," Avery said.

"'Night."

I hung up the phone and poured myself a very large glass of Absolut and waited for it to knock me to sleep.

RETTE

Welcome to My Eating Disorder

There was Ben and Jerry's Chubby Hubby in the house. How was I supposed to do sit-ups or read a book or apply for jobs or concentrate on anything when that chocolately good menace was in the house?

Welcome to my eating disorder. There's not a name for it like anorexia or bulimia, but it's very real and very destructive. Symptoms include being haunted by any fattening food product in the house; I was unable to do anything without feeling its presence, without constantly being hyperaware that yummy food was nearby and waiting to be eaten. A siren luring me to danger.

There were others like me. We just didn't have a clinical name for our illness as of yet. The Food Haunted perhaps. The Chubby-Hubby Challenged.

Some people might be tempted to call my ailment a mere lack of discipline and willpower. Not so. I was strong enough not to buy the Ben and Jerry's in the first place, but when skinny Greg unthinkingly brought it into the house, how could I start a diet until it had been devoured?

Every time I went to the grocery store, I'd have to do damage assessments of each and every item of food I bought. I would have to look at the amount of calories that I would intake if I ate the entire thing in one sitting. Tiny pizzas that totaled less than 500 calories were okay, but the ones that said there were three servings of 300 calories a piece—I mean really, does anyone eat merely one-third of a frozen pizza?—were a no-go. Any kind of ice cream or macaroni product also couldn't come into my home. Clearly no cookies, chocolate, or chips of any kind could be tossed into the cart.

Even if I resigned myself to being overweight, I couldn't eat whatever I wanted because even eating just a little too much meant that every year I'd gain another ten or so pounds until I became so fat I wouldn't be able to get out of bed. I'd need to have my groceries delivered to my home and I'd have to hoist myself out of bed with a specially made device just to lumber to the bathroom or, of course, the refrigerator.

I had reason to believe this was an ailment peculiar to women. Males could have a box of cookies in the cupboard, eat just one or two at a time, and leave the open box there for days while they went about their lives unfettered by visions of chocolate chip cookies.

I explained to Greg long ago that he was not allowed to keep treats in the house. He was required to hide them in some secret place where I couldn't find them. Though sometimes, as with the current Chubby Hubby crisis, he forgot, most of the time he managed to hide his stash. Thus, the back of his truck had become a treasure trove of half-eaten candy bars (*half* eaten!) and bags of chips. His desk drawer was littered with Pop Tart wrappers and stale Chips Ahoy.

No matter how valiantly I tried, I could not push visions of Chubby Hubby out of my head. I went to the kitchen table and began flipping through the classifieds. I looked under "marketing" and "public relations." Who knew, maybe the business world wasn't so bad. I thought teaching was such a noble profession, but I'd had to kiss administrative ass, plus I'd had to placate parents and students. There was artifice and superficiality and politics and bullshit in any career.

The phone rang.

The problem with a cordless phone was that, like a remote control, it got left in obscure places. It rang and I began a frantic hunt for it. I only had three rings before the voice mail picked it up.

Finally I found it beneath the coffee table.

"Hello," I said, out of breath from my phone safari.

"Hello, may I speak to Margarette Olsen?"

"This is she."

"Hi, Margarette, this is Eleanore Neuman, the managing editor at McKenna Marketing. How are you?"

"I'm wonderful, thank you." Holyfuckingshitholyfuckingshit.

"Margarette, we would like to offer you the job of editorial assistant."

"Oh?" I tried to be suave. She detailed the pay ($32,000 a year, she said in a tone that suggested the pay was not negotiable) and the benefits and asked me if I would be interested. I waited for a long moment, pretending to weigh my many career options, and said that the position did seem like a good match. She said that was great; when could I start?

"Does Monday sound okay?" I offered.

"That would be great. We'll see you at eight o'clock Monday morning."

I hung up the phone and waited to feel euphoric. Or at least relieved.

I flopped on the couch, stared at the ceiling, and waited for the news to sink in.

Instead of feeling happy, the first thing I thought was, am I settling? Could I find something better? What if there were another, better job for me? I had taken the first job I'd been offered; no one else had even called for an interview. At least the horror of a job search was over. Writing all those cover letters, amending my résumé slightly for different jobs, dealing with my prehistoric printer that printed out my résumé crooked two times out of three and took about fourteen years to print a single page, spending three dollars at Kinko's every time I faxed a résumé, the godawful interviews and depressing newspaper ads—it was too much.

A job. Finally. Maybe it wasn't ideal, but I'd get some good experience for my résumé. At least my new life was no longer on hold. This was it. Real life.

I called Mom and Dad and left a message. I called Avery at work and got her voice mail. I couldn't tell Greg till he got home from school that night. I had to share the news with someone. I called Jen at her office.

"This is Jen Olsen," she answered.

"I got the job at McKenna!"

"Great! Is it salaried?"

"Yep." Uh-oh.

"Can I ask how much it pays?"

Shit. I should have known. I didn't want to tell her. She made $38,000 a year plus bonuses, which amounted to another few thousand.

"About forty thousand." If you factored in health and other benefits, that was close enough.

"Wow, that's a lot better than teaching! When do you start?"

"Monday."

"Let's get together to celebrate, and you can give me the details."

"Yeah, I'd like that."

"I'm really happy for you," she said.

"Thanks."

"I should get back to work."

"Sure. Talk to you this weekend."

"Later."

Saturday night Jen took me to a sports bar. It was the kind of place she loved and I hated. All the guys there wore turtle necks, J. Crew flannel shirts, and clean baseball caps on top of their neat, short hair, and the women looked like they tried much too hard to look casually pretty. I'd asked Avery if she could come, but she was going to a play in Denver with some friends. I was disappointed she couldn't make it. Jen could always keep the conversation going with fluffy anecdotes and amusing observations, but I liked the occasional intelligent exchange mixed in with tales of Jen's sexual escapades.

We got there early, about nine, so there were still a couple of booths open.

"I'm having such a bad hair day," Jen said.

I cringed inwardly but gave her a little smile and nod. Jen's hair looked stunning as usual. Her long hair was, as always, curled in gentle waves like a model's hair in a shampoo advertisement.

"I just got my hair cut and it's in that awkward first week of a haircut stage, you know?" Jen said. "It's so unfair. Your hair is awkward for the first two weeks of a haircut, it looks okay for about two weeks, and then it looks shaggy and in need of another haircut!"

"It's practically tragic."

"Not *tragic.* Just annoying. I tried a new hairdresser. I don't know if I'll go back to her. I mean she was nice and stuff? But she had dyed her hair black, and she had like an inch of light brown roots. You know I have such *issues* with roots. It's like, my god, look in the *mirror.*"

"Mmm."

"So, how's the wedding coming?"

I shrugged.

"You don't want to go there, huh? I understand. You need to think about something else tonight."

We sat in silence for several moments. Jen let out a dramatic yawn. "Oh my god, I'm so tired. Last night Dave went out to the strip club with his buddies and he came to my place in the middle of the night all drunk and horny and stuff and he woke me up to have sex and I could *not* fall back to sleep for the longest time. He was going on and on about how sexy one of the dancers was, and I was like, I do *not* need to hear this."

"Dave? I thought you two had broken up?"

"We are broken up. I did not mean to let him in last night, but he'd already woken me up so I figured, why not shag? Neither of us are in serious relationships, so what's the harm?"

I nodded as if she made sense.

"So. McKenna Marketing." Jen held her glass of beer aloft. "I'm not sure if I should say congratulations or condolences. Regardless, to being employed."

"To being employed." We clinked our beers together. I wished I could toast with unrestrained joy that wasn't mixed with apprehension, so I tried to push my doubts to the back of my mind and focus on the beer.

"So, tell me the deep dark secrets of McKenna Marketing," I said.

"McKenna has got the usual bullshit," she began. "You'll be working for Eleanore who, as you know, is quite a character. I don't know Eleanore very well, but at least she's not Sharon, my satanic boss. Honestly, they've been hiring so many people there lately, it's crazy. I can't keep track of all the new faces. We're staffing up so we can handle the Expert Appliance account. It's a really big account for us."

"How long is the project going to last?"

"At least several months."

"What happens when the project is over? I mean, won't there be too many people?"

"Well, the idea is that we'll be so successful we'll be able to get a ton of new projects and keep busy."

"What if we don't do a good job with Expert?"

"Well, there'll probably be some layoffs."

"Oh great, and I'll have to go through the job hunt all over again."

"Are you kidding? We should be able to get some pretty decent severance packages. It'll be great. I'll give you the following tip: create a filter for Lydia's e-mails. She was the pregnant nurse at Avery's party? She forwards the most unfunny e-mails you will ever waste your time on. I have my Lydia e-mails filtered directly into their own folder so that when I'm unbelievably bored and I have nothing better to do, I can go through them."

"Filter?" I asked.

"I'll show you how to filter e-mails. Or I can have Tom, the love of my life, show you."

"Love of your life? What happened to Dave?"

"Dave was a tricycle. Tom is L-O-V-E in more of a Harley Davidson motorcycle sort of way."

"Tom is cute. So you two are like a thing now?"

"Well, he hasn't called. He's just sort of friendly to me at the office. He said his ex cheated on him and he's kind of wary of women right now, but I can wait till he's ready. Well, I mean, I'll covertly help things along. I may date other guys, and if they happen to send me flowers at the office, well, I can't help that, and if they don't, well, I can help that, too. I'll just send them to myself and make him die of jealousy."

"Clever."

Soon I was on the lovely precipice between buzzed and drunk, a beautiful place in which life didn't feel quite so stressful and scary, but I wasn't yet feeling ashamed of myself, when two fraternity types asked if they could sit with us. Jen smiled and graciously slid down the booth. The GQ-looking guy sat down beside her. I moved over, too; I had no choice. The skinny one sat down on the very edge of the booth, as far away from me as possible.

"This place is kind of weak," Mr. GQ said.

"No cigars," Skinny Boy said.

"I really want a big old stogy tonight," Mr. GQ said. "You like cigars?"

"Sure, every now and then. Not too often," Jen said. What? Jen? Smoke a cigar? This from someone who said kissing a smoker was like cleaning a toilet bowl with your tongue?

"Have you ever been to Enotekas?" GQ asked.

"Oh, my god, that rabidly yuppie place?" I said. The three of them looked at me as though I had suggested we remove our genitals with a penknife.

"I like that place," Jen said, which was news to me because when we'd gone there together, I thought we'd agreed it was overpriced and pretentious.

"That place has pretty good cigars. You can't smoke them too often," GQ said. "Your taste buds get kind of screwy for a few days."

"Exactly," cooed Jen. "Food tastes a little different for a couple days afterward. But every now and then it's okay."

"Where are you two from originally?" GQ again.

"Minnesota. Just outside Minneapolis. I came out here for school and Margarette followed me."

"Actually, I followed my fiancé."

"Me and Randy grew up right here in Denver," GQ said.

"Really! Colorado natives!" Jen gushed.

"It looks like our friends finally got here," GQ said, looking toward the door. "It was great talking to you. I'll see you around."

GQ and Skinny Boy gave us overly enthusiastic politician handshakes and bolted away.

Jen deflated. "They were nice, huh?"

"I guess."

"Ooh, he's cute," she said, wasting no time. Jen looked at the world like Arnold Schwarzenegger's Terminator, who could scan a room and immediately compute all important data. For Jen, the data she calculated included the presence or absence of wedding rings, approximate income brackets, age, and attractiveness.

She pointed to a guy in a crew cut and army fatigue pants standing at the bar right behind us. Normally I didn't go for military types, but the white T-shirt he wore stretched across a broad, well-defined chest, and his Matt Damonish smile made me forgive the crew cut.

"Not bad," I agreed.

"I'll go get us some more beer," she said, emptying the remains of the pitcher into our glasses and bringing the pitcher up to the bar. She stood beside army boy and pretended to seek out the bartender's attention. It would've taken the bartender half an hour to notice me, but he noticed Jen in moments. "Flat Tire," she said. Then, turning to army boy, "Oh my god, where are your legs? I can't see your legs! They blend right into the surroundings!"

He laughed but said nothing.

"You in the army or something?" she asked.

"Used to be."

"Did they make you wear those pants at all times?"

"Nah." Not the best conversationalist, but his smile put me in a forgiving mood. Wow, Jen was good. Army boy was buying the pitcher of beer for her.

"Well, thank you . . . do you have a name or should I just call you G.I. Joe?"

"I'm Bill."

"I'm Jen. Catch you later, Bill. Thanks again for the beer."

Seconds later, Bill and his scrawny friend followed her to our table. "Mind if we sit down?"

"Please," Jen said. Gorgeous Bill slid in next to her, and, story of my life, I got the weaselly sidekick leftovers. "This is my older sister Rette. She looks like a mild-mannered English teacher, but beneath the calm exterior lies a party animal. I know. We went to college together."

"Oh please. Was I the one who suggested we drive to Chicago to see the transvestite strippers?" I teased. "Was it my idea to steal the keg and throw a party in the dorm lounge, breaking every possible university rule in one night? Was it my idea to steal the plant from, god, what was the name of that bar?"

"Ha! Oh, my god, I forgot about the plant. I needed one for my apartment, right?" she explained to Bill and Scrawny Sidekick. "But I couldn't afford it. So we were at this bar that had all these hanging plants everywhere. It was a dark, small bar, right? Not many people were there. We spent half the night plotting how to sneak out a plant past the bartender and the bouncer. Finally I unhooked it. I covered it with my coat and was like ten feet from the door when the bouncer was like, 'Um, what have you got there?' "

"Jen dropped the plant right there. Dirt flew *everywhere*. She just bolted. It was hilarious." I laughed at the memory. Jen really was the funnest, craziest person I knew.

"You ever do anything really wild?" Jen asked Bill.

Bill paused for a moment. "I killed a man once when I was stationed in Germany. I was guarding camp, you

know, and he snuck over the fence. I just came up behind him and twisted his neck like you do to chickens."
He illustrated the action with his hands. He grunted in
mock effort, his teeth bared menacingly. When he was
finished, he smiled with pride. "So that was pretty wild,"
he said.

Jen and I looked at each other for a long moment.
"Wow, I really have to use the bathroom," I said. "Jen?"

"Yeah. Me, too. Excuse us for just a second, boys."

Jen and I raced to the bathroom. As soon as the
door closed behind us, we doubled over with laughter.
It was the kind of laughter that, spurred by a little alcohol, built on itself, spiraling exponentially until we were
howling uncontrollably. "Oh my god, can I pick the win-
ners or what? Shit! What a psycho!" she laughed.

After several minutes, our laughter died down. I wiped
the tears from beneath my eyes. "How are we going to
sneak out of here without them seeing us?"

"It's a big bar. We'll just hang out by the dance floor.
Too bad we lost all that beer though."

"At least it was free." I sighed and helped Jen up. We
peeked out the door. Bill the assassin and his Scrawny
Sidekick were hidden from view. We snuck out to the
other side of the bar where the dance floor was and
stood at the edge of the floor, weaving to the music
without being fully committed to all-out dancing.

A gorgeous guy came up to me. He had blue eyes,
tousled hair, and a sexy grin. Was he not aware that Jen
was far prettier than I? Why was he looking at me?

"Hello," he said.

"Hi."

"I'm Mark."

"I'm Rette."

"Would you dance with me, Red?"

"Rette. Rette," I said. "It's short for Marg*arette*." I'd had
this conversation many times before. "Sure. I love to

dance. That'd be fun." I left Jen standing there, stunned and more than a little irritated. I didn't feel bad leaving her. She'd done it to me a zillion times before.

Mark was a good dancer. It had been a long time since I'd danced with a guy since Greg didn't like to dance.

Mark's cologne was wonderful. I wished Greg would wear cologne. I'd told him countless times about the erotic effect it had on me, but, despite my pleas, he refused.

Mark danced close to me, sometimes touching me. Briefly, I imagined what it would be like to kiss Mark. It had been more than two years since I'd kissed anyone but Greg, and I couldn't remember what it was like to be kissed by someone else. I suspected that Mark would be a damn good kisser. Not that Greg was a bad kisser. I was perfectly content to kiss only Greg for the rest of my life. Sure, sometimes he lost control of his saliva and my mouth was deluged by a wad of phlegmy liquid, and occasionally I wished he would vary his gentle kisses with stronger, more passionate ones, but he was a caring lover and I was content. Still, there was no harm in closing my eyes, relaxing, and imagining what Mark's lips would feel like.

Mark and I danced for three songs before Jen came up to me and said it was getting late and we should be going.

"It was nice dancing with you," I told him.

He gave a nod and grinned. I felt his eyes follow me as Jen and I made our way through the crowd.

"Do you think he didn't notice your engagement ring?" Jen snapped the moment we got into the parking lot. "He was just after cheap sex. How could you let yourself be used like that?"

"Cheap sex? Are you on drugs? He just wanted to dance."

"You're practically a married woman," she hissed, unlocking the passenger side door and marching to the driver's side, her high-heeled boots clicking sharply against the pavement.

"Christ, Jen, I didn't even touch him. We were just dancing."

Jen snapped her seat belt into place.

"You're sleeping at my house. You've had far too much to drink to drive home," she said.

"Oh, so this is interesting, you and I *split* a pitcher, thereby each consuming the same amount of beer."

"Beer affects you differently."

Whatfuckingever. I weighed more than she did and I had danced most of the buzz off.

Needless to say I drove home the moment we got to her place where I'd left my car. I was extra careful driving home. I didn't want to get into a car accident and prove Jen right.

AVERY

Ben, Entertainer of Anorexics

Ben actually called the day after the party. He asked if I'd be up for going bowling that night. For about three seconds I considered being coy and saying I was busy, but then realized that would be stupid.

"Sure. Sounds like fun." That's when I remembered I didn't like bowling, and it actually didn't sound like fun at all. Oh well, if there was a date number two, I would plan that one.

As I got ready, I had the odd feeling I was cheating on Art. Which of course was ridiculous, since we'd never even met. I didn't know if I should write to him about the date tomorrow. I would see how it went and then decide. If it seemed like this might go somewhere, I'd let him know.

When Ben got to my place, he asked me where the best place to bowl around here was, and I admitted I didn't know, I didn't bowl much. I told him that I hadn't bowled in years, as a matter of fact, so he'd have to just be patient with me.

He wasn't. I had always been a terrible bowler, and it wasn't a deficiency I was at all concerned about. Ben, however, tutored me throughout the endless two rounds. "Keep your arm straight. Don't forget to follow through. Stay focused."

"So, Lydia tells me you work at a hospital," I said between rounds. "What do you do there?" Part of me wanted to bonk him over the head with my bowling ball, part of me hoped he was a surgeon who would ask me to marry him. Maybe I'd been hanging around Jen too much.

Ben worked with anorexics and bulimics in the eating disorders unit. In between barking bowling tips, he entertained me with stories of women puking in purses, garbage cans, and toilets, women whose organs could barely function, women who had false teeth by the age of twenty-two from the acids of their vomit eating away at their teeth.

After the second round, I suggested we forget the bowling and focus on the beer. We went to the bar where the stools and booths were made out of squeaky red plastic and the "decoration" was a spattering of neon beer advertisements.

Over beer Ben told me he had been a leisure studies major in college, a statement I immediately laughed at, mistaking this for his first humorous comment of the night. I stopped laughing when I noticed the pained expression on his face.

"You're joking, right?" I said.

"No."

"Oh. So, what exactly does one do with a leisure studies major?" Was there really such a thing, or was he pulling my leg? He seemed incapable of humor, so I was inclined to believe him.

"There are many career possibilities. In my job, I think of activities to occupy the patients' time. I help them keep their mind off food."

I thought this man, this entertainer of anorexics, was more than a little strange, but by the end of the night I had been plied with enough beers that when he asked to come inside my apartment, I didn't think anything of it. It had been such a long time since I'd been on a date, I'd forgotten how it all worked.

Once we were inside, I was at a loss for what we should do. I got as far as suggesting he have a seat on the couch. I sat beside him and suddenly Ben fell on me in a burst of probing tongue and groping hands and excited murmurings. In moments, we were horizontal and his large, odd-smelling body was on top of me, his jeans grinding against mine. I pushed him off and said that I didn't want to rush things. Anyway, maybe men could be aroused through layers of denim and cotton, but his determined, noisy thrusting did nothing for me. He said he understood.

We sat awkwardly beside the other for a few minutes. "Well, I should get going. I'll give you a call sometime," he said.

"Great," I said.

I walked him to the door, waved a cheery good-bye, and returned to the couch where I stayed for a long time, thinking about everything and nothing at all.

JEN

Dating: More Fun Than a Root Canal (Barely)

I'd lost my touch. Tom hadn't called me all week, and when we saw each other at the office, he acted distant. At the clubs with Rette on Saturday, not a single guy asked for my phone number! Some guy asked Rette to dance. Had even one guy asked me? No! And Rette weighed about fourteen tons. It was all so cruel and unfair.

In any case, my ego was in serious need of bolstering. Plus, Kitty was purring for attention.

Dave had pounded on my door at 12:30 one night last week looking for sex, and while I'd had every intention of chewing him out and kicking him out the door, when I saw him, I melted. I gave a feeble attempt at bitching at him, pointing out that I had been sleeping, thank you very much.

"I know, babe. I'm sorry. I just missed you. I still love you, you know." I could smell alcohol on his breath, mixing with the smells of his cologne and aftershave. He smelled so good, so familiar.

He put his hand on my neck and looked into my eyes. He pulled me toward him and kissed me. When he began kissing my neck, my defenses vanished entirely. Kitty ached for him. I was still mad at him, but it had been so long since I'd been properly fucked that I didn't protest as he shed my clothes.

Afterward, as we lay entwined in each other's arms, I cried. I couldn't help but wonder if I'd ever meet another guy whose touch could electrify me like Dave's could. But I had no choice but to try to find him.

So the next weekend, I called Mary from marketing. I despised Mary, but I've discovered it's best to befriend people as two-faced and viper-tongued as Mary. She was the kind of person who flirted with everyone, even women. She smiled and kidded and patted you on the shoulder. But as soon as you were out of hearing range, she'd attack. She would mimic Jim from sales's lisp or Marty from accounting's limp. She scathingly mocked Teresa from teleresearch's crispy, tortured hair. Mary was the kind of woman you were always on guard with because you knew she'd seize your slightest frailty and turn it against you. Only her closest friends, the people she considered cool and worth her time, were immune from the most scorching assaults, and even then, she could turn on them in seconds flat if she thought they'd committed the slightest infraction against her. I couldn't stand her, but I think I'd managed to get her to think of me as part of the McKenna Marketing in-crowd. Normally you couldn't pay me to go out with her, but I hadn't realized how few close girlfriends I had until I needed someone to go to the bars with me to scam for men. I could only convince Avery and Rette to go out with me every so often. For the last five years, I'd spent so much of my time and energy with Dave, I hadn't put much into my friendships. Now I was paying for it. Even drunk,

Mary was sooo boring, but I needed to get out, and she was willing to go out, and there you are.

Mary was telling me I shouldn't be jealous of Rette getting married, that my time was coming. I insisted that I wasn't jealous, but she'd hit a sore spot. I did wish it were me trying on bridal gowns.

"Anyway, you'll get a guy soon. A guy who can afford a little better ring. I mean my god, she'll have that ring forever, you'd think he could spring for a little more than a diamond the size of a grain of sand!" She laughed at her own hilarity. I focused on sucking down my vodka tonic as fast as I could, hoping that a buzz would help make the evening go by a little faster. What I went through to meet men! "I mean not that my ring is huge or anything. Todd went for *quality.*" She brandished her wedding ring in front of my face. I scanned the bar looking for a fork I could jab into her hand.

"I mean some things, you just have to put the money into it. Quality is important. Like with furniture. Have you seen my new couch? Oh my god, you have to come over. It's divine. It was pricey, but it was worth it. It's going to last us years and it's so elegant."

I nodded, miserable.

Blessedly, just then a guy hit on me. He was short and blond, which was so not my type, but even so, he was a break from Mary, and I gave him my full attention.

He said he was a lawyer and that I was the most beautiful woman he'd ever seen, I should be an actress or a model, I was truly a vision. He wouldn't shut up about what a knockout I was, and believe me, I didn't try to make him. Except for Mike's unfortunate height—he must have been five-six, five-seven tops because I was five-five myself, and with the tiny heels on the boots I was wearing, I positively *towered* over him—he wasn't bad-looking.

When he asked to take me to dinner at Vesta's in Denver and then to a concert at the Bluebird Theater, I couldn't help feeling benevolent and forgiving about his diminutive stature and pale coloring.

The more Mike and I talked, the poutier Mary got. Mike was buying us both drinks, so I didn't see what she had to complain about.

Soon she started whining about how late it was getting. She was right. I had a date to rest up for. I gave Mike my phone number and my most seductive smile. He said he was counting the minutes until we saw each other again. The rush of adrenaline coursing through me kept me wired for the next few hours, but I finally managed to fall asleep, dreaming of what it would be like to be a lawyer's wife.

The next day I spent the entire afternoon primping, so by the time Mike picked me up, I looked *good*. He told me so all the way to the restaurant.

Once we got there and were shown to our seats—out of the way by the window—a pall came over the conversation. He ordered an expensive bottle of Cabernet. We looked over the menu and discussed what looked good. The waitress came and took our order.

Silence. I sipped my wine. More silence. Then Mike began talking about the case he was working on. He said he'd spent weeks going through phone bills and whatever documents to find incriminating evidence to win the case. I waited for a plot, a point to his story, a punch line. It didn't come. The story went on for a hundred years. He spoke in a monotone and was woefully ignorant of concepts such as pacing and timing and a little thing called editing out extraneous, boring details. His voice droned on and on, eventually fading into little more than the *mwah-mwah* voice of adults in Charlie Brown cartoons.

I started in on my second glass of wine and braced myself for the long night ahead.

RETTE

Eau d'Asshole

On my first day at work, Eleanore took me around the office and introduced me to everyone. I promptly forgot their names and what it was that they did exactly.

A big part of my job was simple copyediting, but I had to learn McKenna Marketing style and Eleanore's preferences and the way they marked things up for the typesetter. The training was not exactly stimulating. For several hours I listened to Eleanore prattle on about style and grammar; it took a lot of effort not to yawn.

Finally she left me with some reports to edit. They were focus group studies on what features people looked for in an oven, which were just about as interesting as Eleanore's opinions on the use of hyphens in modern journalism. I drank coffee with abandon, determined to be alert enough to catch every mistake.

The next morning I finished the thermos of coffee I'd brought from home before I even got to the office. I wasn't used to waking up at 6 A.M., and of course I didn't get much sleep the night before because of new-job stress and my previous afternoon's caffeine orgy.

I was already having trouble focusing on my work when Eleanore stopped by.

"How's it going?" she asked.

"Well." I tried to look awake and perky.

"I think you'll really enjoy working here. I've worked here three years."

She looked thoughtful. Was I supposed to say something? Was this supposed to impress me? "Really?" was what I finally came up with.

"The editorial department was really a mess when I got here. We were losing money, the reports were always coming out past the deadline. But I was able to turn this place around." Her tone was defensive as if I would doubt her. "I've put in a lot of hours of overtime over the years to get us here. It can get pretty stressful."

"I bet."

"I run to relax. It's important to have an outlet for stress. I run at least fifty miles a week. Not bad for someone who is forty-six, huh?"

"That's great. Fifty miles. Wow."

"I run in marathons. It's what keeps me in shape. I've never been more than ten pounds overweight in my entire life."

Did she not notice that she was sharing this information with a person who had struggled with her weight her entire life and was quite obviously thirty pounds overweight?

"I gained those ten pounds when my first marriage broke up. Michael was my high school sweetheart. We got married right after graduation. We were married seven years. Then I discovered he was cheating on me. It wasn't the first time either. So for a while I ate a little more than I should. Then I looked in the mirror and said, Eleanore Kelly—my name was Kelly then—I didn't change it after the divorce. My maiden name was Smith; then when I was thirty-two, I got remarried and for six years my name was Chase. Then I married Dwayne, that's how I got the name Neuman. What was I saying? Running. Right. It was the breakup of my first marriage that got me into running. I've never been more than ten pounds overweight in my entire life because I made a decision when I looked in the mirror that day and said, 'Eleanore Kelly, I will not tolerate self-indulgence . . .' "

For more than two hours she went on in gruesome detail about the demise of her first two marriages, every place she ever traveled, all the marathons she'd run in, and about how perfect her current husband, Dwayne, was. I said nothing except for the occasional, "Oh really?" or "How interesting."

"I'm not ashamed of having been married three times. I mean it would be nice if Michael and I could have spent our lives together, but it's not always possible. My therapist thinks that I may have abandonment issues because once, when I was five years old, my parents took me to my grandmother's house and left me for a week-long vacation without saying good-bye."

She had a can-you-believe-it? expression, her eyes large and accusative, as if her parents had sold her five-year-old body to strangers for sex.

"They thought it would be easier for me that way, but let me tell you, it wasn't. Really they just didn't want a scene; they didn't want to see me crying. But I cried all right. That week I cried a lot."

Eleanore continued to analyze this event and all of its perceived repercussions on her life. After a very, very long time, she asked me about my wedding plans.

"We're hoping to have it at the Broker Inn if we can . . ."

She clapped her hands together. "That's where Dwayne and I got married four years ago. Everything was just so perfect. You're going to have a wonderful time. For our reception the food was perfect and the champagne was delicious—normally I don't like champagne! I try not to drink very often. When I do drink, I usually only have one glass of wine. I've never been drunk in my life. Our little niece and nephew were the flower girl and ring bearer and they looked so adorable. Particularly little Josh in his little tuxedo. His sister Nina tried to keep him walking straight down the aisle, but he just zigzagged around with a big smile on his face—he just *loved* the attention. I'll have to bring in pictures sometime."

"Great."

"Well, I guess we'd better be getting back to work. I think you'll really enjoy working here." Eleanore looked at me for a moment. Was she waiting for me to say something or was she deciding if she had finished saying all that she wanted to say? "Well, I guess we'd better get back to work," she repeated and finally left my office. I smiled and exhaled, a survivor of a verbal hurricane. Eleanore was a talker, but she seemed nice.

Funny thing, first impressions.

Eleanore trained me for the first couple of days, but Paige was really the person who told me what needed to get done and funneled work my way. It was odd working under a person who was only a year older than me, but I liked Paige. Eleanore always seemed annoyed with me when I asked questions, especially if she didn't know the answer. Paige was more relaxed.

Paige's voice trailed off at the end of her sentences when she did talk, which wasn't often. She wore braces on her wrists and hands. I asked her if she had carpal tunnel. She nodded.

"Did you get it from this job?"

She nodded again.

"I have a bunion from when I waitressed in college. It still hurts sometimes . . ." I was cut off when Eleanore came into Paige's office and said she had some proofs for me to go over. I took the pages and promptly went back to my office. I sat down and thought, *I have a bunion from when I waitressed in college?* What kind of information was this? I'd meant to strike up a conversation about workplace hazards, and instead I'd delivered a ridiculous non sequitur that had catapulted out of my mouth at a dizzying speed. I couldn't exactly go back and explain to her what I'd meant. Shit. If there were a perfume named after me, it would be called *Eau d'Asshole.*

Eventually I extracted from Paige the information that she took an anti-inflammatory drug for her carpal tunnel. She worked an average of sixty hours a week, and since the assistant before me quit, she'd been working even more, which had done some significant damage to her hands. She didn't complain or seem upset that she was in constant pain for working sixty or seventy hours a week when she was paid for only forty.

Paige was nice, but she was the kind of person who probably didn't get asked to parties very often; she was the type to hover on the edges of the room as unnoticeable and innocuous as dust. But I liked her. Several times in the first few days she told me that I was doing a good job, and a few times when I queried her about something that looked odd she said "great catch." I'd return to my office smiling. Great catch! I'd made a great catch! I'd finally found something I was good at.

I was kept busy because there was too much work for our department, especially with Eleanore's unbelievable verbosity—her endless monologues could easily devour two hours of my day. I had no idea how she managed to get any work done because she felt compelled to share her stories with just about everyone in the entire office.

Eleanore's conversations always had a tirade quality to them. Every story seemed to have the same moral: Everyone in the world was hopelessly flawed except her, which thus put an undue burden on poor beleaguered Eleanore, who always rose to the occasion through heroic efforts.

At first, I didn't mind the heavy workload. I liked having a little stress. I liked pushing myself to see how much I could get done in a day. What I didn't realize was that in my first few days, Paige was keeping my workload to a reasonable level. Soon, however, I was expected to plow through as much work as Paige did, and the stress became overwhelming. One day I worked at such a hectic pace for so many hours on end that when my stomach rumbled to tell me it was almost six o'clock, it was like coming out of a trance, and I could suddenly feel how much my right forearm and wrist ached from the keyboard and mouse, and my neck was stiff and sore. By the time I got home from work, my eye was twitching like a mad scientist from staring at the computer screen so long.

The thing was, my body didn't have a chance to heal. I worked the same long intense hours day after day. In less than a week, I was wearing braces like Paige. I tried to remind myself to look away from the computer screen, but my eye twitch lingered. I was beginning to look like someone who should be named Igor.

In stark contrast to the beaten-down ergonomic wrecks in the editorial department were the people from sales who were positively ebullient at all times, always complimenting me on my gorgeous outfits and asking me questions like how my commute was or how the wedding plans were coming along. They acted as though I was the most fascinating person they would talk to all day. I'd answer politely, but people that happy scared me, and anyway, all I wanted to do was *not* think about the wedding. The fact that we hadn't found a place to have it at was keeping me up at night, as were my dismal prospects of finding a dress that didn't make me look like Snuffalupogous in taffeta.

Unfortunately, all my coworkers knew about me was that I was getting married, so in that polite but distant way coworkers feign interest in you, the wedding was a perpetual topic of conversation, particularly with Paige. She was so shy, I couldn't get past feeling we were little more than strangers. I would ask her about her wedding; she would ask about mine. She'd had a huge wedding and an elaborate reception at an expensive restaurant. Her ring was gargantuan.

"Your ring is so cute," she told me. "It really complements your hand." What did she mean by cute? Did it complement my hand because it was small like my hand? Did she think my ring was dinky and therefore Greg didn't really love me? Cute was a very poor adjective to apply to a wedding ring.

"Where are you going to hold the reception?" she asked.

"We haven't made final plans yet, but we were thinking about going to the Broker Inn."

"Oh, two of my friends got married there. It's a nice place."

Was she insinuating that I was unimaginative? That my wedding would be unoriginal?

"Do you know what kind of food you're serving?"

"Maybe Chicken Kiev. We're not sure if we're going to have a sit-down dinner or a buffet."

"We had a sit-down dinner. People could choose swordfish or prime rib. I think having a choice is nice, don't you?"

"Sure. Yeah." My guests would be lucky if they got chicken nuggets and Spaghettios, but I didn't say this. I didn't like where this conversation was going, so I excused myself to return to the safe comfort of my deluge of work.

It was wonderful to be bringing home a paycheck, but my discontent lingered. I woke up early most mornings—four, five o'clock—and then lay in bed worrying about being too tired to do a good job at work, my eyes stinging from lack of sleep. What if I was so tired I made mistakes and got fired? I couldn't take it. I couldn't fail again. I wanted to be out of debt. I wanted the wedding to be over. I wanted a new car so I could stop stressing out about the next time my car was going to conk out on me. My debt was approaching a number so abstract that it was almost easier not to worry about it now than when it had been merely unmanageable rather than unthinkable, which it was quickly becoming.

I would start my diet on January first. Sure it was cliché, but it was a convenient time for new beginnings. I'd had good intentions of dieting, but my new job was insane, and by the time I got home from work, my hunger was raging out of control. I would put a frozen pizza in the oven, binge on whatever snack food was in the house during the eleven minutes it took to cook, then stuff the pizza down so fast I barely bothered to breathe or chew. Then I would sit on the couch, a moaning, distended ball of flab, unable to move because of my considerable girth.

If I started my diet right after the holidays, I could still lose the weight by the wedding. I could lose a pound a week, times four weeks a month, times seven months was twenty-eight pounds. At the end I could starve a little. My goal had been forty pounds, but thirty-five would work.

I couldn't wait to join a health club. I'd work out for two hours at a time, five days a week, and I'd be svelte in no time.

My hopes that Greg would do more housework once I got a job were not realized. He wasn't home much, but he'd use a few dishes every day and leave the counter a mess. I would say, as nicely as I could, "Are you going to clean those dishes?" He always said he'd get to it. And he would. But the mess lingered until every last dish—including the Tupperware we used in lieu of bowls and plates—had piled up in the sink so I had nothing to eat out of and no cooking pans.

All week I longed for the weekend, but when Saturday finally came, instead of luxuriating in my time off, I spent the morning cleaning, then I went out for several hours casing reception halls. When I came home, Greg had a few of his buddies over. There were beer cans everywhere, dishes (unsoaked, of course) filled the sink and spilled over across the counter. All the food I'd bought had been eaten, so I needed to go to the grocery store again, and the floor I'd mopped was sticky with beer and a variety of mysterious crud. I went into my bedroom and cried. I could hear parts of their conversation, including the word *premenstrual* uttered more than once. My worst fear was being realized: I was becoming the kind of housewifely woman who was the butt of jokes in sitcoms.

One afternoon Eleanore stopped by my office and asked, "What do you think?"

"Of what?"

"I got my hair cut and the color touched up."

I saw no difference whatsoever, but said, "Looks great."

"It's so funny; as I've gotten older, I've watched all my friends' hair get lighter and lighter. They cover their gray with blond, but they used to have brown hair. Every year their hair gets lighter. I was always a blonde, so it's not that big a change for me."

She patted her hair a few more times and was on her way.

I was soon feeling better about the comfortable routine of working as an editor. I would never have exciting work anecdotes to share. (Hi, hon. What a day. Somebody actually spelled "letter" "leter," can you believe it?) I would never have exciting adventures like Tom's tales of being a paramedic, but after the hell of teaching, dull routine wasn't so bad. I enjoyed feeling as though I was improving a manuscript, making things clearer for the reader. I liked getting paid to read, even boring marketing reports. I loved looking up an odd-looking word in the dictionary and having my suspicions confirmed—it was being used as a noun when it should be an adjective. Scandal!

But somehow, I still wasn't happy. Not like I'd thought I would be. Now that I had a job, I couldn't fantasize about all the interesting, challenging, high-paying jobs that I could get. My reality was hopelessly dull.

AVERY

Often, Sometimes, Never

Ben didn't call.

I hadn't exactly wanted him to, but some part of me expected he would. A week had gone by, and he still hadn't called. The more time that passed, the more he grew in my imagination into a Prince Charming-caliber guy—dashing and witty and wise. I tried to remind myself that he wasn't particularly good-looking or interesting or kind, but it's difficult to reason with your imagination.

After getting rejected by Ben, it was comforting to find Art's e-mail waiting for me when I arrived at the office Monday morning. The one good thing about Jen's chronic lateness was that I had a few peaceful minutes to myself when I got to the office. I loved leisurely sipping my coffee and reading my e-mail before the rest of my day crashed down around me in an endless tumult of unrealistic deadlines.

To: Dancinfool@yahoo.com
From: ArtLover@yahoo.com

My mother was in town this weekend. It was fun to show her around. We went to the art museum and to a Broncos game. Mostly we ate too much. She's a neat lady. Very funny, very smart. She has finally started dating again. I gave Mom advice on dating and following her heart. It was cool being the one giving advice. She's spent so much time helping me and giving me advice, it was nice to return the favor. It's nice that our relationship has evolved into an adult friendship.

I was crazy busy with work, but taking a fifteen-minute break to write to Art actually helped me be more productive. After I wrote him, I could attack work with a new energy.

I needed that energy for the Expert Appliance account. Everyone in the company was on edge. Jen and I had finished the first round of reports on ovens, but the deadline for getting the second round on washers and dryers was completely unfeasible, and even more so because Jen put in, at most, an hour of work a day.

Ordinarily, I didn't mind that she came in late and took two-hour lunches and spent most of the day gossiping with coworkers. But now that I was working my butt off nine and ten hours a day and still falling behind, and Jen wasn't even attempting to do her share, there were times her lack of a work ethic was rather irritating.

I didn't like it when I let work stress me out like this. It wasn't worth it. But I really needed to prove myself to have a shot at Sharon's job. I knew I could do it. I couldn't let another promotion pass me by. I was smart enough and hard working enough, I just needed to get my name and face out there in front of the big-wigs who made decisions.

"How are the Expert reports coming?" came Sharon's shrill, accusing voice from the doorway. "You know we have to get the first round of the washer and dryer reports to the editors by Wednesday."

What I wanted to say was that I knew very well when the deadline was and it wasn't necessary for her to remind me every single day, but just because Sharon had pulled this arbitrary, utterly unrealistic deadline out of the air without regard for how long it would actually take to complete didn't make it in any way achievable. Instead, I said nothing and just nodded.

She looked at me suspiciously, as if she had every expectation that I would fail. "Thanks," she said in her faux voice that she ended all of her conversations with to make it clear she was done with you.

There was no way we were going to meet the deadline. Sharon's crystal ball had determined that the teleresearchers could each get twenty-two calls done a day when in fact they were getting about fifteen at best. I wasn't given the budget to give them any rewards for reaching Sharon's goal, nor could I let them work longer hours because my budget didn't include letting them work overtime. Plus, Jen hadn't begun working on her part of the first set of reports, so I'd been doing both our jobs for us when I didn't have enough time in the day to do my own job.

There was no one I could complain to about Jen not doing her share of the work. For one thing, Jen was my friend and I didn't want to get her in trouble; for another thing, there was no way I could bring it to a manager's attention without looking petty.

Even though I knew the teleresearchers were doing the best they could, I walked to their cubicle area as if my presence could spur them to higher numbers.

I listened to Teresa Sanchez as she finished up a survey:

"Do you look in *Consumer Reports* before purchasing a major appliance (A) Often (B) Sometimes, or (C) Never?

"Okay, my last question: Is there anything you can think of that would improve your laundry process?"

"Yeah, we all hate folding!" she laughed encouragingly. "Thanks so much for your help!" Teresa hung up the phone and groaned.

"Hi, Teresa, how's it going? Learning anything exciting about consumers' desires for innovations in laundry?" I asked.

"Yes, everyone would like a machine that folded their clothes. If I hear that suggestion one more time, I'm going to scream."

"I'll let Expert know about that," I joked. The other members of the team were getting busy signals, wrong numbers, and answering machines, so I was able to pull them all aside for an impromptu meeting.

"Listen, you guys are doing a great job, but we're just not pulling in the numbers we need. I technically don't have the budget to do this, but you guys are working so hard, I want to reward whichever one of you can pull in the highest numbers. We absolutely need to get the project finished by the sixteenth." If I couldn't convince Sharon to give a reward, I'd just pay them myself. I was desperate.

"Avery, it's nice of you to offer a bonus, but we're doing the best we can and we just can't get that many calls. The deadline is unrealistic," Teresa said.

Teresa was a talented young woman who could do so much better than phone surveys. She didn't have the money to go to college, and her appearance didn't exactly scream, "I am future management material!" She hairsprayed her bangs into a pouffy sphere that looked like the extended cranium of a Cro-Magnon. She wore a lot of dark eyeliner and lined her lips in a shade much darker than her already dark lipstick. Her nails were always painted an airhorn-siren-loud color.

I liked her. I didn't want her to think of me as the unreasonable tyrant boss. I wanted to scream, *No kidding! It's not my deadline! I'm not the bad guy.* Instead I just said, "I know it's tough, but I know you guys can do it. I appreciate your hard work."

I walked back to my office. The teleresearchers hated me. I hated me. I sounded like such a corporate bullshitter. I had no power to reward them and no power to change the deadline. All I could do was incur the hatred of the teleresearchers and fail miserably in front of my boss.

As soon as I got back to my office, the phone rang. "Avery, this is Jack Webb from Expert Appliance. I wondered how the research was coming."

"Good to hear from you, Jack. Everything is on schedule. We should have all the interviews complete within the next two weeks."

"Super. Have you found anything interesting yet?"

"It's *really* too early to say." So far Expert Appliance had spent fifty thousand dollars to learn that people wanted reasonably priced appliances that wouldn't break down. "I'll let you know!"

"The questionnaire seems to be working okay?"

"No problems. In fact, it seems to be working out really well."

Jack kept me on the phone for twenty more minutes, talking about how much he was looking forward to the results of the project and unrelated ramblings on projects he was working on. I took deep breaths and tried not to think of how much work I could be doing.

* * *

Jen finally strolled in to the office.

"It's nine o'clock, Jen. In case you haven't noticed, we have a huge project we're way behind on," I said.

"What's your point?"

"My point is that I got in at seven this morning. I've been doing your job as well as mine and Jen, I can't do it anymore."

"I'm sorry I haven't been up at the crack of dawn slaving away. I'm only going through the most difficult thing I've ever experienced. In case you forgot, the man I planned to marry viciously dumped me, leaving me with nothing but the credit card debt he got me into."

"Jen, I know you're going through a hard time . . ."

"Yeah, I can see you're just bursting with concern." Jen slammed her briefcase down.

"I'm sorry."

"Gosh, I'd *love* to discuss this, but I have too much work to do to waste time talking." She turned to her computer.

I started to protest, but I didn't know what to say.

Jen did work hard in the next few hours, but the tension was so awkward, I wished I hadn't said anything, just to have her cracking jokes again.

After a while, I got so absorbed in my work I forgot about the tension between us. There were times when I could spend hours designing and reworking a graph, slightly changing the hue of each color, contrasting a pewter blue against a shade of violet against a rich pale yellow. The world was a kaleidoscope of colors and possibilities, a palette of shades to choose from.

I didn't look at the clock until I realized I was starving. It was 1:30 and I hadn't eaten anything but a banana all day.

"I'm going to eat some lunch. Want anything?"

"Some of us have too much work to do to take lunch breaks."

"Fine," I sighed.

In the kitchen, I pulled my salad out of the fridge and brought it to the table where Les was sitting. He looked uncharacteristically unhappy. He was staring out the window, his sandwich untouched on the table.

I didn't know Les very well. Our acquaintance was limited to polite how-are-you-doings exchanged in the hallway, and a few times we'd chatted about things like Boulder's weather and what movies we'd seen recently while he got my ailing computer working. Even though I didn't know much about him, I liked him. Les had a good spirit. Even when he was obviously stressed and frustrated, he just smiled and acted as though helping me was the only thing he had to do all day. When something went wrong with my computer, he didn't blame a coworker's incompetence or declare management's technology purchases cheap like Tom always did. He just fixed the problem. After working with Sharon and Jen for so long, I'd really grown to appreciate people who did their job well.

"Les? Is everything okay?" I asked.

Les turned and smiled wanly. "Everything's fine."

"Are you sure?"

"I'm sure. I guess I just wish there were more hours in a day."

"No kidding. Yesterday I worked till seven, stopped at the grocery store, made some dinner, and it was suddenly nine o'clock and it was all I could do to walk across the room and fall into bed. It's like, gosh, what an exciting life I lead."

"Exactly. I just can't seem to get everything done that I need to. I worked all weekend—twelve hours Saturday, twelve hours Sunday—and I only finished a third of what I'd hoped to. I was really hoping I wouldn't have to work this weekend."

"So don't."

"I have to; it has to get done." Les gazed out the window again, looking very tired.

I started on my salad. In all the silence, the crunch of my cucumbers and carrots seemed to echo more loudly than usual.

Finally Les broke the quiet. "I had this idea that when I moved to Colorado I'd get a less stressful job and go hiking every weekend and get back in shape and have a life," he said. "Read a book every now and then, maybe get a girlfriend. Instead I'm just as stressed about work as ever. I've hiked exactly once. I haven't read so much as the advertising on a *cereal box* let alone a book, and I did meet someone, but she won't give me the time of day."

"Have you asked her out?"

"No, no. It's just a crush. It's silly really."

"Tell me about her."

"She's beautiful and fun and amazing."

"Les, any woman would be lucky to find you." He really did seem smart and funny and kind. But because he was overweight and rather plain, there was no sexual tension, so I didn't feel that awkward, expectant hopefulness I felt when I was attracted to someone and hoped they felt that way about me.

"You know," I continued, "I love hiking and I rarely work weekends, so I have no excuse for not hiking more often. Would you like to go hiking with me on Saturday? I mean if you don't have to work."

"I'd really like that. That'd be great. Much better than coming into the office."

"Great. Why don't we go to Chataqua? There's a ranger's station at the entrance of the park. Let's meet there, say around ten?"

"Sounds good. I'm looking forward to it," he said.

"Good. Well, I guess I should go back to work. I'll see

you Saturday." I took my unfinished salad with me to eat at my desk. Halfway to my office, I stopped midstep. What had I done? What if Les thought I'd just asked him on a date? What on earth would we talk about for two hours on the hiking trail?

I considered e-mailing him to tell him I couldn't make it, but I couldn't think of what to say to get out of it. Well, I did want to go hiking and I did want to get to know Les better. I'd just make it clear I wasn't romantically interested in him, and we could go from there.

My fears turned out to be entirely unfounded. Early on in the hike, I made a point of saying that I wasn't ready for any sort of romantic involvement with anyone, that I was still recovering from my divorce and happy to be single. After I'd made it clear that this wasn't a date, I relaxed, and our conversation came easily. Les kept me laughing for most of the trail.

In two hours, I learned that Les was thirty-three and had never been married, though he'd lived with a woman for a couple of years way back when. He'd changed majors a lot in college, and as a result had gotten an exceptionally well rounded education. He'd taken courses in art history, anthropology, literature, international relations, and economics before finally graduating with a degree in physics. He taught physics in a high school for several years, and he taught himself about computers in his free time. He'd launched the technology literacy program at his high school. He loved the work, but the pay was atrocious, so he got a job at a large Internet company, and for the next two years he rarely worked fewer than seventy hours a week. He was so stressed out all the time that he gained thirty-five pounds in a single year.

He'd always loved Colorado, so he decided to move out here and focus less on his career and more on his life. Except like so many good plans, his was unrealized.

What was perhaps most striking about our conversation was how much I shared about myself. When I'd been with Gideon, I'd grown used to never talking about myself or my feelings. With Les, I opened up and told him all about my years as a dancer and the very unhealthy relationship with one of the musicians on the ship I'd worked on. I told him all about my five years at McKenna Marketing and my marriage to Gideon. I told Les about my passion for yoga and jogging and discussed my favorite writers and artists. Les was also a huge fan of Bosch, Toulouse-Lautrec, and Bracquemond, among others. He seemed to actually consider my babbling interesting.

"This is a reasonable hike," he said as we approached the top of the hill. "This path has a decent incline, but it's not so steep you have to focus on staying alive every second. I like a trail where you can enjoy the view as you go. Maybe the reason I've only gone hiking once since I moved here is because the one time I did go, it was *traumatic.* Tom took me to Rocky Mountain National Park a couple weeks after I moved out here and took me on a trail that was like this." He indicated with his forearm an incline that was nearly vertical. "Now, I'm still not used to the change in elevation, but I certainly wasn't used to it after being here only a couple weeks. I know people who have lived here for a while don't notice it, but let me tell you, there is no oxygen to be found anywhere around here. I could barely breathe when I was just standing immobile on the ground, so you can imagine what it was like to charge up the side of a cliff with über-athlete Tom. So I think we're going on this little jaunt. Turns out it's a *four-hour hike.* By the time we got to the top of the mountain, I was delirious from lack of oxygen. I was completely out of breath." He demonstrated, wheezing comically. His expression was hilarious and I couldn't help laughing. "I'm standing there, clutching my heart like a dying man, and I look over, and there is this obese woman, smoking a cigarette, and she's got two little kids. Granted, I'm not in the best shape, but this woman was *rotund,* and a smoker on top of it, and she managed to get both herself and her two small children up this cliff without apparent difficulty. It was *humiliating,"* he said, smiling. "Oh sure, laugh at my pain."

The climb down the mountain went quickly as we talked nonstop about every topic that popped into our heads. We came to the end of the trail where our cars were parked and turned to face each other. "I had a lot of fun," I said.

"I had a great time. Would you like to get some lunch?"

I hesitated. "Lunch? Sure, but . . . I just want to make things clear. I don't date coworkers." It was a perfectly reasonable excuse. And not a total lie.

"Sure, I understand," he said with a smile.

"I mean, not that you were even interested in me in that way. I mean, I know you're into someone. Why are you smiling like that?"

"Nothing." He shook his head but continued smiling that disconcerting smile. I quickly changed the subject back to lunch.

"You know, I know we just exercised and did this really good thing for our bodies, but I'm craving a big plate of cheese-filled enchiladas," I said. "And maybe a margarita or two."

"Only if we can start out with some lard-laden chips."

"Twist my arm."

He pretended to battle fiercely to twist my arm. "Uh!

There. You know, we shouldn't feel guilty. After expending all this energy, our bodies are telling us we need to refuel with a heaping plate of fried cheese products."

"It's really so important to listen to your body."

"Exactly."

Over margaritas and nachos I asked him to tell me about his mystery crush.

"Avery, I'd really rather not get into it."

"I've told you everything. Come on, spill."

"I told you, it's a silly crush. It's nothing."

"Where did you meet her?" I knew he didn't get out much, so I made a guess. "Work?" I could tell by his sheepish expression I was right. "It's not Jen, is it? Don't be embarrassed. She's very beautiful. And very flirty." My good mood suddenly faded a little. I finished my drink.

"Do you think, maybe if I lost some weight . . ."

"Les, don't lose weight for Jen. Do it for yourself. You could get into great shape. You could get a new haircut, new glasses, new clothes, and Jen still wouldn't be interested. She only goes for pretty boys who treat her like crap."

"Glasses? What's wrong with my glasses?"

I couldn't believe how rude what I'd just said was. "Nothing's wrong with your glasses, I . . ."

"Should I get contacts? I can get contacts."

"Take your glasses off," I said. He did. I looked at his eyes. There were dark brown, like melted chocolate. "You have very beautiful eyes. You need some stylish glasses to show them off."

"These are out of style, huh?"

"Yeah, well, they just aren't exactly flattering."

"And my hair?"

"I'll give you the number to the salon where I go. You know, you should not take relationship advice from me.

I'm divorced and recently—" I didn't know if it was the margarita making me bold or just the way Les made me feel like I could tell him anything, but I decided to tell him about Art. "I've recently been e-mailing a man I met over the personals on the Internet. We've never met and I don't know what he looks like, I don't even know his real name. It's kind of dating training wheels, before I get out there and do it for real. Do you think that's awful and pathetic?"

"Of course not. Not at all. It doesn't matter how you meet someone. You know more about a person you meet over the Internet than you do a stranger in a bar."

"I guess. I still feel pathetic." I stared at a lone chip marooned in the salsa. "Do you believe in true love? Destiny?"

"Yes. I don't believe it's easy, but I believe that somewhere out there is someone who gets you, who will listen to you and support you and be there for you. My father had a saying that it's not the person you are with but the person you become when you are with that person. Certain people bring out your best self. That's who you need to find. A man who brings out your best self."

I'd always envisioned myself falling for a dashing, romantic guy who would sweep me off my feet, but right now the idea of a guy who simply understood me sounded pretty good. "That makes a lot of sense," I said. I slid my finger around the edge of the margarita glass and licked the salt off my finger. I was getting a little tipsy. I had to change the subject before I said something stupid. "Do you have any family out here? What brought you to Colorado?"

"I've been to Colorado several times on vacations, but I moved here without knowing anybody. I've always loved it out here. I wanted a change so I just decided to go for it. The rest of my family still lives in Ohio."

"Are you going to see them at Thanksgiving?"

He shook his head. "I'll probably just make myself something."

"I'm going to my mother's house. Why don't you come? We both would love a little more company, and we're both decent cooks. It would be nice to have more guests. It gets kind of dull with just me and Mom. Sometimes we invite our friends over, but this year everyone is busy and it was just going to be the two of us."

"I'd love to, but you have to let me help. I'm a pretty good cook too, you know."

"It's a deal."

Les's kind smile was infectious. I felt better than I had in a long time.

JEN

Porno Pyrotechnics

Work had become hellish, not only because there was way too much of it, but because Avery was being such a capital *B* Bitch. So I was surprised when she asked how my weekend had been and how things were going with Mike.

"Pretty good. He really treats me right, that's for sure. He always takes me to nice restaurants and calls me when he says he'll call."

"What is he like in bed?"

"I have no idea. He's gotten nothing more than a chaste smooch from me."

"You're kidding."

"No I'm not. I'm following 'The Rules.' You're not supposed to sleep with a guy for at least two months if you want him to marry you."

"I thought you didn't really like Mike. I thought you said he was boring."

"That's really not the point."

Just then, Tom entered our office. "Hey, just want to check in and see how things are going."

"Good. I think you fixed everything," I said.

"Great," he said. "Hey listen, some of us from IT are going out tonight after work for Happy Hour. Would you like to go?"

I thought for a moment. Les would probably be there, but I could risk that to see Tom. "Yeah, that'd be great. Thanks for asking."

"Oh, Avery, you can come, too."

"Thanks. I'm busy."

I waved good-bye and turned to Avery. "I think he just asked me out. I'm sure he did! Finally!"

"Does he know about Mike?"

"No, what would I tell him? Mike and I aren't in a committed relationship or anything." I turned to my computer, but I was much too happy to work.

I'd tried to explain to Kitty that sex should not be used in a medicinal capacity, but there were times when she just didn't listen. Kitty and I had been very good about not sleeping with Mike right away. Mike and I had gone out several times in the last week, and we hadn't gone any further than a few good-night kisses. So by the time Tom asked me out, Kitty was about to explode.

The numerous beers I drank that night at the bar didn't help the situation. Nor did dancing so close to Tom. I lost myself in the flashing lights and pulsating music, in the smell of Tom's cologne, and the feel of Tom's warm skin.

Tom pulled me aside to a dark corner. We finished our drinks and he pulled me close to him, dancing slowly despite the fast music and the thunderous bass. Tom whispered in my ear all the places he wanted to kiss me. Kitty was all ears.

When Tom suggested we go to his place for a drink, I agreed without hesitation.

We'd barely made it inside his apartment when Tom leaned into me, running his hands slowly up and down my back. His kiss was delicious. For a moment, I was extremely, extremely happy to be single. I was looking forward to being a sexless wife and mother, but until such a time, I was going to have *fun*.

Tom wasted no time in peeling off my shirt and bra. For all his promises of how he wanted to kiss me all over, except for some brief but enthusiastic lapping at my breasts, most of my body was woefully ignored, and within moments, he was trying to unzip my jeans. I moved his hand and shook my head no, but a few minutes later he tried again and managed to peel off my jeans in one rapid, expert motion. He slipped his fingers inside my underwear. I closed my eyes and willed myself to relax.

"Tell me how good your pussy feels," he whispered. My eyes popped open and I looked at him quizzically, but his own eyes were closed and didn't notice my discomfort. He told me again to debrief him on the goings on of my pudenda. *Pussy* was not a word I particularly liked, and I felt like an actress being given stage directions, so I pushed his finger out. He promptly began taking off his own clothes and then whispered, "Suck my dick." Had he seen too many pornos in his time? Did normal people actually talk like this?

I went down on him as he'd requested, but the beer must have desensitized him, and after about fifteen minutes, my jaw was getting sore. I told him to put a condom on and come inside me, not so much because I wanted sex but because my jaw was cramping and it seemed like the quickest way to get his dick out of my mouth.

He pulled a condom out of his jeans, put it on, and pushed his way inside me. While he was pumping away, he asked in a breathy voice if it felt good. I could guess at the answer he wanted to hear, but the truth was that I was indifferent. I mumbled an ambivalent "Mmmm." I watched the expressions he made. They had a practiced, theatrical air to them, as if he were putting on a show. Porno pyrotechnics.

He kept encouraging me to tell him how good my pussy was feeling, and finally I said, with about as much enthusiasm as I might muster to discuss laundry, "My pussy feels so good; oh it feels so good."

How to Be a Drunken Slut

Rule #1: Remember your lies.

All at once my social calendar was becoming a difficult balancing act.

I couldn't decide who I wanted to date, and dating two guys was exhausting. It meant constantly doing laundry so I'd always have my sexiest underwear and bras ready to wear. It meant never having time to clean the house or going to bed early enough to get a decent night's sleep.

I couldn't remember who I'd told what. I kept saying, "Have I already told you the story about . . . ?" One night when Mike and I were trying to decide where to go to dinner, I asked him, "Do you like sushi?"

"Jen, we talked about this for half an hour the other night when we were discussing all the different foods we like and the unusual foods we'd eaten. Yes, I like sushi."

It was Tom who didn't like sushi. Oops.

More challenging was remembering my lies about where I was when I was with the other guy. I couldn't remember who I'd used the I-have-to-stay-home-and-do-laundry lie with or the my-girlfriend-broke-up-with-her-

boyfriend-and-I-need-to-be-there-to-comfort-her lie. I'd
told that to Mike one night when I went to the clubs with
Tom. The next day I was complaining to Mike about my
hangover. He said, "I thought you were comforting your
friend."

"Oh yeah, I was. I, uh, we just you know were talking
and started doing shots at her place."

"But I thought you said you were at the Oasis."

"Right, right. That's why we got hungover. We did shots
at her place and then went to the Oasis and started drinking beer. You should never do that, mix hard liquor and
beer."

Mike chose to believe my inexpert lies, so I kept telling
them.

**Rule #2: Do a particularly good job of disposing of tell-
tale condom wrappers.**

I'd hoped that sleeping with Mike would help me decide which guy I wanted. If he'd been a great lover or a
terrible lover, the choice would have been a little clearer,
but as it was, sleeping with him only confused the issue.

If only I could mix the best parts of Mike with the
best parts of Tom, I'd have the perfect man.

On the one hand, Mike was a caring, if dull, lover.
He gave me long full-body massages and he always took
the time to lovingly kiss my neck, back and arms before
and during sex. Otherwise, his hands and tongue weren't
good for all that much. Tom was more exciting in bed,
but he was often too rough and rarely caressed any part
of my body except my breasts and Kitty, and even then it
was perfunctory, like he was impatiently waiting for the
car to warm up in cold weather when all he really
wanted to do was race away.

Outside of the bedroom, Mike took me to nice restaurants and seemed to really take an interest in what I

had to say. He empathized with my frustrations at work and gave me constructive advice on how to advance my career. I talked a lot when I was with Mike because whenever he spoke I became instantly bored. He just didn't know how to tell a good story, how to sift out the uninteresting details to get to the heart of the anecdote. He had a penchant for punning and he thought he was funnier than he was. Tom was funny and entertaining, but whenever I started to tell him about my day he would interrupt or look bored, staring at something across the room. If I could tell him a funny story and get him to laugh it was great, but with Tom I always felt like I was putting on a performance.

Then one weekend, Tom didn't call me for three days straight. I went out with Mike Saturday night, but when he asked me go to a movie Sunday night, I said I had plans. I assumed Tom would call me.

He didn't.

I spent the entire evening at home alone. I didn't know what to do with myself. My life had been so busy lately, and I didn't know what to do with the sudden calm.

My thoughts raced. Was Tom going to break up with me? Had he met someone else?

I called him and got his machine. I called again a couple hours later at around ten and left another message.

I tried to go to bed, but I was sure he'd call me, so I was rigidly alert, waiting for the phone to ring, and I didn't fall asleep for hours.

The next day at work I e-mailed him first thing. By two in the afternoon when he still hadn't returned my e-mail, I went down to his office. He was charging out as I came down the hall.

"Hey," I began.

"Hey, I can't talk. Glenn's computer crashed. Got to keep the VPs happy." His tone was distant, as if there were nothing more between us than the fact we worked in the same building. He brushed past me with cold indifference.

That night Mike begged me to let him come over. I told him I really needed to clean and do laundry and get some sleep. Oh how I craved eight hours of sleep in a row. He said he would bring dinner and leave promptly at eight and I could do my laundry while we ate.

I finally relented and let him come over. He brought brie and fresh French bread and fruit and red wine and paté and decadent pastries from a local upscale market. That was another problem with dating two guys. I'd been going out to eat almost every night. With Mike I always drank a bottle or so of wine to lessen my boredom, and I often went to bars with Tom where I'd drink more beers than my waistline could afford. I was trying not to eat during the day to save my calories for night, but it still wasn't enough. I'd had to purge a meal or two here or there. I wasn't going to get dangerously bulimic again—I was too smart for that—but I also wasn't going to fatten the goose that laid the golden eggs.

Mike gave me a long back rub and said I seemed tense. I told him I wasn't looking forward to going home for the holidays, especially since Rette would be going to her future in-laws for the weekend, leaving me to face my mother alone.

After discussing what had been stressing me out and after the long back rub and a couple glasses of wine, I felt much better, so relaxed. We had slow, delicious sex, and I decided Mike really was the guy for me.

Mike left early as promised; he was out the door by nine. I was in bed asleep by ten. Half an hour later, there was a thunderous knock at my door. At first I thought it was Dave and, despite myself, my heart leapt. Then I remembered that I'd been sleeping, and that he was a jerk for waking me up.

Except it was Tom.

"How'd you get through the security door downstairs?" I asked.

"Somebody let me in. Aren't you glad to see me?" It was obvious he'd been drinking.

"Tom, I was sleeping. I have to go to work tomorrow. Why didn't you call first?"

"I was in the neighborhood. I missed you." He leaned toward me and kissed me, his hand stroking my breast. I didn't mean to get turned on—I was mad at him for waking me up and anyway, I'd decided I was going to break up with him—but I did, and minutes later we were pulling off each other's clothes on my bed. I reached over to the nightstand to get a condom and when I turned back, Tom was brandishing the empty condom wrapper from my escapade with Mike just a few hours earlier that had been left on the windowsill.

I swallowed hard and said, as nonchalantly as I could, "What?"

"Are you sleeping with someone else?"

"Of course not, that's from you the other night."

"We haven't seen each other since Thursday."

"Right. It's from Thursday."

I could tell he wasn't sure, but he was horny and decided not to worry about it, at least until after we'd had sex.

Rule #3: Become an expert at covering up hickies.

The next day Tom was really attentive. Maybe the threat of another man made me seem more desirable. He asked me to go out with him that night since I would be gone for the weekend. I said okay, thinking I would break up with him for sure that night, but as soon as we got to the bar, we started having so much fun I lost my resolve. I never laughed like this when I was with Mike.

That night, the sex with Tom was rougher than usual. After so many shots of tequila, I didn't remember the whole thing all that well, but I do remember thinking that the pain sort of felt good.

The next morning I kicked Tom out early, saying I had to get to the airport and hadn't even packed yet. The asshole never even offered to drive me to the airport. I was going to break up with him for sure. I would've been even madder if Mike hadn't already offered to take me to the airport.

I was so hung over I threw a few clothes in a suitcase and decided that was close enough to being packed. I hadn't even finished drying my hair or putting my makeup on when I heard Mike buzzing to get in.

He took my luggage downstairs to the parking lot where his car was. We had just started driving away when he said, "What's that?"

"What?"

"On your neck. It looks like a hickie."

My stomach lurched as I flipped down the visor and looked in the mirror. It was indeed a hickie. Tom must have given it to me during our drunken romp the night before.

"You gave it to me Monday night." It almost scared me how easily the lie came. I said it with such assurance I almost believed myself.

"Really? I guess I must have," he said. He smiled an awe-shucks smile, like he was pleased with himself. "I haven't given anyone a hickie since high school."

"I have delicate skin, you know, being a redhead and all."

"Your skin is beautiful. You're beautiful." He looked

affectionately at me. He was only three or four years older than me, but I knew I made him feel young. I felt old, and very, very tired.

Sex and Alcohol

Sex and alcohol had not yet filled the cavernous ache, but I kept trying.

RETTE

Ties That Bind

I lay naked and spread-eagle, my extremities tied to the four corners of my bed. Greg sat beside me, his thin body slumped into a nervous question mark, his penis inert against his leg. Plaintively he examined my body: the large breasts that rolled into my armpits, the reddish-brown pubic hair between my thighs, the thick calves with dark, two-day-old hairs poking out.

Greg asked what came next.

"Sweetheart, this was your idea." I was inexplicably nervous, and though I wanted to be supportive, I couldn't quite keep the tension out of my voice. "I think the idea is to experiment," I added.

He nodded, his face crumpled with shame. He said he'd be right back.

Greg knew exactly how to touch me. Our routine was usually effective but dull. *Cosmo* suggested bondage as a way to take our erotic relationship to new levels. Now I was wondering why I was taking advice from a magazine that put the ability to fellate a man as a skill on par with running a country or managing a Fortune 500 corporation.

Would the sex on our wedding night be explosively good? Maybe we shouldn't have sex for two weeks before the wedding to make it all the sweeter. What if we were too tired or too drunk? Our first post-marriage coitus had to be memorable.

A strand of hair stuck to my forehead, tickling me. I shook my head and blew from the corner of my mouth, but it adhered tenaciously. Without other distraction, the tickle became all consuming, tortuous.

Greg returned grinning. He was holding something behind his back. *A videocamera? Hot wax?* My heart raced and not, sadly, from erotic excitement.

"Gregory, get this hair off my face!"

He set what he was holding down on my stomach, and reached to move the hair. I screamed and jerked up, spilling the ice cream sundae he'd brought over my breasts and abdomen. I screamed louder.

"Off! Get it off! Freezing! Freezing cold!"

Greg bolted up. "Shit, sorry. Sorry." He looked around for something to wipe it off.

"Use a pillow case! Anything!"

Greg ran to the bathroom and got a towel to wipe the gooey chocolate syrup and the whipped cream off, managing to leave both me and the bed sticky.

"I thought it would be fun," he said.

"You were wrong. I want to be free. Now."

"But . . ."

"Now."

Greg loosened the knots of the silk scarves that attached me to the bedposts. Was he disappointed with me or himself?

"Do you want to join me in the shower?" I asked. "I'm sorry for screaming. Look, I appreciate you experimenting with me. Now we know I don't like arctic desserts dumped on me. Next time we'll find something we both like."

"I'm really sorry."

"Sweetie, don't worry about it. I'm sorry too." And I was sorry. Sorry that our sex life was on its death bed. He followed me, dejectedly, into the shower.

I relaxed in the spray of the hot water and tried not to think of which bouquet style to order for the bridesmaids.

Trapped in Nebraska

Greg and I had met at my Psycho Landlady's Christmas party two years earlier. I rented a room in a house from her when I first got my job teaching. It wasn't so much what she said that made it clear she was mentally unbalanced, but this way in which she would in one instant treat me like her best friend and in the next look at me like I'd just slaughtered her puppy. I was an emotional, moody person myself, so I had a high tolerance for people whose moods swung dramatically, but her highs and lows were so extreme, so sudden, they could scare someone far braver than I.

I didn't want to go to the Psycho Landlady's Christmas party, but I didn't want her to hate me. After all, she had my deposit. I was just going to pop in and make an appearance and then leave.

Greg worked with one of her friends, which is how he ended up at the party. He was sitting on the couch by himself, and I was trying not to look like the complete friendless dork that I was. I thought that he was cute, but in a nerdy, nonthreatening way that gave me the confidence to sit down and ask him if he was a friend of my landlady. We talked for the rest of the night. We had been talking for hours when his friend came up to Greg and said he was ready to go and Greg said, "Well, it was nice to meet you," and just left. Without asking me for my number. I was crushed; I'd thought we'd really hit it off. But then, a few minutes later, just before I was about to leave, he came back in and asked, all awkward and shy, would I maybe like to go get a cup of coffee sometime? I said I'd love it and gave him my phone number.

By our second date, I knew we were going to get married. We'd gone Christmas shopping together and, as we waited in line at the cash register, he joked around with a little girl who was standing in line with her mother in front of us. He made the girl squeal with laughter. Watching this big, tall guy making these funny faces, making this little girl laugh, not at all concerned with looking hip or cool . . . his sweet grin, the genuine pleasure he got from playing around with her . . . he just seemed like such a sweetheart. Right away I could envision us as an old couple, shuffling along the beach together, arm-in-arm.

Your future in-laws, of course, aren't something you consider when you're busy falling in love. If I'd been smarter, I'd have fallen for a guy whose parents lived somewhere interesting like New York or San Francisco. Greg's family wasn't the most thrilling group of people, and spending a four-day weekend with them seemed an interminable amount of time. I had precious few days off, and this was not how I wanted to spend them. I'd only been working full time for three weeks, but I was already ready for a vacation.

Greg's mom was nice, but she always looked so weary, like life was so difficult and largely horrible and there was nothing she could do about it. She had long ago resigned herself to a dour, joyless life. All she did was talk about recipes, constantly sharing tips with me, which I'm sure would have been fascinating, *if I cooked,* which, as I'd told her more than once, I didn't do. Greg's mom was adamant that we have a church wedding, even though Greg was agnostic and I and my entire family weren't religious. I wasn't looking forward to a weekend of defending why we just wanted a judge and not a minister. And I didn't like Greg's dad, Ralph, at all. The first time I'd met him, Greg's mom, Claire, was busy cooking dinner in the kitchen and Greg hopped in the shower, leaving me and Ralph alone together in the living room watching a sitcom. Just when a punchline was about to be delivered, Ralph flipped to the Home Shopping Network. After a minute or so, he flipped back to the sitcom, and so on, back and forth, totally oblivious to the fact that I might be trying to watch the sitcom and might appreciate being able to follow along uninterrupted. The more I got to know him, the more he proved how rude and self-absorbed he was. It was amazing that Greg could grow up with such a Neanderthal for a father and still turn out to be such a sweetheart. Greg's younger brother, Sean, didn't take after his father, happily, but he was an eighteen-year-old obsessed with videogames and motorcycles, so we never had more to say to each other than polite hi, how-are-yous. The more I thought about spending a long weekend with these people, the more unhappy I became.

Greg and I said nothing to each other for much of the drive, absorbed in our own thoughts.

"You're pretty quiet," I said.

"I'm kind of annoyed. I'm working on a project with three other students, and one of them has blown off three of our meetings, he's not doing any work on it, and all of us are going to suffer. And then one of my professors is behind on his lectures. He can't stick to the point. Anyway, he got all behind, so we have three thundred pages to read for this test in two weeks, and next week we have a fifteen-page paper due. It really bugs me when I suffer for other people's laziness and incompetence." He shook his head. "I'm sorry, I don't mean to complain."

"It's okay, it's nice just having some time to actually talk to you," I said. "I can't wait to go on our honeymoon. We need to figure out where we're going to go."

"And where will we get the money?"

"I have absolutely no idea. Should we go to Hawaii?"

"I always wanted to go to Hawaii. Or what about Mexico?"

"Ooh. Good idea. I cannot wait to be sipping piña coladas by the ocean." Greg and I really needed to get away from school and work, friends and family. We needed to focus on each other. I couldn't wait to go on vacation together and luxuriate in unabashed laziness. I closed my eyes and envisioned making slow love to Greg with the sound of the ocean lapping the shores just outside the windows of our hotel room.

Greg and I got to his parents' place late Wednesday night. We had to share a bedroom with Greg's younger brother. There was a full-size futon on the floor of the room for Greg, and I was supposed to sleep in the single bed Greg had as a kid. I thought the futon was a nice touch. As if Sean's presence wasn't enough, they needed to make it even clearer that Greg and I wouldn't be getting any for the weekend. Yet another of the many things that sucked about having to spend my weekend marooned with Greg's family.

The next morning, Sean got up early, before Greg and I woke up. We had the room to ourselves and Greg crawled into bed with me. Wordlessly he began kissing my neck—he knew I loved when he did that. It had been awhile since we'd had time to just enjoy each other. To my surprise, Greg went down on me. He'd done that maybe seven times in the two years we'd known each other. Not that I minded. Greg's attempts at oral sex had all the erotic flare of a dog lapping at a water bowl. I was trying not to fall asleep when Sean opened the door to the bedroom without knocking.

Greg looked up from my crotch with a look of horror on his face as he dove on top of me. Unfortunately, my leg had been over his arm, so when he propelled his body forward, my leg was shot straight up until my calf was crushed up against my ear.

I waited for Sean to figure out what was going on, excuse himself and close the door. Instead he opted not to notice that my leg was sandwiched between Greg's body and my own, my foot dangling piteously beside my head as Sean asked Greg if he knew what time they were supposed to pick up Grandma.

"I don't know. I think around three since dinner is going to be at five."

"Were you going to pick her up or should I?"

I looked back and forth between brothers. On and on they went, all the time with my leg up by my ear and Greg on top of me. I began giggling and couldn't stop. I pressed my face into the pillow as my body convulsed with suppressed laughter. I didn't stop until Sean finally left, mercifully shutting the door behind him.

"Oh my god," Greg groaned, rolling off me.

I finally unleashed my laughter, and for a moment, Greg tried to protest that it wasn't funny, but then he started laughing, too.

This turned out to be the best part of my day.

The day began with a big breakfast of sticky rolls, eggs, sausage, and hash browns. I never escaped the sickly full feeling as Claire plied us with a steady stream of fattening hors d'ouvres all day.

I tried to help Claire in the kitchen, but she insisted she was fine and I should enjoy myself. Ralph, Greg,

and Sean were busy watching football, so I locked myself in the bedroom and read until the guests started to
arrive.

Most of Greg's aunts, uncles and cousins had had
the good sense to move out of Nebraska, but the ones
who still lived in the state began arriving by the carload,
and their loud voices filled the house. Finally, I put my
book down, put a smile on my face, and emerged from
my sanctuary.

The scene was chaotic. Little nephews and cousins
played videogames in the family room and the distinc-
tive noise of spaceships being zapped to destruction rang
throughout the house. Dishes clattered in the kitchen and
voices fought to be heard over the din.

I didn't feel like talking about the weather, cran-
berry sauce recipes, or wedding plans, so I avoided the
adults and stationed myself on the loveseat near where
Greg's two adorable cousins were playing with Barbies.
Kate was three and her sister, Anne, was four. Each girl
had a huge springy mass of dark curly hair. They were
getting Barbie ready for her job as a fashion model
when Anne declared that she wanted her Barbie back.
Kate pointed out that Anne already had another Barbie.

"It's my doll and I want it," Anne said.

"Mom said we should share."

"Gimmee." Kate held the doll close and glared at
her sister. Anne tightened her hand into a fist and lightly
struck Kate's head. "You are stupid!" she declared. Kate
balled up her fist and bopped her sister on the head.
"You are stupid!" she retorted. They did this to each
other several more times. I tried to suppress my amusement.

"What's going on?" I finally asked, feeling guilty,
thinking that if I were a real adult I would have put a
stop to their bad behavior immediately rather than sitting there being entertained by it.

"Kate stoled my Barbie, but it's mine," Anne said.

"Mom said we had to share," Kate protested.

"Sharing is good. Anne, don't you want to play with another Barbie? Then you can play together," I said.

"But it's mine!" she said. She began to cry.

I was out of ideas. I'd made a child cry. Oh shit. I would make a terrible, terrible parent.

Fortunately, Kate and Anne weren't my responsibility. I slunk away from the crying children and sat at the end of the couch on the other side of the room until at last it was time to eat.

The dinner table was a bright medley of foods dripping with butter. Buttery rolls, mashed potatoes, corn, stuffing. I disgusted myself with how much food I was able to consume. I had an appetite that was entirely unladylike.

"This is delicious, Claire," I said. "You're a talented cook."

"Unfortunately, she eats too much of her work." Ralph laughed, patting Claire's ample waistline. I felt myself falling into a dark mood. It was not the time for an emotional crash, but Greg's family was such a depressing, sad group of people.

"Was it hard to find the food? I read in the paper that there has been a grocery worker's strike in the area," I said.

"She made it hard on herself. She drove over to the next town to buy groceries," Ralph said.

"I want to support the workers," she said, looking at her plate.

"Those whiners. It takes no brains and no skills to do that job, and they want thirteen dollars an hour," Ralph said.

The thirteen-dollar-an-hour figure, I'd read in the paper that morning, was for those who had been working there for years. That still only amounted to $27,000 a year, which was not much money, especially for a mundane job where you had to stand on your feet all day, taking bullshit from cranky customers. But I said nothing. It would be an absolute waste of energy to attempt to change Ralph's mind.

Greg's dad and uncle monopolized the rest of the dinner conversation, discussing the best method of lawn fertilizer and why kids today had such poor math skills.

I looked across the table at Greg. I knew that Greg wouldn't turn out like his father, a man on the periphery of family life, a silent breadwinner, semen donor, and turkey carver. A man who never bought the Christmas presents and forgot relatives' birthdays. It was amazing that Greg had turned out so well, growing up in this cavemanish household.

It took about four hundred years, but eventually dinner was over and the guests went home. Greg and I retreated to his room and collapsed onto his tiny single bed, groaning in pain from the obscene amount of food we'd eaten. Even Greg found Thanksgiving a painfully long day, and he suggested we leave Saturday rather than Sunday. I readily agreed, but Saturday still seemed like an impossibly long time away.

"Want to go for a walk or something?" he asked.

"Yeah. I need to walk for four years straight to lose the weight I've gained this weekend."

"Mom is a good cook, that's for sure."

It was dark out, but the sidewalk was well lit. Greg took my hand and we walked slowly along the path through the quiet neighborhood.

We walked through a park and sat down at a picnic bench. The thick trees surrounding us made the bench feel secluded and private. We began kissing and all at once we were all over each other, kissing and groping frenziedly, and I went down on him. There are times when giving your boyfriend a blowjob makes you feel both benevolent and powerful and you really get into it, and this was one of them. Greg was moaning appreciatively, and I looked up to see his face. His eyes were closed and his head was thrown back. His excitement really turned me on.

I was watching him when suddenly something white and goopy fell on his stomach from the sky. I looked up and saw the bird that had just unloaded on Greg fly away.

Greg was unaware of the gelatinous bird excrement quivering on his belly button, so he was still moaning and groaning while I nearly choked to death from the combination of laughter and his engorged penis in my mouth.

Greg finally realized something was going on. I managed to disengage my mouth from his dick, at which time I was laughing so hard I was crying. Greg, however, didn't think the incident was very funny. "I was almost there!" he protested. For a moment he tried to finish himself off, but my convulsions of laughter did not facilitate the process, and he soon gave up.

AVERY

Get-togethers

Les and I half sat, half sprawled on opposite corners of the couch. I smiled, contented with too much food and wine. My mother was on the recliner across from us.

"I think this is the nicest Thanksgiving I've ever had," I said. It had been a long but wonderful day. Les and I arrived at my mother's house around noon to help her prepare dinner. I'd never had so much fun cooking a meal. We spent the day talking and laughing and drinking spiked cider and eating fattening appetizers as we bustled about the kitchen chopping and cutting and baking and sautéing.

"No stress. No family drama. Just great food, great wine, great conversation," I said.

"To stress-free holidays," Les said, raising his glass in a toast.

"We're going to have enough leftovers for a month. My fridge is packed with food," Mom said.

"I may have gotten a little carried away," Les said. "I love to cook and I just don't do it very often. I guess it's because it seems like such a waste just to cook for one. Isn't that silly? I love to cook but won't do it just for myself."

"I did that for a while," I said. "Looking forward to dating so I could go to nice restaurants with someone and have someone to go to the movies with. Then I thought, this is ridiculous. I'll go to whatever movies I want to see. I'll take myself to nice restaurants. It was hard at first, but then I really started liking it. With Gideon, we'd always 'compromise,' which meant we effectively did what he wanted. At least he liked to dance. That was one thing we agreed on. Before Gideon and I got married, it was usually impossible to get a guy on the dance floor. I went out with guys who rode motorcycles, they'd been in the Marines, they jumped out of airplanes for fun; they thought they were so brave, but they wouldn't get out on a dance floor for anything. Looking stupid was scarier to them than defying death."

I looked into my wineglass and wondered if Art liked to dance. I wondered how his visit with his family back East was going. I wouldn't be able to hear from him until Monday.

"What kind of dancing do you like? Do you swing dance?" Les asked.

"What? Oh yeah, I love swing," I said.

"I've always wanted to learn. I took a few lessons, but I had a different partner each time. It just seemed like I needed to learn with the same partner so she could learn my leads."

"You're doing it again: waiting for a girlfriend to start doing the things you want to do."

"You're right. Would you want to take lessons with me?"

"I'd love to."

"I know a place we can go. I'll sign us up." With that decided, there was a sudden lull in the conversation. I looked around as if to find a new topic of conversation and saw the stack of dirty dishes littering the counters in the kitchen.

"I think I'll get started on the dishes," I said.

"Don't you dare," Mom said. "Leave them."

"Mom, I'm not going to leave them for you to do all by yourself." I stood and started toward the kitchen.

"I'll help," Mom said getting up from the couch. "Les, if you try to help, I'll beat you over the head with a dirty pot. You did most of the cooking and you're a guest to boot, so don't even think it." Les held his hands up in surrender, saucer-eyed in mock terror of her threats.

"Anyway," she added, "we girls need a little time for girl talk."

Mom and I washed dishes in silence for a few minutes. Then Mom said, in a tone so quiet I could barely hear her over the running water, "I like him. He's a great catch."

"Mom, I told you, Les and I are just friends."

"Why? He's sweet, he's funny, he's smart."

"He's all of those things, but it just doesn't click for us in that way. Why can't a man and a woman be friends without everyone trying to make it into something more than it is?"

"Maybe you think he's just a friend, but he adores you, it's obvious."

"As a matter of fact, Mom, he told me he has a crush on another woman."

"When did he tell you this?"

"A few weeks ago."

"Well, he's over her and into you."

"Let's drop it, okay?" I didn't want to tell her that, though I cared about Les, the last thoughts in my head when I went to sleep at night weren't of him but of a man I'd never met.

JEN

Surviving a Weekend with Your Parents: How to Self-Medicate with Alcohol

Rette had given me the number to Greg's parents' house in case of an emergency. Having to spend an entire day with my parents certainly qualified as an emergency. While my relatives began yet another exciting round of Trivial Pursuit, I slipped into the study to make the call.

"How was your day?" I asked when Rette picked up.

"An endless nightmarish mix of dull in-laws, conversations about weather and weed removal, and interfamily fights over such riveting topics as butter versus margarine and whether kids today should be able to use calculators to do their homework. I consumed approximately four pounds of butter today. I'm afraid Greg's mother has never heard of a little thing called cholesterol. Greg's father is such a jerk. He sat on his ass in front of the TV all day while his wife ran around like a crazy person getting ready to feed seventeen people, and he was barking at her to bring him a beer. How was your day?"

"The first thing Mom said to me when she picked me up from the airport was, 'Have you put on some weight?' Then she said, 'You look tired. Haven't you been sleeping?' I was like *Yeah, good to see you too.* We got home around ten in the morning and Mom started making Bloody Marys. She was like *Calories don't count on holidays!* And I was like *Yeah they do, but count me in, there's no way I'm going through the day sober.* I'd nursed a nice buzz all day, and with the help of some brandy, was still pleasantly numb.

"Mom was drinking Bloody Marys at ten in the morning? That's excessive even for her. Does she seem okay?"

"I guess."

"How's Dad?"

"I barely spoke to him. He spent most of his day in his workshop trying to come up with his latest invention that is supposed to make us zillionaires but is really just swallowing up the last shreds of our inheritance. I talked to him for maybe ten minutes at dinner. It was like 'Good to see you, Dad. Glad I flew out to Minnesota to visit.' I'm going out with some friends from high school tonight though. I heard from Wendy that Traci is getting married to *Larry Walker.*"

"No way!"

"I know, I can't believe it. They make such a weird couple."

"I'm so jealous. I wish I were there. I'm trapped with these horrible people for two more days."

"You aren't getting any sympathy from me. I had to face Mom and Dad all alone because of you."

"But they are staying at *my* house for Christmas."

"I'm still mad at you."

"You're right, I'm a horrible sister. Oh shit, Greg is calling me. It's my turn. We're playing charades. Can you believe it? Does it get any worse than this? I'm in a nightmare. A long, painfully real nightmare. I gotta go. I love you. Happy Thanksgiving."

"Love you, Rette. See you Monday."

RETTE

The Funeral

Things had been great between me and Greg over Thanksgiving, but as soon as I started back at work, things went back to the way they were.

When Greg touched me, I pushed him away. Sex was beginning to seem like such a waste of time. What have you accomplished after sex? Nothing. I'd rather get some chores taken care of or read a book. If I did get minor tremors of horniness, I didn't want to extinguish them with Greg. Sex was such a production. The Magic Wand was so much easier.

All the women's magazines talked about how important a healthy sex life was. They always offered tips about how to keep the sex hot in a long-term relationship. Why go to the effort? If I didn't spend my time having sex, I could learn photography or study a new language. Sex was always the same thing, over and over again. The whole thing was so ridiculous.

If something did arouse me, which happened less and less frequently, after a few minutes of making out with Greg, my desire would be distinguished utterly. I had never been an orgasm faker before, but lately I'd had to expedite the process; if it lasted too long, it became painful in addition to boring.

What had happened? It used to be that a mere touch or look from Greg could turn me on at any time or place. I would think about him at work and the southward migration of blood flow seemed so overwhelming I was certain everyone around me knew I was having scandalous thoughts.

Maybe I'd been on the pill too long. I'd heard some kinds of pills actually lowered a woman's sex drive. Probably that was all it was.

Of course, maybe it was something about being responsible for taking the pill every day, buying the $20 pills every month, going to the clinic to get the prescription, and injecting my body with synthetic hormones like a cow at a corporate dairy farm that had diminished my sexual appetite. Or maybe it had something to do with the fact that, after all this, I almost never came with him anymore, while he came all over the place, making me and the sheets sticky and gross.

And who do you think washed those sheets and made that bed?

I had to stop myself from thinking like this. These were the kind of thoughts that were causing friction between me and Greg. I was young, in love, about to get married; I had no reason to mope.

The real villain causing problems between me and Greg was the Magic Wand.

With Greg, orgasm achievement was a convoluted, time-consuming alchemy: one part concentration mixed with two parts luck sprinkled liberally with fantasy. The Magic Wand, on the other hand, with its consistent pulsations, could cause mind-blowing hoo-haas in seconds flat.

I had to face reality. The Magic Wand was destroying my relationship with Greg. I had become too reliant on it. I had to quit using it. Right away. Cold turkey.

An hour after I made this resolution, I read the word *arm,* in a magazine, and I was off, envisioning a faceless man's veiny, muscular arm pulling a faceless woman toward him for a passionate kiss, pressing himself into her . . .

Like a true ascetic, I was determined to see this fantasy out manually, but after a few minutes, I was getting nowhere, achieving nothing but a hand cramp. The Magic Wand called out to me, and, without further ado, I caved.

I could no longer deny that the Magic Wand had to be disposed of. I just couldn't resist the temptation when it was so nearby.

The question was how to properly send off such a dear friend to the grave. It had brought me nothing but pleasure, sheer delight. Its only fault was that it was so efficient, so good, it rendered men obsolete.

I couldn't give it a burial—it could be dug up some lonely Saturday night in the future. I couldn't put it to its final resting place at sea—it would be a pollution hazard and, anyway, we lived in Colorado, as land-bound a place as you're gonna find.

The garbage was the soundest method I could come up with, but that seemed so disrespectful. It didn't seem right somehow, but I couldn't think of a better plan.

Early in the morning on a Tuesday, the day our garbage was picked up, I carefully, tenderly wrapped the Magic Wand in tissue paper, then a paper bag, then a plastic bag (I did not want evidence of my mechanical debauchery in plain sight).

I brought the Magic Wand to the garbage and hid it

beneath a cereal box. I considered saying a few words, something about all the good times we had together, but instead, I just turned and walked slowly back inside.

Later, when I heard the garbage trucks rumble in, I felt strangely sad.

Management by Sticky Note

I didn't sleep well Sunday night, and I was moving through my Monday morning at a disturbingly slow rate. I made some coffee to help spur my brain into action. Too late. When I returned from the bathroom deodorized and my hair freshly fouffy from the hair dryer, I realized I'd neglected to put the pot beneath the spout and I now had a counter full of coffee. All of the appliances on the counter were marooned in brown water, which expanded until the counter could no longer contain it and it dripped onto the floor. I grabbed every dishtowel we had and, in a valiant sweep of the towels, I managed to spray the coffee all over myself, including one of the very last clean outfits I had left. *Crap.*

When I finally managed to clean the disaster, I went to my room and spent a full five minutes staring at my closet in hopes of coming across an outfit that wouldn't make me feel like complete buffalo excrement. I put on a skirt and sweater and then began a hunt for nylons. I finally discovered a pair and struggled to get them on my right leg, then my left. Just as I was trying to maneuver them over my thighs, I heard a hideous tearing sound. *Crap.*

With my only pair of nylons torn to shreds, I resorted to an uncomfortable white shirt and blue pants that made me look like a pregnant hippopotamus.

I was twenty minutes late getting to work. I tried to sneak into my office without Eleanore seeing me. I thought I'd made it safely, but just as I was about to step into my office I heard her say, "Our department is hardly so ahead of its deadlines we can stroll in whenever we feel like it. And we're about to get hit even harder with the Expert account."

"I . . ." I began to defend myself, but gave up. I didn't have the energy to fight.

"I think you should count on doing a lot of overtime these next several weeks."

"Of course." I only had a wedding to plan, a fiancé to spend time with, and thirty pounds to lose.

Crapcrapcrap!

I turned on my computer and began sorting through the e-mail of coworkers and clients asking how the editing of such and such a report or newsletter was coming and did I remember the deadline was Wednesday?

I looked at my to-do list for the day. If I worked my ass off for ten hours and if Eleanore limited her interruptions to half her normal amount . . . I still couldn't get anywhere close to being able to meet the deadlines. Rushing didn't help. If I made a mistake, I was only causing myself more work. I was so stressed I didn't know where to begin, so I began by doing what was least important: going through my personal e-mail.

> *To: MOlsen@mckennamarketing.com*
> *From: ARose@mckennamarketing.com*
> *Rette,*
> *How was Thanksgiving? Let's meet in the breakroom at 12:45. I'd suggest going out to lunch, but I don't even have time to eat the lunch I brought, let alone go out. Much stress. Too much work. Still, want to catch up. OK?*
> *Avery*
>
> *To: ARose@mckennamarketing.com*
> *From: MOlsen@mckennamarketing.com*
> *Dearest Avery, Splendid idea. See you at 12:45.*
> *-R*

I worked at a breakneck pace all morning. At quarter to one I waddled to the breakroom, my body bloated with Thanksgiving-blubber. I sat at the table and attempted to hoist my left leg over my right, but my legs were too bulky to actually cross. I balanced my left ankle on my thigh instead. I bit into my apple and watched enviously as Avery unwrapped a sandwich that looked suspiciously like turkey.

"Is that turkey?"

"Tofurky."

"Is it good?"

"It's great. Do you want to try it?"

"Good god, no."

"How was your Thanksgiving?" Avery asked.

"I gained about four hundred pounds because Greg's family is so unbelievably boring that food was my only source of entertainment. How was yours?"

"It was really fun. Is that all you're eating? You want some stuffing? Some mashed potatoes? Some apple pie? I have a ton of leftovers." Avery, that cruel, skinny temptress, took the lids off the Tupperware containers in which all sorts of sinful, fattening foods lurked. She spread the array of cellulite-inducing delights before me.

"No. Thanks. My diet officially began today. I'm ill from eating so much. How was your Thanksgiving?"

"Les from work came over to my mom's place. We made dinner and had the best time."

"Les?"

"He works in IT."

"Yeah, I know him. He helped me get my computer set up. He seems like a really nice guy. So are you two like a thing?"

"Oh no. I'm not attracted to him. Anyway, he has a crush on Jen."

"Of course he does, what guy doesn't?"

"No kidding. But it's been really fun having a guy friend. We talk and talk about everything. We went hiking last Saturday, and we've talked on the phone every night for the past week for at least an hour or two. We had so much fun making dinner together Thursday. We just talked and talked; he really made me laugh. Then Friday we went out to a movie and Saturday we went to the art museum in Denver and then went out to dinner and saw a band . . ."

"Are you sure you're not dating?"

"Yes, I'm sure. That's what I'm saying. It's better than dating because there aren't any of those annoying expectations getting in the way, but we are good friends who are there for each other."

"Speaking of . . ." I said, indicating with my eyes that Les was behind her.

He limped across the kitchen floor. "Hey," he said.

Avery turned. "What's wrong?" she asked him.

"I worked out yesterday. My body went into shock. Most of my muscles had atrophied pretty severely and weren't at all happy about being dragged back to the land of the living. I can't tell you how excited I am to go home and soak in a bathtub full of Ben-Gay. But pretty soon my muscles will thank me for this. Or thank you I should say. You're quite a good influence on me," he said to Avery as he pulled his lunch from the fridge.

"That's great, Les," Avery said.

"I assume you mean that it's good that I'm working on getting in shape and not that I'm crippled with excruciating pain."

"Right," Avery said with a laugh.

"Well, I'll catch you two later," Les said, taking his lunch with him back to his desk.

"You know," Avery said quietly when she was sure he was gone. "I wish I was half as attracted to him as I was to Gideon. But you just can't force yourself to be attracted to someone. It doesn't matter anyway. He's hot for Jen. Like every other man in the world."

For the rest of the week, I ate lunch at my desk, came in early and stayed late. So much for forty-hour weeks.

I quickly grew sick of cleaning up other people's mistakes. I didn't have time to fix my own. Being an editor is like being a goalie. You never get the glory of making the game-winning goal, but you get blamed for everything that gets past you. At least on the field, spectators can see the catches a goalie does make; they have no idea the spectacular saves we editors make.

I kept expecting Eleanore to come by and give me a pat on the back. Eleanore did finally stop by my office, but not for back-patting. She pointed out a few mistakes I'd made editing a sixteen-page industry newsletter so tiny and insignificant that only a particularly anal editor would notice them. I apologized and promised that things would get better. For all the hours of overtime I'd worked and all the stress and frustration, the only thing Eleanore had to say was, "Yes, I'm sure it will get better. Things can only get better."

She never said anything good about my work, and she reveled in finding my mistakes. When she found an error of mine, she gleefully ran to report it to me.

"My dictionary says this word should have a hyphen but I see you didn't add a hyphen." A satanic grin lurked beneath the surface of her expression. She wanted it to seem as though she were simply casually imparting information, but I could see that secretly she loved catching my mistakes.

I returned to my desk with my lunch to see a stack of reports I'd edited that Eleanore had eviscerated with a patchwork of sticky notes with bitchy comments like, "Have you ever heard of the A.P. Style Guide?" because

I'd forgotten to write out the number nine. She could have just circled the numeral nine, which was the editorial mark that meant "write out." But no, she had to write "Have you ever heard of the A.P. Style Guide?" and draw a menacing arrow to my mistake in a thick red pen that made me think of the lines surgeons draw before they cut open a patient to remove a cancerous organ.

Somehow, when she managed me by sticky note, it decimated my self-esteem even more than when she told me about my many flaws in person. Every morning when I arrived to find my errors in black and white and bleeding red pen, my self-esteem was trampled. Eleanore was constantly doing a clog dance on my ego, turning my insides into bruised mulch.

The thing was, I was catching the vast majority of the errors. There was no such thing as an editor who caught every mistake the first time around. That was why documents were run by a few different editors a number of times. Having Eleanore constantly point out my errors made me wonder if editing was yet another thing I had no talent for. The thought that I could fail at this career too filled me with dread.

AVERY

The Power of the Few

Our graphic designer had come up with three logos, and we were testing them out on consumers, asking them which ones they preferred. One logo had a mortarboard on top of the *e* in Expert and spectacles that made up the middle line of the *e*. It was the corniest logo I'd ever seen. Another had a swoosh symbol encircling the *Expert Appliance* in a karma-wrecking shade of green. The last just had the words *Expert Appliance* in a shiny white and gray. The last one was classy, up-to-date, and offered the high-tech association we were going for. It was clearly the best choice, but everyone in the focus groups was choosing this boring swoosh thing or the bespectacled professorial one that looked like an owl on a kids' TV show who taught children how to subtract two from three or to determine how many licks it took to get to the center of a Tootsie-Pop.

I was getting unreasonably irritated. It wasn't the consumers' fault I was way behind and working overtime, knowing that we were coming up with an inferior product. These people were giving up their time, answering questions over the phone and in focus groups; I should be thanking them for their help.

To: ArtLover@yahoo.com
From: Dancinfool@yahoo.com
It's terrifying how many decisions a handful of people make. Focus groups can be blamed for many of the stupid movie titles, insipid endings, and inane taglines that we're subjected to day in and day out.

Think about it: Are the people who have the time to go to focus groups and are lonely enough to answer phone surveys representative of the rest of us? Are these the people we want in charge of deciding what media get shoved down our throats? Are these the people we want making major business decisions for the largest corporations in America?

Stop the insanity!

To: Dancinfool@yahoo.com
From: ArtLover@yahoo.com
Focus groups are the juries of popular cultures, and they are rarely a jury of our peers.

Your e-mail made me laugh, which I appreciate—I really needed some levity in my life right now. My brother found out his ex is dating another man. This is the lowest I've seen him yet. I guess the finality of their relationship is finally setting in.

I've been reading this book that is supposed to help you help your loved ones get through difficult times. The book said that getting over a death is the hardest thing to deal with, and the second hardest thing is the death of a marriage. But I wonder if that's right. With divorce, no one bakes casseroles or sends sympathy cards. When some-

one dies, there's usually no one to blame. When you get divorced, you review your failings day after day, trying to figure out exactly where you went wrong.

Art was so kind and considerate. It was so nice to see a guy who really cared about his family.

Was he as wonderful in real life as he was online?

Maybe it was time I met him so I could find out for sure. We would meet in a public place of course, just in case he really was a psychopath. A restaurant. A nice one. He'd have gotten there a couple minutes before me. I'd enter the restaurant and see a good-looking man sitting at the bar. He'd turn and look right at me. My heart would race but I would tell myself that there was no way I could get that lucky. He would smile. "Are you by any chance . . ." he would begin. "Avery," I'd finish. For a moment, I'd feel a little awkward, a little shy, but then he'd tell a joke, and we would start talking and laughing and wouldn't stop through the entire six-course meal or through the after-dinner drink at the bar. We wouldn't stop talking until we got on the dance floor. Then, my body, which had been hibernating for the last two years, would come alive again. His fingers grazing my arms would send shivers down my body. I would tremble with anticipation.

We would have lazy Sundays of slow sex and long, giggly conversations. We'd eat bagels and drink coffee and read the *New York Times* and rent videos and fall asleep on the couch, entwined in each other's arms.

I had to start dating soon—I was becoming too stuck in my ways. If it went on much longer, I wasn't sure I'd be able to make room for someone else in my life. I'd gotten a little too used to living alone. It was getting hard to imagine sharing my life with someone. But since Art and Les had come into my life, I remembered that, despite all the work relationships were, there was a lot I'd been missing out on. Art reminded me how nice it was to have romance and excitement in my life, and Les provided friendship and support. In many ways, Les played the role of the boyfriend without the sex and expectations. It was so nice to have someone in my life, someone to review the day's events with each night.

After work, Les and I went to our first swing dancing lesson. For the first half hour, the instructor reviewed the basic steps with us, then she spent the next half hour teaching us a couple of trickier steps and a dip. Les was a better dancer than I would have thought. For all his awkwardness in real life, his slumped posture and uneven gait, on the dance floor he had a gentle but self-assured lead. A couple of times I misunderstood his lead and stepped the wrong way. When Les and I tried to correct ourselves, we careened into another couple.

"Sorry, sorry," I gushed to the couple.

"No problem," the woman smiled.

"I think we're just about ready to go pro," Les whispered to me. "We can call ourselves Twinkle Toes and the Foot Smasher."

"Which one am I?"

"Twinkle Toes, of course."

"I don't know, I think you're a better dancer than you think you are."

"You're too kind."

I had been so ferociously independent for so long, I'd forgotten how amazing it was to be close to someone, to have his warm hand on my back and his laughter in my ear.

After class, Les asked if I wanted to get a drink.

"Sure, but just one. I need to get some sleep. Work's been crazy."

We walked to a nearby bar. I ordered a Chardonnay, and Les ordered a beer. We sat in a dimly lit corner in the back of the bar, at a sticky wood table.

"How are things going at work?" I asked.

He rolled his eyes. "We're about a month behind on the Expert Web site."

"You're joking. Why so much?"

"Mark is just not a good manager."

"Is he a good programmer?"

"Oh god no, he's awful."

"Well how did he get promoted to manager then?"

Les shrugged. "His timing was right. He came to the company when the IT department was in its fledgling stages. They needed a manager, and he was there. He knows how to throw jargon-y terms around, and he sounds so confident in himself that if you don't know anything about technology, he can be convincing. Morgan loves him."

"Mark can be charming," I said.

"I guess. It's kind of funny though, because all of us who work for him know how full of it he is. He says the most ignorant things. Sometimes it's hard not to laugh. He'll say something that makes no sense. It would take more time and more money to do it his way, and the end result will be an inferior, unstable product, and if Rich or I or someone . . ."

"Who's Rich?"

"Another programmer. Really smart guy. Anyway, we'll suggest a better way to do it, and Mark will get really pissed and argue even harder for his stupid idea. I'm not very good at kissing up, but you'd think I could at least keep my mouth shut, but I just can't bear to see things done in such a completely moronic way. He's been making me do tech support stuff. It's ridiculous to have a programmer doing tech support, but it's his way of putting me in my place."

"Why is it ridiculous?"

"I've got a very specialized knowledge. I make a lot more money than a tech support person does. It's just not a good distribution of resources. I mean I can do it, but it makes more sense for me to be doing something that's going to make the company money."

"Mark sounds like such a power freak. He sounds like Sharon. She was a week late giving me the approval on the dishwasher research questions—and by the way, I wrote them and she didn't change a single word, she just kept them on her desk for three weeks collecting dust—and then yesterday she yelled at me for being behind. She sees absolutely no correlation with her holding up the questions for a week and our being exactly a week behind. And she's so snippy about it, you know? It immediately gets me on the defensive. Oh, and then, today she asked me to get this report up onto the intranet. I sent it to IT the second after she asked me to. I even cc'd her so she'd know I sent it. So a few hours later, she forwards me a message from Morgan and cc's him on it, asking me accusingly why the report isn't online yet. So I hit REPLY ALL and added Mark's name to the list and asked Mark if he knew when the file I sent him would go online. I wanted to write, 'the file I sent to you the very second Sharon asked me to.' It was so obvious that Morgan had asked Sharon a few days ago to take it online and she was trying to blame the delay on me. Oh and that Mary from marketing is such a liar. She was supposed to send me this file three weeks ago. When I reminded her, it was obvious from her expression that she'd forgotten. Which is fine, why can't she just say, 'Oops, sorry, I forgot'? But no, she claims she did send it but it must have gotten lost in e-mail. But strangely, she doesn't have a copy of what she sent. Whatever. . . . Why are you laughing?"

"Let's try not talking about work for a few minutes."

I took a sip of my wine. "That was fun tonight, wasn't it?" I said.

"It was a blast. It's been awhile since I've been on the dance floor."

"I wish I could take classes all day. If I didn't have a job, I could take all the classes I wanted. I could take tap and jazz and yoga and Pilates. I'd take drawing and writing. Why can't I just be independently wealthy? Work is so stressful. Oh, did I tell you how Sharon . . ."

We stayed for two more drinks, bitching about work the entire time. I didn't get home till way after my bedtime.

On the bright side: When you have a silly amount of work to do, the day goes very quickly.

"Avery." It was Sharon, who lurked outside my doorway. "I need you to do something. I need you to create a PowerPoint presentation for the meeting tomorrow afternoon that gives an overview of everything we're working on for Expert. Present some graphs of the findings we've uncovered so far. I'll need it completed by ten so I'll have a chance to review it."

What I thought was, *You want me to get this done by ten tomorrow morning? Are you crazy? I'm completely overwhelmed. Why can't you do it? And why didn't you tell me about this sooner!* But what I said was, "Okay, I'll get right on it." If I wanted her job while she was on leave, this was the kind of thing I had to do.

Sharon gave me the project timeline for each department's part of the project, and I spent the rest of my day running around, trying to track down department heads to see where they were and whether they were on schedule.

Everybody seemed to be behind, but the IT department was way, way off schedule. I left three messages
and an e-mail for Mark, but he never got back to me, so
I called Les to try to figure out what was going on.

"Les, according to this project plan, Expert should
already be testing parts of the site. The interface should
be done, the storyboards should be done, the 'Click
here for more information' template should be complete. From what I can tell, nothing's even been started."

"Sure, I'd love to go across the street and get a sandwich. I'll meet you in your office."

I was puzzled for a minute, and then I realized that
of course Les wouldn't be able to talk about it in the office.

We went to the deli across the street and each got a
sandwich. We sat down at a table, and Les leaned in
close.

"Mark hasn't even finished the specs for the Expert
site yet," he said in a hushed tone. "It should have been
finished a month ago, but he's been working on this
other project."

"What does that mean, 'the specs'?"

"Expert needs to approve the storyboards and interface, and then each of the programmers get their spec,
essentially the details of their assignment for the site."

"Doesn't he know how important this is?"

Les shrugged. "I've been in a panic about it, but what
can I do?"

"Does Morgan know about this?"

"Not yet, but he will soon. I asked Mark about it, and
he said the text hasn't been approved yet, which is true,
but that's no reason to be delaying the rest of the project. You can throw copy up in no time at all, it's all the
back-end stuff that takes time."

We talked about work for a few more minutes, scarfed
down our sandwiches, and returned to work.

Sharon left at five o'clock, I noticed bitterly. I stayed until ten, crunching numbers, creating charts and graphs, writing and rewriting talking points. When I finally left the office, I was so exhausted I could hardly see straight.

JEN

Meetings: How to Utterly Squander Precious Hours of Your Short, Sad Life

The monthly company meeting was, as usual, run by the M&M gang triumvirate of power: Marc, Mark, and Mary. Mark demonstrated the new features of the McKenna Marketing Web site. One new feature was an online method of running our return on investment stats, which meant we'd no longer have to bug Marc and Mark about getting us the numbers we needed for our staff meetings. At this everyone cheered. Instead of interpreting this as it should have been, a "Yahoo! We no longer have to try to get you to help us, we can do it ourselves and actually get the numbers on time and without any hassle," he chose to interpret the applause as testimony to his gift as a Web manager, and like a peacock fanning its colorful feathers, Mark beamed under the attention.

Sharon then went through a PowerPoint presentation that lasted about eight and a half years. She overviewed the different areas of the Expert Appliance account. She showed endless slides of our findings so far, fascinating tidbits like how the majority of consumers like dryers whose doors opened down instead of to the side. "The door acts as a shelf so the clean clothes don't fall to the floor," Sharon said, as if this were the most insightful revelation we'd ever hear.

It looked like the Web portion of the project was way behind. Mark stood up right away and said their stuff was right on schedule, they were just waiting for the copy before they could let Expert begin testing.

The graphs were really well done, which wasn't Sharon's style. I figured out why when Morgan told Sharon she'd done a great job on the presentation. Sharon smiled and said a modest thanks, and I heard Avery say under her breath, "I don't believe her." Of course, Avery had done the presentation and Sharon was taking the credit. It was a vintage Sharon move.

After work I went to a dinner party hosted by Dan and Lydia. It was some going-away party for some guy from sales. He'd gotten a new job in New York or New Jersey somewhere, and this was our big sendoff. The guy was cute but annoyingly married.

The party would probably be boring as hell, but I figured it might be a good place to meet single guys. Mike and Tom were okay, but I wanted somebody that had Dave's humor, Tom's sexiness, and Mike's sweetness. I wished I could genetically engineer my perfect mate. This dating shit was getting so old.

Actually, I didn't have much choice but to go by myself. (It was the first event I could ever remember going to stag!) Tom said he couldn't go because he didn't want the entire office to know about us, and I couldn't bring Mike in case it got around that I was seeing someone. I didn't want Tom to think I was cheating on him.

When I got to Lydia's house, my hopes for meeting

the guy of my dreams were quickly dashed. Everyone there was married or coupled off. At the long dinner table, I was sitting next to Mary from marketing and her husband, Mark and his girlfriend, and Sharon and her husband.

Lydia went around the table with a bottle of wine in each hand, asking whether we wanted red or white.

"Red, please," I said. I wanted to grab the bottle out of her hands and drink the whole thing down, straight from the bottle.

While Lydia poured wine, Dan came around with the first dish, a small salad with organic greens and warm goat cheese.

"Your china is beautiful," Mary said to Lydia. "Is it Wedgwood?"

"Yes."

"I thought about getting Wedgwood, but I ended up getting Lenox. Jen, what kind of china do you have?"

China? I didn't even have dishes, except for what I could steal from the dorm cafeteria in college. "I have Lenox, too."

"You're so lucky you don't have a house, Jen. I just spend all my time and money decorating," Mary said.

"How big is your house?" Sharon asked.

"Twenty-four hundred square feet," Mary said.

"Ours is three thousand," Sharon said.

"I'm finally getting around to decorating my new house," Mark said. "I'm having my furniture shipped in from Italy. I've got thirty-seven hundred square feet to fill, so I've got to hope that the stock market holds up." Mark chuckled.

Well, I just love my six-hundred-and-fifty square-foot apartment with a glorious view of a parking lot, thanks for asking.

I felt like I was at a party of drunk frat boys who were

pulling out their dicks—why don't I just run and get the tape measure, boys? I was in yuppie hell. I couldn't wait until I had the biggest house and most expensive china and most expensive furniture to brag about.

RETTE

Letting Go

Eleanore's emetic voice followed me like a swarm of wasps ready to sting at any time. In my nightmares, in my car on the way to the grocery store, during sex with Greg, she was hovering, casting judgment on every move I made. My anger toward her was with me constantly; there was no reprise. In my head, I had calm, rational conversations with Eleanore in which I told her that I was working extremely hard and a little appreciation from time to time might be nice. I knew I couldn't say these things in real life, however, because when I was with her I was so guarded and tense I could barely speak at all.

Every evening I'd lie in bed and instead of escaping into sleep, I'd lie awake mentally cataloging the injustices she had perpetrated against me that day. When I did sleep, I was constantly having strange dreams with Eleanore and Paige in them, or I'd spend the night in a state of restless half-sleep reviewing over and over again what had happened at work that day and what I had to accomplish at work the next day.

This was what I'd been so desperate to attain when I'd been unemployed?

I was unduly excited when the phone rang. A ringing phone held the possibility that someone would transform my mood and help me shake off these depressing thoughts. I leapt off the couch and jogged to the phone in the kitchen.

"Hello?"

"Hi, sweetie, it's your mom." She never said, "It's Mom," she said "It's your mom," as if I wouldn't recognize her voice, as if there were room for confusion.

"Hi, Mom."

"What's up?"

"Nothing."

"Your father and I booked a cabin for the three days after Christmas. Are you sure you don't want to come?"

"Mom, I don't ski."

"How can you live in Colorado and not ski?"

"It is possible."

"So Jen is going to pick us up at the airport?"

"Right. Yes." We'd covered that like eighty times. As if we were going to leave her stranded or something.

"So what's going on with you? How is the wedding coming along?"

"I'm . . ." I noticed a stain at the counter and used my nail to chip it away. "I'm actually not that great. Greg's been kind of distant lately. I feel like he's angry with me and I don't know why." I waited but she said nothing. "And we're so broke and my car broke down again this week. Greg had to drive me everywhere, and it was such a hassle. He's so busy."

"What a shame. I had to put eight hundred dollars on my car. It's only three years old, but it had a leak and it needed new break pads and tires. Cars really are such a hassle. It was in the shop for four days. Your father had to cart me around. It was terrible."

"Yeah. I'm sorry to hear that." Neither of us said anything for a long moment. "My boss is driving me nuts. She will never say anything positive to me and she's really stuck up. I'm so depressed all the time that I can't function. I hate my life and don't know what to do."

"That sounds just like my boss Jack. Oh that man makes me nuts. We were at a seminar and do you know what he did? He introduced me as his assistant! I've worked there longer than he has. I'm a manager. I mean I work under him but not *for* him. I'm certainly no *assistant*. It totally undermined my credibility. I felt totally belittled for the rest of the seminar. The sales associates all looked at me like some kind of secretary or something. It was humiliating. And then when we were at a meeting back at the office . . ."

Mom went on and on for nearly half an hour about all she had to suffer through at her office. I expressed outrage at the proper times. Her boss, Jack, really did seem like a jerk. He'd been promoted ahead of my mother, even though she had more experience and a longer tenure with the company. Still, today I wanted Mom to tell me something, some magic words to live by that would make me less miserable about my job and my life. Mom eventually ended her tirade and changed the subject to her sister's divorce.

"Ron is already dating someone new," she said. "He hasn't even totally moved out yet. I'm sure he was with this new woman before the separation. Lena is beside herself as you can imagine, but I have to say I'm not surprised. I mean what does she expect? She let herself go."

To my mother, a woman who "let herself go" didn't constantly wear makeup, didn't always wear stylish clothes, didn't get new hairstyles regularly, and did let herself get fat. Lena's big crime was having put on twenty pounds over the past fifteen years. I was already thirty pounds overweight—my mother must find it miraculous that Greg would be marrying a woman who'd "let herself go." No wonder Jen and I had such bad relationships with food.

"Mom, nobody deserves to be cheated on and dumped. I feel terrible for her."

I could tell Mom didn't like my little rebuke because she abruptly said she should get going. Then her tone abruptly changed again, and was suddenly buoyed with artificial cheer. "I can't wait to see you," Mom said. "I'm so excited to look for wedding dresses! This is going to be so fun."

"I'm looking forward to seeing you, too, Mom. Love you."

"Love you. Say hi to Greg for me."

"Sure. Sure." I hung up the phone. I tried calling Avery, but she wasn't home. I couldn't think of anyone else to call or a single thing I wanted to do.

It was only eight o'clock, but I got into bed and waited to fall asleep.

Eleanore's Verbal Gymnastics

For my New Year's resolutions, I vowed to eat better, work out regularly, and not let Eleanore get to me. But since New Year's was a few weeks off, I was eating with abandon, doing nary a sit-up, and despising Eleanore with everything I had.

We'd gotten behind schedule because Eleanore had done some miscalculations when she was assigning deadlines. Of course she blamed Paige for not catching the error. It was fascinating to listen to her verbal gymnastics as she assigned blame where it didn't belong.

When Eleanore stopped by my office to chat, I used nonverbal signals to let her know that I was overwhelmed with work and far too busy to chat.

"It seems like everybody is upset about the delay. Even the president of the company put in his two cents," she whined. "He is never around to give me a pat on the back, but if anything goes wrong, he's all over me. When I first got here, the editorial department was a mess. But I turned that all around. I worked overtime, I straightened things out. Once I set my mind to something, I stick to it."

"Eleanore," I interjected. "I'm sorry Morgan . . ." I almost said "reprimanded," but that would imply that she had done something wrong, and in Eleanor's mind, she was perfect.

". . . I have a lot of work, so I . . ."

"Nobody remembers how I turned this place around. These publications used to come in over budget, over deadline, but I got this department running smoothly. It wasn't easy, but once I set my mind to something, I follow through. One time I decided that I would never let myself get overweight, and you know something? I've never been more than ten pounds overweight in my entire life."

This was the four hundredth time she'd told this story. It hadn't been interesting even one of the other 399 times. She had a repertoire of five anecdotes that she repeated over and over again. Did she know? Did she care? Did she have any desire to be remotely interesting?

I gave up on the idea of getting back to work anytime soon. As Eleanore bragged about how she jogged five miles to work almost every day, I tried to look bored, but this, sadly, in no way discouraged her.

Eleanore finally left, and just as I was about to get back to work, Glenn, the director of marketing, stopped by my office.

Glenn was in charge of marketing McKenna Marketing, and he oversaw Pam, who managed the marketing projects we did for other companies. Glenn had worked as a consultant before getting the job here. Eleanore said that if he'd been successful as an independent consultant, he wouldn't need the job with McKenna. She said he'd gone to one seminar on the importance of branding and declared himself an expert. Usually I found Eleanore too judgmental, but in this case she pegged him straight on. Of course I had to find this out the hard way.

"I hear you're an exceptional editor," he said.

It felt so good to get a compliment after so many months of having my efforts ignored or berated, I could barely suppress a smile. "Thanks."

"I know you're busy, but I wondered if you could do me a big favor. I wondered if you could look over these news releases, particularly this one. This one I want to get out by tomorrow. We're sending it to hundreds of journalists at newspapers and trade magazines around the country." He waved a sheet of paper. "I'm starting a big media campaign. The goal is to get journalists to know our name, so maybe they'll write a story or two on us. I'll be sending out a news release every week for the next few months. This is the first batch for the next month. I know how good you are as an editor, and I just wondered if you would mind looking these over."

"Sure, I'd be happy to," I said, feeling honored.

Stupid, stupid, stupid.

* * *

When I'd interned at the newspaper in college, a lot of news releases passed my way. Many of them had been extremely professional, but many were amateurish and riddled with spelling errors. The other journalists and I would make fun of the spelling and grammar errors—newsroom work wasn't always fires and crashes, there was a lot of down time and we had to entertain ourselves somehow. Mocking news releases wasn't a noble endeavor, but it did pass the time, and if an editor can't feel superior to a bad writer, there would be no joy at all in an otherwise thankless job.

I read the first of Glenn's releases, which was about how he'd recently joined McKenna Marketing and what an alleged amazing guy he was. It was the worst news release I'd ever read. His other releases were just as bad. They were sloppy, poorly written, dull, and full of grammatical errors. Journalistic writing was supposed to be brief and to the point. Glenn's releases were wordy and convoluted. His headlines, which should never be longer than a few words, were nearly a paragraph long.

As the head of the marketing department, he had to be making about three times my salary, yet he couldn't even write a grammatically correct, let alone well-written, sentence. It took me an hour to correct the first release. I took the time to write down tips such as basic rules to Associated Press style, how hyphens were used, how paragraphs should be no more than thirty words long and headlines should be just a few words. I wanted to tell him an interesting news release would probably produce better results, but I didn't know how to say that nicely. I went on to the other releases. Most of them were about how McKenna's market research had saved companies scads of money, but we couldn't use the names of the companies we helped because of client confidentiality. It was true that overworked journalists used press releases to create about 50 percent of their stories, but they were not going to write about what a good company McKenna Marketing was without an angle to make it at least appear like news. I didn't want to hurt his feelings, so I tried not to change what he'd written too much, but even so, by the time I was done, I'd saturated the releases with sticky notes and corrections.

Working on his releases put me way behind schedule, and I'd already been slammed with work. I was thoroughly annoyed by the time he stopped back down to check in.

"Did you get a chance to look at them?" he asked, smiling the fake, fake smile of a marketing VP who made three times my salary by faking his way to the top.

"Yeah, I made some notes."

Glenn looked over the release. "There's an awful lot written here. I can't really even see your changes. Would you mind inputting the changes? The releases are on the shared network drive in the folder marked Releases."

"Um, well." I did not want to be considered a non-team player. I would already have to work overtime. That was the way to succeed. To work endless hours and forgo a life. "Sure."

"Great, great. I need them done by tomorrow." He left without thanking me.

I rewrote his releases entirely. I had to stay three hours late to finish up my own job. The only solace I had was that writing news releases would be one more thing I could add to my résumé.

Soon, I was hiding not only from Eleanore, but from Glenn as well. He brought a marketing brochure down to my office for me to "edit," which, practically speaking, meant rewriting.

"Doesn't Pam do the copy writing for the company?" I asked.

"She used to, but now that we've grown, she'll write exclusively for our clients. I've been hired to focus on moving McKenna's marketing efforts forward."

"Uh-huh," I said, though I didn't understand at all. Pam was a talented writer, and Glenn was a feckless dweeb.

I skimmed over the text. The opening sentences were "McKenna Marketing is at the forefront of innovations. We enable you to stay ahead of today's ever-changing business world."

It was astonishing to me how many clichés could be packed into two small sentences, and if anyone could tell me what the hell it meant that we were at the forefront of every possible innovation, I'd be the first to thank them.

It was going to be a long, long day.

At the company meeting two weeks later, Glenn announced that the release he'd sent about his joining the company had made it in a newsbrief in the *Denver Post.* Of course the *Post* always published newsbriefs when an executive joined a company. I didn't point this out, naturally. Everyone congratulated him. He said it would take awhile, but eventually word about McKenna would spread, and this was really just such a great start. I waited for him to thank me for my "help," but he said nothing. He stood there and smiled as Morgan McKenna gave him a slap on the back and said McKenna Marketing was really going places, and it was an exciting time for McKenna Marketing, wasn't it?

Shoveling Shit

I longed for escape from my thoughts. I longed to escape into sleep, but I was lucky to struggle through a few unrestful hours a night. I continued waking up every morning well before my alarm clock. I stayed in bed, trying to fall back to sleep, but the tempest of my poisoned thoughts made rest impossible.

In my little free time, I tried to read *The Jungle*, hoping to escape into a well-written book. It had been eight years since I'd read it the first time. I found it difficult to concentrate, and I read the same paragraphs over and over, but, slowly, I did make progress.

It was more depressing than I remembered. When Jorgen couldn't get work anywhere else, when his health and spirit were damaged beyond recognition and he had nowhere else to go, he takes a job shoveling manure. It was the lowest possible job, but he couldn't get a job doing anything else. Slowly, arduously, he adjusted to the stench, the toxins that made his head swim, the blinding muck. It was an apt metaphor for my hours with Eleanore. I did feel like I shoveled shit all day. At least it was metaphoric, not literal, shit.

AVERY

The Vortex

First thing Friday morning I logged into my e-mail account. I smiled when I saw I had new mail.

> To: Dancinfool@yahoo.com
> From: ArtLover@yahoo.com
> *Did you have a nice evening? I've spent all my free time these last few weeks fixing up the house for some relatives that are coming for a visit. I haven't had any time to paint. (Oh well, I guess that's what being an adult is all about.)*
>
> *Would you ever like to meet in real life? Just for coffee or dinner or something. Or maybe dancing. I know I won't be anywhere near as good of a dancer as you, but I'm willing to make a fool of myself to see you on the dance floor. Or course you have to promise not to laugh. What do you say?*

After a two-month courtship, he finally wanted to meet me in real life. I loved that he would go dancing with me, even though he wasn't good, just because he knew I liked it.

> *To: ArtLover@yahoo.com*
> *From: Dancinfool@yahoo.com*
> *My evening was relaxing, which is to say dull. Yes, I'd like to meet you. Coffee or dinner or dancing . . . any-thing sounds good. Let me know where and when. How will I recognize you?*

I sent the e-mail just as Jen burst into the office. "It's eight-forty-five, and I somehow have to survive the entire day at work. Why isn't it five o'clock yet? Why? Why? I couldn't be more depressed."

"I have some news that might cheer you up."

"I doubt it. What is it?"

"Art and I are going to meet in real life. He's going to tell me where and when."

Jen suddenly appeared to break out of her cocoon of self-absorption and seemed legitimately interested in what I had to say.

"That's great! You know, I have a good feeling about this," she said.

"I thought you said he was going to be an organ-eating murdering rapist."

"Well, he might be, I mean you need to be careful, right? But you know what I really think, I think that he's probably really sweet, but maybe not that great looking, but he'll make a great husband and a caring lover."

"Why don't you think he'll be good-looking?"

"Why would he be surfing the Net if he were halfway decent looking?"

I gave her a look.

"Oh shut up, you're gorgeous and you know you are," Jen said. "You just can't meet decent guys at the bars."

"Did you consider the possibility that he can't meet decent women either?"

"Anyway, when is he going to write you back?"

"He usually checks his mail at least once a day, so, I don't know, later today, I'd guess."

Every hour on the hour Jen pestered me to check my e-mail. I pretended like it was no big deal, I'd get to it when I got to it, but I had my eye on the clock. I couldn't believe that only fifteen minutes had passed; it was killing me not to check every ten minutes. When I did check it and there was no message, both Jen and I were disappointed. When he hadn't written back by noon I started to worry. Maybe he'd changed his mind.

I checked again at 2:00 and was so ridiculously relieved to be told I had new mail I accidentally let out a little squeal. I'd wanted to read his note in private, but, upon hearing my excitement, Jen rolled her chair over to my desk.

"What did he say?" she asked, peering over my shoulder.

> *To: Dancinfool@yahoo.com*
> *From: ArtLover@yahoo.com*
> *How does next Wednesday work for you? I know a great little restaurant. It's kind of out of the way, but the food is great. Let's say eight o'clock at the Full Moon Grill on Arapahoe and Fulsum. Over the weekend I'll try to dig up a picture of myself that I can scan in and e-mail to you Monday so you can recognize me.*

This was what romance was about. This rush, this excitement, this inability to keep a smile off my face.

Jen and I spent a good part of the rest of our day discussing what I should wear and what he might be like. I kept telling myself not to get too excited, that he was probably unattractive and dull, but I couldn't remember the last time I'd felt so alive, and I couldn't help being giddy with anticipation.

After work, Les and I went to the mall, purportedly to do some Christmas shopping.

The mall was crowded, but Les and I strolled along at our own pace, not yet panicked about buying presents. We stopped in front of a hip men's clothing store.

"Let's just say you were going to buy some clothes for a guy who looked like me, and was my height, weight, and coloring. What would you get him?" Les asked, eyeing the trendy clothes.

"Why, Les, are you asking me to help you pick out some new clothes? Why I'd love to," I said in an affected Southern accent. "We girls are trained from a very early age to dress things. Of course as children it was Barbie dolls we were clothing, but the lessons still apply." I helped him pick out several new pairs of pants and shoes, sweaters and shirts. Then we went into an eyeglasses store, where he asked me to help him pick out some frames.

He tried on a pair of frames and looked at me. I shook my head. We did this several more times, him turning, waiting for me to shake or nod my head. "Les, you're not even looking in the mirror," I said, laughing.

"I trust you. I'll look in the mirror before I buy them. I'm just developing a pile of maybes first."

"Um, no," I said, vetoing a squarish frame. "So guess what? Art and I are going to go on a date next week. He's going to send me his picture tomorrow. Can you believe it? An actual date."

"That's great," he said without enthusiasm.

"Those are okay. Put those with the maybes. Ugh, definitely a no." Les put the glasses I disliked back on the shelf. He stared at them for a long moment.

"I'm kind of scared," I continued. "What if he doesn't

think I'm attractive or interesting? I don't particularly want to deal with any more rejection. Les, is something wrong?"

"No. I'm happy for you. That's great. I really hope it works out."

"Put back on the thin gray frames. I think I like those best."

"These?"

"Yeah. I think those are the ones."

He looked into the mirror. "I think you're right. These feel great."

"Do they? They look really good." He tried on several more pairs, but we both liked the thin, stylish metal frames the best.

After he paid for the glasses, I continued talking as if I hadn't been interrupted. "I'm trying not to get my hopes up, but part of me really hopes this works out. I would really love it if I didn't have to go to yet another office holiday party stag. I can't tell you how I've been dreading the party."

"We can always go stag together."

"That'd be great," I said, feeling guilty that I hadn't remembered that he'd be going to the party alone, too. We walked out of the store and lingered at the railing, looking at the shoppers on the floor below.

"I spent several hundred dollars on myself today and didn't buy a single gift for anyone else. Next time I come to the mall I'm really going to have to increase my gifts-bought-per-hour ratio or I'll never be ready for Christmas," he said.

"We were just kind of scoping out the scene tonight. Mapping out our strategy, seeing what we want to get people. Next time we'll actually buy gifts. You want to get some ice cream?"

"No thanks. I should be getting home. I've been trying to get to bed early so I can work out before I go to work. I know you're saying, Les, get a life, why do you have to work on a Saturday, but I do have to go into the office for awhile."

"What a drag. Well, have fun with your workout."

"I will. I've actually been having fun. I feel a lot better. And it's so cool how in just a couple weeks I can already see such an improvement. Last week I could only jog for a few minutes at a time without stopping to walk. This week, I mean my pace is pretty slow, but I can jog without stopping for twenty minutes. I know that probably doesn't sound like much . . ."

"No, Les, that's great. I'm proud of you."

"It's a step in the right direction." Les got quiet after that. He didn't say anything as we walked through the mall out to the parking lot. Les seemed strangely distant.

The next morning as I opened the newspaper and turned right to my horoscope, hoping it would give me some insight into whether things were going to work out between me and Art, the phone rang.

"Hello?"

"Hi, may I speak to Avery?" There was considerable static, but through the crackling line, the voice sounded familiar.

"Speaking."

"Avery! It's Kestrel."

"Kestrel! Oh my god! How are you? How'd you find me?"

"I called your mom. She gave me your number. I'm great, how are you?"

"I'm good. What's that static?"

"Sorry, I'm calling from a cell phone. If I didn't have a cell phone, I would never have time to talk to anyone. I'm on the road all the time now. I'm in sales."

"Still selling your jewelry?"

She laughed. "No, I'm an account manager for a major advertising agency now. You're never going to believe it, but Avery, guess what? I'm getting married!"

I tried to imagine Kestrel, a bisexual vegan who, for a while, had actually made a living as a modern dancer and jewelry maker, working for an advertising agency and getting married. Then I wondered if maybe she was "marrying" a woman in a commitment ceremony or something. That would be more her style. I kept my question vague to allow for the possibility. "Congratulations, that's great. Where did the two of you meet?"

"He works at the same agency I do. He's a regional sales manager."

So she was really marrying a man. Kestrel, with her five tattoos and her nose ring, had fallen in love with a regional sales manager? "Wow, sounds like a lot of changes are going on in your life. Are you still dancing?"

"No, I don't have time. I got sick of being broke and living like a bohemian. Listen, the wedding is going to be in June. You're going to get an invitation, but I wanted to give you enough time to make plane reservations if you can come. Do you think you'll be able to make it?"

"Definitely. I'd love to. Kestrel, I'm so happy for you."

"Ouch!"

"What's wrong? Are you okay?" It was hard to hear her with the sound of the ambulance blaring behind her, but it sounded like she said something about her high heels.

"You wear heels?"

"I know, isn't it crazy? I wear business suits and heels every day, just like a grownup or something! Hey, how's Gideon?"

"Oh my god, it really has been a long time. Gideon and I are divorced. We've been divorced for about two years. It was hard for a while, but there's somebody special in my life now. I'm doing okay."

"Divorced! You two were perfect for each other."

"It was an amicable parting. Our lives were just being pulled in different directions."

We talked for twenty minutes about her new house in the suburbs with a Jacuzzi and a two-car garage. She talked about how she wanted to have kids right away because, at thirty, she just didn't have any time to waste.

By the time we hung up, my emotions were reeling. It was so hard to believe that Kestrel of all people had gotten swept into the vortex of middle-class life. Maybe it was inevitable that we'd all get sucked in, until one by one our ideals and our dreams fell away.

JEN

Girls' Night In

I was experiencing testosterone overload. I never thought it could happen, but I was officially getting sick of men. Both Tom and Mike asked me out for Saturday night, and I told both of them I was having a slumber party, girls only. It was a lie, but the idea grew on me. I liked the idea of spending a night without having to hold my stomach in, a night without having to laugh at unfunny jokes, a night of eating too much and laughing till my stomach hurt.

Avery brought wine and foccacia, marinated skewers of tofu and vegetables, and grilled potatoes; Rette brought salsa and baked chips; I brought brownies, chips, dip, and guacamole.

We promptly changed into our own version of PJs: I put on a tank top and my faded University of Minnesota shorts, Rette was in her sweats and wool socks, and Avery wore flannel pajama bottoms and a T-shirt. I brought a pitcher of margaritas to the living room, where we'd spread our sleeping bags over air mattresses.

"Avery, you're looking really good," Rette said.

"I'm feeling really good. Les and I have been dancing twice a week, and then two or three times a week we've been going to the gym together to take this Bikram yoga class."

"Which is?"

"They turn the heat up in the room to more than a hundred degrees, so you sweat out all the impurities. You leave feeling really cleansed and recharged."

"That sounds like punishment, but whatever," I said. "Okay, here are the rules: Everyone has to start the evening doing two shots of tequila. It's my party and you'll get wasted if I want you to." I gave slices of lime and a salt-shaker to Avery.

Avery did a shot and her face contorted like she'd just eaten a roach. "Gaa! Oh my, I'm way too old to do shots."

"There is nothing more juvenile than drinking to excess. I'm just trying to get you in touch with your inner youth. Now drink up," I said, pouring her next shot.

"Yes, these are Jen's rules. We always had to do two or three shots before going to the bars when we were in college," Rette said.

"And we always had fun, didn't we?" I said. "And, I might add, saved having to pay those inflated club prices for drinks."

"You're so right," Rette admitted with a smile.

"Do you know how bad alcohol is for you? It's like voluntarily going to the desert and baking in the sun until you're delirious with dehydration. That's why you feel buzzed: The alcohol zaps all the nutrients in your blood and dehydrates you. That's why your pee is bright yellow the morning after you drink. Your pee should never be bright yellow."

"Yeah, that's very interesting. Thanks for sharing." I handed the lime and salt to Rette. "Drink."

"Did Jen tell you about the assassin who bought us free beer?" Rette asked.

"Yikes, he was scary," I said. "But cute. Very cute."

"True. But you're used to cute men surrounding you in droves. How is it that your men would give you a night off to spend with the girls?" Rette asked.

"I just told them I was busy."

"Jen saying 'no' to a guy? That's unprecedented," Rette teased.

"Ha ha. Seriously, you guys have to help me decide which guy to date. Dating two guys is exhausting and I can't choose, so I need you to choose for me."

"Maybe you can't choose because neither guy is really right for you. Maybe you shouldn't be dating either of them," Avery said.

"I've thought of that, but that means I'll have to find someone else, and I don't really have that kind of energy."

"Dating is exhausting," Avery said. "I couldn't sleep at all last night. I kept thinking about meeting Art. I try to remind myself that it probably won't work out, but I don't know, I just have a really good feeling about this. I've planned all these trips we're going to take together, all these candlelit dinners we're going to have, weekend getaways with champagne and a Jacuzzi in a cabin in the mountains."

"That sounds so awesome," Rette said. "I miss dating."

"Oh my god, I don't even want to hear it," I said. "You've got it made. You'll never have to diet again and you'll always be sure of getting laid."

"Are you kidding? Trying to make a relationship work is hard work," Rette said.

"She's right. The trouble just starts when you say 'I do,'" Avery said.

"Even before sometimes. I don't know, I don't like

what's happening between me and Greg. When we were first dating he was always doing nice stuff for me, and now he doesn't ever even cook a meal or do his own dishes. We're not even married yet. I need to whip him into shape. Any suggestions?"

"Rette, I'm not the one to be asking for marital advice," Avery said.

"Dave only did nice stuff for me after he did terrible stuff, like when the stripper he hired for his friend's bachelor party broke my coffee table. He didn't buy me a new one, but he went down on me for like half an hour, and I never really liked that coffee table anyway, so I forgave him."

"Once, I guess we'd been dating maybe three months at the time," Rette said, "I'd been grumbling about how my favorite author had just published a new book, and it would be a year until the paperback version I could afford came out, and I was sick of making the slave wages of a teacher. At school the next day the book was on my desk with a ribbon on it and a card that said 'To the most beautiful woman in the world from the luckiest man in the world.' A gift just because. I just couldn't believe I could find such a wonderful guy. But he hasn't done anything like that for a while."

"He's busy with school, you're busy with work," Avery said.

"Oh my god, no kidding, it's ridiculous. I thought I put in long hours when I was teaching. I had no idea that corporate America was a sweatshop filled with people in suits. And the worst thing is that I wouldn't have to put in these obscene hours if it weren't for the grotesque incompetence of management. It reminds me of this thing that happened over Thanksgiving. We were at Greg's parents' place, and Greg's two little cousins, they were three and four and cute as can be, they were bopping each other on the head, saying, 'You! Are! Stupid!'

It was adorable. They could say exactly what was on their mind. You can't do that at the workplace. You can't just bop stupid people over the head and declare them stupid. But let me tell you, in my head, I'm giving a whole parade of stupid people a good thwap on the noggin every day. There's Eleanore, and Glenn, and all of the project managers who think I have nothing else to do but edit their reports as though they are the only people whose material I clean up. It just seems like everyone is out to irritate me. All day long I think, 'You are stupid! You are stupid!' I know, very mature. I'm not proud. The worst thing is that I really need this stupid job."

"Why don't you look for another job?" Avery said.

"I am looking, but do you remember how long it took me to get this crappy job? I'm not sure I'll even be able to get another job because Eleanore will give me a terrible reference. For the rest of my life, this bad experience is going to haunt me. Every time I look for a new job, I'll worry the HR person will call McKenna Marketing and find out that my boss and I hated each other. I feel ill just thinking about it."

"You're not the first person not to get along with your boss," Avery said.

"I know. I just feel like such a failure. I wasn't on very good terms with the head of the English department at my last job, and now there's Eleanore. I'm the common denominator here. I just don't get along with stupid people very well."

"There are personalities like that at every job," Avery said. "There are always these egos you have to deal with no matter where you work. It's like a family. Your parents can drive you crazy and your siblings know exactly how to push your buttons, but you don't have to spend eight plus hours a day five days a week with your family. You don't want to stay in a job that makes you miserable, but you have to know that wherever you go there are going to be personalities like Eleanore and Sharon and Glenn."

"I used to think I would have an interesting life," Rette said. "I was just going to be a humble schoolteacher, but I would have summers off to travel to exotic places and have affairs with good-looking men with accents. So how does my life turn out? I got myself the dullest job on earth, and even if I could save up enough money to travel, I'd never get more than two weeks of vacation at a time."

"Why not? Why can't you? Why don't you just save your money and go?" Avery asked.

"I just told you. I mean I can take little trips here and there, but I'd always thought it would be fun to just backpack across Europe for a few months. Or take a road trip across the United States for a couple months."

"What's stopping you?" Avery asked.

"Well, let's see. For one thing, I can't even pay off the debt I already have, let alone save up enough money to travel for six months, and for another thing, oh yeah, I have a job. I can't just call in sick for six months. Anyway, Greg wouldn't want to backpack through Europe, and it wouldn't be fun to travel alone."

"Why do you put up so many barriers to your happiness, Rette? You make it sound as though unless all these many things go just like you want them to, you can't possibly be happy," Avery said.

"I'm just saying I wish I'd made different choices in my life."

"You're twenty-seven. You make it sound like you have no control over what your future brings, and you know what, Rette? It ain't so."

They blathered on and on about boring, abstract stuff like happiness, totally ignoring the very real problem of me dating two men.

* * *

We finally fell asleep around two or three in the morning. At six, we were jarred awake by a sound I couldn't immediately identify. It took me a minute to figure out that it was a combination of creaky bedsprings, moans, and a headboard crashing against a wall.

"Aah," Avery said groggily, "There's nothing like the sound of neighbors having sex to drive home the point that you ain't getting any. Thank you! I know! I'm a loser! Nobody wants to have sex with me! It's been eight million years since I've had sex. Thank you so much for the reminder!"

"She must be a prostitute. Real women don't sound like that, do they? I don't sound like that," Rette said.

"I think their bed is going to break," I said, listening to the bed creak rhythmically. "God, I'm jealous. I can't remember the last time I had wake-the-neighbors sex."

"I don't think I've ever had sex like that," Rette said.

"Thank goodness!" Avery laughed.

The racket went on for a million years, and even after it ended it took me forever to fall asleep. Something about the whole thing struck me as oddly sad, and, for the life of me, I couldn't figure out why.

RETTE

Lessons in Doing Absolutely Everything Wrong

I woke up with a start early Saturday morning. Disoriented, it took me a minute to figure out where I was—I opened my eyes and saw Jen and Avery in their sleeping bags, and remembered we'd stayed up till three in the morning. I was exhausted and sick to my stomach—my liver had spent the night marinating in tequila and my stomach was gorged with brownies and guacamole.

The noise that had woken me at that ungodly hour, I eventually figured out, was Jen's neighbors romping. The caterwaul woke Avery and Jen, too, but they were able to fall back to sleep. I couldn't, so I got dressed and drove home, my eyes stinging from lack of sleep.

That night, I went to the grocery store and when I stopped in the meat section, looking at all the meat sliced and wrapped in plastic, I began to cry, right there in the store. Not quiet, small tears, but huge, embarrassing blubbering sobs. I didn't even particularly like meat, but I bought it to make Greg happy. I cooked it to make Greg happy, and this was what I was going to have to do for the rest of my life to keep our relationship running smoothly. For the rest of my life I'd have to go to the grocery store once or twice a week; I'd have to cook and do dishes and mop and sweep and clean the muck out of the bathtub.

I dried my tears and continued my shopping, reminding myself that I wasn't a victim of war or famine or a brutal car accident that left me crippled and my flesh mottled and scarred. I wasn't living in a cardboard box.

I was, however, decidedly a failure. My career was a joke. I'd already blown my first attempt at a career, and now I was failing again. The only thing I was good at was doing absolutely everything wrong.

Why had I ever thought I could enjoy a career? I'd believed the myth that if I went to college and studied hard I would get a challenging, enjoyable, well-paying, fulfilling career. I had no reason to believe this was a reasonable expectation. It's not like Mom, Dad, Greg, Avery, or Jen had ever come home exclaiming about what a wonderful, fulfilling day they'd had. Instead, they came home exhausted, griping about the bullshit they put up with, about their incompetent bosses, about the injustice of their coworkers being promoted above them. We all go through life praying for the weekend and our two weeks off a year.

AVERY

Behind the Digital Armor

Monday morning I was so nervous, it took me an extra-long time to get ready for work. I seemed to move in slow motion, forgetting what I was doing, distracted and jittery. When I finally got to the office just after eight, Jen was already there.

"What are you doing here so early?" I asked.

"Are you kidding? I'm dying to see Art and your expression when you finally get to see him."

I'd wanted to have the big moment to myself, but Jen rolled her chair across the floor so she could get a good look, and I knew it was a losing battle. I took a deep breath and logged into my account.

> To: Dancinfool@yahoo.com
> From: ArtLover@yahoo.com
> *My picture is attached. How will I recognize you? I'm really looking forward to meeting you. See you Wednesday.*

I stared at the icon at the bottom of the e-mail that indicated he'd attached a graphic.

"Finally, we get to see what this guy looks like!" Jen said.

I clicked on the attachment. We waited for an interminable length of time as the picture downloaded. When it finally did, Jen and I stared at it in silence.

"Holy shit," Jen said at last.

I couldn't say a word.

"I don't believe it. What a creep. What a cheating sleazebag creep," Jen said.

Lydia's husband, Dan, smiled out at us from the computer screen.

JEN

The Plan

It was a slimy, conniving, cruel coincidence worthy of one of the soap operas I'd once been so addicted to: Avery's digital paramour was married to a coworker.

"What are you going to do?" I asked.

"I think I'm not going to think about it for a while. I think I'd like to forget this ever happened."

"You're going to tell Lydia, aren't you?"

"No, I'm not going to tell a six-month pregnant woman that her husband is getting his kicks with women he meets through the Internet. I don't believe this."

"If your husband was cheating on you, wouldn't you want to know?"

"He hasn't cheated that we know of. Maybe he just wanted some attention, a little harmless flirtation."

"We have to find out so we know for sure."

Avery said quietly, "You know what? Except for one glaring thing, I don't think he lied about anything. He is a painter. He did live back East somewhere before moving here. He and Lydia do have dogs. I can't remember if their names are Holden and Phoebe, but I'm sure they are. He probably has been fixing the house up for a certain 'relative' who will be 'visiting.' With his talent, it's probably a beautiful nursery. You've seen his paintings. Remember? We saw them when they had that dinner party for Dan's birthday? There were two watercolors and that oil painting. They were really good."

I didn't know what to say. Then an idea occurred to me. "Have you ever told him what you look like?" I asked.

She thought a moment. "No."

"Not even how tall you are or that you have blond hair?"

"No."

"I have an idea. Dan has never met Rette. We could send Rette in your place. If he puts the moves on her, we'll have to tell Lydia she's married to a sleazebag. If he's just looking for some attention, we don't have to tell Lydia a thing, and our consciences will be clear."

"I don't think that's a good idea."

"Why not? Come on, my plan is brilliant. We just have to convince Rette." I picked up my phone and dialed Rette's extension.

"Are you busy?" I asked.

"Extremely."

"This is an emergency. Avery and I need you in our office right away."

"What is it?"

"Just get down to our office."

When she got to our office, I closed the door behind her and told her the whole sordid story.

"I don't believe it," she said. "What a creep. And when she's pregnant. Avery, I'm so sorry, you must be so disappointed."

"Dan's always seemed like such a nice guy," Avery said.

"So you see our dilemma. We have to figure out if he really intended to cheat on Lydia, or if he was kind of bored and this was just a relatively harmless cyberfling," I said.

"How are you going to do that?" Rette asked.

"Well, he's never met you. Avery's never told him what she looks like. We can send you in her place. If he puts the moves on you, we'll tell Lydia what kind of guy she's married to."

"And break up a marriage? That's a great plan," Rette said. "I can't believe you want me to seduce another woman's husband. That's ridiculous. It'll never work. Anyway, did you forget I'm engaged?"

"Like I could forget. No! It's not like you have to sleep with him or anything. A few kisses. Maybe let him get in a grope or two," I said.

"No way, absolutely not."

"But Rette," I began.

"No, no, no. I'm going back to work."

"It's for the best," Avery said after Rette left. "I'll tell him I've met someone else and stop e-mailing him, and we can forget this ever happened."

"Just hold off on writing him back. We'll talk her into it, you'll see. We'll scan in a picture of her, and if he still wants to meet her, believe me, she'll change her mind."

"I don't know . . ."

I didn't let her think about it. I grabbed the picture I kept of me and Rette from my desk and ran down the hall where the graphic designers, and thus the scanners, were. I smiled sweetly at Joseph.

"Could I use your scanner for just a teeny little second?"

He grinned and looked at me stupidly, which I took as a yes.

"Thank you so much. Actually, I don't know how to use the scanner. Could you help me?"

The picture was from my freshman year in college, just before we were going to hit the clubs together. Rette and I had done a few shots, and Rette looked relaxed and really happy. The picture captured her long hair and stopped just below her ample cleavage, mercifully leaving her thighs well out of sight.

Joseph e-mailed me the picture, and I cropped myself out of the photo (finally, a reason to use the Photoshop poor Tom had reinstalled four times!) and convinced a reluctant Avery to e-mail Dan asking if he was still interested in meeting her. A few hours later, he wrote back that he was "very interested" in meeting "such a beauty."

When I told Rette what we'd done, she responded predictably. She pretended to be outraged, but being called a beauty, even by a lying cheating scumbag, was flattering. Eventually, I broke her down, and she agreed to do it.

Wednesday night, Avery and I helped get her ready for her "date." Avery brought a small microphone that we taped in Rette's bra so we could listen and record their conversation.

"It itches. It's poking me," she complained.

"Sorry. But isn't this exciting?" I asked.

"A little," Rette said.

Avery had been the technical adviser for the spying part of the plan, but when it came to the beauty consulting, I was entirely in charge. I did Rette's makeup and hair and dressed her in a low-cut crushed-velvet blouse and black jeans.

"Don't you think this is a little too revealing?" she asked. I stood behind her, brushing her hair, watching her looking worriedly at her image in the mirror. "I've never had so much cleavage exposed in my life," she griped.

"You've got it; we're flaunting it." I watched her give her reflection the slightest smile. Good. We needed her to feel like a gorgeous temptress to make our plan work.

Avery had given Rette copies of all her and Dan's e-mail so Rette would know everything Avery knew about Dan, at least according to what he had written.

We told Rette that her goal was to get him to reveal if he routinely cheated on his wife, in which case we were telling Lydia about this for sure. The other possibilities were less clear cut. If he wanted just a one-night stand, our action was uncertain. "Just be as trampy as you can be, and we'll decide what to do later," I said. Rette looked queasy.

"Are you sure you're up to this?" Avery asked.

"No. This is never going to work. I'm going to say something that'll give me away or the microphone will fall out or . . ." Rette said.

"Could you ever try to consider the bright side of things?" I asked.

"No," she said. She sat in the chair in front of the mirror awkwardly, her hand covering her chest.

"Stop hiding your cleavage. This is no time to be shy!" I said.

Avery and I borrowed Avery's mother's SUV and got to the restaurant early. Rette was driving her own car to make things look legit. Avery and I parked the truck and got into the back, hiding on the floor so no one could see us through the windows.

Avery turned on the volume to the receiver that was connected to Rette's microphone. All we heard was a sound like wind through a tunnel.

"Is it working?" I asked. "This is great. Probably all we'll hear is the sound of Rette's tits sweating."

"We tested it at home. It's going to work."

Just then, we heard a high-pitched noise that sounded

like a mouse hiccupping. Then we heard Rette whisper, "He's here! He's parking his car. Shit!"

"Hi," we heard Dan say a minute or so later. "It's nice to finally meet you."

"Hi. It's nice to meet you. I've been looking forward to it."

"Wow. You know, you look familiar. You look like someone I know."

Avery and I both stopped breathing for a moment. Rette and I did have the same shaped eyes and the same unusual shade of hair. Why hadn't I thought of this before?

"Really?" she squeaked.

"We've never met?"

"No, I'm sure we haven't."

"Huh. Well, anyway, ever been here before? It's good, I think you'll like it." We heard the door swing open.

Dan requested a table for two. There was some shuffling, some mumbling I couldn't make out.

"Do you like wine?" Dan asked.

"I love it."

"How does a bottle of Merlot sound?"

"Perfect."

"The duck here is quite good. And so is the filet mignon," he said.

"Filet mignon!" I said. I hadn't eaten all day and I was famished. I wanted to be the one in there getting wined and dined.

"Shhh!" Avery whispered, as if we had any reason to be quiet.

I made a face at Avery, but she didn't see me. She was listening too intently to notice me.

We listened to them order. After the waiter left, Dan babbled on and on about how much he'd enjoyed her e-mail and how intelligent she was. I was squashed uncomfortably on the floor of the SUV between the seats, my legs crumpled beneath me as they talked. Rette tried to keep him talking, asking him all about himself. When he asked her what she'd do if she weren't working in marketing, she stuttered, "Well, I . . . love dancing and romance novels. I do crafty kinds of stuff." She was sighing deeply as if her life depended on her response. She was way too hyper. Always had been. Fortunately for her, Dan was also into artsy-craftsy things, and he launched into some story about this desk he'd made and all the challenges that went along with making it.

"The wine is so wonderful," Rette said as she poured herself more. "Should we get another bottle?"

"Absolutely."

"I'm starving!" I complained. "*I* want the autumn harvest salad with jicama and pine nuts and a flavorful sauce. *I* want the duck a l'orange. She's not getting him to admit anything, she's just scamming a free dinner!"

"Would you be quiet! Listen," Avery said, more huffily than was necessary.

For about a million years, all we heard was Rette eating a very loud, crunchy salad and them discussing how good the bread was and how delicious the wine tasted.

By the time their dinner arrived, I was salivating over the thought of getting home to a bottle of wine myself. They chatted endlessly about nothing, and soon I was spacing out, not hearing anything much amid the clinking of silverware and the hum of conversation. Suddenly, Dan said something interesting enough to catch my attention.

"I've really enjoyed writing you these last couple of months. You are even more beautiful then I'd imagined," Dan was saying. "You really are gorgeous. It's amazing that someone like you hasn't landed a husband by now."

"Funny you should mention that. I sort of, listen Dan, I sort of have a confession to make. I'm engaged."

Avery and I looked at each other, horrified. What the hell was she doing?

"Engaged?" Dan asked.

"I'm not looking for anything serious. I love my fiancé. I can't wait to spend the rest of my life with him. I guess I just wanted one last fling. You know, when you're with someone for a while, they stop taking you to fancy dinners. They stop calling you beautiful and gorgeous. I guess I kind of missed that. Do you think I'm horrible?"

Neither of them said anything for a moment. Then Dan said, "No, I know what you mean." There was a long stretch of silence. Shuffling. Breathing.

"What? What's going on?" I asked. "She's blowing it. That's it. It's over."

"Rette, I'm married myself," he said.

"Really?" she said.

"I hadn't intended on cheating on my wife, in fact, I still . . . I guess my wife has been a little preoccupied with her work and some other things . . . I just sort of put that ad up there, not as a joke exactly, out of boredom really. Only one other woman responded, but her e-mails just weren't interesting at all, so I told her I'd started dating someone. But you, I don't know, I really enjoyed e-mailing you. You are smart and funny and insightful. You're really something. I hadn't intended to meet you in real life, but then . . ."

I looked over at Avery. She was crying. I reached over and took her hand.

"Do you ever miss kissing anyone else?" Rette whispered. "Do you ever wonder what it's like to sleep with someone else?"

He laughed. "Yes. Definitely. But I don't regret marrying my wife. Not for a second."

"Do you want to go somewhere tonight? Just the two of us?"

My eyes nearly popped out of my head. I was dying to hear what happened next, but the next thing we heard was the waiter asking if they wanted coffee or dessert.

"Rette? No dessert? You're sure? I guess just the bill then," Dan said. About a century and a half later, he finally spoke again. "Your offer is tempting. Very tempting. But I can't. I shouldn't have come here tonight. I don't know what I was thinking. I've been wracked with guilt ever since we started e-mailing each other."

"You've never cheated on your wife?"

"No. Not once in seven years. I'll get this."

"You don't have to . . ."

"I insist."

After a couple minutes of silence, Avery and I listened to the heels of Rette's shoes clicking against the floor, then the pavement.

"Rette, I really want to thank you for tonight. You're not disappointed, are you?" Dan asked.

"No. In fact, I think this evening couldn't have turned out better."

"Would it be okay if I e-mailed you every now and then? I'd love to know how the wedding goes."

"I uh, I'm not sure if that's a good idea. We'll see, okay?"

We heard a car door open, then close. After a minute or so, Rette said into the microphone, "Meet me at my apartment." The engine turned and we heard her tearing out of her parking spot.

Avery and I waited a full five minutes before moving from our spots below the truck's windows and heading over to Rette's place.

I charged up the stairs to Rette's apartment, threw open the door, and yelled, "You blew it!"

Rette was sitting on the couch; she'd already changed from her sexy clothes and was wearing a T-shirt and shorts.

"I did not. I thought if he thought I had something to lose by sleeping with him, he'd know I'd have to keep our affair secret and he'd be safe in sleeping with me." She got up and went into the bathroom. I followed close behind. Avery stood against the wall, her arms crossed, her eyes on the floor. "He'd know it wouldn't turn into a fatal attraction thing and that I wouldn't expect him to leave his wife," Rette said. "I don't know, playing it that way just came to me. I didn't have a script to work from, you know."

"You did fine," Avery said quietly.

Rette pulled her hair up in a ponytail, turned on the faucet, and began scrubbing all the makeup off her face.

"No, no," I said, exasperated. "You were supposed to get him drunk and then lure him to some out-of-the-way place and then run your hand up his leg while kissing him lightly on his neck. My god, doesn't anyone know how to seduce a man anymore? Avery, you read romance novels, you know how it goes. You're not supposed to be honest and admit you're getting *married*, for god's sake."

Rette rinsed her face, then patted her face dry and walked into the living room.

"Are you okay, Avery?"

"You did fine. Look, it's over, he didn't cheat on his wife. Let's just drop it, okay? I'm going to bed." Avery stood and made her way toward the door.

"Bed? It's like only nine o'clock," I said.

"I'll see you guys later. Thanks for the help tonight," Avery said. The screen door swung shut behind her.

The Midday Romp

Why do relationships have to be so complicated? Poor Avery was taking the Art/Dan thing really hard. My own love life was as confused as ever. Things were strange between me and Tom. At work he acted nothing more than distantly polite to me. He didn't always call me when he said he'd call, and when he did want to get together, it was always at the last minute. In a way, I was glad I had Mike in my life. It kept me busy and not always just waiting around for Tom. But when Tom and I did get together, we always had fun.

The whole situation was tricky. I didn't know who to fantasize about before I fell asleep at night. I tried to give them each a 50/50 split of my fantasy time, but memories of Dave usually crowded them both out of my mind.

One morning, I couldn't stop thinking about sex with Dave, and I got so crazy horny, I e-mailed Tom suggesting we take his Excursion, find a secluded spot, and have a little lunchtime nookie. A few minutes later he arrived at my office door, grinning.

"Ready for lunch?" he asked.

"Am I ever," I said, smiling.

"It's not even eleven," Avery said.

"We want to beat the crowds," I replied.

Tom and I drove to the farthest end of a Wal-Mart parking lot and parked next to a field near the Dumpsters in the back of the Wal-Mart. We climbed in the backseat and I unbuttoned his jeans and pulled them and his boxers down to his ankles. I took him in my mouth. Keeping him in my mouth, I pushed my skirt up and awkwardly worked out of my underwear—no easy feat in such a small space. I didn't want him to come before I had a chance, so after a couple of minutes, I straddled him, putting him inside me.

"I don't have a condom," he said.

"Just pull out," I said. I'd just had a period. I'd probably be fine.

I came after a few minutes. Tom guided me to change positions so I was sitting on the edge of the seat, reclined awkwardly, and he was kneeling on the floor. When he came, he pulled out and sprayed my stomach with his cum.

He sat next to me. "Here," he said, giving me some Burger King napkins that had been lying on the floor. They looked clean enough, so I cleaned off as best I could. We dressed in silence.

I could have washed up better once we got to the office, but in an odd way, I liked having the sticky remnants of him on my stomach. The thought of our midday romp kept a smile on my face for the rest of the day.

After work, Mike took me out for a dinner that must have been at least $200, considering all the wine we had. Being taken to a nice meal always made me feel especially generous, and when we got home, I gave him a long, particularly delicious blow job, then snuggled up next to him to fall asleep. In the minutes it took to fall asleep, images of Dave kept popping into my mind. Dave laughing, Dave coming, Dave flashing me that smile of his.

How was it that I could be dating two guys and still feel so lonely?

RETTE

Pellets and Punishments

The fact that my mother was coming for a visit dramatically compounded my yuletide-and-work-induced stress. When Mom was around, I felt like a lab mouse trapped in an experiment I learned about in college. In the experiment, there were three different groups of mice. A lever was set up in the mice's cages. When one group pressed the lever, they would be rewarded with a pellet of food every time. In another group, the mice would never be rewarded, and in the last group, the mice were rewarded sporadically. The first and second groups quickly grew bored with the game, but the mice that were in the third group just couldn't stop themselves. They would do anything to get that periodic reward. They'd press the level until their paws bled. That's how I felt with my mother: I alternately felt stung and loved by her, and I couldn't always tell what I'd do to elicit one response or another. It was exhausting constantly being wary, trying to brace myself to keep from being wounded by one of her comments or disapproving looks. But every now and then I'd be rewarded with an unexpected compliment.

Part of it was that we were so different. Even as a little girl, when she tried to dress me in frilly pink dresses and hair ribbons, I considered it the gravest, cruelest punishment imaginable. She'd cajole, then she'd pull the I'm-your-mom-and-you'll-do-what-I-say card. I'd kick and scream and tear the ribbons out of my hair at the first possible opportunity, causing my mother much frustration and gritted teeth. It was a battle that would continue in a slightly different form for the rest of my life.

When I was a teenager, as my curves developed without permission from me, I took to wearing enormously oversized clothes to hide my burgeoning figure. Mom hated my outfits and told me that if I didn't wear such muumuu-ish clothes, I wouldn't look so much like a circus tent. (She actually said that. *Ouch.*) But every now and then, I'd buy an article of clothing that Mom liked. She'd smile and tell me how nice I looked. *Ka-ching!* Pellet. You'd think I'd keep trying for more pellets, and I did, to some extent, but there was also that teenage rebelliousness in me that said, *Yeah, you want me to be skinny and starve myself like you do? Screw you!*

Okay, this backfired on me much more than on Mom, I see that now, but doesn't most teenage rebellion?

Part of me wanted to be into clothes and doing my nails and learning how to accessorize myself in a dazzling manner, but if something didn't challenge my intellect, I just couldn't bring myself to care. Jen did a much better job of garnering Mom's approval. Jen got pellets up the ying-yang, but of course she couldn't eat them because she was on a perpetual diet.

At least Mom paid attention, right? Unlike Dad. With Dad, Jen and I could have been doing cartwheels while on fire and he wouldn't have noticed. But for some reason, Dad being in his own little world didn't bother me nearly as much as Mom picking on me like a monkey mom at the zoo, picking straw and whatever the equivalent of lint is in primate circles off her monkey baby.

Jen and my relationship to food had a lot to do with what we learned from Mom's relationship to it. She knew the fat content and calorie count of every food on the face of the earth. Any time she had the tiniest sliver of cake at the holidays, she would ruin it by talking the entire time about how bad she was and how fattening it was and how much more she'd have to work out the next day to burn it off. She could never just enjoy anything.

She thought of food as an insidious enemy, an unfortunate necessity of life. Maybe it had something to do with the fact that she never prepared good food. Instead of fresh baked bread we had Wonderbread. Instead of brie, we had Cheesewhiz. Instead of filet mignon, we had Hamburger Helper. Instead of fresh pasta we had Mac 'n Cheese. You'd think someone as calorie conscious as our mom would have made things with fresh fruits and vegetables, but since food wasn't a pleasure to my mother, she just wanted to get dinner on the table and over with as fast as possible.

Maybe because Mom never kept any kind of snacks in the house—even low-fat pretzels or fresh fruit—potato chips and candy bars became my forbidden fruit. While other teenagers snuck alcohol in an effort at rebellion, I snuck junk food. The pounds added up slowly over the years, but I wore such baggie clothes, it took me awhile to notice. One day I noticed an unfortunate sprawl of my thigh and realized that I was not comfortable moving in my body (not that I ever had been). I thought, I've become a disgusting fat pig, how did this happen? So I'd starve myself in penance, then binge in an oh-screw-it-I'll-just-be-fat moment of frustration.

I knew my body disappointed my mother, and I couldn't blame her, it disappointed me, and no matter what I did, it always would. I learned that I would never be good enough from the first magazine I ever read with tips on how to find the right bathing suit to cover our "flaws": short waist, long waist, a bust that's too large or too small (they never say there is a size that's just right because this isn't Goldilock's porridge; when it comes to women's bodies, there are no just rights, just flaws and imperfections that need to be covered and hidden). I learned that my pores would never be small enough, my clothes would never be fashionable enough, my hair would never be shiny enough, and my house would never be homey enough. Somehow, I also managed to learn that stuff like that wouldn't make me happy. It would, however, make seeing my mother for Christmas considerably less stressful.

There wasn't much I could do about it now. An alcoholic or a drug addict can get wasted behind locked doors and still make it into the office or onto the movie set the next day. Being overweight meant I advertised my addiction every moment of every day. I publicized my sorrow in every angry stretch mark, in the ungainly, rolling heft of me that couldn't be covered or hidden away.

AVERY

Widows and Orphans

Sunday morning, I awoke to a day that was gray and cold and as listless as I felt. I had to shake my mood. I'd been in a funk since I'd seen Dan's face smiling back at me from the computer screen earlier in the week.

I lit aromatherapy candles and tried to do some yoga, but I just couldn't concentrate.

I pulled my journal out from beneath my mattress, sat at the kitchen table, and waited for the words to come. Usually, struggling to get my thoughts on paper had a cathartic effect, but I couldn't even begin to describe why I felt so hurt. I grabbed the phone from the end table and called Les.

"Hello?"

"Hey, you. How's your weekend going?" I asked.

"Pretty uneventful. I squeezed a workout in yesterday, but otherwise I've pretty much been one with the couch all weekend. I just can't seem to get motivated. How about you? You sound a little glum. Is it because of Dan? Are you disappointed?"

"I'm disappointed. I'm disappointed in Dan. I thought he and Lydia had such a great marriage. I mean she's pregnant with his child, and instead of Dan being supportive, he decides he's not getting enough attention. It's just so sad." I close my eyes, trying to blink away the tears. "I really thought I had something real with Art. We didn't even know what the other looked like; it was a relationship based purely on the fact that we seemed to really get each other. It seemed substantive and real. But maybe what makes something romantic are the details you don't know, the imperfections you aren't yet aware of or can overlook. In the missing details, you fill in your own, making him into what you want him to be."

"What about in *When Harry Met Sally?* There, the only obstacle was that they didn't realize they were meant to be together. They knew all of each others' faults and it wasn't until they were ready to see just how well they fit together that they were able to start living happily ever after."

"Or maybe they just got sick of dating and settled for each other."

"Maybe that's what true love is: Giving up your illusions and loving the reality of an imperfect person."

"I guess. It just doesn't quite seem as exciting."

"That's why it's so hard. Exciting takes no work whatsoever; it just carries you along. A serious relationship, one that keeps getting deeper and better, that's hard work."

The next morning, it took me a long time to drag myself out of bed. I went through the motions of showering and dressing and drove to the office on automatic pilot. I walked past the cubicles padded like the walls in an asylum, along the institutional gray carpet. The hum of the computers, the click of fingers tapping at the keyboards, the sound of voices on the phone fused with artificial enthusiasm, into my tiny office where I spent most of my waking hours.

I sat down, turned on my computer, and went to the kitchen, coffee cup in hand, ready to dutifully poison myself to be a productive employee.

I lingered in the kitchen, drinking my coffee until I was finished. I put the mug in the dishwasher. I was too restless to go back to my office, and I couldn't exactly hang out in the kitchen all day. I went to Rette's office instead.

"How are you doing?" I asked.

"Oh, I'm just great. Eleanore just yelled at me for half an hour about widows and orphans."

"Which are?"

"Something no one but a fascist editor would care about. They're when you have a column that begins with the last line of a paragraph or when you end a paragraph with a small word. We get rid of them to make copy look better, so I missed a paragraph that ended with a four-letter word when Eleanore *has already told me* never to end with *anything fewer than five letters*. Then, to help my day get even better, I got five e-mails in the last hour from marketing people who have copy for me to edit. They all mark their e-mails highest priority, with the subject line 'Due today' as if it's my fault they waited till past their deadline to finish it and as if every other marketing person didn't also just send me a high-priority e-mail. And do you think people thank me for changing their *Illicit* to *Elicit*? No, they don't thank me for what I catch, they just blame me for what I miss. God forbid I don't catch everything. I'm the fall guy for every mistake. I've made just a stellar career choice."

"You like writing, don't you? Maybe you could work in the marketing department writing releases and ad copy."

"Yeah, but then I'd have to deal with Glenn. Eleanore's a monster, but at least she's a good editor. Glenn is shockingly talentless. You can deal with people who have egos all out of proportion to their talent, but I can't. I do not get paid enough to put up with any of this."

"I know. It's almost Christmas. I need time off, not overtime. And it's not helping that your sister is not pulling her weight on the Expert project. I mean I know she's your sister and all, but I'm doing maybe ninety percent of the work and I just, gosh, I mean I need more help."

"She's probably too busy with Sharon's stuff."

"What do you mean?"

"She's helping Sharon with the budget and some other stuff so she can take over for Sharon while she's on maternity leave."

I looked at her blankly for too long a moment. "Really. I didn't realize she was going for that position. I wouldn't think she'd want a more stressful job."

"She doesn't. She wants more money."

"Don't we all." I tried without much success to keep my tone light. "Well, I guess I should probably get back to work."

"See ya."

I made my way unsteadily to the women's bathroom and locked myself in a stall. I leaned against the stall wall, hugging myself, starring at the gray tile floor until the tears blurred my view.

Stop it! I told myself. *You have too much work to take time out to have a breakdown.*

This was my fault. I stupidly thought that my hard work would be rewarded even though none of my efforts had been rewarded in the past. Sharon and I had started

working at McKenna at the same time. Even though I
had a lot more people skills than Sharon did, she'd moved
up the ladder faster. She knew how to brag about her
hard work. Every bit of work she did she played up to seem
like she was a workaholic who accomplished an amazing number of important tasks for the company. She
knew what it took to succeed, while I waited quietly and
patiently for someone to notice my work and reward me
for it.

I dried my tears. It wasn't too late. The announcement
hadn't been made yet; it wasn't official. Even if I didn't
get Sharon's job, I needed to let the higher-ups know I
was ready to take on more challenges.

I emerged from the stall, thankful that no one else
was in the bathroom. I patted my eyes dry, but I couldn't
get rid of the telltale red eyes. All I could do was hope
no one saw me and ask what was wrong. If they did, I
knew I'd burst into tears again.

I went back to my office. It was almost nine and Jen
still wasn't in, and I was grateful. I took a few deep breaths
and composed an e-mail to Sharon.

> To: SHall@mckennamarketing.com
> From: ARose@mckennamarketing.com
> *Hi Sharon, I wondered if you would have some time
> available this week so you and I could meet. I'm inter-
> ested in seeing if there are any additional challenges I
> can take on at McKenna, and I'd love your input on
> any ways I could enhance my skills while benefiting the
> company.*
> *Thanks,*
> *Avery*

I waited eagerly all afternoon for her response. She
never wrote back.

Holiday "Cheer"

What I wanted to do when I got home from work was hide under the covers and never come out. Unfortunately, I had to go to the company office party. I thought about skipping it, but this was a prime opportunity to rub elbows with the bigwigs. I was going to network and befriend and suck up—whatever I needed to do. I was going to try anyway.

At least I had Les to go with as my "date."

"Avery, my god, you're gorgeous," he said when I opened the door to let him in. "I mean you're always gorgeous, but you really look beautiful tonight."

"Thanks, Les." I had bought the dress almost a year ago during the post-holiday clearance sales, and I hadn't had an opportunity to wear it until tonight. It wasn't the typical sort of thing for me to buy; it was much too risqué, much too Halle-Berry-goes-to-the-Oscars. It was a gold silk dress, a color that matched well with my dark blond hair; sheer gold-colored fabric lined the scooped neck and plunging back like a thin, translucent scarf. The dress didn't reveal cleavage but threatened to do so. It did show off my neck and back, and the silky fabric was very sensual and might have made me horny if I hadn't been so damned depressed. "You mind if we stick around here for a little bit? I'd like to finish my glass of wine before we leave."

"Is something wrong? Is the Dan thing still bothering you?"

"Les, there have just been so many things disappointing me lately, I hardly know where to begin. Let's just say my coworkers are the last people on earth I want to spend the evening with. Do you want a glass of wine?"

"I'm good."

While I finished my wine I told him about the Jen/Sharon situation. He said all the right things about how

I still had a good chance of getting that job or something even better, but I was in a bad mood and nothing anyone could say would get me out of it.

When we got to the banquet room of the hotel, Mary came up to Les and me to greet us.

"Here are your drink tickets," she announced, handing us each two. Then, in a conspiratorial whisper she said, "Let me know if you need any more. I had them print up a couple hundred extra!"

Before I could even thank her, she was moving on to the next guests.

"Can I get you a drink?" Les asked.

"Yes. Please. Chablis."

With Les waiting in line, I was by myself, feeling awkward and alone in a group of people I saw everyday. I looked around for someone to talk to and spotted Jim from sales crying in the corner. He gripped his drink close to his heart, like rosary beads he was praying over. I crossed the room to meet him.

"Jim, what's going on? What's wrong?" I asked.

"My wife left me. She took everything. All my money, my stereo, my computer, my TV, my VCR, my microwave, most of my clothes."

I hadn't even known Jim was married, let alone long enough to have gotten a divorce. Then he said, "I don't even know where she is, whether she's still in the States or if she went back to the Philippines," and I remembered our conversation over the coffee maker a few months earlier when he'd told me about his mail-order bride. As his tears started with a renewed vigor, I patted Jim on the shoulders and told him the usual stuff about how everything would be all right. I did feel bad for him. Part of me, however, wanted to high-five the bride and tell her, "You go, girl!"

After a few minutes, I saw Rette making a "come over here" gesture to me from across the room. She looked worried. Anyway, I was happy to have an excuse to get away from Jim. I parted ways as politely as I could and made my way through the crowd.

"What's going on?" I asked Rette when I reached her table.

"It's Jen. She just slammed two drinks in a row, and I think she'd been drinking before she came. She can hold her liquor pretty well, but I think we need to get her out of here before she does something she's going to regret. Something that we're going to regret, for that matter."

"Is she upset about something?"

"She'd planned on coming here with Tom, but then he gave her some excuse about not wanting to go public with the whole interoffice romance thing, and she wasn't sure if she should ask Mike in case that would mess things up with Tom, as if that relationship wasn't already in shambles, but . . ."

I waited for Rette to continue, but when I looked to see what she was looking at, I understood why she shut up so quickly. Jen was walking toward us. She looked beautiful in a backless black dress. Her red hair was swept up in a dramatic, complicated style. She was a little unsteady, but I wasn't sure if it was from the preposterously high heels or from having a drink or five too many. I was so focused on Jen, it took me a moment to notice someone was walking beside her. I caught my breath, unable to move.

"Hey girls, look who's here," Jen said, slurring her words. "Dan, I don' think you've met my sister, Rette, yet. She started workin' in our editorial department a couple'mosago. And you remember Avery. Of course, you may know her better as Dancinfool."

Dan looked confused, then nervous.

"Rette, would you mind coming with me for a second?" Jen said.

Rette looked at me, slightly panicked. I was too stunned to send out a "Please don't go!" signal, and she and Jen left Dan and me alone. At that moment, I hated Jen. Why had I ever confided in her?

"I think I missed something," Dan said with a forced laugh. "I'm confused."

All of my feelings of hurt and disappointment turned into anger. "I'm Dancinfool, Dan. I'm the one who's been e-mailing you these last few months. When you sent your picture, and we learned who you were," my voice faltered, "we wanted to know just how far you'd take it— we were looking out for Lydia—so we sent Rette in my place."

"You didn't say anything to Lydia, did you?"

What a weasel. "No, Dan."

"I didn't mean anything by it. I didn't mean to cheat on her. It got out of hand. I would get lonely sometimes when she was on the road, and I just wanted someone to talk to."

My face grew hot with anger. I knew that Lydia hadn't been traveling as much in the past three months since Dan and I had started e-mailing each other, but even if she had—what kind of excuse was that?

"I mean nobody got hurt, right?" Dan's childish whine grated my nerves.

"No, Dan, somebody did get hurt. When I responded to a stranger's personal ad, I knew that I had to be careful, but somehow, I don't know, you managed to hurt me anyway. Watching you lie to your wife, watching you lie to me . . . God, when I think about how many personal things I told you about myself, I mean, it's just humiliating. I know you think these past few months have been harmless fun, but I think your behavior has been vile."

I strode off in a fury. I didn't know whether I felt like crying or screaming. I nearly knocked Les over I was so blind with rage.

"God, Les, I'm so sorry."

"I'm fine. Are you okay?"

I straightened up and saw that Tom was standing next to Les.

"I—not really, I just bumped into Dan." I was just about to say that I was going to call it a night when Jen stumbled drunkenly toward us.

"You told him, didn' you?" Jen said to Les. She turned to Tom. "Tha's why you haven' called, isn' it? Les told you we slept together, but it was before you and I were goin' out. I was drunk, I was going through a rough time . . ."

"You slept with Les?" Tom said.

"You slept with Jen?" I said to Les.

"Are you a nymphomaniac or something?" Tom asked. "Is there anyone you won't sleep with?"

At once, I was annoyed with Les, sad for Jen, and mad at Tom.

Then Jen said, much too loudly, "I'm not a nymphomaniac!" Then she ran crying into the bathroom. I ran after her.

Mary from marketing was in the bathroom touching up her makeup. Jen and I stumbled past her. Jen pushed open a stall door and vomited into the toilet. I pushed my way in after her, closing the door behind me.

"It's okay, Jen," I said.

"No, it's not okay, I really like Tom and I blew it."

"No, Jen, you don't really like him. If you did, you wouldn't be dating Mike. Obviously neither of them is right for you."

"I don' wanna be alone. I've never been alone before."

"You're a strong woman; you're going to be fine. Hang on a second." I opened the stall door and peeked out. I caught Mary looking directly at me. "Would you mind leaving us alone?" I asked nicely.

Her eyebrows rose, and she made this *eh* sound that indicated how very rude she thought me and how very put-out she felt, but she packed up her makeup and left.

I turned back to Jen. "When did you sleep with Les?" I asked.

"That night at Rios. Drank too much. He drove me home. I was lonely. I don' remember anything."

With that, she retched violently again into the toilet.

When she was done, she rested her head on her arm on the toilet seat. She stayed there quietly for several minutes. I thought she'd passed out, but then she said, "I miss him. I really miss him." It took me a second to figure out that "him" was Dave. Tears slid down her cheeks and in moments she was weeping in choking sobs that sounded so sad, so plaintive, I wanted to cry, too. "I know he wasn't good for me, but the way I felt about him was so strong, so intense. We didn't always have good times, but the good times were really, really good, you know? What if I never feel like that with anyone else again?"

I didn't have an answer for her. I just rubbed her back as she cried, feeling helpless to help her. Then I thought about Les. I couldn't believe what he'd done. He'd never struck me as the kind of guy who would take advantage of a woman who'd had too much to drink.

After a while, Jen's tears softened to a dull moan, and I finally noticed the disgusting stench of vomit and urine. I picked Jen off the floor. "Come on, let's get you home. We'll get a cab." Jen nodded and tried to compose herself the best she could. She put her arm around me, and together, we walked awkwardly toward the entrance. Les was waiting outside the women's room for us.

"I'll grab my car," he said.

"I think you've done enough," I said.

But as I supported her right side, he took her left, and together, we managed to get her ambulatory enough to make it down the corridor to the parking lot.

When we got to the entrance, Les said, "I'll pull around. I'll just be a second."

I was furious with Les, but I couldn't very well stand there all night with Jen hanging on me, hoping a taxi would happen by, so, when Les pulled up, I reluctantly helped Jen in and climbed into the backseat myself.

It was a short drive to Jen's apartment, and I insisted that Les stay in the car while I helped her get to bed. I lingered after helping Jen to bed, but finally I couldn't avoid Les any longer.

He was waiting in the driveway. I slammed the passenger side door behind me. "Well, it looks like Jen is dating one less guy," I said, not looking at him. "Now's your opportunity."

"Jen isn't the woman I want," he said softly into his lap.

"Oh really, who is your latest object of affection?"

"You."

It wasn't until he said it that I realized it was the answer I was looking for.

JEN

How to Make a Total Ass of Yourself and Destroy Your Career at the Same Time

If there is a better way to shoot your career in the foot than getting wildly drunk at an office Christmas party, I'd sure like to know about it. No, better not. I'm sure I'd try that, too. If it's something that can damage my career and utterly humiliate me, I can't seem to help myself, I have to do it.

Blackouts can be blessed things. All I remember of that cursed night are two images. In the first, I'm yelling at Les for telling Tom about how we'd slept together, and in the second, I'm draped over a toilet bowl and Avery is comforting me. Those brief frozen snapshots were all I remember of the entire night. I chose to believe that no other coworkers saw me in my inebriated state, nor did anyone hear my unfortunate confessions. Thus, by process of elimination, the only people I could never face again were Les, Tom, and Avery.

It was cruel and unfortunate that the holiday party had been on a weekday. It meant I had to go into the office the next day, pretending to be conscious while try-

ing to recover from my losing battle with the shot glass
the night before.

I didn't eat anything for fear of continuing my all-
night puke marathon, but I was so exhausted I did
something drastic: On my way to work I stopped and
bought a nonfat double latte. I'd only had coffee once
before, and I thought it tasted like nuclear waste. I put
in three packages of Sweet'n Low and it still tasted rancid, but I sucked it down as penance.

When I got to work, I walked down the hallway to my
office as fast as I could. I expected my coworkers to
make snide comments, but they just smiled as if nothing
unusual had happened the night before. Maybe only a
couple people saw me and my little alcohol-induced
temper tantrum.

Then I saw Mary. "Well, looks like you had fun last
night! Feeling better? You were a riot!"

I smiled. Evil, evil, vile, cellulite-ridden bitch. May you
get premature crow's-feet and may your husband go
bald and impotent before he turns thirty.

"I'm fine," I mumbled, continuing on to my office. I
collapsed into my chair, booted up my computer, put
my fingers on my keyboard and pointed my closed eyes
in the direction of the computer screen to make it look
like I was working while I napped.

"How are you doing?" Avery asked. I was extremely
relieved to know Avery was still talking to me. It meant I
couldn't have been *that* bad the night before.

"I feel like rat shit. Don't tell me anything I did last
night. I don't want to know."

"I'm here for you if you want to talk about anything."

"Thanks, Avery, I'll be okay."

I spent my day trying to avoid Tom and push memories of the night before out of my head. The image of
me yelling at Les, Tom's disgust, and Les's expression of

surprise and guilt kept popping into my mind. I groaned in embarrassment at the memory.

I could never face Tom again.

The stress of the Expert account splintered through the office. Just about everybody was rescheduling the days they'd planned to take off for the holidays. Everyone was putting in such long hours, no one had time to Christmas shop or decorate for the holidays. Tempers were short and the tension was a palpable buzz of negative energy.

Sharon let us know, in no uncertain terms, that we were expected to be in the office over the weekend to catch up on the Expert reports.

Saturday came and I dragged myself into the office, simmering with bitterness and self-pity. I spent a good portion of my day drawing stick figures of a very pregnant Lydia, the vile salesperson who sold all this to Expert and promised such unreasonable deadlines. There was exploding Lydia; Lydia impaled by a Zulu's spear; ebola Lydia, in which I did a particularly nice job rendering realistic oozing wounds; and AIDS Lydia, complete with lesions.

Despite all of my doodling, Avery and I did manage to get quite a bit of work done. By the end of the day, we were exhausted, the good kind of exhaustion you feel when you work hard and actually have something to show for it.

We got right back to work early Monday morning. At noon, Sharon and Morgan came into our office with the first draft of the report we'd sent to Morgan the week before for approval. Right away, Morgan began talking excitedly. "This report," he said, brandishing the draft we'd given him, "just isn't acceptable. It's like any other research report. We're not just any market research company, we're McKenna Marketing. We need to go the extra mile. I had an idea about how we can stand out. I spoke with Jack Webb from Expert this morning and he loves the idea. We're going to give them more than just statistics and numbers. We are going to give them qualitative data as well as quantitative so the reports read like a story."

"A story about the features people want in their dishwashers?" I asked, trying to keep the sarcasm out of my voice.

"Morgan," Avery said, "we've been working on these reports for weeks. The teleresearchers' questions were geared to gather quantifiable data. We do have some qualitative comments, and we've incorporated those into our reports, but primarily our data are quantitative. Even if we had the data we needed . . . I'm concerned that if we make such a drastic change so late in the game we may not be able to meet our deadline."

"We can do it and we will do it," Morgan said.

What I wanted to know was, what exactly was he doing that permitted him to include himself in "we." Avery and I, the teleresearchers, the programmers, and the marketing department were doing all the work; I don't remember him doing squat.

"It's imperative that all deadlines are met. There's never an excuse to miss a deadline," Morgan continued. "We need to go the extra mile to give them the product they deserve. The deadline is December thirty-first. It's not a suggestion. The final product needs to be on their desk before the end of the year. That's what we've promised, and we're not going to go back on our word. Nothing else is acceptable."

Sharon nodded in agreement.

Morgan launched into one of his "pep talks" about going the extra mile, which only succeeded in making me more bitter. When he left, I angrily began scribbling versions of malignant carcinoma Morgan and leper Morgan and torture chamber-victim Morgan.

While I doodled, Avery said, "He just negated weeks' worth of our work. Just about everything we've done for the last month, all of the hours of overtime, everything has just been scrapped."

"Wait a minute," I said, pausing mid-doodle and looking at Avery over my rendition of skin-cancer Morgan, "are you saying I worked on a Saturday for nothing?" I was glad I hadn't worked very hard until just the past couple weeks. At least I didn't have as much work to throw away.

"When you make huge changes at the last minute like this, you're just asking for mistakes and an inferior product," Avery said. "The *research* on the dishwashers isn't even close to finished. There's no way we can even do the reports by the eighteenth, let alone get them to editing so they can get them to the printers, by"—she tore through the papers on her desk to find the sheet that contained all the deadlines—"oh my goodness, the twenty-first. What about Christmas? How will the printers be able to finish them all by the thirty-first?"

"The printer is charging us extra, so it's worth it to them to put in the hours over the holidays."

"Worth it to whom? The boss or the people who actually have to work instead of spending time with their families?" Avery said.

"They probably get overtime so maybe they don't mind," I said, without conviction.

Avery and I spent the next several minutes trying to figure out how we could possibly get this all done by the twenty-first. We decided to try not to show Morgan anything until the last second so he wouldn't be able to make any more "suggestions." We'd give him everything at once so he couldn't go through any one report too closely. We divided up work: Avery was the better writer, so she would do the introductions and tell "The story." I would work on the graphs and data that supported "The story."

If we worked twenty-four hours a day, we still couldn't get everything finished, especially since the research on the dishwashers wasn't even close to done. Avery asked the teleresearchers when they would be finished with the calls, and they said that if a miracle happened, they might be able to get through the calls by the end of January.

"We're either going to have to convince Morgan it can't be done—I mean getting them one section of the report at a different time than the others shouldn't be a big deal," Avery said.

"Or?" I asked.

"Or, we're going to have to make up information," she said in a whisper.

Our office was silent except for the perpetual background buzz of typing and talking from other offices. "We'll deal with that later," I said. "We'll just get done what we can get done and the teleresearchers will get done what they can get done."

She nodded, as if we'd made a good plan.

RETTE

'Tis the Season

Monday morning my period arrived three days too soon. I had to be a tampon mooch. I hated that. When I asked Eleanore if I could bum a tampon, she was kind enough to let me know that *she* was *always* prepared.

I took a couple of Advil for my cramps. I'd heard that in places like Africa where women got enough exercise and didn't consume caffeine or chocolate or artificial flavors, the symptoms of PMS didn't exist. But was avoiding cramps really worth forgoing chocolate? Why not drink coffee and eat chocolate and simply pop a Midol? This was the kind of thinking that made America great. Why deny yourself when you could simply create a product that mimicked health while still enjoying all that your heart desired?

And can we talk about bloat? I'd forgotten what a landmine of fattening foods the office was around Christmas. For the entire month of December, there were chocolates and baked goods around every corner. I tried to be strong, but for every few brownies or cookies

I successfully avoided, there was a baked delight I absolutely had to try.

As if my day weren't heinous enough, I had to go Christmas shopping amidst mobs of rabid consumers. Every year I put off Christmas shopping in hopes I would mysteriously come across some money with which to buy gifts, which of course never happened. Plus, I had to spend a ton of money because I needed Mom and Jen to think that I was better off financially than I was.

Dad was both impossible to shop for and easy to shop for. Impossible because I could never think of something that was just right—something interesting and original that he would love. But he was easy to shop for because he was equally unexcited by any gift anyone got him.

Mom was a challenge, even though I knew what she liked. She liked expensive clothes and expensive jewelry and a lot of it. Jen also liked expensive stuff. Both Mom and Jen always bought themselves whatever they wanted. It was difficult to buy gifts for people who liberally pampered themselves. Getting Mom a day at the spa for a manicure, pedicure, facial, and massage would have been a good gift if she didn't spend one day every other week doing exactly that.

Greg was the hardest of all to shop for. I could get him books and CDs and cologne and a watch and some new shirts (which he desperately needed), but I couldn't think of something original, something he would love but wouldn't buy for himself. And I only had a single weekend to get inspired.

Avery was easy. I got her some handmade candles from a local artist, a framed picture of me and her from her Halloween party, and a book of poems by Adrienne Rich. She was the only person whose gifts I was excited about. For everyone else, I bought uninspired gifts just to have something for them to unwrap.

I got home from the mall tired, hungry, and depressed.

"How'd shopping go?" Greg asked.

"Don't ask. I'm only halfway done and I've already spent three hundred dollars, and I'm not particularly excited about anything I got anyone." I still had to buy a tree and decorations and enough groceries and liquor for five people for four days of festive overeating and drinking.

"Maybe this isn't the right time to ask you," Greg said.

"Oh god, what?"

"Well, I was wondering if you might be able to pick up something for my parents and brother. I'll give you the money of course."

"Why can't you go out and buy their gifts? You're out of school for three weeks, I work full time."

"It's not like I'm sitting around. I have a lot of reading to do, and I have an incomplete to finish. I figured if you had more shopping to do, what's the big deal with picking up a couple more things? If I pay and you buy, then the gifts will be from both of us."

"What do you want me to get them?"

"Whatever. I don't know. Get my parents a juice maker and Sean a beer maker. A beverage theme."

"You need to pay me cash. I'm not putting anything else on this credit card." I refused to even look at how much interest I was being charged each month. I couldn't believe I had become one of *them*: a typical American with revolving debt. I'd been living paycheck to paycheck; then suddenly I needed to put in several hundred dollars worth of work on my car, and then there was my four-month bout of unemployment, and then along came Christmas—and well, there I was. Paying sky-high interest rates and falling victim to inescapable debt.

* * *

I shopped all weekend. What an evil, evil holiday. I'd been suppressing my inner capitalist for months. I hadn't bought myself new clothes, new books, new CDs, nothing, not the smallest treat for myself since we'd moved to Colorado in June. Now I was overcome with desire. I wanted jewelry, makeup, pajamas, bras, underwear, and new shoes. I wanted new outfits for work and more clothes for hanging out at home. I wanted expensive face creams and facial cleansing systems. I wanted dishes, bath towels, wineglasses, candles, and decorations for the house. I had a good reason to look at my clothes, my home, and myself with a critical eye: My mother was coming for a visit.

Mom of the never-chipped nails and always-immaculate home. I wasn't looking forward to her seeing my cramped apartment. I was twenty-seven with a college degree and still had chipped, mismatched dishes and ancient Goodwill furniture. Sure, Greg and I were just starting out, and when Mom and Dad were starting out they were broke, too, but by the time they were my age they had two cars, a house, two kids, and took a vacation every year. They didn't lollygag about through their twenties deciding which poorly paid occupation they wanted to try out. They just earned and saved and stayed at the same miserable job accruing benefits year after year.

I blamed them for my misery. They were the ones who led me to believe if I worked hard and got good grades I'd grow up to get a rewarding job that paid enough that I could go out to a movie every now and then without breaking the bank.

All morning I looked forward to lunch, even though my lunch consisted of a Weight Watchers frozen dinner. I started every day with the best of intentions, then by about 5:30, I felt so deprived I spent the rest of my day making up for it—lavishly.

Paige was ahead of me in the line for the microwave. "Mine will be done in thirty seconds," she said.

"No problem."

Eleanore burst into the lunch kitchen, all smiles. "I just got my hair touched up." Her voice was as welcome as the shrill of an alarm clock in the middle of a deep sleep.

I nodded but said nothing.

"It's so funny," Eleanore said, "because as I've gotten older I've watched all my friends' hair get lighter and lighter. But I was already blond, so it's not that big a change for me."

Paige said quietly, "I was thinking of getting my hair dyed the color of Margarette's hair. What do you think? I think your hair is gorgeous, Margarette. I read somewhere that tons of women are dying their hair to get the shade of red you have naturally."

Eleanore offered what was probably supposed to be a smile but looked more like the expression of someone charged with changing a particularly rancid diaper. "I'm sure that would be lovely," she said. Eleanore got her Tupperware dish out of the refrigerator, and with a curt nod, exited the kitchen.

At once, my mood improved considerably. I didn't even bother to hide my smile.

AVERY

The Bullshit Hits the Fan

Sharon never got back to me about my request to pursue new challenges. Instead, Monday morning, the first e-mail I read had the subject line "Congratulations, Jen!" It was sent from Sharon to the entire office, and it announced that Jen would be the interim manager while Sharon was on maternity leave.

I called Les's extension and asked him if he could meet me outside by the picnic table.

I slipped on my coat and went outside to wait for him. I didn't know how to handle his declaration of love for me, so I decided to ignore it. I hoped he wouldn't bring it up again and everything would be the way it had been between us.

I watched Les come outside and cross over the yard to the bench where I sat.

"What's up?" he asked.

"Did you get the e-mail?"

"What e-mail?"

"Sharon announced today that Jen, who never does any work, gets to take over for Sharon while she's on maternity leave. I can't believe this place." I waited for Les to say something, anything to make me feel better, but he didn't. "So don't you have any reaction?"

"I'm sorry you didn't get the job. You deserved it."

"Les, what's up? Is something wrong?"

"Avery, I can't do this."

"Do what?"

"I can't just pretend I don't have any feelings for you. I just can't be your buddy. This is too painful. I love you, Avery. I've never met anyone like you."

"What are you saying, that we can't be friends anymore?"

"I hope we can be friends again. I just need some space. I can't talk to you or see you for a while. I'm sorry."

"What about our dance lessons? What about yoga?"

"I'm sorry, you'll have to go by yourself. I can't see you for a while." Les walked inside, leaving me alone in the cold.

After work, I came home and made myself a tofu and broccoli stir-fry and listened to the very loud silence of the phone not ringing. I ate dinner, listening to myself crunch. Eight o'clock, nine o'clock, and still no word from Les. He couldn't be serious about not talking to me, could he? For the last month, Les and I had talked on the phone or gotten together every night, often talking for hours at a time. I kept thinking of stuff I wanted to tell him. Plus, I really needed to talk to someone about this Jen thing. I obviously couldn't call Jen or Rette. Mom would listen, but she wouldn't really understand.

I picked up the phone. I set it down again. He would get over me soon enough, right? He'd find someone else and then we could be friends again. Of course if he found someone else, he'd be busy with her all the time, and I'd be in the exact same place I was now.

At a little after noon the next day, I was approaching Pam's office to pick her up for lunch when I heard Mark's sharp voice.

"The deadline was Monday. That was five days ago. We can't wait any longer!"

She said calmly, "Mark, Expert hasn't approved the copy yet."

"It's your job to see that they do."

"I sent it to them three weeks ago. I've followed up three times this week, gently reminding them that the deadline was Monday, but if they don't approve the copy, we can't go live with it. They are the client; if they don't have time to approve it just now, we have to accept that."

"You're just going to have to give me what you've got. We can't wait any longer because you can't meet your deadlines."

"But what if Expert has changes? Won't that just be more work for your programmers to have to put it up and then replace it with new text?" she said calmly.

"Yes, but I don't see that we have any choice."

"Okay, I'll e-mail you what I have. I'll give Expert another call and see if I can impart the urgency of the situation."

Mark stormed out of the office, nearly barreling into me.

I apologized even though it wasn't my fault. He rolled his eyes.

"That sounded fun," I said to Pam.

"He's a little passionate, but at least he cares," she laughed.

"Do you have time for lunch?"

"No, but I never have time for anything. I do need to eat. I've really been looking forward to catching up with you."

We went to a deli nearby. I told her over sandwiches and chips that I'd be interested in moving into her department if there were any openings. I told her I enjoyed writing and reworking the research reports, and I'd love to do something a little more creative like write copy.

"I don't have a ton of experience in writing, but I've been reading up on writing persuasive copy," I said. "I've kept a journal for years. I wrote for my school paper in high school. I know that's not much, but I did enjoy it. And I read a lot."

"I don't have any openings right now, but I'd be happy to give you a shot at writing a brochure. Writing copy isn't easy. Unlike graphic design or computer programming, everybody thinks they can do it, and they're not shy about letting you know their opinions. But if you're serious about it, I think you'd be great."

"I'd love some new challenges. I haven't been doing a very good job of moving up the ladder here, and I don't quite understand what I'm doing wrong. I work hard. I have good people skills. I've been here as long as Sharon has, but she keeps getting promotions so much faster than me."

Pam studied her sandwich. She looked like she felt guilty about something.

"What?" I prodded.

"Of course I didn't work here at the time—" she began, "but I've heard that Morgan's had some concerns about you since you sent a brochure to the printer without his approval? Apparently there were some errors in it, and it turned out to be quite an expensive mistake. He expressed some concerns that maybe you weren't a team player."

"What are you talking about? I never—wait, do you mean the time *Sharon* sent a brochure to the printer without his permission?"

"That's not the way I heard it."

I felt sick to my stomach. Suddenly, it all made sense. Why Sharon had been promoted ahead of me: She'd pinned the brochure debacle on me. For four years, Morgan had thought I'd deliberately thwarted his authority. Morgan rarely had occasion to work with me directly. He spent far more time with Sharon, who could tell him anything she wanted to about me, and obviously did. She could, say, take credit for work that I did. And I let her get away with it.

I spent the afternoon in a daze. When I got home and unlocked the door to my apartment, I paused for a moment, looking at the empty, quiet rooms. I couldn't face another long evening alone.

I had to talk to someone. Les was the only one who would understand. I'd feel better if I could talk to him. But he'd been avoiding me at work.

I missed him. I missed our friendship. I missed talking to him and hanging out with him.

I picked up the phone and dialed his number. I got his voice mail. Was he really not there or was he screening his calls? "Hi Les, it's Avery. I really want to talk to you."

He didn't call back. I went to bed around midnight, but didn't sleep. My spirit felt bruised.

I went to work the next day bleary-eyed and groggy. As soon as I walked in the door, Mary charged toward me, stopping me in my tracks.

"Did you hear?" she asked.

"Hear what?"

"They fired Pam. They're making her take the fall for Expert backing out of us doing their Web site."

"Pam? It wasn't her fault IT was late in development."

"Mark said she was behind on the copy, which delayed the rest."

"But Mark could have done the initial specs and storyboards without the copy . . ."

"I saw Pam with her box of stuff going down the elevator," Mary interrupted. "It was so awkward. I just wanted to die. It's so sad, isn't it?" she said, not looking at all upset about it. "I guess that's the way it goes sometimes."

JEN

I'll Drink to That

Mike wanted to take me out to celebrate, but the prospect of spending the night with him was about as desirable as getting my clitoris pierced. (What is that *about* anyway?)

Anyway, I had a bajillion presents to wrap. I got a quart of light eggnog and a bottle of rum and spread the presents, wrapping paper, tape, scissors, and ribbons out in front of me. To save calories, I poured drinks that were more rum with a splash of eggnog than vice versa, but it was festive nonetheless. I hadn't bothered to do a whole Christmas tree deal, but I did adorn my living room with sparkling lights.

I held my glass up to toast myself. "To more money and new adventures." I drained my glass. Actually, I didn't get a raise right away, but it would come. I did have more power at least. I could see myself as a managerial dominatrix: "Get that report on my desk by five!" *Whitcha!* My whip would crack across their desks.

The phone rang. I looked at the clock. 9:45. "Hello?"

"Hey, babe, how are you?"

For a moment, I wasn't sure who it was. I knew it wasn't Mike, and I didn't think it was Tom. Then I knew: Dave.

"I'm good. How are you?"

"I miss you."

My heart didn't race. In fact, I felt a little annoyed. I knew exactly how this was going to go: He'd ask to come over, we'd have sex, and then he'd leave and I wouldn't hear from him again for weeks. "Guess what? I got a promotion."

"Congratulations. That's great. Can I come over? I'll bring champagne, we can celebrate."

"No, Dave, you can't come over."

"Are you busy? Is someone there?"

"I am busy, but that's not why you can't come over. We've been broken up for almost five months now. You can't call me whenever you get horny and expect me to do cartwheels over the chance to see you."

"Jesus, what's up your ass? If you don't want to see me that's cool, you don't have to be all bitchy about it. Merry fucking Christmas." With that, he hung up. Hung up! On me. What a jackass.

But whatever, it had taken me five years, but he was out of my life now, and that was the important thing.

The phone rang again, and I figured it was Dave calling back to say something bitchy, so I let the machine pick it up.

"Hey Jen, I heard the good news! Congratulations!" It was Rette.

I picked up. "Thanks!"

"Oh, hi. So, I hear you'll be the big woman on campus while Sharon is gone. I'm so happy for you. You deserve it. You worked hard for it."

"Thanks. I'm excited. It feels good."

"Are you drinking?"

"I'm celebrating."

"By yourself?"

"Yeah. So?"

She didn't say anything.

"So do you have a point or what?" I said.

"I just—when's the last time you went a night without drinking?"

I thought for a second. I couldn't remember. "I don't know."

"Jen, I'm worried you might have a problem."

"What do you mean?"

"I mean I think you may be an alcoholic."

"What the fuck? God, can't you just be happy for me? Are you so jealous of me that you have to insult me like that? God, you are such a buzzkill."

"Jen, I'm very happy for you. I'm just worried about you. You've been drinking so much lately. Alcoholism runs in the family, you know."

"Nobody in our family is an alcoholic."

"Except Mom and her father, Grandpa Bob."

"What? What are you talking about?"

"I've been worried about Mom's drinking since high school, so in college I did a report on alcoholism to learn more about it. I did a lot of reading and research and interviewed a rehab counselor. I asked him whether someone who comes home every night and promptly makes a martini and then two or three more and spends every night in a hazy blur of alcohol was an alcoholic, and he said yes. He said the person is a high-functioning alcoholic, which means they can hold down a job—often a high-status one—and they can get wasted every night but still keep things together enough to keep their job and family and a house—at least for a while, unless things get worse. I also asked Mom if anyone in our extended family drank too much, and she said her dad was a raging alcoholic. He got four DUIs back in the days when you could rack up DUIs like trophies and never spend a day in jail."

"Huh. Well whatever. I'm fine, Rette. I've just been going through some tough times. I know I've been drinking too much, but I'll stop. Why did I never notice that Mom had a problem?"

"I don't know, maybe because you're a self-absorbed bitch?"

"Oh yeah, right. So, did you ever confront Mom?"

"Yeah. She nearly tore my head off, telling me to mind my own business and that I should concentrate on my own problems and take a look in the mirror and lose thirty pounds—those were her exact words. It was a fun night altogether."

"So you thought you'd piss me off too?"

"What am I going to do? Watch my little sister drink herself into the grave? You're a pain in the ass, but you're the only sister I've got."

I knew Rette was right that I'd been drinking too much, but I'd deal with it just like I dealt with my weight: I'd just be stricter with myself. I'd never have more than a drink or two at a time.

Even though Sharon hadn't left yet, work was already a lot more stressful. Sharon was giving me all her work, and I was already too busy to get my own done.

I left the office at seven, too late to catch a Tae Bo class. I got home from work full of restless energy. I paced around the room feeling wired and edgy.

I called Rette and Avery, and they agreed to meet me at the Mountain Sun for some dinner. It was kind of a granola place, but they had great—oh shit, they had great beer.

It's fine, it's okay, I could go there and not order a beer.

Forty-five minutes later, when the waiter came and asked if we wanted anything to drink I think, *I don't want any skanky tap water, I'll get a beer, but just one. I'll nurse it for the whole night.* Rette gave me a look. I ignored her.

"I am so bored," I said to Rette and Avery after the waiter, a skinny white guy with a scruffy beard and Rastafarian dreadlocks halfway down his back, left. "I just don't know what to do with myself without Dave. When I was living with Dave, we were always going out, going to the bars to play pool or darts or hanging out with friends. We were always having people over or going to our friends' places. I've just never faced all these empty nights by myself before."

"Can't you still hang out with those friends?" Avery asked.

"I lost them in the breakup. They were mostly Dave's friends from when he worked as a ski instructor or bartender. I never really made my own friends here."

"Maybe you can join a book club or a pottery class," Avery offered.

"A book club? Pottery? Yeah, that'd be a big no."

The waiter brought our food. Rette had a veggie burrito. Avery had a vegetable sandwich, and I had a salad with light Italian dressing.

"I'm having a thirty-and-a-half crises," Avery said.

"Say what?" I said.

"When I turned thirty, everyone asked me if I was upset about it, and I wasn't. Everyone said they had their crises at thirty-one or thirty-five or forty or whatever, as if a crisis were inevitable. They weren't happy with the way their lives were going, and whatever birthday they were having during this tumultuous time in their life was just this milestone that made them stop and reflect on their lives, and that's what brought on the crisis. Well, yesterday it was my half birthday, and I realized that I failed in my dream of being a dancer, my dream marriage was a disaster, and in general my life is a huge flop."

"Avery, I think you've been hanging out with me and Jen too much. You've become a total downer," Rette said.

"I just don't understand these feelings I'm feeling," Avery said.

"It's called depression. You're just not used to it, but I know all about it," Rette said. "Still, your melancholy is like my ecstatically happy."

I went to take a sip of my beer and realized it was empty. Shit. How'd that happen? Where was the waiter? What was I supposed to do, die of thirst?

I tried to concentrate on the conversation, but I was dying for another beer. Finally the waiter came back and asked if I wanted a refill.

"Yeah, please."

"Avery, just a couple weeks ago you were telling me that I had my whole life ahead of me and I could do whatever I wanted with my life. Hello? Sound familiar?" Rette said.

"Yes, but the thing is, how can I do whatever I want with my life when I don't know what it is I want to do?"

As promised, I limited myself to two beers, but by the time we were done talking, the nice buzz I had worked up was wearing off. I was starting to feel edgy again. I stopped at the liquor store for a pint of Absolut Citron, but not to get drunk or anything; I just needed a little help falling asleep.

I woke up the next morning with an excruciating hangover. How did I get from promising not to have anything to drink to waking to a blinding hangover?

When I got to work, this e-mail was the first thing I saw:

> To: *JOlsen@mckennamarketing.com*
> From: *MOlsen@mckennamarketing.com*
> Subject: *Favor*
> *Take this test, for me. Please?*

She sent me a link to a Web page. I had an idea what it was about, so I didn't click on it right away. I decided to wait until Avery went to work out. She and Les had been going to this Bikram yoga class deal three days a week. Les wasn't talking to her anymore, but she still went to the class alone. It started at 11:00 and went till 12:30, but with showering and driving back from the gym, she didn't get back until 1:00. It was really strange for her to take two-hour lunches. I think maybe she was mad at the company about something, maybe about working so hard for so long for slave wages or something like that.

When Avery left for class, I opened up Rette's e-mail and clicked through to the page, which was titled, "Am I an alcoholic?" It contained the Michigan Alcoholism Screening Test.

> 1. *Do you feel you are a normal drinker? (By "normal," we mean you drink less than or as much as most other people.) (No, 2 points.)*
>   Yes.
> 2. *Have you ever awakened the morning after some drinking the night before and found that you could not remember a part of the evening? (Yes, 2 points)*
>   Well, duh, yes, everyone had. But I took a piece of paper and marked down 2 anyway.
> 3. *Does your wife, husband, parent, or other near relative ever worry or complain about your drinking? (Yes, 1 point)*

Yes, my stupid sister did, which was why I was taking this stupid test. 1

4. *Can you stop drinking without a struggle after one or two drinks?* *(No, 2 points)*

I thought about last night at the Mountain Sun. Maybe not. 2

5. *Do you ever feel guilty about your drinking?* *(Yes, 1 point)*

I've felt guilty about things I've done while drinking—like Les—but not about drinking itself. I didn't mark anything down.

6. *Do friends or relatives think you are a normal drinker?* *(No, 2 points)*

Well, Rette didn't, but she's only one person, and a total lunatic clearly. I marked down just 1. This was definitely not as much fun as taking the "Is he hot for you?" or "Will it last forever?" tests in *Glamour* or *Cosmopolitan*, that was for damn sure.

7. *Are you able to stop drinking when you want to?* *(No, 2 points)*

This was totally cheating—they asked this same thing in question 4! Whatever. 2

8. *Have you ever attended a meeting of Alcoholics Anonymous?* *(Yes, 5 points)*

No.

9. *Have you ever gotten into physical fights when drinking?* *(Yes, 1 point)*

No.

10. *Has drinking ever created problems between you and your wife, husband, parent, or other near relative?* *(Yes, 2 points)*

No—wait, what about all those fights Dave and I had when we'd been drinking? But we fought all the time. And we drank all the time. Who knows which led to the other? I marked down 1, 'cuz that seemed like the fairest answer.

11. *Has your wife, husband, parent, or other near relative ever gone to anyone for help about your drinking? (Yes, 2 points)*

   Not that I knew of.

12. *Have you ever lost friends, girlfriends, or boyfriends because of your drinking? (Yes, 2 points)*

   No. Well, there was the Christmas party, and Tom hadn't spoken to me since my drunken confession . . . I gave myself 1 out of 2 again.

13. *Have you ever gotten into trouble at work because of your drinking? (Yes, 2 points)*

   If holiday parties count, which they shouldn't, since everyone gets wasted there, then yes. 2

14. *Have you ever lost a job because of drinking? (Yes, 2 points)*

   No.

15. *Have you ever neglected your obligations, your family, or your work for two or more days in a row because you were drinking? (Yes, 2 points)*

   No.

16. *Do you drink before noon fairly often? (Yes, 1 point)*

   No.

17. *Have you ever been told you have liver trouble? Cirrhosis? (Yes, 2 points)*

   No.

18. *After heavy drinking, have your ever had delirium tremens (DTs) or severe shaking or heard voices or seen things that weren't really there? (Yes, 2 points)*

   No. Woo-hoo, I'm totally going to ace this thing! Take that, Rette!

19. *Have you ever gone to anyone for help about your drinking? (Yes, 2 points)*

   No.

20. *Have you ever been in a hospital because of drinking? (Yes, 5 points)*

   No.

21. *Have you ever been a patient in a psychiatric hospital or on a psychiatric ward of a general hospital where drinking was part of the problem that resulted in hospitalization? (Yes, 2 points)*
No.

22. *Have you ever been at a psychiatric or mental health clinic or gone to any doctor, social worker, or clergy for help with any emotional problem, where drinking was part of the problem? (Yes, 2 points)*
No.

23. *Have you ever been arrested for drunken driving, driving while intoxicated, or driving under the influence of alcoholic beverages? (Yes, 2 points)*
No.

24. *Have you ever been arrested, even for a few hours because of other drunken behavior? (Yes, 2 points)*
No.

I added up my points—12—and clicked the NEXT button on the screen to get to the part where they told me what it all meant. I guessed it would probably tell me that I'd been drinking a wee bit much lately, but I was totally fine, and one day soon I'd get a husband and have kids and stop my—totally normal for my age and marital status—partying ways.

"Scoring: Add up the points from your answers. A total score of 0-3 points indicates no alcoholism; 4 points is suggestive of alcoholism; and 5 points or more indicates alcoholism."

What the hell! That's the harshest grading ever! This is worse than high school. Where's the curve? Where's the extra credit opportunities?

I went back through my answers, and marked off all the ones that I so generously awarded 1 out of 2 points to. I was still at 9, which, according to this totally biased and bullshit test, still put me well into the category of flaming alcoholic, but it was all total crap. I didn't buy it for a second.

On the way home from work that night, I stopped off at the liquor store to buy a bottle of wine to prove that I could easily have just one glass of wine with dinner like anybody. A glass or two of red wine was supposed to be good for you; it cleared your heart out or something like that.

At home, I poured myself a glass of wine and tried to figure out what I wanted to eat. I had no food in the house except some frozen broccoli and a can of tomato soup. That did not sound like a yummy dinner. I decided I'd fill up on one more glass of wine—one or two glasses were totally fine.

I sat on the couch, flicked the TV on, and changed the channels until I got to some show that didn't look totally horrible. I felt restless, anxious. Why was I not experiencing that relaxed feeling I normally felt after a couple of glasses of wine?

I probably hadn't poured enough in the glasses, I probably hadn't really had two full servings yet. I'd pour just a little bit more, just to get me to the standard two-glass size.

I filled up my glass halfway and returned to the couch. It was Friday night, and I was home alone watching TV. How could I possibly be home all alone on a Friday night? I wished I were still in Minnesota, where all my girlfriends from high school and college still were. I could be out with them right now if I hadn't followed stupid Dave out here to Colorado.

Although maybe that wasn't exactly true. Would things really be different if I were still in Minnesota? Jill and Wendy were married. Traci was engaged. Laurie and

Deb lived with guys, and even Liz was dating someone seriously. None of them would be free to go out; they'd all be with their men. At best all I could do would be to elbow my way into their plans for the evening as some pathetic third wheel. I was the only twenty-five-year-old on the entire planet who didn't have a significant other.

Why didn't I feel relaxed? If anything, I felt more wound up. My heart was racing. It was probably because I'd only had two glasses of wine. Wasn't that why it's called a "pick me up"? The first couple glasses actually make you feel more awake. I just needed one more glass, and then I'd feel relaxed. I poured myself one more glass, and suddenly somehow the bottle was empty. That was weird, weren't there normally like five glasses per bottle? It must have been smaller than usual. I stole a glance at the clock. I'd been home for an hour.

Houston, We Have a Problem

I slept fitfully, on and off through the night. In those horrible moments when I was sort of awake, I wanted to die. My head felt like someone has drilled thick steel bolts through either temple.

I got out of bed and staggered to the kitchen, clutching my head with both hands. I poured myself an enormous glass of water and noticed the empty bottle of wine. *Wait, I thought I was just going to have a glass or two, how did it get empty? Whatever, I'll worry about it later; right now, I need more sleep.*

I stayed in bed, sleeping on and off, until three o'clock in the afternoon. Yeah, this was exactly how I wanted to spend my Saturday. I'd wanted to get groceries and do laundry and clean the house. I wanted to spend hours working out at the gym and looking adorable until some great guy asked me out.

Was it possible that maybe I did have a teensy problem? There was probably some medication that a doctor could prescribe, some herbal treatment or something to help. Take three vitamin C, do an Indian rain dance, and call me in the morning—you'll never drink too much again.

I called Rette. "Hey, if I did have a problem with alcohol, which I don't, how is it treated? Is there medication for it?"

"No."

"What do you mean no?"

"I mean there's Antabuse, which makes you throw up if you drink alcohol, but doesn't change the fundamental problem. The only treatment is to stop drinking."

"What do you mean to 'stop drinking'? You mean like totally stop?"

"Totally stop. Forever."

"Fuck that."

"AA can help."

"Triple fuck that. I'm not going to any AA meeting."

"It's not like you have anything to be ashamed of. Robert Downing Jr., Ben Affleck, Grace Slick—and I mean like a million of some of the greatest writers of our time have struggled with alcohol."

"I'm not struggling. I mean I'm struggling but not with drinking. My life just hasn't been going the way it's supposed to lately."

"Can I come over?"

"No."

"I'm going to come over anyway okay?"

"Whatever."

I hung up the phone. No more drinking *ever*? Was she kidding me? No more margaritas at Rios? No more beers after work at the Oasis? No more wine with dinner? I loved wine with dinner! No more cosmopolitans or martinis or sex on the beach? No more White Russians or Bloody Marys or Mimosas? What kind of life would that even be?

What would this do to my social life? What guy would ever date me if he knew I had a drinking problem? What guy would marry me?

I had been drinking too much, but I could stop. Right? Then again, when was the last day I'd gone without drinking? I drank to celebrate when I had a good day; I drank to console myself when I had a bad day; I drank when I had a day, any day. I drank to relax after work with friends or by myself; I drank when I went out with my friends; I drank when I wanted a romantic evening; I drank when I was home alone and bored and had nothing else to do.

But that was normal. Everyone drank, why did Rette think there was something wrong with me? *Never drink again.* Rette was full of shit.

The buzzer went off. I managed to make it to the intercom and buzz her in. I opened the front door for her and stumbled back to bed.

"Jen?" I heard her close the door behind her. I couldn't call out to her or my head would explode. It was a small place; she'd find me.

"Jen? Are you okay?"

"No, I don't know. Physically I'll be fine." Out of nowhere, tears filled my eyes. I blinked and they rolled down my cheeks. "I don't want to not drink for the rest of my life. I really like drinking. No, I didn't mean it like that . . ."

"I know."

"I don't think that this never drinking again business sounds very fair at all."

"Alcoholism is like diabetes—it has to be treated carefully for the rest of your life."

"At least diabetics get to eat *something.* I'll just have to be stricter with myself. I'll manage it better."

"I have no doubt that you can go for years drinking as you are Jen, but . . ."

"Well, good, then I will."

"But if you keep drinking like this, do you ever think you're going to fall in love, have a good, healthy relationship with a healthy guy? Or is it just going to be years and years of more Daves and Toms?"

"I loved Dave."

"Did you really? You and Dave . . . you guys were drinking so much when you were together and the alcohol created all this drama. I mean, do you think it's possible that you mistook that drama for passion? Alcoholics tend to choose to be with other alcoholics. You and Dave never thought your drinking was excessive because both of you and all your friends drank like crazy."

That last thing she said sort of struck a chord. It was true that Avery, Rette, the people from work, Mike, none of them drank nearly as much as Dave and I did or the couples Dave and I hung out with when we were still together. Even Tom—he drank a lot, but compared to Dave he was a lightweight.

"How do you know all this?"

"I wrote a paper on this, I told you. It was a sixty-page paper. I got an *A* on it."

"Of course you did." I rolled my eyes.

"Here's the thing. You can spend the next thirty years of your life half awake in a fog of alcohol and hangovers like Mom does . . . although actually, Jen, I think your problem has already gone way past Mom's. She spends every night tipsy, but I don't know that I've ever seen her drunk. The way you drink Jen, I wouldn't be surprised if you died in a few years from a drunk-driving accident or I don't know, Senator George McGovern's daughter, she battled with alcohol all her life and when she was forty-five or so, she wandered out into the winter cold drunk and died of exposure."

"I don't want to die when I'm forty-five," I said. "But I don't want to not be able to drink either. Rette, I'm the fun one. I'm the party animal. Who am I going to be if I'm not Jen the Party Girl? Who am I going to be? I'm always the first person invited to every party. They can always count on me to make things fun."

"Jen, you're totally insane when you're sober. You have nothing to worry about there. You've been the life of the party since you were three. I remember at some Christmas party Mom and Dad had, you were two or three at the time, and you were in the center of the room screaming, 'jingle bell, jingle bell, jingle bell rock' into your thumb, like your thumb was a microphone. You looked so adorable and everyone was smiling and oh-how-cute-ing, and I just hid in the corner feeling like a lump."

"You were always getting the good grades and being little Ms. Perfect."

"Yeah, but Mom didn't care, she always liked you more."

"She always liked *you* more." At this, we both cracked up. Then I started crying again and Rette started crying, too, and in about eleven seconds it was a great big snot and tears festival.

"How come you're not an alcoholic?" I sniffed.

"I don't know; it's possible that I may be. It hits people at different times. Some people don't show any signs until they turn sixty, and then they drink themselves into the grave within a couple of years. Alcoholism is genetic, but it doesn't mean everyone in a family will be an alcoholic. I have eczema and irritable bowels and tension headaches, and you don't have any of that."

"Thank *god.*"

Neither of us said anything for a minute. I still felt

like shit, even after about a zillion gallons of water and Advil and two multivitamins.

"Rette, I'm really tired, would you mind leaving me alone so I can take a nap?"

"Sure. But Jen I . . . I went online and printed off some meeting times to AA meetings nearby. You . . ."

"I'm not going to any goddamn AA meeting!"

"Okay, that's fine. Just hang on to these, please? Just in case."

RETTE

Christmas. Ugh.

Mom and Dad arrived the day before Christmas. Jen used a personal day to get off work, but I didn't get fancy benefits like that for another month. It was hard to believe I had only worked there for two months. I'd enjoyed the job for about two weeks before becoming bitter and disenchanted. It seemed as if I'd been there an eternity. But I didn't mind having to work that day. For one thing, I got out of making the long drive to the airport to pick up Mom and Dad, and for another thing, Eleanore had taken the day off, so work was like a vacation.

I'd finally finished Christmas shopping the night before; then I'd wrapped gifts and cleaned the house until one in the morning, so I was exhausted by the time I got home from work, and I had dark circles under my eyes that would not go unnoticed by Mom, no matter how much makeup I used to conceal them. I was strung out on caffeine, and the looming parental visit did nothing to calm my jittery nerves.

When I got home from work, Greg was making dinner. Mom stood beside Greg with a nearly empty martini in hand. Dad was sitting at the kitchen table reading the newspaper. Jen was across from him, staring into her martini glass, looking bored.

Mom looked beautiful. She was laughing, her head thrown back, her manicured hands touching Greg lightly on the shoulder. Every time I saw my mother, I was struck anew by her beauty. Why couldn't she get bags under her eyes like a normal forty-six-year-old?

"A man who cooks. He's such a catch!" Mom said, finally noticing me.

Greg was making baked chicken, baked potatoes, store-bought rolls, and frozen mixed vegetables. In this family, that was the equivalent of a gourmet meal.

I hugged Mom, then Dad. After that we looked at each other, unsure what to do or say next. Mom made herself and Jen another round of martinis.

When dinner was ready, we sat down at the table and served ourselves in silence. I wanted to think of a funny story or interesting conversation topic to ensure everyone had a great time, but I couldn't think of a thing to say. Dad was the first to speak.

"It was a nice flight in," Dad said. "Right on time. No turbulence. A good sandwich for lunch, too."

"Don't bore them," Mom said. "Who wants to hear about our flight? Honestly. Any progress on the wedding plans?"

"Not really. I've been so busy with my job, and Greg's had finals to study for. Things will calm down soon, I hope," I said. "We can focus on it then." I watched Mom as she "ate." She had a way of making it look like she was a hearty eater without actually eating anything. She would put a heaping amount of food on her plate, make a big deal of how magnificent everything was and how stuffed she was from eating so much. Tonight she'd eaten most of the vegetables, a couple bites of potato and a few bites of chicken without the skin. She'd taken a roll and torn it in half, but she'd never actually taken a single bite.

Alcohol, however, she consumed incessantly. She never got drunk, but she carefully nursed a steady buzz throughout the night. By eating so little, Mom saved her calories for her alcohol. By eating less she could also drink less since there weren't any nutrients in the way of her getting buzzed.

After dinner, we sat in the living room, talking about nothing in particular. The TV was on to fill in the awkward silences and to spur conversation topics. An ad for an upcoming episode of *Ally McBeal* got Mom, me, and Jen talking about our favorite TV shows. Over the course of the evening, Mom drank prodigious amounts of brandy. Jen finished off the wine. I nibbled at the remnants of German chocolate cake we'd had for dessert, and Dad retreated to the balcony where he smoked cigarette after cigarette. Greg, the only viceless one among us, sat across from me on the other side of the room. He caught my eye and gave me an "it-will-all-be-over-soon" smile.

Finally, Jen said she was beat and she should be getting home now. Mom and Dad slept in our room, so Greg and I set up an air mattress in the study for ourselves. Earlier I'd bragged about how much personality our apartment had, but now I saw the place through Mom's eyes, and I was embarrassed by the flaking paint and strange layout. (There were no hallways, just one room opening up into another room. To get to the bathroom you had to go through our bedroom.) The place seemed small and old and poorly decorated.

Christmas morning I woke up early. I lay on the air

mattress, staring at the ceiling for a long time, willing myself to go back to sleep, thinking about how dealing with my family would be slightly less horrendous if I weren't sleep deprived. But finally I gave up, put on my robe, and padded through the house, turning on the Christmas tree lights. I made coffee, settled into the battered reclining chair and stared, mesmerized, at the lights on the tree that blurred into a comforting haze.

By the time Jen got to our place Christmas morning, I'd eaten two sticky rolls to quiet my rumbling stomach. When Mom noticed the missing sticky rolls she said, "Jesus, Rette, just one of those things has your fat calories for an entire day. Do you want to look like a whale in your wedding dress?"

There's nothing like being equated with the world's largest mammal by your mother to start the day off right.

It took about a thousand years, but eventually Christmas did end. I was counting down the hours until Mom, Dad, and Jen left to go skiing. But like a biblical superhero or prisoner of war, I had many hurdles yet to face before freedom was mine. Like trying on wedding dresses with my mother.

My stomach was knotted with anxiety. I hated my body enough without looking at it through my mother's eyes.

We spent an exhausting couple of hours trying on dresses before breaking for lunch. Being seen in my underwear by my mother had miraculously diminished my appetite. We both ordered wine and house salads.

"Did I tell you what Jack did?" Mom said between sips

of wine, sharing yet another story about the long-time villain in Mom's office drama.

"No, what?" I said.

"I was in a meeting with my entire staff *and* two of the senior managers—I mean we were in the middle of a discussion—and he just comes barging in with the letter I'd finished earlier in the day, and he says, in front of everyone, *everyone*, 'So I see here the deadline was yesterday. Yesterday. I think you mean the twenty-second, not the second. Why don't you pay a little more attention to detail? I shouldn't be your copyeditor.' On and on he goes. I was *humiliated*. It was just a little typo. I was rushing to get it done because *he* was three days late getting the specs together, and instead of thanking me for my prompt work, he announces my error in front of everyone. Why couldn't he just fix it? Why didn't he have his secretary type it up in the first place? It's her job, not mine." Mom speared a tomato from her salad. "I hope a car bomb kills him."

"A car bomb? Wouldn't a nice little heart attack or a job transfer do?"

"No, I want him to die a painful, gory death. Every day I imagine his head being blown to smithereens. I want his limbs torn off slowly one by one. I want him to die a slow, agonizing death after lingering for several weeks, months maybe, with eighty percent of his body charred with third degree burns, his face a mangled heap of puss-filled horror, all red and gooey."

I laughed and Mom winked at me.

I was in a better mood after lunch. It helped somehow to know that it wasn't just me who had trouble dealing with authority. It wasn't that I was so difficult to get along with or so touchy; it was that, by and large, managers were idiots.

Without hope, I tried on the next dress. It didn't

seem particularly striking on the hanger, but when I turned to look at myself in the mirror, I felt transformed. If Jen were here, she could explain what magical equations of fabric and fashion architecture made me look so good, but whatever it was, all I knew was the tight bodice and the way the fabric flowed around my legs flattered my body beautifully. The bodice sucked my breasts in and made them look higher and firmer than they actually were. The dress left part of my shoulders bare, but had short sleeves connected to the bodice that had the delightful effect of covering the matronly heft of my upper arms and revealing only my small, delicate wrists.

"You look gorgeous," Mom said. We both stared at my image as I turned to inspect the front, the back, and the sides.

"I'm so proud of you, Rette," Mom said. "I wish your sister would find a decent guy. I don't understand why she's always falling for these losers. I'm a little worried about her. It's not really fair. You got her same beauty, but you also got all the brains and the talent."

"Talent?" I asked.

"Yes talent. You sound shocked. You've always been the brain of the family, you know that." Mom fussed around with the dress some more and caught my gaze in the mirror. "Well, what do you think? I think we've found our dress. It's perfect for you."

It was perfect. I felt gorgeous in it. Maybe the wedding wouldn't be a complete disaster after all. Then I looked at the price tag. "Eighteen hundred dollars. Oh my god. That's a thousand more than I was planning to spend."

"This is your dress. There's no question."

"Mom, don't be ridiculous. Eighteen hundred dollars is just the beginning. It'll be another two hundred for alterations, two hundred for the shoes, the veil, the gloves. It's too much, we have to be reasonable."

"I'm going to buy this dress. This dress is made for you. I never had a wedding. I want you to have the fairy tale wedding I never had."

Fairy tale wedding. As if princesses in fairy tales suffered from stress-induced gastrointestinal woes and chronic insomnia.

"Mom, that's really generous, but—"

"I'm sorry Rette, but I'm buying this dress."

"I'll feel so guilty. It's so extravagant."

"Well, you'll just have to get over yourself because my mind is made up."

"Thank you, Mom," I said, hugging her.

"You're welcome."

It was all so silly, all this money we were spending for just one day. On the other hand, the wedding pictures would last forever.

AVERY

Surprises

I looked through the phone book for a psychic. I needed guidance to help me figure out what to do about Les, my job, and my life.

Les's absence left a huge void in my life. I'd gotten so used to talking to him about what was bothering me that now that he wasn't around, the stress built up until the negative energy seemed palpable, metallic and sharp to the touch like rusty barbed wire scraping my insides, stopping all the positive energy flow.

I tried talking to Martha about my feelings about Pam getting fired, but all she said was *"Mrow?"* She looked at me as if she were genuinely trying to understand what I was saying.

"What would we do if I got laid off? I only have two weeks of savings in the bank. I'd have to start eating your kitty food."

"Mrow?"

I don't think she got the joke.

* * *

I missed the way I laughed when Les was around. He got me so much better than Gideon ever did. So why wasn't I rushing into Les's arms? Because he wasn't as pretty as Marcos or Gideon? Surely I wasn't that superficial, was I? In any case, where had pretty ever gotten me?

Everything happened for a purpose. People came into your life for a reason, to teach you something. Maybe Les had come into my life to teach me not to judge a book by its cover. But I'd spent my life appreciating things that looked good on the outside, like the ballet dancer on *pointe,* looking lovely and lithe while beneath the beautiful costume, her toes bled, her tendons ached, her stomach rumbled with perpetual hunger. Maybe it was about time I stopped caring so much about appearances and started caring about what was going on beneath the superficial facade.

It seemed so sad to have Christmas with just my mother. I wanted spouses and grandparents and sugar-saturated nieces and nephews bouncing off the walls.

Mom and I made coffee and sat beside the Christmas tree. Since there were only two of us, unwrapping presents didn't take long. Mom bought me a sweater, some handmade pottery, an abstract watercolor of a dancer.

"This is beautiful," I said.

"It is pretty, isn't it? I got it at the People's Fair last summer and thought of you." Mom gathered up the wrapping paper and ribbons. "Well, should we make breakfast?"

"Sounds good." I stood and followed her to the kitchen, shuffling along in my wool socks and flannel pajamas.

"So I rented a couple of videos—tearjerkers of course," Mom continued. "Then we have dinner reservations at the Q and tickets to the Nutcracker tonight."

"Sounds great." Mom held out the pot of coffee. I held my cup out so she could fill it.

"Would you peel the potatoes?" Mom asked, handing me the peeler. "So I finally met a man through my dating service. He's good-looking and has a good job. We went on four dates and I had a lot of fun. I broke it off with him last week."

"Why?" I asked.

"I think it's because he doesn't get me, and he's never going to. He was disappointed, but I had to do it. We just didn't feel right. When I was with him, I didn't feel like I could really be myself. Like he didn't get my jokes, so I stopped telling them. With your father, bless his heart, with him, we laughed all the time. Your father really brought out my sense of humor."

"That's so weird. Les said almost the same thing to me back when he was speaking to me. He said you need to find someone who brings out your best self. It's not so much the person you're with as the person you become when you're with him."

"Why isn't Les talking to you?"

"He told me that he's in love with me. I told him I care about him, but I'm not attracted to him. He said it was too painful to talk to me or be around me right now."

"Are you sure you don't love him? I saw you two at Thanksgiving. The way you laughed with him, the way the two of you talk and joke with each other, I really thought something was going on. He certainly couldn't take his eyes off you. The way he looked at you . . ."

"Mom, I'm not sure about anything. I miss him so much, it's ridiculous."

"Avery, maybe you need a little space from him so when you see him next time, you'll have a little distance—it'll give you a better perspective. I'm going to tell you a story."

"Somehow I don't think I'm going to like this."

She stopped making the eggs and looked at me. I put the potato down and returned her gaze. "When I was fifteen years old, this boy had a crush on me. He was a good friend of mine, really kind and funny. He was a great artist. One of the girls at school told me he had a crush on me. At the time, I had a crush on the best-looking guy in the class, Fred."

"Fred? Fred is not the name of a romantic love interest."

"Shh, dear, this is my story. Anyway, even if it weren't for Fred, I just thought of the other guy as my friend. So one day, he walks me home from class, and he's kind of nervous, kicking around the stones in the driveway, and I think, uh-oh, he's going to ask me out. So I say real fast that I just think of him as a friend and it will never be anything more and I'd better go inside now and then I run inside. Shortly after that, he went away to prep school, and I dated Fred—for about three weeks. The first time Fred and I kissed, it was all over. It was . . . how do I describe it? It was like kissing a rabid dog whose mouth was filled with foaming slobber. It was like he hocked a loogie in my mouth."

"Ah!"

"I know. And when the other boy came home from school, he was dating this girl, and I was crushed. I wanted so badly to tell him that I regretted what I'd said, that I wanted to take it back."

"Was he better looking? Had he changed?"

"No, he hadn't changed at all. *I* had changed. I wasn't scared anymore. I realized that being friends first wasn't a bad thing. Who wants to have a relationship with someone who *isn't* your best friend? Why did I think that because we were friends, we couldn't explore being something more?"

"So what happened, did he end up marrying the other girl?"

"No, he ended up breaking up with the other girl—and marrying me."

"Dad?"

"Yes, of course, Dad."

The office was deserted that week after Christmas. Everyone had finished their part of the Expert project except us (IT had nothing to do since that part of the project had been pulled from them). The researchers were only halfway done with their surveys on dishwashers. Jen and I decided we had no choice; we had to fill in the rest of the surveys ourselves. I filled out several myself, I sent some to my mom, some to my friends. I looked at the surveys that had been completed and repeated trends consumers had mentioned. We worked late every night that week. We did, however, manage to get the project done by the deadline.

I began my report with the suggestion that Expert target its message to the busy working mother, who probably didn't have time to cook and clean like her mother had, but still wanted to show her love to her family through wholesome domesticity. This woman was probably better educated than women of previous generations, and might be a whiz in the boardroom, but felt like a klutz in the kitchen. This upper-middle-class mom was Expert's ideal demographic, because she was the one who could afford Expert's steep prices. Thus, the Expert campaign should communicate that its products would make anyone an expert in the kitchen and a dazzling washer of clothes. Plus, these appliances were easy to use and did all the work for you, but you got all the credit.

Les and I hadn't spoken for nearly two weeks. I couldn't take it anymore. I called him, and this time, he wasn't screening his calls. As soon as he answered the phone, I felt better.

"Hey," I said. "What are you doing for New Year's?"

"Tom invited me to a party, but I think I'm going to stay home and watch a video. Maybe order a pizza."

"Jen and Mike are going to a club for drinks and dancing. I'd really like it if you came."

"Avery, I . . ."

"Les, this is the only end of the millennium we're ever going to see. Don't stay home with a video."

He didn't say anything, so I went on.

"Les, I don't know exactly how I feel about you or what I'd like to happen between us. I just know I really miss you and I really want to see you. I think we need to talk. And you never know. We may even have some fun."

He considered this. "Okay."

I exhaled, relieved. "Great. We're meeting at my place at nine."

Les was a little late arriving, and by then Jen, Mike, Rette, Greg, and I had already had a couple of glasses of champagne each. Jen, in that way she did, kept everyone laughing riotously with her silly antics and funny comments. The mood around her was festive, and as soon as Les arrived, he was swept into it too.

We piled in Mike's Mercedes. It was way too small for six people, but we decided to rough it to minimize the number of designated drivers. I sat in Les's lap and Rette sat in Greg's lap and Jen took off the panel of the sunroof so she could shout "Happy New Year!" at the top of her lungs to whoever was listening.

"Jen is such a riot," I said, "I think I'm going to pee in my pants."

"Please don't," Les said dryly, which cracked me up all over again.

It only took a few minutes to get to the bar. I'd expected it to be standing room only, but it wasn't nearly as packed as I thought it would be, and we had no trouble finding a table. Rette and Greg sat across from Les and me, and Jen and Mike took off to get drinks for us all.

"Come on, Les, let's hit the dance floor, show them what we've learned," I said.

"There's hardly anybody out there."

"Don't be chicken. Come on!"

As soon as we got out there, Les lost his inhibitions. We'd only taken a few lessons, but we'd learned a few spins and dips that looked harder than they actually were, and I thought we looked pretty good together.

After several songs, Les suggested we go to the balcony to cool off. We had the balcony to ourselves.

"You're looking great," I said.

"I feel good. I'm working out regularly, and I've lost some weight."

"You seem lighter, but I don't mean pound-wise. Your spirit seems lighter than it was when we first met, like you're carrying less emotional weight. Go over there, in the light. I'll read your aura."

"Read my aura?"

"Don't make fun. You can't say anything. I have to just look at you for a minute."

I looked at him, trying not to focus on any one part

of him, to let him blur so I could see the colors surrounding him. But instead I focused on his kind eyes, his small dimples, his grin. That grin said so much. It wasn't like Gideon's I-know-I'm-a-totally-sexy-hunk smile; it was not at all arrogant, but it was self-assured. There was something so sexy about someone who was self-assured.

"So what do you see?"

"Nothing. I'm not doing it right. I'm supposed to let your features blur." I continued looking at him, at his features bathed in the soft glow of the moonlight. "Instead, I think I'm actually just getting a clearer view."

Neither of us said anything for a long moment.

"What are you thinking?" he asked.

"Lots of different things. I was thinking about how I always fall for guys with dark eyes and dark hair. I like the contrast of my light to his dark."

"You can totally use me for my looks. I completely support that."

I laughed and looked away, glancing at the bodies dancing inside beneath the lights that flashed off and on, off and on, darkness then light.

"What else were you thinking?" he asked.

I looked at him again. I paused, considering my words. "I was thinking that I wonder what it would be like to kiss you."

"You can find out."

"What if it turns out I don't feel about you the way you feel about me? I don't want to hurt you."

"I'd rather get hurt than never give you and me a try."

"What if it doesn't work out and we're not friends anymore? I don't want to ruin our friendship."

"We can never go back to being just friends. It's already too late. I already love you."

Maybe he was right. Maybe I really didn't have anything to lose.

"Don't you think it's a bad idea to date a coworker?"

"Is it going to be any more awkward between us at work than it already is now?"

He had a point. Plus, if we gave this whole relationship thing a try, I wouldn't have to wonder anymore if there was a possibility for something to happen between us. What would his kiss be like—too cautious? Awkward? Fishy-lipped? If it was terrible, at least I'd know, at least I would have given it a try.

Les walked toward me, leaned in, touched his fingers lightly across the back of my neck, and pulled me toward him.

His kiss surprised me with its intensity, with its—there's no other way to put this—skill. It was the kiss of a man who knew what he wanted; there was nothing hesitant about it.

I stopped thinking, and let myself just feel, feel every sensation: the smell of his soap, the taste of his minty breath, the feel of his lips against mine.

Later, when I could think again, I'd think that it was like Sleeping Beauty's kiss—the kiss that finally woke me up. Was it really that Les didn't look like a movie star that had made me so afraid, or was it that I knew I could really love him and be loved by him, that this relationship could be something real and deep and, therefore, scary? Maybe I lived in my fairy tale world because there, I had nothing to lose.

We waited to go back to my place until just after midnight. When we kissed at the stroke of twelve, Jen and Rette cheered. *"Finally,"* Rette said.

We spent the rest of the night making love. Les's body was so different from Gideon's. His stomach was a little pudgy and his shoulders were so much broader, his legs were so much more muscular. In the embrace of his thick, strong arms, I felt safe—spiritually, emotionally, and physically. I felt like everything was going to be okay.

We slept most of New Year's Day and woke up famished late that afternoon. We made vegetable risotto and ate it picnic-style on a blanket we threw on the living room floor. We spent the evening giving each other back rubs and drinking cheap wine and watching old movies.

It wouldn't be for a few more weeks that I'd look at him sitting across the couch from me, a smile on his face, and realize that I loved him.

The wonderful, relaxing feeling I felt all New Year's Day vanished abruptly when I returned to work the next day. First thing in the morning, Morgan stopped by my office with a copy of the report on features customers wanted in refrigerators that I'd done for Expert.

"Did you write this?" he asked. I couldn't read his tone exactly, but it wasn't friendly. It seemed accusing.

"I wrote parts. The introduction and transitions. But most of it just pulls directly from what the clients said in the surveys."

The cell phone he wore on a clip on his hip rang. He checked the number to see who was calling. As he answered the phone he gave me a nod and was on his way. I thought about his cryptic nod good-bye. It seemed like it was a "we'll talk more later" nod. But was it to talk about how I would be fired for wasting time rushing through my work and delivering a substandard product or to talk about what a good job I was doing and how he appreciated my attention to detail? I had the uneasy feeling it was the former.

JEN

Reflections

Tom hadn't spoken to me since the holiday party, and you know what? I didn't miss him.

I broke up with Mike on New Year's Day. He took me out to a nice dinner, and I started to do what I do to make a dull baseball game go faster: I started working on getting a buzz. I told the waiter to bring me two martinis right away because I knew the first one would be gone before he stopped back. In fact, both were gone by the time he returned with our salads less than five minutes later. I was so embarrassed that when he asked if I wanted another, I said no even though I really did. That's when it finally hit me: Was going to nice restaurants worth dating a guy I had to be drunk with to stand being with?

I broke up with Mike after dinner. He didn't take it well—he bargained and pleaded and promised he'd change. There were mercifully no tears, at least.

I decided to take a break from dating for a while, at least until I caught up on my laundry and my sleep.

* * *

These last few weeks, I'd been crying at every turn, for any excuse or no excuse at all. Frankly, I felt sorry for myself. I felt like I'd been diagnosed with some terrible disease. Which maybe I had.

I drank every night for the first two weeks of the New Year. I figured if I had to give it up forever, I might as well enjoy it while I could. But drinking so much was making me sick. I was exhausted and I could just feel the brain cells dying, my head hurt so bad. One morning I woke up and I felt so vile I vowed that I'd try an AA meeting, just to see what it was like.

I suffered through the day at work, not getting much accomplished. That night, I decided I was too tired to face going to a meeting, but I promised myself I'd definitely go the next day. I fell asleep on the couch before seven.

It's amazing how easy it was to vow that I'd never drink again when I was hung over and feeling like a steaming pile of dog shit. But the next day, right about the end of the day at five, I was really, really craving a beer. I knew a beer wouldn't get me buzzed though, and I couldn't afford the calories of a whole six-pack, so I decided I'd pick up a half of a pint of something to accompany the beer.

I pulled into the liquor store parking lot, put the car in park, and then just sat there in the driver's seat. I really wanted a beer, something to make the tension go away, make the night alone easier to face, but I didn't want to be hung over tomorrow.

I sat in my car for several more minutes, arguing with myself about which I wanted more, a beer or to feel okay tomorrow.

Fuck it, maybe I'd go to one meeting, and then I

could stop at the liquor store. That was fair. I'd keep my vow about going to a meeting, but nobody ever said you had to stop drinking right after your very first AA meeting. I'd probably have to stop drinking someday, but that didn't mean it had to be today. I went home without buying any alcohol first. I could pick up anything I wanted after the meeting. I looked at the printouts that Rette had given me. There was a meeting half an hour from now close to my house.

I was expecting the people in the meeting to look like they were teleported directly from a Montel Williams set—all mullet haircuts and Kmart clothes and from-a-box-blond hairdos. There were a couple of trailer trash types, but out of the ten people there, the majority looked completely normal.

I sat in one of the metal folding chairs arranged in a circle and listened without saying a word as people talked about what was going on in their lives and shared horror stories from their drinking days. One of the guys was a well-dressed, good-looking middle-aged man. The deal was that he used to be a doctor, but because of his drinking he lost his job, his wife, and his kid. He'd been trying to get his kid to talk to him, but the kid didn't believe he was sober, and could he blame her? After what she'd been through?

There was a middle-aged woman who was dressed like a successful business woman—no-nonsense hairdo and expensive clothes—a biker guy with thick tattooed arms, a young mother with pockmarked skin and eyes that hinted that maybe she hadn't had the easiest life, and a cute guy who looked like he was in his mid- to late-twenties.

Nobody made me talk, which I appreciated. If I spoke, I was afraid I'd start crying and never stop. If I said the words out loud, if I admitted I had a problem, that I couldn't seem to stop drinking, there would never be any going back. It would be a fact, not just a possibility.

At the end of it all, we grabbed hands and said that "God grant me the serenity to accept the things I cannot change . . ." prayer. I was sitting between the biker and the young mother. I expected to be grossed out by holding their hands, but when I reached out and took their hands, it turned out I wasn't grossed out at all. Their hands were warm, and strangely comforting, the soft, small hands of the mother, the gruff hands of the biker, and me in the middle, feeling like maybe I wasn't so different from them after all.

But the meeting was a bunch of bullshit because I was still stressed and feeling crappy, and I still wanted to go home and drink something.

Metal folding chairs scraped the concrete floors of the church basement as people stood and folded their chairs to put them away. My chair was stuck or something because I couldn't get it to fold.

"Can I help?"

"Please." I looked up. It was the cute younger guy.

"This is the first time I've seen you here."

"It was my first meeting." *First,* as if there would be more, which there would not, since this was a great big fat waste of time.

"My name is John. It's really good to have you here. I hope I see you again sometime." He walked over to the wall and stacked my chair against the others. As I was leaving, I heard him say, "Hey!"

I turned to look at him.

"Just so you know, it's not like you come to one meeting and poof! that's it, you'll never want a sip of alcohol again. But the meetings, they can help, I promise."

I nodded. "Okay. Thanks."

I stopped at the liquor store, went home, got tanked, and cried myself to sleep.

When I woke up, I felt nauseated and I thought, this is probably what it feels like to be pregnant. Then I thought, when exactly was the last time I had my period? Wasn't it around Thanksgiving? That was seven weeks ago.

I thought about that condomless romp Tom and I had shortly after that. But he'd pulled out. I just felt crappy from drinking. Right? I'd skipped periods before. My freshman year, when I was dieting pretty heavily, I only got two periods that whole year. I never understood women who got all concerned when their periods were a few days late. My period had always been inconsistent and flaky, kind of like me. I probably just hadn't been eating as much as I should, that was all.

I went to meetings off and on during the next couple of weeks, though I was still drinking regularly. The only requirement for attending the meetings was a desire to stop drinking. I didn't really want to stop drinking, I just wanted to stop drinking so much, but from what I was learning at the meetings and from the literature they gave out, it seemed like maybe finding a way to just drink less wasn't an option. My efforts to stop after two drinks certainly never seemed to work, that was for sure.

Through it all, I felt really low, maybe even worse than after Dave and I broke up. All I could think was, *This is not how my life is supposed to go, this is not how my life is supposed to go.*

At the meetings and in the stories of people in books I read, I heard some truly incredible stories. Stories about losing jobs and millions of dollars and loved ones. But some of these people, they seemed so happy. This one guy actually said that he was so happy with his life now, he was glad he'd become an alcoholic because AA had helped him get in touch with his feelings, which improved his relationship with his wife and kids, and he was living a life more fully and deeply than he had ever imagined possible. Maybe that was what kept me coming back. I wanted that, too. I wanted to live life fully, to be able to have good relationships and generally go through life with my shit together instead of the alcoholic, bulimic, debt-getting-into ways I normally dealt with my problems. I really, really wanted to believe that a different life was possible.

I admit, too, that I did like seeing John. He was cute and always friendly to me. I didn't flirt with him at all, though; I felt so vulnerable, so exposed, I didn't feel confident enough to flirt.

Flying Lessons

"Alcohol gave me wings to fly then it took away the sky."

—Anonymous

Freshman year. Jill Sandy's house. Peach schnapps and orange juice—a fuzzy navel. Probably like point zero two percent alcohol, a laughable amount these days, but back then after a drink or two, all was right with my world. Everything seemed funner, funnier, better, including me.

I'd spent thirteen years trying to get that feeling back, one drink at a time. It had been a long, long time since alcohol had been fun. A long time of me thinking, "I think I'll have a drink," as if it were me making the choice, and not my addiction, this messed-up chemical imbalance of my body that made every part of me scream for another drink, just one more sip, craving to capture that moment of peace and happiness and self-acceptance I'd felt at Jill's house, just for a second, one single instant, just one more time.

After one meeting, John asked me if I'd go for a cup of coffee with him.

"Um," my voice came out in a quiet, husky squeak. I was crying all the time—in the car, at home alone, at nearly every meeting—and the constant crying was making my voice raspy. My old confidence had disappeared entirely. "Yeah, okay."

We went to Penny Lane. I ordered a chai with skim milk; he ordered a green tea. We sat in a table in the corner, quiet and out of the way. I wanted to hide from everyone, including myself.

"How long have you been going to meetings?" I asked him.

"Six years."

"Six years! How old are you?"

"Twenty-eight."

"So you've been going since you were twenty-two? God, am I going to have to go to these stupid meetings for six years?"

"A lot of people go for the rest of their lives on and off. I've been going fairly often lately because I've been going through a hard time."

"Why?"

"It's the second anniversary of my fiancée's death. Car accident."

"Drunk driver?"

"Icy road."

"God, I'm so sorry."

"Yeah, so am I. I've been really bummed lately. I've been thinking stuff like, I'm going to spend the rest of my life alone so what does it matter if I start drinking again, that kind of thing."

I sipped my tea, feeling awkward, wishing it were a cosmopolitan.

"I've wanted to get to know you better since the first time I saw you," he said. "You never say anything in the meetings."

"I'm not someone you want to get to know better, trust me."

"You're so funny, so pretty. You're a little shy . . ."

"Ha! Shy, that's a good one," I laughed. "I guess it's possible, who knows." This conversation was not making me comfortable. "So, what do you do for a living?" Ack! God, would I ever stop fishing for economic information to determine if I could comfortably raise his kids?

"I'm a photojournalist for the *Denver Post.* I do some freelance work for magazines as well. How about you?"

"I work in marketing."

"Do you like it?"

"Oh my god no . . ." I told him what a cesspool my company was, and how poorly managed it was. I told him about how I dealt with my frustration by depicting salespeople and executives with hideous diseases, and soon John was cracking up.

"So what's it like at your office?" I asked.

"It's like any job. I have some great friends there and some people I'd be completely content to never see again. Isn't every office like the dysfunctional, Jerry Springer side of the family?"

I laughed. "I guess so."

"But who would we sleep with and gossip about if it weren't for our coworkers?"

I laughed again and it felt good, really good. I almost felt like my old self and it was so nice, sitting here, laughing with a cute guy. There wasn't a trace of alcohol anywhere in sight.

We talked for a few hours until they were closing the place up, and John walked me to my car and asked if we could do this again sometime.

"You mean, like on a date?"

"Exactly like a date."

"I don't know. You're cute, and nice and funny, but I . . . my last few relationships have been total wrecks, they've been like sewage waste, and I want a relationship that's like, a clear nonpolluted stream, something that's beautiful and healthy and going somewhere, and I just feel like I have to be healthy, and I have to get my shit together and the deal is, my shit is just not together yet."

"I'm in no rush. I'd like to hang out with you sometimes if it's okay. We can just be friends."

"Friends?" What a novel concept. Getting to know someone before I slept with him. I liked John. And he was a recovering alcoholic. He didn't seem like a total mess at all. He seemed healthy, like he had his act together.

"Jen, are you okay? Why are you crying?"

"All I do these days is cry," I said. "It's nothing, I'm fine."

If John could get sober and stay sober, even through his fiancée dying, wasn't it possible that I could, too?

"Tell me it's possible for me to stop drinking. Tell me it's possible that I can have a happy life and do it without alcohol," I said, sniffling.

"It's possible. You have to learn how to do everything all over again. How to deal with stress and social situations and sadness. You have to learn how to feel—when you're drinking, you're numbing your feelings, and when you stop, you suddenly feel all this stuff, some of it is good, and some of it's not, but life sober is better; it's much, much better."

RETTE

Rediscovery

With the Expert account finished, I was much less busy, and I hardly knew what to do with myself. I was actually able to stay on top of my workload and leave at five every day. I was so used to working at the fastest possible pace, it was hard to slow down.

I told Glenn I could no longer help him with his projects. I told him that I needed to focus my efforts, but I sure did appreciate the opportunity to learn new things.

I sent out a few résumés this week. I did it at work so I didn't feel like I was wasting my own precious free time. Also, it felt delightfully subversive to look for another job while on the clock. I realized that I might need to put in a year here before I was attractive to other employers. I thought of my days with Eleanore as something I had to survive, and the experience would ultimately make me a stronger person.

The good news was that since Avery was promoted to Marketing Communications Manager in Pam's place (Morgan liked the copy she wrote on the Expert research reports), she'd been giving me brochures, e-mail copy, Web content, and other things to write. (Except unlike Glenn, I asked her for the work so I could get some experience and get a better job. Plus, Avery would always tell people stuff like, "Didn't Rette do a great job on that brochure?" Can you imagine? A manager who actually gave credit where credit was due?) Avery said I was doing a great job and that if a position opened up in her department, she'd do her best to see that I got the job. I'd report to Avery who reported to Glenn. At least there would be a layer of competence between me and him.

When I started to get pissed off about all the crappy management and bad decisions McKenna Marketing made because of the reckless incompetence of our managerial team, I'd think, *What does it really matter in the grand scheme of things if McKenna Marketing squanders resources and generates an inferior product. This isn't a cure for cancer or the launch of a world war. This isn't as important as world hunger. What do I care if McKenna Marketing goes under? I can get unemployment.* But it was no good. I was an editor. I had to care about every comma, every syllable, every character. Not caring would be worse than caring too much.

With a reasonable workload, I experienced the strangest thing: I wasn't exhausted when I went home at night. I suddenly had hours to myself in which I could read and think.

One night, Greg was home from school, studying at the kitchen table, rubbing his neck.

"Is your neck sore?" I asked.

"It's killing me. All my stress seems to lodge itself right here."

"Want me to give you a back rub?"

"Are you kidding? I'd love it."

"Let's go in the bedroom."

I followed him into our room, where he took off his shirt and lay down on the bed. I rubbed his shoulders, his neck, his back. I was in no rush, and it was so nice, just feeling his warm skin and listening to him murmur with gratitude. As I worked my way down his back, I told him to slip out of his pants. I continued massaging his legs and feet.

"Now you," he said, propping himself on an elbow.

He spent a good half-hour giving me a full-body massage until I felt utterly, completely relaxed. Greg gently pushed my legs apart, running his fingers along my inner thigh, then slipping them inside me.

We made love, slowly. It had been such a long time since I hadn't felt stressed out and in a rush to get to the next task, I'd forgotten how nice it was just to give myself over to pleasure.

"**T**hat was so nice. I wish I didn't have to have a stupid job, and then I could just be your full-time masseuse and geisha girl," I said.

"I need to figure out a way to become independently wealthy."

"Then you and I can just travel around Europe. We'll go to Paris, and Venice, and Amsterdam, and London . . ."

"And Athens. And Australia."

"I feel it's relevant to point out that Australia's not in Europe, but we should definitely swing down there for a month or so, while we're at it."

"Since we're zillionaires, we might as well."

I smiled and looked at Greg. God how I loved his smile. How I loved *him.*

Why did I love him? I was going to have to articulate it when I wrote the vows. But why do we love anyone?

It's one part attraction; one part being able to laugh together even after two years together when you've already told all your best jokes; one part not being able to wait to rush home and share every part of your day and find out how his went. I loved Greg because of his goofy smile that made me smile, no matter how cranky I felt. I loved him because he knew what things like VPNs, Bluetooth technology, firewalls, and calipers were, so I'd never have to. I loved him because he wasn't as reserved as my dad and was nothing at all like his own dad. I loved him because when I said, "Who do you really think is prettier, me or Jen?" he always gave me the right answer.

If I could have it my way, I'd feel this rush of love for Greg every moment of every day, I would be able to shed the stress of work with a snap of my fingers and be able to luxuriate in a lazy reverie with great sex every night. But if every moment with Greg was clear-the-table-with-a-sweep-of-your-arm-to-make-mad-passionate-tear-your-clothes-off sex, these unplanned, stolen moments of rediscovering how much we loved each other wouldn't be quite so startling, so wonderful.

AVERY

Shift F7

Being a marketing copywriter means becoming intimately acquainted with your Shift F7 thesaurus option. All I did all day was think of new ways to say Company *X* is the greatest! Use Company *X* and make oodles of money!

Still, this job was more creative and called on more of my intellect than my previous job. Also, my raise made a world of difference. It was amazing how having just a little money in the bank made me feel more secure.

It really shouldn't have come as a surprise to me that I ended up in marketing. I only liked pretty things, dealing with the positive side of things. In marketing, you never pay any attention when the company you're promoting failed a customer miserably, you only quote the customers who liked the service and you only profile the instances in which the company saved a client time and money. In marketing, there were no "problems" only "challenges to overcome." It's not such a bad way to view the world.

JEN

Unhappy Hour

It had been at least nine weeks since I'd gotten my period. I hadn't had a drink for two weeks, and I hadn't felt nauseated since that last bender, so that seemed like my little bout with nausea probably wasn't morning sickness. If I *were* pregnant, the little fetus had probably been mutated from all the drinking I'd done since the romp with Tom. I was definitely going to have to figure out a way to beat this alcohol thing if I wanted to be a Mom and bear a healthy kid, and I did, I really did. Just not right now.

Marty from accounting brought my expense check to me himself. He seemed surprised to see Sharon, who had been in the middle of bitching at me for something that was her fault. Sharon watched the situation gravely as Marty and I exchanged smiles and thank-yous and see-you-laters.

When Marty left, Sharon said, "That's not the check for the expense report you turned in yesterday, is it?"

"Yes it is."

"It took him thirty days to get me my expense check."

I shrugged.

"Well, clean up that section we talked about," she sputtered.

"Will do."

Sharon stalked off.

Yes, there are definite perks to being beautiful.

I looked at the clock. Five o'clock at last! I called Avery, who now had a new office—one all to herself. "Hey, let's go." It would be my first sober happy hour. I hadn't had a drink in fourteen days. That might not seem like much, but to me it seemed huge. I loved how good I felt, I loved life without hangovers, but even so I spent every single night focusing on nothing except talking myself out of drinking. It was completely irrational. It was exhausting. I wanted so much just to go get a bottle of something and not worry about it, just get drunk and not think twice about it. That seemed so much easier.

"See you out front," Avery said. "I just have to shut down and I'll be there."

I buzzed Rette. "Ready?"

"Hell, yes."

The three of us met in the front of the office and walked downtown to Rios. It was already crowded, but we managed to get a table. When the waitress stopped by, Avery said, "We'd each like a margarita on the rocks with salt."

"Actually, I'll just have a glass of water with some lemon." Avery looked at me. "I'm on a diet," I said. "So how are you liking your new job?"

"It's okay. I enjoy writing," Avery said. "Pam was right,

though, everybody thinks they can write. One client I wrote some collateral for just loved what I did, and we went to press with it right away. With another client, though, I had dozens of meetings with two male VPs, a male CEO, a sales guy, and the marketing director. We went over every sentence dozens of times. They'd contradict each other, go back to the way we had it a week earlier, constantly change their minds. You'd think you wouldn't want to use up so much staff time on a brochure and some letters. I mean think about how much money a VP and a CEO make per hour, and all those hours we spent changing a few words around! They spent so much time arguing with each other about which bullet point to put first. You know how men are. It was a total territory war. Since our last meeting, they've changed their minds yet again about the kind of message they want, who their target audience is, what tone they want to take. It's kind of frustrating, but we get paid for every hour I work, so their egos are costing them a lot of money."

"Have you heard from Pam?" Rette asked.

"Yeah, actually I have some news: She's started her own company. She got a couple big projects right away, and she said she was looking for part-time help. She's hoping to hire a couple full-time people by the end of the year. She said if either of you are interested in making some extra money doing some marketing and publicity writing, to give her a call."

"Extra money! Hell yes, count me in," Rette said. "I'm not that busy at work right now, so I could work part time for Pam while I'm at the office—it'll be perfect!"

"I know, isn't it ridiculous, I'm so bitter, even with my promotion," Avery said, "That I'm taking two-hour lunches and stealing office supplies, as if taking three sticky notepads and eleven pens equals all the mental anguish I've experienced over the past five years."

"And if she does have a full-time position open up, oh my god, I'd take it in a nanosecond," Rette continued. "Are you going to work for her?"

"Actually, I've finally figured out what I want to do when I grow up. It's a major change, and it may sound a little crazy . . ."

"What?" Rette said.

"My plan is to save five thousand dollars, and then go to this nine-week program in California where I'll become certified to be a Bikram yoga instructor. I figure that with doing some work for Pam and saving like crazy, I'll be able to quit McKenna in six months and fly out to California."

"A yoga instructor! Jesus!" Rette said.

"I know, it sounds a little nuts, but I've been thinking about what it really is I want to do with my life, and I know it's not sitting at a desk all day. I want to be active and use my body, and yoga instructors—I won't get rich, but I'll be making as much as I make now, and I just know I'll be so much happier. I figure sometimes you need to give destiny a little hand, you can't just wait for it."

"Well that's great, Ave. I think that's a great plan," Rette said.

"Yeah, congratulations," I said. Avery had barely even taken a sip of her margarita. How could she just sit there, apparently indifferent to the drink in front of her? I looked around the room at all the people enjoying their margaritas, their beers, their wine. They'd have one or two, and then stop. They wouldn't go home and do several more shots to "help them sleep." *Why can't I just stop at two? Why can't I stop at two? Fuck you people who get to enjoy all that wine and beer and margaritas, fuck all of you.*

"How about you, Jen, are you interested in working for Pam?" Avery asked.

"I don't think so, not right now anyway. Right now I'm making enough major changes. I have to focus on some stuff before I can think about changing jobs."

Avery looked at me. "What kind of major changes?"

"I'd rather not talk about it right now."

Rette reached out and squeezed my hand in hers. "You know we're here for you if you ever want to talk."

"I know." I could feel the tears coming up again. Probably the crazed hormones of a pregnant woman. "I have to go to the bathroom. I'll be right back," I said. I leapt off my stool and quickly wove my way through the restaurant to the bathroom. I opened then locked the stall door, pulled up my skirt and pulled down my underwear and saw the most beautiful thing I'd ever seen: blood.

I closed my eyes, exhaled. Then, of course, I started crying.

Maybe it's the tears that have been welling up inside me since my freshman year in college, when drinking hard and regularly became part of my routine, when I started drinking for fun and drinking to mask how much pain I was in. Maybe part of the reason I'm crying all the time these days is that one of the twelve steps in AA is to make a searching and fearless inventory of ourselves. I've always tried not to reflect too much about the stupid shit I do. The truth is, I don't like to reflect too much on my life because when I do, I don't like what I see.

I'd done so many stupid things in my brief twenty-five years on this planet. My period being MIA for almost four weeks was a little reminder that actions have consequences, but I was being given a second chance. I couldn't mess this up. I would live a life where I didn't do this stupid shit anymore. A life where I'd remember who I'd slept with when I woke up in the morning. The next time I thought I was pregnant, I'd know for 100 percent certainty who the father was. But it was here now, like an old friend that I was very happy to see.

I returned to the table feeling a little better, as if I'd been given a gift I didn't necessarily deserve.

"So how are things with Les?" I asked.

"Really good," Avery said and smiled.

"He's looking pretty good these days. I mean you wouldn't mistake him for a star of *Melrose Place*, but he's obviously been working out," I said.

"We're going out dancing a lot and doing yoga together," Avery said. "My life these days is just filled with small but really wonderful moments. Like we rented this horrible movie the other night, and we both groaned at the same time, and it made me so happy. I just thought, yes, *finally*. How about you, Jen? How many men are you fighting off these days?"

"I have no life whatsoever. I go to work, to Tae Bo, and to sleep." I inhaled sharply.

"What's wrong?" Avery asked, following my gaze.

"Oh, phew. I thought that was Mary. It's not. Did you guys hear she's sleeping with Mark with a *k?*"

"I believe it," Avery said. "I saw her sitting on his lap in his cube at the office."

"You're kidding. She's married. He has a live-in girlfriend," Rette said. "Scandal!"

"It's true. I just can't believe Pam is okay with getting fired when it was so clearly Mark's fault we lost the Expert Web site account," Avery said. "It's this gross injustice, and there is nothing I can do about it. Well, I can take two-hour lunches and steal office supplies and plot how I'm going to get out of there, but I mean, there is nothing I can do to change what happened."

Avery took a sip of her margarita. Would there ever be a day when I didn't notice stuff like this? When I didn't count every sip of alcohol that I didn't get to take?

"You know what I think? I think a job is like a marriage. The interview is like a first date," Avery said. "You smile and only show your best self. You wait eagerly for him to call. When he does, your heart races, your future seems to have unlimited opportunities. You have your good days and your bad days. After having your ideas rejected and the credit for your work stolen by another, you feel betrayed and cheated on. The good days get fewer and fewer. Eventually, you quit or get laid off and you become a bitter divorcée. Then you get a new job and start the process all over again."

"Except for it's really more like an arranged marriage," Rette said. "How much do you know after a half-hour interview? You make these huge life decisions with very little information to go on. There's no way I could have known what an evil bitch Eleanore would be. And I was so desperate for a job, what else could I have done even if I did know? When you take a job, it's like bungee jumping off a cliff blindfolded. You have no idea what's going to happen, but you can guess the outcome is not going to be good."

RETTE

Maybe Someday

Greg and I were married three weeks ago. I was not the svelte goddess I aspired to be, but I looked pretty damn good. Also, I didn't trip making my way down the aisle nor was I catapulted down a flight of stairs mere moments away from the wedding, which seemed a good omen. On the other hand, there was much hand-wringing and stress over the flowers on the left side of the veranda, which refused to hang perfectly symmetrically to the right side. Also, in his sweaty palm-induced stress, Greg dropped the ring right when he was supposed to slip it on my finger. It bounced around, and Greg and the minister and the best man, Greg's brother, searched around for thirty of the longest seconds of my life, bumping heads and looking generally like bumbling idiots, until Greg found it—by pulling up my dress. Only a few inches, but the audience laughed and *whoo-whooed* as I did my best not to keel over and die of embarrassment. Everyone assured me it was adorable and one of the things that makes a wedding memorable, and maybe a few years from now I'll be able to laugh about it. I'm not there yet.

Jen, who attended the wedding with her boyfriend, John, didn't take a single drink of alcohol during dinner and the party, not even at the champagne toast. I was so proud of her, but I didn't know how to say it, so I just hugged her and told her I loved her.

Les and Avery are still together. When asked about the *m* word, she says she thinks he might ask her over Christmas, and she'll say yes, but she wants to be engaged for three years and live together during that time to make sure it's right. She figures that after three years of living with someone, she'll know him as well as she ever can.

Avery's teaching yoga full time and loving every minute of it. I've been working for Pam on the side, and the extra money has reduced my stress tremendously. Unfortunately, with the market the way it is now, the work is unsteady and it's not quite time for me to make a permanent move. Jen, however, got a great tip about a job opening through someone at AA. She landed the position and loves her new job. It doesn't hurt that she's also making a lot more money. I'm thinking of joining AA just for the networking opportunities. I mean really.

In a different happy ending, maybe I'd have lost all the extra weight and gotten into great shape. Maybe I'd become the kind of person who genuinely liked vegetables and didn't even crave chocolate and pizza. Maybe I'd fall in love with working out and get the kind of hypothetical body that flexes triumphantly in Bally's commercials. Maybe I'd find a fulfilling, challenging, well-paying career in which I never had to work overtime. Maybe Greg and I would someday develop the kind of relationship in which the sex never got routine and the conversation never faltered, and Greg would always do his share of the dishes without being asked. Maybe someday I'd even find myself sexy enough to star in my own sex fantasies.

But this is my happy ending we're talking about. The best I can tell, the most romantic, idyllic, passionate moments are usually dashed with hearty dollops of bird-shit or the metaphorical equivalent thereof. But our friends and lovers help us through the endless crap hurtling our way.

I've been thinking that the people you know are not just the key to success in business, they're the key to success in life, too—the friends we make, the people we love, the laughs we share, the lives we touch.

Please turn the page for an exciting sneak peek of
Theresa Alan's next new novel
THE GIRLS' GLOBAL GUIDE TO GUYS
coming next month in trade paperback!

I

Boulder, Colorado

"It couldn't possibly have been that bad."

"Oh, but it was. I saw his you-know-what within an hour of knowing him, totally against my will."

"He flashed you?"

"Not exactly. We stopped by my apartment after dinner before we went to the club because we'd gone for Italian, and I had garlic breath, and I wanted to brush my teeth before we went dancing, even though I knew within four seconds of meeting him that it could never go anywhere. I don't know *what* Sylvia was thinking setting us up. But to be polite I had to go through the charade of the date anyway, even though I wasn't remotely attracted to him. So I started brushing my teeth, but I wanted to check on him and make sure he was okay, so I came out from the bathroom into the living room, and he was just sitting there on the couch, naked."

"No!"

"Yes. Naked and, ah . . . You know, aroused." I'm stuck

in traffic, story of my life, talking on my cell phone, which is paid for by the company I work for, making it one of the very, very few perks of being employed by Pinnacle Media. "I mean I know it's been a while since I've dated anyone, but isn't the whole point of dating and sex to kind of, I don't know, enjoy this stuff *together*? Like getting turned on by the other person's touch, and not by the sound of someone brushing her teeth in the bathroom?"

"So what did you do?"

"Well, I looked at him like the maniac he was, and he realized that I was appalled and said that he'd assumed that when I said I was going to the bathroom to brush my teeth, what I really meant was that I was going to put my diaphragm in."

"I don't . . . Is English his native language? I don't see how anyone could possibly come to that conclusion."

"Right, Tate, that's my point. The guy was a loon. So I reply, quite logically under the circumstances I think, my mouth foaming with toothpaste, 'No, I willy was bruffing my teef.' And this whole situation strikes me as so wildly funny. I mean in the past six months I've dated a bitter divorcé, been hit on by a string of lesbians, and now this. How did my dating life go so tragically wrong? Anyway, I just lost it. I crumpled to the ground in a fit of hysteria. I mean I started laughing so hard I literally couldn't stand, and he looked all put out and confused and out of the corner of my eye, as I was convulsing around like a fish out of water, I see him get dressed, and then *he stepped over* my writhing body and said, '*I don't know where things went wrong between us* . . .' "

"No!" Tate howls with laughter.

"Yes. He said some other stuff, but I was laughing too

hard to hear him. I mean, hello, I can tell you *exactly* where you went wrong, buddy."

Tate and I laugh, then she says, "Did you tell Sylvia about how the guy she set you up with is a kook?"

"Hell, yes. I called her up and I was like, 'um, thanks for setting me up with a sexual predator.' And you know what she said? She said, 'I knew it had been a long time for both of you, and I thought you might just enjoy each other's company, even if it never got serious.' I don't think you need to be an English lit major to read the hidden meaning in that sentence. I mean, obviously Sylvia thinks I'm such a sad schlub who is so desperate for sex I'll have a one-night stand with a scrawny, socially inept engineer."

"Jadie, look at it this way: you can put all these experiences into your writing. Maybe you'll write a book one day about all the hilarious dates you've been on."

I groan. "Oh god, please don't tell me I'm going to go on enough bad dates to fill an entire book."

"There's a guy out there for you, I know there is."

"Maybe. I'm just pretty sure he's not in Boulder, Colorado."

"He's out there. I know he is. Somewhere. Look, I gotta go. I'm going to be late for my shift."

"Have fun slinging tofu."

"Oh, you know I always do."

I click the phone off, and now that I have nothing to occupy myself with I can focus completely on how annoyed I am at sacrificing yet another hour of my life to traffic. Why aren't we going anywhere, why?

I can't wait until the day I can work full time as a writer and won't have to commute in highway traffic twice a day any more.

I'm a travel writer, though most people call me a "creative project manager for a Web design company."

Personally I think this shows an appalling lack of imagination. I *have* published travel articles, after all. Several of them, in fact. Granted, all told, in my five years of freelancing I've only made a few hundred bucks on my writing and my travel expenses have come to about ten times more than what I made from my articles, but it's a start. (By the way, in case you're wondering, "creative project manager" is a fancy title for "underpaid doormat who works too hard." Essentially, my job is to manage people who do actual work. I make sure the copywriters, graphic designers, and programmers are getting their pieces of the puzzle done on time. Every now and then I get to brainstorm ideas for how to design a Web site, and those are the few moments when I actually like my job, when I get to be creative and use my brain, letting the ideas come tumbling out. But mostly my job feels ethereal and unsubstantial. The world of the Internet moves so quickly that by the time a Web site gets launched, the company we created the site for is already working on a redesign, and within months, any work I did on a site disappears. That's why I like writing for magazines. I do the work, it gets printed with my byline, and I have the satisfaction of having something tangible to show for my efforts.)

Finally I see what has been holding traffic up—a car that's pulled over to the side of the road with a flat tire. Great. Forty extra minutes on my commute so people can slow down to see the very exciting sight of a car with a flat tire.

Eventually I make it home, grab the mail, unlock my door, and dump the mail on my kitchen table, my keys clattering down beside the stack of bills and catalogs advertising clothes I wouldn't wear under threat of torture. I sift through the pile; in it is the latest issue of the alumni magazine from the journalism school at the University of Colorado at Boulder, my alma mater. I flip idly through it until I see a classmate of mine, Brenda Amundson, who smiles up at me from the magazine's glossy pages in her fashionable haircut and trendy clothes. As I read the article, my mood sinks.

I know I'm not the first person who has struggled to make it as a writer, but sometimes, like, oh, say, when I get my alumni magazine and read that Brenda Amundson, who is my age—twenty-seven—and has the same degree I have, is making a trillion zillion dollars a year writing for a popular sitcom in L.A. while I'm struggling to get a few bucks writing for magazines no one has ever heard of, my self-esteem wilts.

I change into a T-shirt and shorts to go for a run—I need to blow off steam. To warm up, I walk to a park, then I start an easy jog along the path by Boulder Creek. It's 7:30 at night, but the sun is still out and the air is warm.

Boulder has its faults, but it's so gorgeous you forgive them. No matter how many years I've lived here, the scenery never stops being breathtaking. As I run, I take in the quiet beauty of the trees, the creek, the stunning architecture. The University of Colorado at Boulder is an intensely gorgeous campus. Every building is made out of red and pink sandstone rocks and topped with barrel-tiled roofs. Behind them are the Flatirons, the jagged cliffs in the foothills of the Rocky Mountains that draw rock climbers from around the world and help routinely put Boulder on "best places to live" lists in magazines.

I jog for about half an hour, then walk and stretch until I've caught my breath. I sit down on the grass and watch three college students playing Frisbee in one corner of the field. Across the way, two young people with dreadlocks and brightly colored rags for clothes are playing catch with a puppy.

The puppy makes me smile, but I realize as I watch it that I still feel tense. My jaw muscles are sore from clenching them, a bad habit I have when I am stressed, which is most of the time these days it seems.

I need to get away, to relax. I long to hit the road.

I've always loved traveling. Since I was a little kid I always wanted to escape, to find a place I could comfortably call home and just be myself. In the small town where I grew up, life was a daily exercise in not fitting in.

The fact that I was considered weird was mostly my parents' fault. They ran a health food store/new age shop where they tried to sell crystals to align chakras, tarot cards, incense, meditation music, that sort of thing. I'm fairly certain that no one ever bought a single sack of brown rice or bag of seaweed from their grocery store. They got by because of the side businesses they ran in the shop—Mom cut hair and Dad built and repaired furniture. Yes, I know, a health food/new age/hair salon/furniture shop is unusual, but when I was growing up, it was all I knew.

My mom was the kind to bake oatmeal cookies sweetened with apple juice and honey and would rather have me gnaw off my own arm than eat a Ding Dong or another processed-food evil. You can imagine how popular the treats I brought to school for bake sales and holiday parties were. About as popular as me. Which is to say not at all.

I sat through years of school lunches all on my own, eating carob bran muffins and organic apples while every other kid had Ho-Hos and Pop-Tarts and peanut butter fluff sandwiches washed down with Coke or chocolate milk. And as I would eat in solitude, I would dream of getting away. I longed to see the world. I ached to find some place where I could be whoever I wanted to be and wouldn't be the weird kid in town.

I found that place in Boulder, Colorado. Boulder is a place where pot-smoking, dreadlocked eighteen-year-olds claim poverty yet wear Raybans. Boulderites believe themselves to be one with nature, but own some of the most expensive homes in the country and drive CO_2-spewing SUVs without irony. It's a place that manages to be somehow new age and old school. A place where yuppies and hippies collide and where, inexplicably, people think running in marathons is actually fun.

My life is equally mixed up. It feels like a pinball machine—I'm the ball, getting flung around in directions I couldn't foresee and never considered. Like how I ended up working for Pinnacle Media. I thought that after graduation I would become this world-renowned journalist covering coup attempts, international corruption and intrigue, the works. But after I got my degree, I couldn't get a job writing so much as obituaries for some small-town newspaper. Frustratingly, papers like the *New York Times* and *Washington Post* seemed to be doing okay even without my help, and nobody from their respective papers was banging down my door begging me to write for them. They didn't even glance at my résumé, just like every other newspaper in America, no matter how small or inconsequential. So I took a job doing Web content at an Internet company during the height of Internet insanity, when every twenty-year-old kid with a computer was declaring himself a CEO and launching an online business determined to get rich quick. The company was living large for a while, but then the economy started to turn. I could tell we were going down, and I felt lucky when I landed the job at Pinnacle.

That feeling lasted, oh, twenty-eight seconds.

I've been looking for a new job since about the day after I started with Pinnacle, but with the economy the way it is, there have been almost no jobs advertised that I'm qualified to fill. My mantra is *someday the economy will get better and I'll be able to find another job. Someday the econ-*

omy will get better and I'll be able to find another job. But until then, my situation feels a lot like being trapped.

I travel to get away whenever possible, taking a handful of short trips each year to cities in the United States, Mexico, or Canada. I've been saving up money and vacation time to go on a real trip, something longer than a four-day weekend, but I keep waiting for some flash of insight that will tell me where the best place to go is, some location that will prove a treasure trove of sales to magazines.

Although maybe it doesn't really matter where I go, whether Barbados is the happening spot this year or if Madagascar is the place to be, whether the Faroe Islands are going to be the next big thing or if Malta will be all the rave. After all, the articles I have sold haven't come from the short trips I've taken but from living in the Denver/Boulder area—stuff about little-known hotspots in Colorado and how to travel cheap in Denver. Mostly I write for small local newspapers and magazines. I've gotten a few pieces published in national magazines, but the biggies, the large circulation publications that pay livable wages like United Airlines' *Hemispheres* or Condé Nast *Traveler*, remain elusively, tantalizingly out of reach.

In the past year, depressed about my career, I decided I would try to get another area of my life in shape—my love life. It hasn't exactly gone according to plan.

First, there was the bitter divorcé. I didn't know he was bitter until we went out on our first date. I knew he was divorced; he'd told me. I just didn't know how frightening the depths of his contempt for his ex went.

I met Jeff at the Greenhouse, the restaurant where I used to work when I was in college. My friend Tate still works there, and I was waiting for her to get finished with her shift when Jeff and I got to talking. I was sitting at the table next to him, and as another waitress, Sylvia, brought him his shot of wheat grass, he said something that made me laugh, and he kept on cracking me up with little quips and witty remarks. I don't even remember what we talked about, just that he seemed like a nice guy, and when he asked if he could have my number, I told him he could. I started to write it down, and he said abruptly, "Before you give me your number, there is something you should know."

I immediately thought he was going to say that he was out on bail for murder charges or something.

"I'm divorced and have two kids."

I waited a beat. "And?"

"And what? That's it."

"That's your big secret? You're divorced and have kids?"

"Yeah, that's it."

"I think I can handle it."

(Of course that really wasn't his big secret. His real secret was that he was a complete psychopath whose rage toward his ex festered in a frightening and unseemly way.)

The fact that he had kids appealed to me. He told me he saw them—a three-year-old girl and two-year-old boy—every other weekend. I imagined Jeff and I getting married, and I would be able to help raise these kids and watch them grow, but on a convenient part-time basis without any of that painful pregnancy and birthing business.

But then I went out on my one and only date with Jeff and that fantasy was blown to bits.

Things started well enough. Then in the middle of a nice meal after a couple of glasses of wine, I asked him something about his ex. Something like if they'd managed to stay friends or why they broke up, I can't remember exactly. Jeff got this maniacal look in his eyes and said, "That lying, money-grubbing bitch. I hate her. Women—all they want is your money. Lying . . . cheating . . . manipulative bitches. But sometimes you get sick of porn and want the real thing." He laughed about that last thing, as if it were a joke, but it very clearly wasn't. And when I looked at him wide-eyed and open-mouthed, he seemed to come out of his trance and our gazes met. I was blinking in shock, and I think he realized that, like an evil villain going around disguised as a good guy, he'd accidentally let the mask slip off and some serious damage control was in order. He smiled. "Just kidding. It was rough going there for a while, but we're friends again." He saw my incredulity. "No, really. I love women." *Yeah, to have sex with. "Sometimes you get sick of porn and want the real thing" . . . unbefuckinglievable.*

So that was the end of Jeff.

Now you'll want to know about the lesbians. Their names are Laura and Mai and they live in my apartment building.

We'd always been polite when we'd met in the hallway or at the mailboxes over the years. Then a few months ago, as I held the front door to the building open for them, they asked me what I had going on that night. It was a Friday, yet I had a whopping nothing to do and no place to be. They said they were going dancing at a lesbian bar that night; did I want to go with them? I said sure, it sounded like fun.

Laura and Mai are both big girls and very pretty. Laura looks like Mandy Moore would if Mandy were a size fourteen. And Mai has a build like Oprah—busty and curvy and strong. And they have the cutest style. Their outfits wouldn't be featured in *InStyle* or anything, but I think they have a certain bohemian charm. And can we talk accessories? Clunky, colorful jewelry to die for.

We hit the club a few hours later, dancing our little

hearts out. For some reason I didn't think it was strange that they kept buying drinks for me and plying me with alcohol. After all, they knew I was straight, I knew they'd been dating each other forever—what was there to worry about?

It was late when we got back.

"Do you want to come to our place for a nightcap?" Mai asked.

"No. Can't drink no more. Alcohol . . . too much."

"Why don't you come inside and we'll give you some water so you won't have a hangover," Laura said.

I was too drunk to protest—or really even to know what was happening. As I staggered into their apartment, I noticed that the hide-a-bed had been pulled out. I remember thinking, *I didn't know their couch had a hide-a-bed.*

We sat on the edge of the hide-a-bed, the two of them flanking me on either side. In an instant, Laura was blowing in my ear and Mai was kissing my neck and stroking my breast. It took me a moment to process what was happening. My brain was working in slow motion. It was like I'd gotten stuck in a sand trap, and no matter how much I tried to accelerate, the wheels of my brain just went around and around and never got anywhere. But eventually I realized that my breast was being stroked by a woman. I found this information to be very confusing.

Once I finally noticed what was going on, I seemed to sober up instantly. I sprung up off the couch. "I'm . . . I'm . . . I'm straight!" I yelped.

"There's no reason to be locked into these artificial constructions . . . these meaningless boundaries . . ." Mai began.

"Like boundaries! Boundaries good!" My English skills, despite my degree in journalism, had been reduced to the level of a two-year-old. That's when I began backing up toward the door. In moments I was sprinting backward at Mach-10 speed, a blur of a human at break-the-sound-barrier velocity.

Unfortunately, I hadn't noticed a coffee table between me and the door to freedom.

Any other person would have stubbed her leg on it, or perchance been knocked sideways. Me? I was going so fast I became airborne and did a back flip—my head hit the corner of the table on my way down. I knocked myself semi-unconscious.

They say fear evokes two responses: fight or flight. No one ever said that knocking yourself unconscious was an appropriate reaction to an uncomfortable situation. But there you have it. I'd turned myself into the perfect victim. I had no way to defend myself. I was at their mercy.

Fortunately, Laura and Mai weren't rapists. They'd put the moves on me, been rebuffed, and now they were a flurry of concern, hovering over me and wanting to know if I was okay.

In my half-conscious state, I was dimly aware that the two of them were dragging me over to the hide-a-bed and hoisting me onto it—managing to knock my head on the metal frame as they did. I quickly fell into a merciful sleep.

In the morning, I didn't remember where I was or what had happened, I just knew my head was in excruciating pain. In addition to a bruise the size of a plum on the back of my head from the coffee table, I had a searing pain just above my ear from where they'd knocked me against the bed frame. On top of all that, I had a blinding hangover.

I groaned in pain. Moments later I heard the patter of bare feet against the wood floor, and I opened my eyes in an attempt to figure out where I was and what was going on.

It was Mai and Laura, who'd run to check on whether I was all right. They were naked, hovering over me like oversized Florence Nightingales, so that when I opened my eyes all I saw was tit. Four large, ponderous tits, encircling me in a mammary orbit.

I promptly shut my eyes and wondered, *how did my life start to read like a* Penthouse *letter?* Sure, some people—guys, no doubt—might like a life that read like a *Penthouse* letter. I was not one of those people.

Laura and Mai still smile at me when we pass each other in the hall. Once they even asked if I wanted to go dancing with them again. (I replied that if I got one more head injury, I'd need to go to the hospital for sure, so it was probably safer if I didn't go out with them anymore.)

A few weeks later I had yet another tangle with a lesbian—that night also involved alcohol and confusing and misguided tit-groping, though thankfully no head trauma—but if you don't mind, it's still too painful and embarrassing to think about, so I'd rather not tell the story in all its gory detail.

Add on the sexual predator from last night, and you have the sum total of my love life in the last six months. And it was no romance novel before that, I can assure you.

I wonder if there is a place where this whole dating and romance thing is easier. Some country where the men aren't as psychotic as the men in America all seem to be. If so, I'm moving there post haste. I just need to find this magical la-la land. I'll search the globe until I find it. . . .

I smile at the idea, then I wonder how dating *is* different in different parts of the world. I know some places have arranged marriages, but where? How are African wedding ceremonies different from Swedish ones or Chinese ones? Do other countries do blind dates? Double dates? Internet dating? Do Russians sweat how many days to wait to call after a first date like Americans do?

I vow to research the cultural differences of mating and love, and that's when it hits me: *if I'm interested in how romance is different in different parts of the world, maybe other people would be too. Maybe that could be my angle when I pitch stories; maybe it would be unique enough to get me in the door of the major magazines.*

The ideas zip through my head, and I have internal arguments with myself about where and when I should go. One part of me really wants to just take off. For months I've been fantasizing about how different my life will be if I can just get away for a while so I can rejuvenate my brain by filling it with art and culture and recharge my body by having lavish amounts of salacious sex with a handsome stranger with a sexy accent. But the other part of me knows for a fact that I'll lose my job if I leave. There have already been numerous rounds of layoffs at my company. I'm the lucky one for still having a job. Well, that's what I tell myself anyway. *I'm lucky to have my job, I'm lucky to have my job.* I know a lot of people who have been out of work for months. As a single woman with no more than a couple months' worth of survival savings in the bank, I'd be in the poorhouse in no time if I got laid off, so I *am* lucky to have a job. But since the layoffs began, everyone at work has been worried they'll be next and they are resentful, tense, and hostile. Looking for other jobs while at the office is a generally accepted practice. The bitterness factor went through the roof when we survivors were doing our own jobs plus the jobs of the people who'd been let go. These days the opposite problem has hit— there's almost no work to go around, and somehow that's even worse, at least for me. The strain of trying to pretend to look busy is much worse than the strain of actually being busy. For one thing, I'm constantly bored, and for another thing, I live in constant terror that someone is going to figure out I don't have anything to do and that they could easily get along without me and they're going to fire my ass.

But the thing of it is, I hate my job, and there is a part of me that would love to get fired despite the economic strain. I'd finally have the time I need to pursue my real dreams and goals. Anyway, I've been wracking up vacation time for months—I should take it before the company goes under and I lose it all.

But taking a trip would be so impractical. . . .

But is "practical" the kind of person I want to be? No! I want to be adventurous. I want to take risks and follow my dreams.

I jump up and run home. There I strip out of my sweaty clothes, take a quick shower, throw some fresh clothes on, and sprint the four blocks from my apartment to the Greenhouse, where Tate is working tonight.

Tate has just finished taking an order from a table and is heading to the kitchen to give it to the cooks.

The Greenhouse specializes in food for diners who have wheat allergies, are lactose intolerant, and so on. Vegetarian, vegan, whatever your dietary oddity, the Greenhouse is here to serve. The Greenhouse does pretty well, what with it being located in Boulder, one of the most health-conscious cities in the universe. Boulder attracts skiers, hikers, mountain climbers, and marathon runners up the yin yang. A Boulderite is as likely to eat red meat as to stir-fry a hubcap for dinner.

The Greenhouse is brightly painted. One wall is purple, one red, one deep blue. The ceiling is pale green, and the work of local artists decorates the walls.

When I worked here during college, I was the only member of the waitstaff without multiple body piercings or a single tattoo. Tate has several of both. Her belly button and nose are pierced and her ears are studded with earrings. She has a tattoo of a thin blue and white ring encircling her upper right arm that looks like a wave, a rose on her ankle, and the Chinese symbol for harmony on her breast. (Only a special few have seen this one, and one drunken night she flashed me and I became one of them. It was a shining moment in an otherwise disappointing life.) Today she is wearing her long black hair in a loose bun that is held together by what looks like decorative chopsticks. She's petite, but so thin her limbs seem long and she looks taller than she is, with the graceful, lithe muscles of a ballerina. It would be fair to call Tate's look exotic. My looks, with my honey-blond hair and dimples, would be best described as wholesome-Iowa-farm-girl.

I follow her into the kitchen.

"Tate, you're a genius."

"What are you talking about? Lance, leave the onions out of this burrito."

"Just write it down," Lance booms.

"I did. I just don't want a repeat of last time. I lost that tip because of you."

Lance, the cook, just grunts.

"Your idea for the book," I continue. I follow her over to the refrigerator, where she pulls out a couple of cans of organic soda. "What I'll do is write a book about romance and dating around the globe. I'll interview women all over the world and find out their most hilarious dates ever. I'll find out about differences in dating and marriage in different cultures—the works. I'll be able to sell tons of articles, based on my research, to bridal magazines and women's mags. You know—stuff like,

'Looking to make your wedding original? Borrow from traditional Chinese or Turkish or Moroccan customs to make your wedding an international success.' Or for *Cosmo* I can write about different sexual rituals around the world, or for *Glamour* I can write something like, 'You think the dating scene in America is grim? At least you don't have to do like the Muka-Muka do—they have to eat worms and beat each other up to see if they're compatible.' "

"Who the hell are the Muka-Muka?"

"Well, that's just to illustrate. I don't know the worst mating rituals in the world yet—that's why I need to write a book about it. I'll be like the John Gray of international relations between men and women. I'll be like an anthropologist studiously researching the most important issue known to humankind: love."

"And along the way, as you're doing all this important academic research, you might just happen to stumble on Mr. Right."

Damn. Sometimes it's a problem that this girl knows me so well. "Well, you know, if it just so happens that way . . . But you have to come with me. You have money saved."

She pushes the kitchen door open with her butt and delivers the sodas to her table. She drops off a bill at another, then clears off the plates at yet another. I hover at the doorway of the kitchen, waiting for her.

"How much do you have saved?" I ask her as soon as she gets back.

"Order up!" Lance says.

Tate checks the order and starts balancing the plates on her arms. "I'm not sure exactly. Maybe five thousand."

Five grand! And she makes a lot less money than I do. Granted, she doesn't need a car, she lives with four roommates, and she doesn't need to spend a dime on her wardrobe for work, but still, I'm impressed.

"What are you going to do with it? What could be better than traveling the world with your friend? Come on, Tate, we need some adventure. We need to shake things up a bit."

"Where were you thinking about going?"

"I don't know. I'd like to see the whole world, but I don't have nearly enough vacation time saved up for that. How about Europe—the countries are small so we knock out a bunch at once. Paris . . . Italy . . . Germany . . ."

"But we don't speak those languages."

"So? It'll be an adventure. You're not scared, are you?" Okay, I admit I'm being manipulative. I know Tate well enough to know that the best way to get her to do something is to accuse her of being scared to do it.

"Of course I'm not scared!" She stomps out of the kitchen and delivers the order. When she returns, she pulls me aside conspiratorially. "What about our jobs?"

"I'll work it out with my boss, ask if they can hire a temp for a while or something. And Jack will understand. His waiters are always taking off on road trips for weeks at a time."

"That's true."

"So you're thinking about it?"

"When are you thinking of going?"

"As soon as possible."

"You'll plan everything?"

"Of course. Come on, it'll be the adventure of a lifetime. And maybe you'll find your soul mate. Another free spirit just like you."

She bites her lip. "It might be fun."

"It'll be a blast."

"Do you really think we could do this?"

"Of course we can."

She nods. "This is crazy."

"You love crazy."

She's still nodding. "Tell me when I should show up at the airport."

"Yes!" I give her an enormous hug. "It's going to be the experience of a lifetime," I assure her.

It's a big promise, but there is no doubt in my mind that it's a promise I can keep.

BOOK YOUR PLACE ON OUR WEBSITE AND MAKE THE READING CONNECTION!

We've created a customized website just for our very special readers, where you can get the inside scoop on everything that's going on with Zebra, Pinnacle and Kensington books.

When you come online, you'll have the exciting opportunity to:

- View covers of upcoming books
- Read sample chapters
- Learn about our future publishing schedule (listed by publication month *and author*)
- Find out when your favorite authors will be visiting a city near you
- Search for and order backlist books from our online catalog
- Check out author bios and background information
- Send e-mail to your favorite authors
- Meet the Kensington staff online
- Join us in weekly chats with authors, readers and other guests
- Get writing guidelines
- AND MUCH MORE!

**Visit our website at
http://www.kensingtonbooks.com**

Contemporary Romance By
Kasey Michaels